REFLECTIONS

Then she caught sight of her reflection in the mirror. A frightened, distracted woman looked back, an image so very different from that of the glamorous fashion model. 'Why am I leaving?' she asked the mirror. . . . Why was she running away from Michael – because she could not cope with the feelings and emotions he invoked? Did that mean that she could never be able to handle a full emotional relationship? Was she no more, in reality, than the constant reflections she saw of herself – a smiling celluloid face, of no depth, no substance . . .?

Also by Deborah Fowler

SOMETIME . . . NEVER

Reflections

DEBORAH FOWLER

SPHERE BOOKS LIMITED

For Alan –
with all my love

SPHERE BOOKS LTD

Penguin Books Ltd, 27 Wrights Lane, London W8 5TZ (Publishing and Editorial)
and Harmondsworth, Middlesex, England (Distribution and Warehouse)
Viking Penguin Inc., 40 West 23rd Street, New York, New York 10010, USA
Penguin Books Australia Ltd, Ringwood, Victoria, Australia
Penguin Books Canada Ltd, 2801 John Street, Markham, Ontario, Canada L3R 1B4
Penguin Books (NZ) Ltd, 182–190 Wairau Road, Auckland 10, New Zealand

First published in Great Britain by Severn House Ltd 1987,
by arrangement with Sphere Books
Published by Sphere Books Limited 1987

Printed and bound in Great Britain by
Cox & Wyman Ltd, Reading
Set in 10/11 pt Compugraphic Plantin

Prologue: CRETE, August 1943

Two naked bodies lay stretched on a goatskin rug. Sheltered from view in the mouth of the cave, the sun warmed them, the sound of the sea soothed them. They were strangely alike, the same suggestion of youthful vigour, the same restless strength. Both were deeply tanned by the sun – but here similarity ended, for one was the golden brown of the Anglo-Saxon, while the other had the smooth olive skin of the Latin. Pale fair hair rested beside wild, blue-black curls – they were an extraordinarily beautiful couple.

'Tassoula?' Jonathan Richardson propped himself up on one elbow. 'Tassoula.' His voice was gentle, chiding, as he shook the sleeping girl.

At his touch, her eyes snapped open. She had been living with danger for too long now to ever sleep soundly. 'I was asleep. Oh Jonathan, what a waste.' She rolled over, never taking her eyes from his. For a moment their expressions were sombre, full of shadows.

Then Jonathan smiled. 'Yes,' he agreed. 'You are very badly behaved.' He spoke in English, slowly. Since their marriage, earlier in the year, he had insisted on her learning his own tongue. She had worked hard, and now her English was almost as good as his Greek. He chose the moment for a brief lesson in colloquialism. 'In England you would be called Lazy-Bones,' he said.

She laughed, delightedly. 'Lazy-Bones? Really?'

His eyes shifted from her face, as slowly he let his gaze wander down the length of her body. Unlike most women of her race, she showed no tendency of going to fat. Her body was as lean and hard as a boy's, except for her magnificent breasts, now, already, responding to his gaze. He buried his face in them, nuzzling, nipping like a young puppy. She caught his head in her hands and held him to her, as her body moved under him in the beginnings of abandonment. Suddenly, she stiffened. 'No Jonathan, there's no time, you'll be late.

His expression was almost angry as he raised his head to hers. 'Then time will just have to stand still for us, won't it?'

He took her, swiftly, strongly, with a strange defiance that she was later to understand. Always before he had been painstakingly considerate, anxious to please her, gentle – almost too gentle in his desire to give her pleasure. But not this time. Roughly he forced her legs apart, despite her struggles and weak protests. He was huge and bruising, she cried out in pain, yet the moment their bodies were fused, heat pulsed through her, and with it came an excitement which was completely new. Joyously, her body rose and fell with his, every muscle straining, their bodies slippery with sweat. When she climaxed, she cried out as never before – a hoarse, frantic, animal cry that seemed to echo round the hills before joining the sounds and sensations that this place had been witnessing since time began. Nothing was new to these mountains – for this was the land of the Ancient Greeks – of Zeus, of Theseus, of King Minos, Ariadne and Ikarus . . . mortal man was of little significance here.

They dressed quickly and silently, words an unnecessary burden. She watched without comment as he carefully loaded the stolen German Luger, packing the remaining precious ammunition into his pocket.

'I love you, Tassoula.'

'I love you, Jonathan,' she replied, simply.

He left her and started down the hillside, taking great strides as he went. At the turn of the valley he stopped, swung round and raised his arm, in a tentative half wave. It was out of character – he was a man of the moment, not given to looking back. For the rest of her life, Tassoula was to wonder whether he had known at that moment, what she herself, had not . . . that they would never meet again.

As the valley closed in around him, Jonathan heard a shrill

cry in the clear blue sky above. A golden eagle swept in a wide arc and landed, with infinite grace and skill, on a small promontory of rock. Jonathan paused to watch the bird – his mission, even his wife, forgotten in the beauty of the moment. Then, he continued on his way.

Less than a quarter of a mile away, the boy, too, saw the eagle. Preoccupied as he was with the terrifying task that lay ahead, he nonetheless watched the bird's flight as he scrabbled down the cliff face towards the German garrison – towards treachery and betrayal. . . .

. . . Two hours and forty minutes later, Jonathan Richardson was dead. The ambush he had so carefully planned, had been expected. He and his men were mown down before they had even taken up their positions. One bullet had destroyed a lung, another had ripped apart his stomach, but Jonathan fought for breath as he was loaded into a German truck, his body thrown on the heap of his dead and dying comrades. As the vehicle lurched its way along the dusty track, his last sight of earth was of the olive groves, and the mountains beyond. The last sound he heard was the warning song of the cicaders, and his last thoughts were of Tassoula, her body arched to meet his. Then there was nothing but blackness, and with it came the merciful release from pain.

In Sitia, the news travelled fast. Dr Georges Pappadis sat in his surgery, head bowed, tears pouring into his stubbled beard, as he listened to what his old friend, Vaselli Koykoyrakis, had to tell him. It was bad enough that Jonathan Richardson and his band of guerrilla fighters had been killed, but the failure of their ambush had far wider implications. Jonathan had planned to intercept the transport of some Cretan prisoners who the Germans were intending to shoot in front of their whole village – a reprisal for former guerrilla activities. Full of bloodlust from having routed the ambush, the German soldiers had then gone on into the village and shot not only the prisoners in their charge, but all the inhabitants. Georges shook his head in disbelief. 'Is there no one left who needs me?'

'There is no one,' Vaselli replied. 'They killed everyone, even the babies.'

The two men sat in silence, totally overwhelmed by the horror of what had occurred. It was Georges, at last, who rallied. 'My family and I must leave for the mountains at once.'

Vaselli seemed surprised. 'Is that necessary?'

'I think so,' Georges replied. 'Whoever betrayed Johnny Richardson, and someone surely did, may well have spoken of this family's connection with him. We cannot take the risk. I can work in the mountains, perhaps be of even greater use, and there is my wife and family to think of.' He frowned, suddenly. 'Is Tassoula here?'

'Yes, she is with your wife.'

'Does she know?'

'Not yet,' Vaselli replied.

'Then you had better send her to me,' Georges said, heavily.

Tassoula studied her father with mounting terror. 'Is he hurt?' she asked.

'No,' Georges replied. 'He is dead.'

Tassoula searched his face. He could see her willing him to say that there was some hope of her husband having been captured alive, that perhaps he was just wounded – anything but that it was over. 'I am afraid it is true, my child. There is no doubt – his body was left in the village with the others.'

'Did he . . .' she began.

'He must have died very quickly.' Georges had been ready for the question.

Much to his astonishment, his daughter's face remained impassive.

'What is to be done, Father?' she asked, after a pause.

'We must leave, and leave now. We have to go into the mountains, there is no other way. You must look after your mother, she will find it very hard to leave her home. Go now and help her.'

Rightly, Georges sensed that keeping the child busy was the answer, and thanks largely to Tassoula's efforts, under cover of nightfall, the Pappadis family left their beloved home, on the harbour front at Sitia, and headed for a desolate and desperate life in the mountain caves.

It was just after dawn, the following morning, when Tassoula crept from the place in which her father had chosen to camp, stumbled to the coastline, and from there to the cave that had been her husband's home for the past two years. His pitiful few possessions lay where he had left them – the rug, a few crude utensils, one or two items of discarded clothing, dusty and crumpled, and his journal – a black, leather-bound book, which contained all that was left of Jonathan Richardson – his thoughts, hopes and dreams.

Tassoula picked up the book and clutched it to her chest, trying desperately to stem the pain that was gathering there. She ran blindly from the cave, to the edge of the cliff. At twenty, life without Jonathan stretched ahead. There was nothing but darkness – the future, a hopeless burden.

The sun was rising fast now. The sea, blue and apricot in the morning light, was heart-breakingly beautiful, but Tassoula saw none of it. At the very edge of the cliff, she barely hesitated, determined now to seek oblivion from the pain.

It was the sun's reflection on the thrashing water that saved her. For a precious moment, she paused, straining her eyes to see what was causing the turmoil in the sea far below. And then she saw them – dolphins, not several, but many – ten, twenty, perhaps. They leapt high into the air, twisting this way and that, their bodies glistening, playing for sheer joy. Tassoula sank to her knees, Jonathan's journal still held to her. She stared downwards, her eyes round with disbelief. 'No,' she murmured, 'no, not the dolphins, not today.'

Although the waters of the Cretan Sea contain many dolphins, they are rarely seen so near the coastline. To generations of Cretans, the sighting of so many, so close in shore, has only meant one thing – good luck in the future to the beholder. Tassoula began to moan, her moans turned to sobs, to shouts and screams, as her grief came pouring out. 'Why today, why today?' she demanded of the silent hills. There was no reply.

She raged against fate, she raged against the death of her young husband, and she raged that this symbol of good fortune should come to mock her now. Yet as the pain and horror flowed from her, so the danger passed. She did not want to live without Jonathan, but she was not ready to die.

It was some weeks before Tassoula came to understand the dolphins' message. When she did, she realised that their appearance had saved not only her life, but another's. For she was expecting a child, Jonathan's child, conceived on the day of his death.

On May 6th, 1944, Tassoula Richardson gave birth to a son. The boy, born in a cave, delivered by the hands of his own grandfather, became a symbol of hope to the local people, from his first cry. This Englishman's son showed that out of death could come life, out of despair, a new beginning. In deference to his father's race, Tassoula named her son. . . . Michael.

Chapter One: LONDON, May 1985

Miranda heard the helicopter, rather than saw it. The noise was like that of an angry bee and she wondered, idly, whether the aircraft's reappearance heralded time for lunch. Then the sound of the engine changed – subtly, at first, almost imperceptibly. Miranda assumed it meant the helicopter was already on the ground, but a sudden spluttering and coughing followed by a breathtaking silence, made her abandon her sunbathing and sit up. An immediate sense of unease propelled her from the terrace, where she had been lying, to the front lawn of the house. There she found her hostess, May Hardcastle, already anxiously searching the sky. Miranda joined her, and instinctively the two women clutched each other as they heard the engine cough into life again. Suddenly the helicopter came into view, apparently rising from out of a little copse at the end of the garden.

'He's too low,' May said, hoarsely, and at the precise moment she spoke, one of the blades thudded sickeningly against the huge chestnut tree which stood a little apart from thc copse . . .

Everything went into slow motion. The nose of the helicopter tipped forward, in the beginnings of a somersault, the engine shrieked uselessly and the machine literally dropped out of the sky like a stone. As it hit the lawn, it burst into flames – the flash of heat so violent, that, involuntarily, Miranda and May were forced to run back towards the house to shield themselves from the blaze.

As the wreckage burnt before their eyes, Miranda began to scream. She screamed and screamed, and it was the sound of her own voice and the choking sensation in her throat that finally woke her – to the knowledge that yet again, she was reliving the nightmare.

She lay in bed, sweating, trembling, tears running down her cheeks. It was seven years since the accident, seven years since she had watched helplessly as her husband had burnt to death. Yet the nightmare never dimmed. If anything, its very familiarity made it more vivid than it had been in reality, when shock had numbed her senses.

Wide awake now, Miranda snapped on the light and sat up in bed. Squinting at her alarm clock, she saw that it was twenty past three. 'Oh shit,' she said, aloud. Her alarm was already set for five since she had to be outside the Tower of London, by seven, for a modelling assignment. *Contact* magazine seemed to think that early morning at the Tower of London, was the ideal backdrop against which to photograph some current evening wear.

Sighing with resignation, Miranda eased herself out of bed. She slipped a long T-shirt over her head and padded in bare feet towards the kitchen. The light in the room proved far too bright and Miranda grumbled under her breath, as she filled the kettle. She ran her hand through her rumpled hair – she felt tense, nervous, and now, very far from sleep. She paced the floor while waiting for the kettle, cold and agitated, and when she had made her coffee, she almost ran back to the warmth and comfort of bed.

Never free of her nightmare, recently it had become more frequent, sometimes happening two, three – even four times a week. Propped up in bed, Miranda sipped at her mug, her face creased in a heavy frown. Seven years was a long time – surely by now the memories should be fading. At twenty-eight, she knew she should be looking to the future, not harping back to the past. She had so much compared with other people – her own mews house, a Porsche, enough money to buy the clothes she wanted, to take holidays when she felt like it. To cap it all, she had a job that was not only highly lucrative, but which still, even after all these years, she genuinely enjoyed.

Yet her life was sterile. She said the word out loud, trying to make sense of her predicament. Women across the world admired and envied her. Once, like them, Miranda had resented the obscurity of her mundane existence, but unlike them, she had fought against it . . . and won. Yet won for what? There were days when she wondered whether she would not have been happier back in Yorkshire, marrying a local boy, and dreaming of fame and fortune, instead of turning it into a reality.

'OK, darlin', let's try it again.' Bill's voice sounded weary. 'That's it, that's better. Come on, sugar, for gawd's sake give me all you've got. Turn your hips a little, that's it! Now pout, no I mean pout. Hate me a little, hate me a lot. Jesus Christ, can't you loosen up, girl? At this rate, we're going to be here all fucking day – I mean, *all fucking day*.'

Miranda didn't blame him for his outburst. Most fashion photographers were *prima donnas* and Bill Barnes was no exception. However in this instance, it was the uncomfortable truth that his agitation was totally justified. It was now nine o'clock. They had taken two hours over a shot which should have been completed in under an hour. 'Could we have a break, Bill?' Miranda asked, weakly.

'Why not?' said Bill, his voice tight with anger. 'We're so over time now, we might as well take as long as we bleeding well like.'

'I'll go and get some coffee,' said Bill's assistant – a tall, lean young man, who clearly got on Bill's nerves.

'Yeh, and don't fuck around,' Bill shouted after him. He sighed and leaning back against a stone wall, began reloading film. 'What's with you, then, Miranda?' he said, after a pause, not taking his eyes from the film.

'I'm sorry, Bill.' There was nothing else she could say. She felt tired and listless – her normal intense professionalism seemed to have deserted her.

'Have a heavy night or something?' Bill persisted.

'No, though I did sleep badly.'

Bill gave her a shrewd look. 'You need a holiday, girl, or a new fella . . .' He smiled for the first time, easing the tension between them. 'Are you open to offers?'

She smiled back. 'I'm not your type, sweetheart.'

'Too true,' Bill replied. 'Me mates think I'm having it away with models all the time in my job, but, it's the honest truth, I never touch fucking models. Neurotic, moody bunch, always worrying about how they look, even when they're flat on their backs. Me current lady works down the local chippie – she's a real goer, and she cooks the best chips in town. I might even marry her, one day.'

Miranda laughed. 'Good for you,' she said.

'Yeh.' They were silent for a moment. 'So what are we going to do about this shot, then, Miranda? It's impossible to take a bad picture of you, you know that, but I want a bloomin' marvellous one, and if you would just get a fucking move on, we could all go and have a bleeding good breakfast.'

'Egg and chips?' Miranda teased.

'Yeh, why not.'

Bill's assistant came into sight, dodging across the traffic, precariously balancing three paper mugs of coffee.

'Look, Bill,' said Miranda, suddenly. 'Give me five minutes – I need a cigarette, that coffee, and then I'll give you your bloomin' marvellous shot. Half an hour from now, I guarantee you'll be eating egg and chips. OK?'

'There's my girl!'

Of course, she was magnificent, when she was on form, Bill thought, as he was packing away his camera twenty minutes later. Every frame he had just taken was a winner. As usual, Miranda Hicks had turned what could have been an ordinary fashion shot, into something special, something unique. She made a fashion page look like a party. People always smiled when they saw her pictures. Bill had noticed it many times, even on the faces of hard-bitten advertising men. She was beautiful, glamorous and sexy, but she exuded fun, good humour, kindness – and somehow, despite her amazing looks, the average woman could still identify with her.

Bill straightened up. He had only worked with Miranda twice before, but on both occasions, she had been wonderful from the start. It had been odd, her behaviour, first thing this morning – quite out of character with his experience and her reputation. She had been lucky that no fashion editor was present or there could have been trouble. These days, Miranda's legendary insistence that she worked alone with the photographer, was usually respected – for no one could argue with the results. She always styled her own hair, chose her own accessories, and heaven help the art director who tried to tell her how to move in front of the camera. She would take direction from no one but the photographer. Bill walked thoughtfully to his car – well, every dog has its day, and was Miranda Hicks perhaps coming to the end of hers, he wondered.

'Hi Jenny, how are you doing, love?'

Jenny Marchant looked up from her desk, and as always, the sight of Miranda surprised and delighted her. The amazing blonde hair, that was too extraordinary to be anything but natural. Those big brown eyes – *brown*, with hair that colour! The high cheekbones, the turned-up nose, the big mobile mouth, which should have looked out of place in the perfect oval face, but somehow managed to be incredibly sensual. And despite ten years in London, Miranda always looked as fresh and healthy as if she had just walked off the Yorkshire moors that had bred her. Jenny had been a models agent for twenty-two years, yet she had never met anyone who could touch Miranda Hicks – she was in a class of her own. Quick scrutiny of Miranda now, though, told Jenny she was tired and edgy, for over the years that Jenny had represented Miranda's interests, the two women had become close friends, as well as colleagues. There was little they could hide from one another.

'You look a little peaky, darling. Let's go out to lunch. Are you working this afternoon, I can't remember?' Miranda shook her head. 'Good, then we'll split a bottle or two of wine and sort out the world.'

'You said you had some news for me, when we spoke on the phone yesterday.'

'I have, darling,' said Jenny reassuringly, 'but let's organise the pleasures of life first and deal with business second. Right?'

They lunched at Julie's. They always did – partly from convenience, as it was just round the corner from Jenny's office, but also because it was much frequented by famous faces, and famous faces tend to leave one another alone. If they had chosen a restaurant in Covent Garden or the Kings Road, Miranda would have been mobbed by autograph hunters and the usual string of young, hopeful girls, wanting to know how to break into modelling.

Jenny steadfastly refused to talk until the meal had been ordered and the wine poured. 'Now, darling,' she said, raising her glass. 'What's wrong with you?'

Miranda shrugged. 'I don't know, nothing really. I'm a little tired, perhaps. It's been a hard year, so far.'

'No harder than any of the others.'

'Then perhaps I'm getting old,' Miranda suggested.

'When were you last screwed?' Jenny asked, suddenly.

Miranda had the grace to blush. 'Bloody hell, Jenny, what a question. It's none of your damn business.'

'Of course it's my business, you are my business. Don't evade the question. When?'

'Oh, I don't know, five or six months ago.'

'Six months!' Jenny slammed down her glass, slopping wine all over the table. 'Did you say six months? Jesus!'

'Keep your voice down,' Miranda said, starting to laugh. 'Do you have to tell the whole bloody restaurant about my sex life?'

Jenny continued to shake her head. 'Six months . . . six months! God, I couldn't last six days.'

'Yes, well we all know about you,' said Miranda, lightly.

'Seriously though, darling, no wonder you're feeling a bit off colour. Celibacy is not a natural state, you know.'

'It seems to come naturally enough to me,' Miranda said. There was a slightly plaintive note in her voice, despite her smiling face.

'And that's the trouble,' Jenny said, warming to her theme. 'I know it's a touchy subject, darling, but David has been dead for seven years now and there's been precious little fun in your life since – and even fewer men.'

'That's rubbish,' Miranda said, hotly.

'Well, let's think about it,' said Jenny. 'There was that dreadful Hooray-Henry man.'

'Charlie, Charlie Devonshire. He wasn't dreadful, he was very sweet and kind and he wanted to marry me.'

'Well, of course he did,' said Jenny, reprovingly. 'Then there was the Egyptian – what was his name, Raoulf?'

'Yes, that's right.'

'I envied you him. He was gorgeous, in fact he's been the best of the bunch, in my view.'

'I grant you he was very attractive,' Miranda said, 'but he was somehow too physical.'

'Too physical, how can a man be too physical?' Jenny demanded.

'Very easily, if he's not the right one.'

'Sugar, I know we've had this conversation many, many times before but you've put David on such a pedestal, he's wrecking your enjoyment of other men.'

'Perhaps he is,' Miranda admitted. 'I don't know. All I do know is that I've had a number of affairs since he died and no one's been right for more than a few weeks. Now, somehow, I've got to the point where it's almost easier not to try. I have good friends who mean a great deal to me, so do I need all the hassle these sexual encounters inevitably seem to cause?'

'Perhaps you need some extra hormones.'

Miranda was about to laugh, but then saw that Jenny's face was serious. 'You're joking?'

'No, I'm not. There has to be something wrong with you. There can't be a man in the country who doesn't lust after you – you can have anyone you want.'

'Perhaps that's the trouble.' Miranda's face was suddenly serious, too.

'Shit, Miranda, stop moaning about it. Jesus, what I wouldn't give for your body and your looks. What a time I'd have.'

Miranda grinned. 'You don't do so badly.'

'That's true,' Jenny grinned – her lean, angular face showing not a sign of repentance.

'Jen, don't you ever wish you'd married and settled down, had kids and all that stuff?' Miranda asked.

'I had a phase when I thought it was what I wanted to do,' Jenny said. 'I was probably about your age at the time, but I soon grew out of it.'

'What happens when you're old?' Miranda asked, none too gently.

'I'll collect penknives.'

'You'll do what?'

'You must have heard of that particular piece of female initiative,' Jenny began to shake with laughter.

Miranda shook her head. 'No, tell me.'

'It's what every ageing woman who loves men, should do – collect penknives.'

'Why?' said Miranda.

'Because one day, when she's too old and ugly to attract the average man, just think of all the boy scouts in the world who would do anything, literally anything for a good pen knife.' Both women collapsed into laughter.

'Jenny, you're incorrigible,' Miranda spluttered.

'No, just practical,' she said, 'and don't think I haven't noticed your subtle change of subject – suddenly we're talking about me instead of you. Let's get back to business.'

'Business I'm happy to talk about,' Miranda said, hurriedly. 'It's this analysis of my personal life I can do without.'

'OK,' said Jenny, helping herself to vegetables. 'How does ten days in Crete sound to you?'

'Not bad,' Miranda said.

'Not bad, not bad! A cloudless blue sky, wine-dark sea, hot Greek sun, even hotter Greek lovers – and you're even getting paid for the privilege.'

'When, who and how much?' Miranda said.

'It's Masons mail order catalogue, they want you to go the week after next.'

'Oh, no,' said Miranda, 'not mail order . . .'

'Wait, just wait a moment,' Jenny interrupted. 'They're launching a new range of up-market garments. A leaflet will be inserted in the main catalogue as a special pull-out section and they want a real classy dame – i.e. you – to launch it for them. The rest of the catalogue is being shot in Manchester, amongst plastic palm trees, would you believe, but they have decided to go for the real thing when it comes to your supplement. They are also prepared to pay double rates – am I getting through to you?'

'Who else is going to be on the trip?' Miranda asked, clearly unimpressed.

'Your reputation goes before you, so there'll be no make-up artists, stylists or dressers. It will be just you, the photographer, the art director – oh, and Chris Brewer from Masons.'

'Jenny, you know I can't stand it when clients hover around.'

'Don't be touchy, darling, and don't bite the hand that feeds you. Miranda Hicks may have come a long way from little Miranda Higgins, hot off the Yorkshire moors, but you know the saying – the higher you climb, the higher the fall. Besides, I haven't told you who the photographer is yet – that will make all the difference.'

'Who is it?' Miranda asked.

'Jake Berisford.'

A shadow flitted across Miranda's face. Jake Berisford had been David's partner. She had met them both as young photographers, struggling to build a reputation. Jake had known David as well, if not better, than Miranda herself, and he alone, of all her friends, was always happy to talk about her husband, without making her feel she was being morbid. If she was honest, Miranda had never really liked Jake, but he represented her main link with David, and as such he was vitally important to her. 'You win,' she said, smiling at Jenny. 'If Jake's going, count me in too.'

'I thought that's what you'd say,' said Jenny, smiling with relief. 'It's an easy schedule. There are only six shots and ten days to do them in. It should be a piece of cake. It's just what you need, darling – a little sun on your back and a change of scene, and don't spend the whole time talking to Jake about the past. Find yourself a gorgeous Greek lover.'

'I thought all the Greeks were small, dark and hairy.'

'Little men are very sexy,' Jenny insisted.

'Not when you're five foot ten,' Miranda said, ruefully. She frowned suddenly. 'Ten days is a long time to leave Paul. He's used to coping for two or three days on his own, but since he's been with me, I haven't been away on a long trip.'

'Dear heart, your brother is no longer a child.'

'I know, but boys of his age are so hopeless. They need clean shirts and hot meals, and have no idea how to acquire either for themselves.'

'How old is he?' Jenny asked.

'Seventeen.'

'Seventeen! Shit, Miranda, he should be able to fend for himself by now – you did at his age.'

Miranda shrugged. 'Well, I suppose he was spoilt rotten by Mum because he was the baby and the only boy, and I've just carried on the family tradition.'

'I'll look after him,' Jenny said, suddenly.

'You!' Miranda burst out laughing. 'Firstly, I'm sure it's not safe to leave my baby brother in your hands, and secondly, I'm perfectly certain you haven't the slightest idea how to iron a shirt or cook hamburger and chips.'

'Miranda, darling, I may not be blessed with your Northern practicality, but there are such things as laundries and take-aways. Leave Paul to me. I think I might rather enjoy playing the role of mother hen – provided it's on a temporary basis.'

'Well, if you're sure,' said Miranda, doubtfully.

'Of course I'm sure, darling. You just concentrate on taking Crete by storm.'

It was of Paul that Miranda thought, as she drove from Bayswater to her Chelsea home. It had been quite a gamble taking him on, but it had worked out extremely well. The situation had arisen just eighteen months before. On one of her increasingly rare trips home, Miranda had fallen into conversation with her mother, while they were preparing Sunday lunch. Half an hour earlier Paul had rudely slammed his way out of the house, saying he did not know if he would be back in time for the meal.

'What's wrong with Paul these days, Mum?' Miranda had asked.

'The problem with our Paul is he's too sharp by half,' her mother had replied. 'I think he's frustrated, I really do. The trouble is there's nothing I can do for him, love. He's just going to have to work it out for himself.'

'How do you mean frustrated?' Miranda asked.

'He's as bright as a new pin, that one. Maths is his subject. They all say at school there's nothing more they can teach him. He's already sat his A level, and they say he'll get top marks.'

'A level – but he's only fifteen! Why didn't you tell me about this before?'

'Well, there's nothing to be done, is there?' her mother replied, defensively. 'Besides which, you're never here.'

But there was something to be done. A talk first with her parents, and then with Paul's headmaster, quickly established that a couple of years of private education, combined with extra tuition in mathematics, should ensure her brother a place at Oxford or Cambridge.

'I don't see him going to one of them posh boarding schools,' Miranda's mother had said, with characteristic shrewdness. 'He doesn't have the right background, they'd laugh at his accent. It might have been different if he'd gone at twelve, but at sixteen, kids are very conscious of these things.'

'Then how about a day school, if not round here, then in London?' Miranda had suggested.

'I can't see why you're suddenly taking all this interest in your brother – you've never seemed to care a jot for him before.'

The remark hit home. 'Of course I care,' Miranda could not keep the hurt out of her voice. 'It's just that I've never really had a chance to get to know him.'

Her mother was not to be mollified. 'You breeze in here just when you fancy and then turn our lives upside down. It's not right.'

Miranda put an arm round her mother. 'Look, Mum, you can't deny him this chance. I know it means he'll probably never take over the farm, but he's so clever – it would be wrong to hold him back. I can afford to pay for his education, he can live with me, and I'll take good care of him, I promise.' She planted a kiss on the top of her mother's head. 'And I'll send your baby boy home to you every holiday.'

Charlotte Higgins gave a sad little smile. 'Don't worry, you've won, you always do – it's just that once Paul goes, there'll be no one left but your Dad.'

Miranda thought of the long, bleak winters of her childhood and felt a moment's disquiet. Her mother would be lonely, yet surely like herself, Paul deserved his chance.

And so it was arranged. Paul was interviewed by St Paul's and immediately accepted. Miranda paid the school fees and her brother came to live with her. All her friends said she was a saint having a school-boy cluttering up the place, and thank heavens it was only for two years. In reality, Miranda loved having him. There was nearly eleven years difference in their ages but as their mother could have told them, they had a great deal in common. They were both bright, ambitious, good-looking and in a hurry, and they immediately recognised these characteristics in one another. It was also good to have someone to come home to, and though Miranda's flat was now cluttered with teenage mess and merciless pop music, it was great to have him about.

Miranda parked the car and ran up the steps to her front door, a smile on her lips. Paul would be amused by the concept of being looked after by Jenny. He had met her several times and clearly adored her – she flattered him and treated him as an adult. Miranda flung open the door. 'Paul, Paul?' There was silence and then she saw a note on the hall table.

'*Sis*,' it read, '*Taking in a film with some people. See you around midnight. Love, P.*' Miranda let out a sigh and dropped the note, dejectedly. She was pleased really – for Paul. He had found it difficult to adjust socially during his first two terms, but now he had a good circle of friends, and increasingly, he was out in the evening, and at weekends. Wearily, Miranda slipped off her coat, went into the kitchen and poured herself far too large a Scotch. Then she wandered, disconsolately, up the stairs to her bedroom – a long evening stretched ahead and it was Friday night, too.

Idly, she wandered over to the window and then gasped at what she saw. Across the street, an enormous new poster was being pasted onto a hoarding. Two workmen, both with brushes and ladders, were struggling with it. 'Oh no,' groaned Miranda aloud, 'they do pick their places.' For the poster in question was an enormous shot of her own head and shoulders. It was an advertisement for a cosmetic house – the photograph had been taken three or four years before, but it was still in regular use. The poster was so large that from where Miranda stood, the workmen appeared to be about the size of one of her ears, and she watched in fascination as they ran their brushes backwards and forwards, pasting it into position.

At last they were done, and with one final look at their handiwork, they went on their way, leaving Miranda staring eyeball to eyeball at the monstrous reproduction of herself. The more she stared, the more unfamiliar the face became. Impatiently, she turned away from the window, only to catch sight of herself in the dressing-table mirror. Over the bed there was a picture of her shaking hands with Princess Diana. On the chest of drawers, there was an enlarged snap of herself and her family, taken just before she left home. On the wall, there was a series of framed photographs presented to her by the company who had first employed her . . . Miranda glanced back out of the window, and then drawn by the need to seek reassurance, she walked over to her dressing-table, sat down and stared into the mirror. 'Who are you, Miranda Hicks?' she asked her reflection. The reflection seemed unable to reply.

Chapter Two

Miranda Hicks was born Miranda Jane Higgins, on November 12th, 1958. Her birth was tinged with both drama and regret.

The drama was caused by Miranda's apparent reluctance to leave the warmth and comfort of the womb. The resultant protracted labour nearly killed her mother and as if that was not enough, Miranda almost choked herself to death on the umbilical cord.

'Our Miranda caused more trouble being born than the rest of them put together, and she's never looked back since,' Lottie Higgins was fond of saying – not without cause.

The regret was with regard to her sex. The Higgins already had two children – Ann and Sarah, who were eleven and seven respectively at the time of their sister's birth. What the Higgins needed was a son – a boy to take over the family farm in due course – another girl merely represented another liability. Yet, when Jack Higgins looked at his third daughter for the first time, at her tiny perfect face and her extraordinary white gold hair, he found it hard to wish the child any different.

The Higgins were Dale farmers, the family had farmed the same land for three generations. They were not wealthy, the land was too poor for that, but they made a living. Their home was a solidly built, four-bedroomed square stone house, on the edge of the moor and they owned just over a hundred acres of arable land, the rest being scrub on which they kept sheep. For the children, it was a good, healthy life. They were well fed and cared for, and if, it being the Northern way, they went a little short on open demonstrations of affection, they nonetheless never doubted that they were loved.

Whilst Jack Higgins longed for a son, he would have been the first to admit that in Ann and Sarah he had the next best thing. They were cheerful children, strong and willing. From an early age, they would come out on the moor with him, rounding up the sheep in all weathers – they could split logs, fork hay and shift muck. Not so, Miranda. Having nearly throttled herself at birth, she seemed hell-bent on a course of self-destruction. By two, she had survived croup, measles, bronchitis and a mild form of meningitis. She was clearly determined to be a sickly child. While her sisters roared in and out of the house, seemingly oblivious to the cold, Miranda would sit shivering by the fire. She was different from them in build, too. Her sisters had stockily built, sturdy, little figures, whereas Miranda was fine-boned, her skin ivory pale compared with their rose cheeks.

'It's as though she was begat by a fairy,' Jack said, one night, watching his wife carrying the child upstairs.

By Miranda's fifth birthday, it began to seem likely that they might rear her. She was far from robust, but the tenacity of her character suggested that there was no way she would easily release her grip on life. She had also established her place and worth in the family – she was the entertainer. She might not have the strength to bring in the coal, she might be too afraid of the dark to shut away the chickens, but once the family was seated round the fire, she kept them endlessly amused with her chatter, her laughter and her childish jokes. Her vivaciousness brought a new sparkle to the farmhouse, where before their talk had been mainly concerned with the next day's chores.

Miranda also had the capacity to be a good listener. There was a genuine kindness about her and a very real interest in other people, which, as she grew, made her the butt for everyone's confidences. She knew all the details of Ann's first kiss, of her father's secret weekly flutter on the horses, and perhaps most influential of all, of her mother's long abandoned hopes and dreams, of being a famous dancer.

Charlotte Napier had met Jack Higgins, backstage at the Leeds Playhouse, in 1946. Lottie had been just twenty, willing to dance anything and everything from classical ballet to the chorus line. She was ambitious, hard-working and enthusiastic about her future career, but she had bargained without Jack's persistence. Having spotted her on stage, he waited for her at the stage door, persuaded her to go out to supper with him, and from then on met her every night after work. He did not say a lot, but he was kind, caring, reliable, and handsome, too, in a way. When the company moved on to Scarborough, Lottie had a clear choice – and she chose Jack. It had been a happy marriage, despite the hard, predictable drudgery, but it would have been unrealistic to have imagined that Lottie could entirely abandon her dreams. Instead, she transferred them to her children, though it soon became all too obvious that Ann and Sarah did not share her interests. It was only when little Miranda was born that she found a soulmate – the child would sit for hours, listening to stories of the theatre, dreaming dreams of a glamorous world, light years away from the drabness of their daily lives.

So gradually Miranda assumed a very special position within her family. She was, without doubt, her parents' favourite, allowed extra privileges because of her ill-health and frailty – the place nearest the fire, the last sandwich to build up her strength . . .

Then, in 1968, when Miranda was ten, everything changed. At forty-one, much to her surprise, Lottie found she was pregnant again. After nine months of perfect health, and an easy labour – so unlike Miranda's – she gave birth to the much-longed-for son, who they named Paul.

Miranda certainly did not dislike the baby. In fact, quite the contrary – she loved looking after him. He was a placid, easy child, given to smiling and laughing a great deal. What did she mind, in fact resent most bitterly, was the sudden and abrupt loss of her privileged position. She was no longer the youngest, no longer the centre of attention. Jack could not conceal his pride and pleasure in having a son at last. He was a man's man and all his hopes and dreams for the future now rested with Paul. It gave him a new energy for building up the farm – he had someone to pass it on to now, and his preoccupation with the boy was plain for all to see.

Lottie was more aware of Miranda's sudden loss of status. She tried to be even-handed in the amount of time and affection she afforded her children, but she could not help but find Paul quite irresistible. As Miranda became increasingly morose and difficult, so Lottie lavished more time and affection on the happy, gurgling baby. As for Ann and Sarah, nothing worried them. They had their friends, they had each other, and like everyone else, they adored their little brother. The more difficult their sister became, the more they ignored her, so that Miranda became increasingly isolated.

The problem was aggravated by the fact that at only eleven, before most of her contemporaries, Miranda started her periods, and the boys at school, noticing her budding breasts, did not hesitate to pass comment. Up until then, Miranda had considered being pretty an advantage. Now, suddenly, she saw it as a handicap, an embarrassment, something to be covered up at all costs. She began dressing in a drab and slovenly way, she rarely bothered to wash her hair. Having always had a small appetite, she began gorging herself on chips and sticky buns, with the result that by fourteen, not only was she overweight, but she had a fine crop of spots.

Certainly she achieved the desired effect – boys no longer showed the slightest interest in her. She never attended local dances nor mixed with other children outside school hours – she was the despair of her parents. In this, at least, she achieved a measure of success in regaining much of their attention, so worried were they by what was happening to their beautiful child.

Yet another metamorphosis was in store for Miranda in the summer of 1974, when she was sixteen years old. Her parents, appalled by the prospect of a long summer holiday stretching ahead, with a sulky, bored teenager on their hands, were at their wit's end as to what to do with her. By this time, Ann was married with two babies of her own and living in Bingley. Sarah, at twenty-two, still lived at home, working part-time on the farm and at the local riding stables. It was she who had the idea. 'About our Miranda,' she said, one night. Sarah and her parents were sitting round the kitchen range, the two younger children having already gone to bed. 'I've been thinking,' Sarah continued, 'what that girl needs is someone of her own.'

'If you're suggesting we marry her off, I'm all for it,' said Jack ruefully. 'Trouble is, who'd have her? Still, there's white slavery, I suppose – does it still exist?'

'Don't Jack,' Lottie said, reprovingly, 'that's no way to talk.'

Sarah laughed. 'I hadn't thought of marrying her off, though that's not a bad idea. No, what I had in mind was a puppy.'

Jack frowned. 'A puppy! We've got three dogs here already, love.'

'Yes,' said Sarah patiently, 'but they're sheep dogs, they're working dogs, not part of the family, particularly since they're not allowed to live in the house. I'm talking about a real companion for Miranda, a dog she can take for walks, you know, be a bit of company.'

'I won't have dogs in the house,' said Jack, firmly.

'All right, so what's the alternative? Have you got a better idea?'

'I think it might work,' Lottie said, slowly. 'I think our Sarah's on to something, Jack.'

'It just so happens,' Sarah continued, 'that the Delafields have a litter of flatcoat retrievers about ready to leave their mother. The Colonel was telling me about them today when he came back from his ride.'

'Flatcoats – they're crazy dogs,' Jack grumbled.

'Not if they're properly trained, Dad. I've done a lot of extra work on the Colonel's horses in the last few months and I reckon he'd let us have one for nothing, or next to nothing, anyway. If I fixed up for Miranda to go along and see them, then she could make her own decision – not feel pressurised by us, or anything. What do you say?'

'I say yes,' said Lottie. 'Jack?'

'I'm surrounded by nagging women,' he said, knocking his pipe against the hearth. His response might not have sounded encouraging to an outsider, but his family knew it meant they had won.

'I'm not going to the Delafields on my own,' Miranda said, 'they'll turn their noses up at me. They're right posh.'

'They're no better than you are,' Ann said, 'besides which, I've made an appointment for you. I can't go and cancel it now, it would be rude.'

'I can do without you organising my life,' Miranda said, angrily.

'Don't be so ungrateful to your sister. It was very kind of her to think of you,' Lottie said, firmly. In response, her youngest daughter slammed her way out of the kitchen.

Secretly though, Miranda was rather intrigued at the thought of paying a visit to the Delafields. Their house, Barnley Manor, was a couple of miles the other side of the village. She had been there once, years ago, when the village fete had been held in their grounds. She had a dim memory of a beautiful white house, shimmering in the heat of an early summer's day.

Then there was the question of the puppy. The idea was not without its appeal. She adored animals and although she had spent her whole childhood surrounded by them, she had never had anything of her own.

So on the appointed afternoon, Miranda took unusual care with her appearance. She washed her hair so it hung in soft, shining curls round her face, she wore a well-cut pair of jeans and a baggy shirt to hide her over-large hips. All this unaccustomed grooming took some while, and it was after three by the time she left home. It was a hot afternoon and to hurry would have made her sticky and uncomfortable, so she walked slowly. By the time she reached the gates of the Delafield's home it was nearly four – her appointment had been for three-fifteen.

From the moment she started to walk up the drive, Miranda forgot her own self-consciousness in the fascination of what she saw. From either side of the beautifully kept driveway, rolling parkland fell away. The Queen Anne house, so very different from most of the local architecture, stood imposing, yet oddly welcoming – the white walls she remembered, sparkled in the afternoon sunshine. She was so struck by the order, by the natural grace and style of the Manor, that she had already rung the door bell before wondering, in a panic, who would answer it. A butler or a maid seemed appropriate, so she was greatly surprised when instead, the door was opened by a boy. He was fair, stockily built, and about her own height. He had an open, honest face, good eyes – bright periwinkle blue – and a spattering of childish freckles over the bridge of his nose. He looked about seventeen or eighteen. He smiled, shyly. 'Are you Miranda Higgins?' Miranda nodded, completely tongue-tied. 'We've been expecting you. My stepmother couldn't wait any longer, she had to go out, but she's left me in charge. I'm to show you the puppies, and if you want one, you can take it home with you.'

'Thank you,' Miranda spluttered.

'Come on,' said the boy. 'They're in one of the stables at the back of the house. Oh, my name's Mark Delafield, by the way.' He grinned, engagingly. 'How do you do.'

'Hello,' Miranda muttered, puce with embarrassment now.

The stable was mostly used for storing hay, but at one end, it had been cordoned off with bales to provide sleeping quarters and a play area for the mother and six puppies. Her shyness temporarily forgotten, Miranda cried out in delight. 'Oh, they're beautiful.'

'Here, let me help you over the bales.' Mark held out a strong, brown hand. Miranda took it, her own trembling slightly. He held her tightly until she was in the dog's pen, and then released her, leaving her unaccountably hot and shaken. She felt awkward, alone with the boy in the semi-darkness of the barn – awkward yet exhilarated. 'Four dogs and two bitches,' Mark was saying. 'We're going to keep one of the bitches for breeding, so we've put a puppy collar on her to make sure we don't get muddled. Look, there she is.'

They crouched down together in the straw as, one by one, Mark passed to Miranda the squirming, fat little bodies for her inspection. As he did so, she watched his hands – strong, capable hands, that were nonetheless incredibly gentle with the puppies. She longed to reach out and touch them, to have them touch her, and the thought bewildered her. Hurriedly, she looked up at his face as he talked about the puppies. He was very tanned, but she saw that where his shirt collar fell open, the skin of his chest was pale. Somehow it made him look vulnerable, and far less intimidating. She realised, suddenly, that he was asking her a question. 'Sorry, what?' she said, blushing with confusion.

'I was asking why you wanted a puppy. Is it going to be a working dog for your father?'

'No,' said Miranda. 'My family seem to think I need a friend – you know, a sort of companion, a dog of my own – they think I'm . . . well, lonely.' She ended lamely, now acutely embarrassed. She hung her head, wondering what on earth had possessed her to make such a confession.

Mark was genuinely bewildered. 'You – lonely, and needing a friend? Surely not, you must have all the friends you could want, you're so . . .' It was his turn to be self conscious. '. . . so pretty.'

Miranda stared at him in amazement, which quickly turned to distrust – he was clearly laughing at her. 'There's no need to be unkind,' she said, standing up abruptly, and brushing the hay from her jeans.

'I'm not being unkind,' Mark said, jumping up too. 'I mean it, honestly. You're the most beautiful girl I've ever seen.'

'Then you must be blind,' Miranda turned away angrily. 'I'm fat, I'm spotty, and no one ever wants to go out with me.'

'Then it's them who are blind, not me.' Mark's face shone with sincerity. 'Look, Miranda, lots of people put on a bit of weight in their teens, especially girls, and as for spots. . . . I've only just grown out of mine. Look, I've still got the scars here on my chin.'

The light in the stables was dim, and Miranda had to move close to see where he pointed.

'I can't see any,' she said doubtfully, but her tone was less hostile, and she met his eye as she spoke.

They stared at one another in silence, the atmosphere becoming increasingly tense. Excitement, exhilaration, terror were all there, yet they stood apparently locked into immobility – unable to move or speak.

At last, tentatively, Mark put a hand on Miranda's arm, as if to steady them both, and it was this simple gesture which lit the fuse. In an instant she was in his arms, as he covered her face with inexpert kisses, his hands gripping her painfully. If she had wanted to cry out, she could not have done so – she was too shocked by the suddenness of the boy's reaction.

For a long time they stood returning each other's kisses, gaining in confidence, passion mounting between them. At last, dazed, Miranda allowed Mark to guide her to one of the stalls at the back of the barn, where the fresh hay was stored. She watched, transfixed, as he spread out an old horse blanket carefully on top of the hay. Then he took her hand and gently pulled her down on to the rug beside him. Neither spoke a word.

His kisses grew more urgent, and now his hands roamed her body. She felt him struggling with the buttons on her shirt. She knew she should stop him, but instead she helped him take off her shirt and unhook her bra. She was shy now, not because of her bare breasts, but because of the role of fat at her waist, caused by the tight jeans, so she was almost relieved when she felt him working on the jeans button and then the zip.

Curiously, when she was quite naked, she was not the slightest self conscious. She felt free, and somehow her ample figure seemed less unattractive in the soft lighting which crept through the wooden slats of the roof. She felt strangely confident and relaxed as she pulled Mark to her, as he sucked at her breasts and his fingers explored between her legs.

'I want you,' he croaked, 'I want you so much.'

It seemed a long time since anyone had wanted anything Miranda had to offer. If this boy wanted her, why not, she thought, her mind perfectly clear, and already made up.

'It's all right, you can if you want to,' she whispered.

'I want to, want to . . . oh God.' Mark sat up suddenly and began peeling off his clothes, while Miranda lay watching him.

Coming from a house full of sisters and a baby brother, Miranda had never seen the adult male organ before. It seemed huge to her, yet consumed with curiosity she put out a hand and touched it, as Mark turned back to her, and was astounded at how it reacted to her fingers.

'I've never done this before,' Mark said, his voice still strained and hoarse.

'Neither have I,' Miranda whispered, but she was not sure if he heard, for now he was on her – heavy, panting, hard against her as he parted her legs.

It hurt more than she could possibly have imagined and just when she thought she would scream with the pain, Mark suddenly tensed, shuddered and groaned, and she realised to her astonishment that it must be over.

There was a long silence during which neither of them spoke. Then Mark propped himself up on one elbow, gently eased out of her, and kissed her tentatively on the cheek. 'I'm – I'm sorry,' he said, 'I'm so terribly sorry. It's not supposed to be like that, only. . . .' He looked close to tears and suddenly Miranda felt the strong one, able to cope with the situation where he clearly could not. 'It's all right,' she said, with an apparent wisdom and knowledge she did not possess, 'I'm sure it's always awkward the first time.'

'Yes, but we've only just met. You came here to look at a puppy and I shouldn't. . . .' He shook his head, and then sat up and began dressing, his face creased with misery.

'It was as much my fault as yours,' Miranda said, desperate to relieve his distress in some way. She sat up too and began putting on her shirt, her unhappiness rising to match his.

They dressed in silence, carefully avoiding looking at one another, not knowing what to say or do.

Dressed at last, dishevelled in mind and body, they stood awkwardly together.

'Now about this puppy . . .' Mark began at last, and suddenly, miraculously, they were laughing – laughing as though they would never stop – children again, mercifully released from the adult world.

They chose a dog for Miranda, whom she decided to call Jolyon, Jolly for short – she had been reading the *Forsythe Saga* at school. Mark carefully prepared for her a bag of puppy meal, then loaded her and the puppy into his little MG Midget and drove her home.

By the time they reached the farm it was still only half past six, but to both of them, it seemed that their lives had changed irrevocably.

'Can I see you tomorrow?' Mark asked. 'We could take Jolly for a walk over the moor.'

'I'd like that,' Miranda replied. They were easy with each other now – more like old friends than new lovers.

'I'll come for you at eleven. I could bring a picnic lunch,' Mark suggested, earnestly.

'That would be great.'

They smiled shyly at one another. Miranda planted a clumsy kiss on his cheek and scrambled out of the car, the puppy clutched to her. 'Goodbye then.'

'Goodbye,' Mark called.

And so began the pattern of Miranda's summer. Every day, she and Mark walked, talked and played with the young pup. At first, still shattered from the violence of their initial encounter, and terrified lest Miranda should be pregnant, neither of them seemed anxious to pursue the sexual side of their relationship. However, once they knew that Miranda was not pregnant, Mark announced shyly one day that he had fixed himself up at the chemist's. So, from time to time, on an old rug which Mark provided, they experimented with the art of love-making. For Miranda these sessions were never as she imagined love should be and sometimes, she was shocked to realise, she was glad when they were over. But it was a small price to pay for Mark's company – she loved him – he was the best friend she had ever had. She loved their talks, and for the first time since Paul's birth, she found she was able to freely communicate, to amuse and entertain. She rediscovered her charm.

She learnt a great deal about Mark as well as herself – she learnt, too, that people were not always what they seemed. To all the world, Mark, in his flashy red sports car, with his Southern accent, beautifully cut tweed jackets and big house, seemed the very epitome of the confident young man. In fact he was far from that. His parents had divorced seven years before and his father had re-married – a woman Mark loathed, and who had subsequently borne his father two more children. They were both boys, who, even at seven and five, seemed a great deal more confident than Mark himself.

Mark was an academic failure, a fact of which his father

never missed an opportunity to remind him, and in the autumn he was being packed off to Tasmania for a year, to stay with relatives and gain practical farming experience. From there he was going to Cirencester Agricultural College for three years. 'I don't even like farming,' he confessed to Miranda, 'but anything's preferable to trying to go against my father's wishes.'

While she was growing in confidence and understanding, physically Miranda was changing too. The long walks had the desired effect on her figure, and she shed nearly a stone during the course of the summer. Sex and sunshine cleared up her complexion, and wanting always to look her best for Mark, she developed an interest in clothes. Her tastes were expensive, and when it became clear that her parents were not prepared to finance her, she took a Saturday job in Lewis's to pay for her new wardrobe. It was a very different girl to whom Mark Delafield said goodbye when he left for Tasmania, from the dumpy, dowdy teenager who had come to ask about a puppy.

In the years that were to follow, Miranda always looked back to Mark with affection and gratitude – she owed him so much. Yet despite a tearful farewell, and the promise of loving one another for ever, once Mark left the country, they never met again. By the time he returned from Tasmania, Miranda had already left home for a very different life.

Over the years she would see his photograph from time to time in the society pages, at hunt balls, Ascot, Henley. . . . Ironically, the nearest they ever got to being linked together again was when Mark's wedding was faithfully recorded in the same edition of *Harper's & Queen*, that carried Miranda on the front page. Both Mark and Miranda kept a copy of that magazine all their lives, but at no time did they ever attempt to make contact again. Both knew instinctively it would be a terrible mistake.

Back in 1974 though, Mark's departure left Miranda miserable and lonely again. She faithfully wrote him long, loving letters each week, but was disappointed in the response – Mark's letters were dull and scanty, and eventually their correspondence petered out altogether. However, her new appearance had a dramatic effect on the local boys.

They were all clambering to go out with her and whilst she did accept the odd date, and even allow the occasional good-night kiss, she was in no hurry to become involved in another sexual relationship. Indeed, she joined in so wholeheartedly with the other girls' ignorant giggling on the subject that after a while she found it hard to believe that she had any experience at all.

Jack and Lottie Higgins were flummoxed but greatly relieved by the change in their daughter. She was a bright girl and all set to take three A levels – she might even get to university, her teachers told them. Then, halfway through the academic year, Miranda dropped another bombshell. She did not want to stay on at school, she wanted a job. She had been at school long enough in her view. It was too childish and she needed to put it all behind her. They pleaded with her to stay on, but it was hopeless, and so at just turned seventeen, she left school and went to work at a branch of Lloyd's Bank in Bradford. It was there that she met Eric Fairfax . . .

Chapter Three

Eric Fairfax considered himself to be something of a lady's man. In fairness, he was not unattractive, in a rather brutish, thickset way. His hair was thinning a little on top, but he had kept his figure, and bearing in mind he was nearer fifty than forty, he was reasonably well-preserved. He was the kind of man who appeared to be most at home in a pub, drinking a large gin and tonic and chatting up the barmaid. As he was overly fond of saying, it was his job to keep a look out for a pretty face. He was in advertising – an art director working for Jackson & Smythe, a large agency, with offices in London and Manchester – and he used this position, exhaustively, in order to ingratiate himself with any young girl looking for a career in some aspect of the industry.

Eric Fairfax made the discovery of his life one wet and blustery July day. He was in Bradford, on his way home to Manchester, after visiting his sister and her family in Skipton. It was Friday, and realising he was short of money for the weekend, he stopped at Lloyd's Bank on the Skipton road.

He saw the girl the moment he walked through the doors. It was her hair that attracted him first – extraordinary white-gold curls – there was no way it could be natural, and yet. . . . He joined the queue for her cash desk, watching her intently as she worked. Apart from her wonderful colouring, her face was perfect. He knew her bone structure would photograph like a dream, and there was a freshness and vivacity about her, which was quite irresistible.

When it was his turn to be served, Eric feigned ill-temper. As she handed him his money, he made a considerable fuss of counting it. 'You're ten pounds short,' he said, belligerently.

She smiled at him pleasantly, completely self-assured. 'I don't think so, sir, but would you like me to check it again?'

'So that you can slip in ten pounds and pretend you haven't made a mistake?'

'No,' she said, 'just to see which of us is right.'

She could not be more than seventeen or eighteen, he judged, yet her poise was uncanny. Still, looking as she did, every able-bodied man in the district must be at her beck and call – she had every reason to be confident.

Slowly, in front of him, she counted out the money. It was correct, of course, but she showed no pleasure at having been right. 'It's quite an easy mistake, sir,' she said, 'the notes stick together so.'

God damn it, she's wonderful, Eric thought, as he walked back to the car and she would be a dead ringer for PIPPA, he was sure of it. PIPPA PAINTS was a new range of cosmetics, being launched by a large conglomerate, aimed specifically at teenagers. The launch was being handled by the London office, but so far as Eric was aware, they had yet to find the right model. Whoever they chose, quite clearly had to be entirely unknown, since her face needed to be used exclusively on PIPPA products, at any rate, until after the launch period. Eric glanced at his watch – it was still only 1.45 – a few pints, a girl for the afternoon, and then he would meet the little bank clerk when she came out of work. Suddenly, the prospect of the afternoon ahead seemed enormously attractive.

Eric was outside the bank at 4.50, feeling decidedly jaded. He had drunk too much, and the decision to take a pair of girls to bed for the afternoon, though undeniably exciting, had proved exhausting. What he needed was a few hours sleep. All fatigue left him, though, as soon as Miranda came out through the door of the bank. Purposely, Eric had positioned himself across the street, so that he could watch her walk. She was much taller than he had imagined, which of course was a positive advantage. Her walk was smooth and graceful, like a cat. He watched her, entranced, and then to his horror, he saw her step forward to hail a passing cab. A bank clerk hiring a cab – he had not bargained for that. Nearly killing himself, he ran between the rush hour traffic and reached her just as she was about to enter the waiting taxi.

'Wait a moment,' he said, breathlessly, 'I must speak to you.'

She looked at him blankly for a moment and then he saw recognition flood into her face. 'I did give you the right money.' Unprotected now by the bank counter, she seemed younger, more vulnerable.

'Oh, I know, I know,' he said, impatiently. 'I just made all that fuss to test your reactions. Look, we need to talk.'

She smiled slightly. 'No we don't, if you'll excuse me, I'm in a hurry.'

'Wait a moment, please – at least hear what I have to say. I think I've got a job for you, a fantastic job.' He noted her expression was now tinged with cynicism. 'No, really, I'm not trying to pick you up, I promise.' Just for a split second, she hesitated, and that was all he needed. 'I won't take no for an answer – I'll be back here every day, I'll wear you down until you at least agree to hear me out. If you're worried that I have some ulterior motive, perhaps one of your colleagues from the bank could join us for a drink.'

'I don't need chaperoning, I can look after myself.'

Eric didn't doubt it, and he realised that if he was not careful he was going to lose her. Suddenly, inspiration struck. 'Where are you going in the cab?'

'Only home,' she replied, hesitantly.

'In that case, how about a drink and then I promise I'll drive you home – it will save you a fare.'

'It rather depends on how the drink goes,' she replied, stiffly, and Eric knew he had won.

He took her to the Queen's Hotel, imagining, rightly, that the quiet opulence of the bar would please her. Once drinks were ordered, he stalled her questions by asking one of his own. 'How come, on a bank clerk's wages, you can afford to take a cab home every night?'

'I don't, every night,' Miranda replied, defensively, 'just on Fridays.'

'Why?' Eric asked. He saw a flicker of irritation cross her face. 'I'm sorry to be so blunt, only I'm intrigued,' he explained, gently.

'There's nothing wrong with being blunt,' Miranda said, 'but what I do with my time is my business. Why don't you tell me what you want and why it's so important that we have this talk.'

It only took Eric a few minutes to outline his idea that Miranda should audition for the PIPPA PAINTS job. It took him considerably longer to answer her questions. She left no stone unturned – how much money would she earn, would she be restricted from doing any other modelling, would she have to live in London, when would she start. . . .

'Look, love,' Eric was forced to say after a while, 'I can only put you up for the job, I'm not promising you're going to get it. There'll be stiff competition.'

'I know that,' said Miranda, 'but it seems only sensible to know what I'm in for if I do get the job. After all, there's no point in going for the audition at all, unless I go with the idea of winning.'

Her straightforward common sense delighted Eric. He was amazed by her, and would have been even more so had he known the true reason for Miranda's weekly cab ride. When Mark Delafield went to Tasmania, he left behind him a legacy. Through him, Miranda had glimpsed what she judged to be, a better life than her own – where young people had cars, ate out in restaurants, took holidays in the sun. Miranda's burning ambition now was to escape her background. The job at the bank was not much, but it was a starting point – and the best way to keep her ambitions alive was a constant weekly reminder of what life could be like. So, every Friday she spent a vast amount of her wages on sitting blissfully in a taxi, which took her home in ten minutes, rather than fight with the Bradford crowds for a seat on the bus, which took an hour and a half to travel the same distance. Miranda was ripe for a chance to escape, and clearly Eric Fairfax represented that chance.

Eric wasted no time. It was not difficult to sense Miranda's immediate excitement at his proposal, and rather than run the risk of her being talked out of her enthusiasm, he suggested running her home, and talking to her parents straight away. She agreed.

The interview was far from easy. Clearly he had an ally in

Mrs Higgins, but Miranda's father was apparently immovable in his condemnation of Eric's proposal. In the end, they reached a Mexican stand-off. The Higgins family would think things through over the weekend, and Miranda would ring Eric in his Manchester office on Monday morning with their decision.

It was a turbulent weekend at the farm. Miranda tried her utmost initially to be tactful and persuasive, making sure to keep her temper, even when provoked, and putting forward what she believed to be good, plausible arguments. Initially, her mother backed her, but as the weekend wore on, Lottie's resistance began to slip. 'Your dad's a stubborn man, Miranda, always has been. I've never been able to stand up to him and it's too late for me to start now. You'd better do as he says, love, and forget the whole idea.'

'I can't and I won't,' Miranda said.

The crunch came on Sunday evening. Miranda confronted her father and told him that if she was unable to audition for PIPPA with his permission, then she would simply do so without it. Jack was far too dismissive in his response, which only served to fan the flames of her determination. 'Don't be silly, love,' he said, 'what will you live on in London? Let's face facts, it's very unlikely you'll be successful with the audition, and if you're not, what are you going to do about a job – the bank won't have you back. Go if you must, but you'll be back with your tail between your legs in thirty-six hours – mark my words.'

So she went, stealthily down the back stairs, at four in the morning, just an hour before her father got up for milking. In the village she caught the first bus to Bradford, from Bradford, a train to Manchester, and by nine-thirty, she presented herself at Eric's office.

He listened, cautiously, to her story. 'So, you've left your job and your home, all on the strength of an audition?'

She nodded. 'I was looking for an excuse to leave, anyway.' She sounded a great deal more confident than she felt.

'Did you leave your parents a note?' he asked, casually.

'No, but they'll guess what I've done.'

Alarm bells rang in Eric's head. The last thing he wanted was any sort of trouble – perhaps the parents would ask the police to trace the girl. She had said she was eighteen in two months' time, but was it true? It was hard to tell with these young girls – he had experienced one or two narrow escapes with under-age kids before. 'I think I should ring your parents, tell them you're safe and that I'll look after you. I think it's only fair to them, don't you?' He smiled kindly. 'And don't worry, love – if you don't make the PIPPA audition, I'm sure I'll be able to fix you up with some fashion modelling, if that's what you want.'

'It is what I want,' Miranda said, fervently.

'OK, go and wait out in my secretary's office and I'll speak to your father. Will you give me the number?'

Jack Higgins was brief and to the point. He had washed his hands of his daughter, he told Eric. If she wanted to throw her life away, to give up her good steady job for pie-in-the sky day dreams, it was up to her – she had caused her mother enough worry and trouble in her short life as it was. He asked Eric to ensure Miranda wrote home, with her address if she settled in London. Other than that, he had nothing to add, except to say that if Eric ever showed his face near their home again, he would knock his teeth down his throat.

Eric replaced the receiver, well pleased. Clearly the Higgins were not going to make any trouble. What Miranda was trying to do was totally alien to their world. They simply could not cope and so they had washed their hands of her, which was entirely satisfactory.

Miranda cried herself to sleep that night, in the dingy little hotel Eric had found for her, prior to their departure for London the following day. She missed the warmth and familiarity of home, she missed the comfort of Jolly's devotion, and above all, she missed her mother. She hated hurting Lottie – all she could hope was that somewhere, deep down, her mother understood.

Eric by contrast, was in high spirits. Twice divorced, he lived alone when in Manchester, in a comfortable flat in Sackville Street. He spent the evening making plans. As things were, they could not have turned out better. Miranda was friendless and vulnerable, dependent on him for everything. The next few months were suddenly full of delicious promise.

Chapter Four

Jenny Marchant stood in the doorway, surveying the room with distaste. She hated agency parties, but Jackson & Smythe, the hosts, were one of the more influential advertising agents, and were responsible for passing her a great deal of work. She could not afford to be missing.

'Darling!' Pete Smythe appeared out of the crowd, swept her into an embrace and kissed her on the lips. He smelt of gin. 'Now you've arrived, the party can begin,' he said. His smile was wide and welcoming, but it never reached his eyes, and Jenny wondered idly, how many times he had used that particular phrase during the course of the evening.

'Darling Pete, how lovely to see you,' she said, smiling sweetly. 'Be a pet and fetch me a drink, and then I'd like you to introduce me to someone I haven't met before – preferably male, and of pleasing appearance.'

Pete stood beside her and joined in her scrutiny of the room. 'The tragedy is, darling, I don't believe there's anyone here you don't know – though some, of course, you are more intimately acquainted with than others.' He leered. 'Wait here, Sugarplum, I'll be back in a moment with a nice drinky poos.'

Pete smiled as he elbowed his way through the crowd towards the bar. He was well pleased with himself. Jenny Marchant's appetite for men was legend. Years ago, he had nearly scored with her himself one night, when they had all been at some dreadful conference in Torquay. Her rejection of him had been less than tactful, and since then he had never turned up an opportunity to bitch at her.

Pete's words were water off a duck's back to Jenny. The

moment he disappeared into the crowd, she forgot him. She realised, suddenly, that there had been no time for lunch and that she was terribly hungry. She could see a buffet table at the far end of the room – perhaps some food would make her feel less morose. She began easing her way through the crowd, calling out greetings here and there as she went. She had almost reached her goal when, suddenly, she noticed a head which stood out from all the rest. The girl had her back to Jenny. Her hair was long and fine, hanging in glossy curls, but it was the colour that was so amazing – white gold. It had to be natural – no such colour could come out of a bottle.

The girl stood a little apart from the group talking round her. She was obviously feeling nervous and confused by the din of the party. Then, as if sensing Jenny's eyes upon her, she turned and glanced over her shoulder. Jenny caught her breath, the face was stunning – the profile, the cheekbones and those enormous, sad brown eyes. Food quite forgotten now, Jenny covered the short distance between them. 'Hello,' she said. 'My name's Jenny Marchant. Who are you?'

'Miranda,' the girl replied, smiling with relief, 'Miranda Hig . . . Hicks.'

Jenny held out a hand. 'Pleased to meet you, Miranda. I couldn't resist coming over to talk to you. I run a model agency, and I was aware that I haven't seen you around before. I take it you are a model?'

'Only just.' The girl gave a disarming smile, tinged with humour – a model who could laugh at herself? Jenny, who always formed instant opinions of people, warmed to her immediately.

The girl stood head and shoulders above most of the other women in the room, Jenny observed, and as yet she had not learnt to stand properly – she was still somewhat self conscious of her height. Yet, she had flair. She was dressed in a black cat suit, tucked into red boots, with a red belt and scarf to match. She looked exotic, dashing, yet, Jenny judged, she was little more than seventeen. 'Who is your agent?' Jenny asked, without preamble – this girl, she must have.

Miranda looked uncomfortable. 'I don't have one, exactly, but Eric Fairfax is looking after me.'

Inwardly Jenny shuddered, but her expression remained impassive. Eric was one of the more obnoxious members of Jackson & Smythe, and briefly, Jenny wondered what sort of relationship he had with the girl. Instinctively she felt none – as yet. There was a freshness about her, and she was certainly far from street-wise. 'Where do you come from?' Jenny asked. 'Where is your home, I mean.'

The girl smiled. 'You mean you don't recognise my accent?'

Jenny frowned. 'Well, I realise you have a slight accent, but no, I can't place it.'

'Then the elocution lessons are working,' the girl laughed delightedly, and Jenny joined in her laughter.

'Why elocution lessons?' she asked. 'I thought it was trendy to have a regional accent these days.'

'It was Eric's idea,' Miranda replied. 'I've been chosen for the launch of PIPPA. Of course, most of my work will be photographic, but I will have to do a certain amount of promotional work, as well – you know, visit stores, that sort of thing. Eric thought my accent was a bit strong for that.' She grinned again. 'I'm straight off the Yorkshire moors, you see.'

Jenny laughed. 'How long ago did you escape?'

Miranda grimaced. 'Only five weeks ago. I'm still a little shell-shocked, and as for London . . . I don't know whether to love or hate it.'

'Have you found somewhere decent to live?' Jenny asked.

'Not bad. A bed-sit, just off Holland Park Avenue. Eric organised it, along with everything else.' Her face suddenly looked tired and strained. 'I'm taking lessons in make-up, I go to dance classes, then there's the elocution, and the hairdressers every day. Eric insisted on my buying a completely new wardrobe. I've had to throw away all my old clothes – even my jeans.' Miranda shrugged. 'It must all be costing an absolute fortune, but Eric says the agency are paying for it, and that they'll get their money back once the PIPPA contract is underway.'

I bet they will, Jenny thought. Poor little thing – there will be precious little money left for her by the time the agency had taken their cut. She smiled reassuringly. 'Don't you worry about how much the agency spends on you. Once PIPPA takes off, you'll be a hot property and they'll more than get their money back.' She opened her bag and pulled out a distinctive black and gold business card. 'Look, here's my card, Miranda. If you want any help at any time, don't hesitate to contact me. I mean that. My office is near Holland Park Avenue too, so drop in any time.'

Miranda took the card gratefully. 'Thanks a lot.'

'And be careful about your contract. Read all the small print. It's not just a question of money, you want to make sure that you are not committed to working either purely through this agency, or for PIPPA. With your looks, sweetheart, you could go a long way, and you don't want to be restricted from doing so.' Jenny grinned. 'I'm sorry, I'm clucking like a mother hen, but it's not an easy business, this one.'

'I'm grateful for the advice,' said Miranda, 'truly.'

'And one final thing,' said Jenny, 'watch that rat, Eric Fairfax.'

'Oh, I will.'

'I must circulate,' said Jenny. 'Nice to meet you, Miranda. Good luck.'

'Thanks.'

As Jenny pushed her way through the crowd, she was acutely aware of the haunted look in Miranda's eyes, but she knew it would be dangerous to stay talking to her longer, or someone from the agency would suspect her of trying to poach the girl . . . and represent Miranda Hicks she would, sooner or later – of that, she was determined.

The party at the agency was the culmination of five of the most difficult and bewildering weeks in Miranda's life. To have been awarded the PIPPA contract was wonderful, and she was desperate to do her very best, but there was so much to learn about modelling. Eric seemed so ambitious for her, packing her every day full of activity. She was grateful for his guidance but she was kept so busy she never had any time to be alone to assess what was happening. Although the contracts were still being drawn up, she was already doing daily shoots for PIPPA and this was more than enough for her to cope with – yet Eric insisted on her undertaking other fashion assignments as well. 'You need the practise, love,' he assured her. And he guarded her so jealously – never leaving her alone for more than a moment. Indeed, Jenny had hardly left her side before Eric was at her elbow. 'What did she want?' he asked, venomously.

Miranda was glad she had slipped Jenny's card into her bag. 'Oh, nothing. She was just introducing herself. She seemed nice.'

'Nice . . . she's a viper, don't you have any dealings with her. Jenny Marchant is one of the toughest women in the business. She makes and breaks people's careers without giving it a thought.'

It was all so confusing. Who was she to believe? Every day someone warned her about Eric, yet he always turned the tables on them, stressing that he was her protector, and so far, there was no denying, he had looked after her interests well.

The morning following the Jackson & Smythe party, Miranda presented herself at their offices, at nine-thirty sharp, as she did every day unless otherwise instructed. Eric was in a jocular mood. 'A new challenge for you, Miranda,' he said. He leaned back in his chair, squinting at her through his cigarette smoke.

Miranda's heart sank. 'Oh yes,' she said, trying to sound enthusiastic.

'You have to be sunkissed by Thursday – a company I know want you to model some beachwear.'

'Don't they want to see me first before they decide?'

Eric shook his head. 'No, I showed them some pics of you and they're dead keen.'

'Which company is it?' Miranda asked.

'Oh, one of the mailing houses, I can't remember which now. Anyway, the point is, we need you browned up a little, so I've booked you a course on a sunbed – five sessions should be enough. You'll have to put cottonwool pads over your eyes, rather than goggles – there mustn't be any marks on your face bearing in mind PIPPA – and don't overdo it, just a light tan. The first session is in ten minutes, just round the corner from here, so quick march. Here's the address.'

His manner irritated Miranda. She felt tired and resentful.

'How much am I going to earn for modelling this beachwear?' she demanded.

Eric looked surprised. 'Three, maybe four hundred pounds,' he said. 'It depends on how long it lasts.'

'Good, then perhaps you could let me have some of it on account, because I've decided I'd like to go home for the weekend.'

Eric stood up, his eyes suddenly steely. 'Look, Miranda, I don't think you quite understand the position. In normal circumstances, models are given nothing until their agents are paid. In your case, I'm giving you twenty quid a week and paying for your flat, and so far you've earned me precisely nothing.'

'Why are you suddenly saying I and me?' Miranda asked. 'You told me the agency were meeting my expenses.'

'They've paid for your clothes, certainly, and your various lessons, but I'm paying your board and lodging, and providing you with the twenty pounds.'

'Why?' Miranda asked. She supposed she should feel grateful but for some reason she felt angry and humiliated.

'Because if I hadn't, you wouldn't even have been a contender for PIPPA. You have no resources of your own, and without my backing, you would have been forced to turn down the offer – just think about it for a moment.'

'You're making me sound like a charity case,' Miranda said, angrily.

'Sweetheart, you are a charity case. Frankly, I'm taking a considerable risk with you. At any time until that contract is signed, PIPPA could change their mind – or after three months, they could decide not to renew. You're a pretty girl, but we don't know yet whether you've got what it takes. I'm willing to take the risk, because I like you and I want you to succeed, but it's time you looked at the big, bad world with your eyes open. Think of that good old Yorkshire expression – owt for nowt? I've demonstrated my faith in you – now what you have to do, darling, is come up with the goods.'

'I think I *am* fulfilling my part of the bargain,' Miranda said, morosely.

'Up to a point, yes, but I still don't feel you're really committed. Certainly if you were, you wouldn't be wanting to swan off to Yorkshire for the weekend. And in answer to your original question, no, I'm not prepared to fund your trip. I need you here – now – to take advantage of all the offers that come your way. Besides which, I didn't think there was much love lost between you and the Yorkshire moors.'

A sudden mental picture of the farmhouse kitchen came into Miranda's mind – of her mother, bending over the Aga, her father sitting at the kitchen table reading a newspaper, Paul doing his homework, Jolly grunting contentedly in front of the fire. At that moment she would have given anything to be back in that safe, secure world. To her horror, her eyes filled with tears, but if he noticed, Eric chose to ignore them.

'Well, are you going to stand there sulking, or have you anything more to say?'

Miranda glanced at the card – Paula's Beauty Salon, 31 Baker Street – it read. She sighed. 'To find this place, which way do I go when I leave the building?'

'That's my girl,' said Eric. 'Come along, I'll walk there with you.'

Eric's manner was immediately friendly and relaxed again, now he had won, but the exchange left Miranda with a feeling of unease. She had seen a side of Eric she didn't like, though later, analysing what he had said, it was hard to justify her feelings. It was true, he was behaving very generously towards her, so why not just settle for being grateful? Somehow the situation did not seem that simple.

Miranda's feeling of unease continued all week, but by Thursday, as Eric had requested, she had a light tan which suited her well. The beachwear was being photographed at studios in Earlham Street. Miranda was told to present herself at eleven-thirty and ask for the photographer, Joe Chang.

Joe Chang was far less Chinese than his name suggested. He had the straight black hair of the oriental, but he was tall with an aqualine nose, and a deep suntan. His appearance was exotic – a cream silk shirt, black trousers, Cossack boots and a large gold earing dangling from one ear.

'Sweet child,' he said, kissing Miranda on both cheeks.

'Eric told me, of course, that you were a pearl, but nothing could have prepared me for this. You are wonderful, a positive jewel.' Before Miranda could think of a suitable reply, Joe draped an arm round her and ushered her through the front door.

Miranda had already become accustomed to the fact that photographers' studios could be somewhat bizarre, but Joe Chang's was in a different league from anything she had visited before. The predominant colours were black and silver – black walls with silver stars. Silver fabric was draped across the set, which was dominated by a king-sized silver bed. Gentle music hummed in the background and there was a sweet fragrance in the air, which Miranda, in her innocence, did not recognise. Instead of blinding her, as was usual, the studio spots gave off low, subtle lighting. Joe, arm still firmly about her, led her onto the set. By the bed there was a table on which stood a bottle of champagne.

'A glass of champagne, dear,' Joe suggested.

Miranda, used by now to coffee out of cracked mugs from the average photographer, was taken aback by this VIP treatment. 'Isn't it a little early?'

'It's never too early in the day for champagne, and a girl like you should never drink anything else.' Joe poured them both a glass. 'To you, Miranda,' he said, with a slow smile, 'and to your future. By all accounts, according to Eric, it's going to be quite something. Now I've met you, I have to admit the old bugger's right.'

'Thank you,' said Miranda. 'This place is amazing,' she said, staring around her.

'Fun, isn't it?'

Miranda frowned. 'I can't see much evidence of sea.'

'Sea? What on earth's sea got to do with it?' Joe said. 'Here, let me top you up.'

'No, I'm fine,' said Miranda, but he ignored her, filling her glass until it was almost overflowing. 'I thought I was supposed to be doing some bikini modelling.'

Joe hesitated for a split second. 'So you are, dear, so you are, but bikinis don't just look good on the beach, you know. Come on, I'll take you to your dressing room. Shall I lead the way?'

Miranda watched Joe as he walked ahead of her down the corridor – broad shoulders, narrow hips, amazingly elegant. He was quite different from the photographers she was used to – so often scruffy, tactless and of questionable temper. She was impressed with Joe Chang.

The dressing room was small but warm and well lit. Joe solemnly handed her a small black and silver bikini and told her to take as long as she wanted to get ready. Miranda settled herself down at the mirror and began, what was becoming for her, the routine preparation. It was only as she worked, she suddenly realised that the bikini she had been given matched the set. Had the set been especially created for her? Surely not, it must have cost a fortune.

The bikini fitted as though it had been made for her – the tiny silver diamonds in the fabric were a perfect foil for her hair, which trailed down her back in long, silky ringlets. When she was ready, she slipped on a robe, picked up her glass of champagne for support, and walked out onto the set.

The bed was now piled high with black and silver cushions. 'Well done, you're ready, that was quick!' Joe stepped out of the darkness.

Clearly, he must have assistance with a studio this size, Miranda thought, fleetingly, but there seemed to be no one else about.

'Take off your robe and make yourself comfortable against those cushions, dear,' he said. 'Here, let me top up your glass.'

Miranda reclined back on the cushions, as she was bid, sipped her champagne and gazed around, while Joe adjusted the lighting. She felt relaxed and confident. The studio was warm and the surrounding inky-blackness gave it an intimate, almost cosy feel.

'OK, dear, are you ready?' Miranda nodded, and Joe removed her champagne glass. 'Lovely, now just relax. That's it, turn a little to me. Now look to your right, chin down, perfect . . .'

For ten minutes, perhaps quarter of an hour, they worked, Joe giving gentle, clear instructions. He was an easy man to work for Miranda decided, dreamily, as she turned this way and that.

'OK, darling, that's great,' said Joe, at last. 'Now let's do some without the top.'

In an instant, Miranda was alert, her sense of calm evaporated. 'What did you say?' she asked, peering into the lights.

'Take off the top, dear, and let's have a look at those gorgeous boobs.'

'No, I won't,' said Miranda, her heart beginning to beat double quick time.

'Don't be silly, dear, I haven't got all day.' Joe walked out from behind his camera, and as he came into view, Miranda could see his smile was not so gentle now.

'I'm supposed to be modelling a bikini – at least that's what Eric told me.'

'You are, dear,' said Joe falsely patient, 'but haven't you ever heard of topless beaches? Stripping off in front of me is no big deal. God knows, I've seen it all before.'

'It may be something you're used to, but I'm not.' Miranda was sitting up now. She reached instinctively for her robe to protect herself.

'Didn't Eric tell you that you'd be expected to go topless?' Miranda shook her head. 'Well, that's too bad of him, he should have done, but anyway, it's too late now. Come on, let me help you.'

'No!' Miranda shrank from him, scrambling across the bed. She pulled her wrap clumsily around her and ran down the corridor towards the dressing room. Once inside, she slammed the door, and leaned back against it, breathless and trembling. Across the room from her was the mirror – she stared at her reflection and saw the face of a frightened child staring back.

She was still standing by the door when Joe came in, carrying a steaming mug. 'A hot toddy for you, dear, to help you relax,' he said, pushing the mug into her hands.

'What's in it?' Miranda asked, suspiciously.

'Brandy, honey and lemon juice, topped up with boiling water,' said Joe, neglecting to mention the three sedatives he had also added. 'Look, my darling, I do sympathise, I really do, but you're not being very professional, are you?'

At his words, Miranda slumped into her chair and began sipping the drink. 'I-It's just I've never done this sort of thing before. I-I didn't expect I'd have to. I can't, I just can't.'

'Tell me,' said Joe, 'what are your ambitions? What do you want to achieve from your career?'

Miranda looked up, surprised by the sudden change of subject. She shrugged her shoulders. 'I suppose I'd like all the things my parents didn't have – particularly my mother. My mother missed out dreadfully. She was a really good dancer, until she married. Then she gave up her career and has spent the rest of her life cooking and cleaning – I don't want that.'

'So,' said Joe, quietly, 'you want money, and plenty of it, in order that you need never live the sort of life your mother was forced to?'

'Y-yes, I suppose so.'

'Then, dear, you're going to have to brace up and grow up,' said Joe. 'If you want to get rich, you have to work for it and as I said just now, that means being professional, and doing what the client wants.'

'I am trying to be professional,' said Miranda, plaintively.

'Then prove it, by taking a deep breath and doing this shot for me.'

'I can't.'

'You can and you must. Look, there's no one here but me. If I have to go back to the client – come to that, if I have to go back to Eric – and say you've refused, it could well be the end of your career. To be a model these days you have to be prepared to go topless.'

'I don't see why . . .' Miranda began.

'How long have you been in this business?' Joe interrupted.

'I expect you know,' Miranda mumbled, 'about five and a half weeks.'

'I've been in it for twenty years, so don't argue with me – I know what I'm talking about. If you don't come across with the goods, today, it will be all over the industry tomorrow. There's too much money involved in this game for models to get away with pissing about.' He stood up abruptly, his face hard and determined. Standing over her, his long, lean figure seemed suddenly predatory. 'I'm going to wait for you out by the camera. You drink up your hot toddy and think about what I've said very carefully. It's up to you – it's your decision – but in my view, if you don't do this shot, Miranda Hicks, you're finished.' Without waiting for a reply he left the room.

Finished, before she had hardly started. Miranda hunched into her wrap and continued sipping the warming drink. All her upbringing, all her life to date, when used as a yardstick to define right from wrong, made the decision easy – this was something she could not, and must not, do. Yet were her old values of any relevance here? Hadn't she forsaken her old way of life for a new one? Heavens above, this was 1975 – things had changed a lot since her parents' day. On a practical level, whatever magazine she was due to appear in, surely her mother would never read. She continued to sip at her drink, and as she did so, she began to relax again. A warmth crept through her body, her limbs felt heavy and languid. When she stared into the mirror, her eyes seemed enormous. Mechanically, she began repairing her makeup, not recognising the gesture as a sign of commitment. When she had finished, she studied her reflection, and then smiled. The girl who smiled back was light years away from the one who had run frightened to her dressing room half an hour before. This one was confident, sophisticated, and had she but known it, drugged to the eyeballs. 'You can do it,' she told her reflection. 'You go out there and show him.' She took a deep breath, stood up, and with head high, walked out onto the set.

Joe came forward to greet her, his smile warm and paternal. 'There's my girl,' he said, taking her wrap. 'Now come over here.' He settled her again on the cushions. 'I'll just check the lights.' While he was away, it was all Miranda could do to keep awake. It seemed sometime before he was beside her again. 'You're not dropping off, are you?' he asked, kindly.

She forced her eyes open. 'No, but I do feel tired, I don't know what's wrong with me.'

'It's because you're feeling relaxed and not worried any more. Sit up for a moment.' He unhooked her bra, with all the clinical efficiency of a doctor, and with about as much interest, or so it appeared to Miranda. 'Now lie back in the cushions again, as you were,' Joe commanded. He smiled down at her. 'That feels all right, doesn't it?' Miranda nodded. 'Now, dear, all you have to do is relax.'

From behind the camera, Joe's voice floated into Miranda's consciousness.

'That's wonderful, my darling. Smile, that's it, you're feeling really good now, aren't you? Right then, so show me how good. OK, now stretch, hands above your head, a big stretch – that's right – now relax again, lovely. Darling, you're pure magic.'

In Miranda's drugged mind, it seemed that she could respond instinctively to Joe's commands, moving her hips this way, then that, rolling around on the cushions with ease and grace. After a while Joe turned on the music again – gentle, seductive background stuff, which heightened Miranda's feeling of relaxation. Time became meaningless – she could think of nothing outside this incredible room, the strange sensations in her head and Joe's gentle voice telling her again and again how wonderful she was.

She was never to know at what point he came and lay beside her – she became dimly aware of his voice being closer, then of his amazingly soft hands on her body and of his lips trailing across her face, her neck, her breasts. It seemed only natural, purely an extension of the photography. Sometime later, she realised that she was naked and so was he. His hands were everywhere – he sucked her nipples, making her squirm with delight, then he let his tongue run down her stomach – down, down. She felt his hot breath between her legs and cried out with pleasure, lifting her body to him. She was his, he could do what he liked with her so long as he did not stop.

From the dark shadows of the studio, Eric Fairfax watched the scene on the bed. He ran his tongue over his dry lips, the pain in his groin almost unendurable. He was desperate to join them, yet he suspected it was too soon for Miranda – the last thing they must do was to frighten her at this stage. From the moment he had first seen her, Eric had recognised her sensuality. Those voluptuous breasts set against her innocent, childlike face and otherwise coltish body, were every man's fantasy. He groaned and began feverishly struggling with the zip of his trousers. As his body jerked in spasms, he promised himself that next time, he would have his share.

Miranda lay spreadeagled on the bed, her hands clutching at the sheets, her face contorted. Joe's tongue worked on her, bringing her to the first climax of her life . . . and her screams of ecstasy drowned all sounds of the whirling camera.

Chapter Five

Three sensations hit Miranda simultaneously. Sunlight, streaming through the bedroom window blinded her as she tried to open her eyes, with it came the realisation that she felt very sick, and as she staggered from the bed to her tiny basin, the pain in her head was so profound that for a moment she did not know whether she was going to be sick or faint. She was sick.

Weak, cold and shaking, she crawled back between the sheets and lay with her eyes tightly shut, until the pain in her head eased a little. Then, like a cancer, memory assiduously began seeping into her brain. She remembered Joe and a taxi driver helping her up the stairs to her room. To the taxi driver's concerned enquiry, she remembered Joe's suave response that she had drunk too much at an office party. She remembered her sense of outrage at the time, but despite a struggle, her apparent inability to speak. Earlier, she remembered waking on the silver bed, to find Joe fully clothed, leaning over her, a look of concern on his face, and his careful explanation that he was going to take her home.

Of what happened before that, she tried to close her mind against the memories, but there was no escape. How could she had done those things? How could she have let Joe do what he had done to her? She remembered her own hoarse cries of pleasure, of her begging for more – it was a nightmare. Shame washed over her and she began to sob. She sobbed until she was forced from the bed to be sick again and then collapse once more, drained and exhausted.

Mercifully she must have slept, for when she woke again, her clock told her it was early afternoon. Feeling a little stronger now, she swung her legs out of bed and tentatively stood up. 'I must go home,' she muttered, 'I must get away, now.' Without further thought, she lifted down a case from the top of the wardrobe and began packing feverishly – not the new clothes that Eric had bought her, none of those, just odd personal things. It was when she picked up the photograph of her parents that she stopped and, gingerly, sat down on the bed again. She studied the familiar faces, gazing back at her, open and honest. How could she go back to them now? She was corrupt, sick. How could she ever look her mother in the eye after what had happened? Her home represented everything that was good and wholesome – and she would never be that again. She let the photograph fall onto the bed and for a long time she simply sat, staring blankly ahead of her. No, she could not go home, not for a long time, if ever. With this realisation came a mounting anger, initially with herself and then, as she thought through what had happened to her, with the man who had caused it all.

Eric Fairfax was a worried man. He paced his office in an agony of indecision. They had gone too far with Miranda yesterday, much too far – he was now painfully aware of that fact. Joe had overdone the drugs so that, temporarily, her normal personality had been completely destroyed, and her behaviour had been that of a stranger. The trouble was, at the time, rational thought had been impossible – it had been so damned exciting – he had never been so aroused before. All he could hope was that she remembered little of what had happened. And bloody hell, where was she? He should have stayed with her in her room until she woke up, just to make sure she did nothing stupid. So why hadn't he? Remorse was not an emotion one could normally apply to Eric Fairfax but at that moment he came as near to the emotion as he would ever do in his life. He knew her background, he knew the kind of girl she really was, and after what had happened, he felt ashamed to face her. A telephone call first thing had established that Miranda was still in bed, or so her landlady informed him. When he rang later, there was no reply. He did not want to leave his office in case she was on her way over to him, yet it did not seem right for her to be alone in her room.

It was nearly three o'clock before it appeared that his gamble had paid off. His secretary announced on the intercom – 'Miss Hicks is in reception to see you.'

'Thank God for that,' Eric murmured. 'Show her. . . .' He never finished the sentence – Miranda burst through his office door, slamming it behind her. Her face was unnaturally pale, except for two spots of colour on her cheeks. There were dark shadows under her eyes, which were bloodshot and puffy. Her hair was tousled. She looked dreadful. 'Miranda!' said Eric, feigning surprise and moving forward to take her arm.

'Don't touch me and don't speak.' The venom in her voice, the look in her eye, rooted Eric to the spot. 'You bastard,' Miranda spat. 'You bloody bastard. Just what are you trying to do to me?'

'I . . .' Eric began.

'Shut up,' Miranda said. 'You set up what happened to me yesterday, didn't you? You arranged that phoney photography session. There was no bikini modelling to be done, no client, you just wanted to corrupt, to destroy, to turn me into. . . .' Here she hesitated as tears burnt her eyes, but anger still had the upper hand. 'Well, you've succeeded. You've destroyed me. I don't know how he made me do those things – he-he must have put something in my drink – but I tell you this, it would have been kinder to kill me.'

Eric smiled, an easy, self-indulgent smile. 'I'll admit Joe told me that you and he got, well. . . . a little friendly, but you can hardly blame *me*, sweetheart, if you decide to sleep with your photographer.' It was a stupid, ill-timed remark.

All control gone now, Miranda lunged at him, her nails raking at his face, kicking, clawing. He was a strong man and it took only a few moments for him to restrain her narrow wrists in the grip of one hand, while he drew back the other and slapped her across the face with all his strength. She screamed and collapsed on the floor, sobbing.

There was a frantic knocking at the door and when Eric, still stunned himself, did not reply, two white-faced secretaries burst in. 'What's happening, Mr Fairfax?' said Joan, his ever faithful, if critical, assistant.

Eric looked up at her, with shocked, unseeing eyes. She had never seen him so disturbed. Then she turned her attention to the sobbing girl on the floor.

'M-Miranda became hysterical,' Eric managed to say at last. 'I was forced to strike her. Could you bring her some coffee and an aspirin?'

'What's wrong with her?' said Joan, bending over the girl. 'Is she ill?'

'No, she's not ill,' Eric bit back. 'Now just do as I say and leave us.'

'I'm not sure . . .' Joan began.

'If you want to keep your job, you'll do as you're told – just piss off and fetch the sodding aspirin.'

When they were alone again, Eric helped Miranda off the floor and onto a chair. She was still sobbing uncontrollably and showed not the slightest resistance. Searching in his desk drawer, he found a box of tissues and handed them to her, but she simply held the box in limp hands, as the tears streamed down her face.

Joan arrived, her face set with disapproval, and slammed down the coffee pot and a box of aspirins on the desk. Eric's rudeness to her now occupied her mind too fully for her to worry unduly about the girl. Models were always a hysterical bunch anyway.

Eric poured the coffee, amazed to see his hands were trembling. Carefully he mixed two aspirin in a glass and then bent over Miranda. 'Here's some coffee and aspirin, sweetheart – take them, it will do you good.'

She raised her head, all her beauty now obliterated by her misery and despair. With a single gesture, she knocked the glass and cup from Eric's hands, sending a dark stain across the cream carpet. 'Do you think I'd ever accept anything from you again?' She spat out the words, then slowly, unsteadily, she stood up. 'I can't go back to Yorkshire, because I can't face my parents after what has happened, but one thing's certain, I'm going to make damned sure I never set eyes on you again. We're finished. You can stuff your PIPPA contract, all those sodding lessons and your so-called charity. You and I are through. I'll make my own way. Even if I end up cleaning public lavatories, it'll be more honourable than working with you and your kind. You stink, you're rotten, filth. How many other girls have you done this to besides me? Quite a number, I bet – your kind are too perverted to be able to stop. Well, this time you've got it wrong – you may have ruined my life, but that doesn't mean it's yours to play with. I've checked out of my room and told the landlady to look to you for a month's rent. I'm walking out of here now, and out of your life. You may wonder why I came to see you once more. Well, I'll tell you – to look evil in the face, so I will always remember what it looks like. If you try to contact me ever again, I swear, by God, I'll kill you, and don't make the mistake of doubting that I mean it.' She turned and started towards the door.

Eric walked leisurely in the opposite direction, to behind his desk. He pulled open a drawer. 'Before you start threatening me, Miranda, perhaps you'd better take a look at these.'

She turned, one hand on the door knob. From the look on his face, the tone of his voice, she had no alternative but to come back into the room. She was drawn like a magnet as he pulled from his drawer a sheaf of black and white photographs, which he threw onto the desk, carelessly, as though they were of little importance. With a trembling hand Miranda picked them up. They were of her and Joe in every conceivable position. There was nothing subtle about them – they were crude, immensely detailed, aimed specifically at corrupting and debasing the act of love.

Miranda swayed, dangerously, and put a hand on the desk to steady herself. 'So, someone else was there all the time?' Her voice was almost a whisper.

Eric smiled slightly. 'Joe's assistant. Yes, he used his time well – he made a video, as well as taking these stills of the, er . . . the proceedings.'

Miranda stared at him, a dreadful realisation beginning to dawn. 'You!' She pointed an accusing finger at him. 'You were there too, weren't you?'

Eric had not expected this but thinking quickly, decided that there was no harm in her knowing – in fact it might even be an advantage. 'Yes,' he said, smugly, 'I was there.'

'And what are these for,' Miranda said, 'to blackmail me, to make me do more, to make me hand all the PIPPA money over to you?'

'Nothing so base, sweetheart,' Eric said, 'but having seen how good you look, you must admit it would be a crying shame not to do any more. After all . . .' he paused, to give emphasis to his words, 'you did enjoy it, didn't you? I saw that for myself.'

'You bastard,' Miranda screamed, and searching wildly around her, she picked up the first thing that came to hand – a marble paperweight from Eric's desk. She hurled it at him with all her strength. He tried to avoid it but it caught him a glancing blow on the temple. He groaned, his knees buckling under him, but before his body hit the ground, Miranda was already out of the office and halfway down the stairs.

The café was seedy, but at least warm. Miranda sat at a greasy table, watching the skin form on her third cup of coffee. Her dramatic exit from the agency meant that she had forgotten her suitcase. All she had in the world was just over two pounds, and a Lloyd's cheque book for her old account in Bradford, in which she knew there were no funds. She stared round at the other inmates of the café. There was an old tramp, jabbering away to himself in the corner, a couple of pale-faced youths sat smoking and passing comments about her, nudging one another and laughing. Ordinarily she would have been embarrassed, but she found she was able to ignore them completely. Behind the counter, the bleary-eyed proprietor kept up a non-stop dialogue with the waitress – both were happily engaged in the character assassination of a mutual acquaintance.

What to do? Where to go? In twenty-four hours she had been reduced to having no money, no home, and above all, no self-respect . . . and she was so tired. She wondered whether she had the nerve to book into a hotel, but it was late now – after eleven – and without luggage, she doubted she would be accepted. In any event, she had no money to pay the bill.

The old man in the corner began a desperate and prolonged coughing fit, and suddenly Miranda could bear it no more. She opened her bag and began scrabbling around for some change to pay for the coffee, and it was then, she saw it. Slowly, carefully, she pulled Jenny Marchant's now crumpled business card from her bag and studied it. The card quoted an address and a home and business telephone number. Did that mean Jenny lived on the premises? It was hard to tell and in any event, how could she call on someone she had met once, briefly, at this time of night. She stuffed the card back into her bag, got up resolutely, paid the bill and left.

The cold air seared through her thin coat as she stepped outside. Since her dramatic exit from Eric's office, she had walked the length and breadth of Oxford Street, in a hopeless turmoil of mind. Now she took a side street, vaguely heading towards the bright lights and perhaps another café, aware that as a girl on her own, she was vulnerable in the shadows. She had chosen Wardour Street, and in moments she was plunged into Soho, with its dreadful reminders of what had happened to her the previous day. Everywhere she looked there were sex shops, strip shows, movies, prostitutes openly plying for trade. By now it was sufficiently late that most of the respectable restaurant diners had left the area – now vice was king, and would remain so until dawn. She turned, and began to retrace her steps hurriedly. A man stepped forward and blocked her path. 'What's the hurry, darling? Why don't you and I go somewhere quiet. I know just the place.'

'No,' Miranda screamed. 'No.' She stepped into the road, dodging round him and then ran for all she was worth, back towards the comparative safety of Oxford Street. As she reached it, a vacant taxi glided by. Without hesitation, she hailed it. Trembling and out of breath, she climbed inside, and sank back on the seat.

'Where to, miss?' the driver asked.

Fumbling in her handbag, Miranda drew out Jenny's card and gave the address. There was nothing else to do.

She had just enough money to pay the cab, with two pence to spare. The driver looked disbelievingly at her tip, shrugged his shoulders, muttered something uncomplimentary, and drove off into the night, leaving Miranda alone in the cold, dark street. Jenny Marchant's house was one of a row of charming Georgian terraced houses. There was no sign of a business being run from it and in the half-light of the street lamp, Miranda checked the address to make sure she had the right place. Then, with a deep breath, she climbed the steps and rang the bell. The house was in darkness but somewhere, in its depths, a dog barked. To Miranda, the noise was infinitely comforting – something normal, in what otherwise had become, for her, a world gone mad. She waited, but no one came. Suddenly she remembered it was Friday night. Perhaps Jenny had gone away for the weekend, yet surely she would not have left her dog. Perhaps she was just out late? Miranda hesitated, she would try once more. This time, she kept her hand on the bell longer and the dog's barking was more persistent. Still, though, no one came. Tears welled up again, and with them came a wave of exhaustion. She could not walk another step, she knew, and what did it matter anyway? She no longer cared what happened to her. She felt her knees begin to sag and she slid into a half-sitting, half-lying position, propped against the door.

Jenny Marchant had spent a wonderful evening. For five years, she had indulged in a very part-time relationship with a TWA marketing executive. Jason Lyons spent no more than three weeks a year in London – he was actually based in Chicago – but when he had a few hours to kill, he never failed to call her. If she was free, they would spend the time together in his hotel suite, always accompanied by a bottle of champagne and a tray of smoked salmon sandwiches. He was nearly ten years younger than Jenny – lean, tanned, a marvellously energetic lover. Normally, Jenny had little time for the American male, but Jason was different – he was sophisticated, cultured and, miraculously he had a marvellous sense of humour. Jenny frankly adored him. That particular evening, he had tried to persuade her to spend the night with him – something they rarely did – since, normally, he was never in the country long enough. Although tempted, Jenny had declined. She recognised the dangers of getting to know Jason Lyons too well. He belonged to the rare breed of men with whom she knew she could fall in love, and there was no way she was prepared to take that risk. Besides which, she told herself as she parked her Lotus, she had a mound of work to catch up on and a quick glance at her watch told her it was already past three.

At first, Jenny assumed that someone had left a pile of rubbish outside her front door, but as she drew closer, she realised, with a quickening heartbeat, that this was human debris – a tramp, presumably. She was frightened. Perhaps the person was drunk or drug crazed. She hesitated, edging forward for a better look. Suddenly, the light from the street lamp reflected on a few strands of hair escaping from the otherwise shapeless heap, and curiosity got the better of Jenny. Quietly she started up the steps, searching her bag for her front door key, and the little torch she always kept with her. She found it, and hesitantly trained the beam on the bundle.

Miranda lay on her side, her face half obscured by her coat collar, but Jenny recognised her instantly – that incredible girl, Miranda. . . . something, the one she had met at the Jackson & Smythe party. An immensely practical woman, Jenny did not pause to wonder why the girl was there, nor what had happened to bring Miranda to her doorstep. It was a freezing night, there was no time to be lost. Quickly, she opened the front door, switched on the porch light and then began shaking Miranda vigorously. She was rewarded by the girl stirring and then opening her eyes. She stared up at Jenny from the pavement, making no attempt to move. 'W-where am I, what's happening?'

'It's all right, love, it's Jenny, Jenny Marchant. You went to sleep on my doorstep. Come on, I must get you inside before you freeze to death.'

Half carrying the girl, Jenny managed to ease her through the door, and then guide her into the sitting room. There Miranda collapsed in front of the gas fire.

'I'm going to run you a bath,' Jenny said. 'It's the only way to warm you up. You must be chilled through to the very bone.'

Miranda gave no indication that she had heard. Now she

was properly awake, the cold had her shaking uncontrollably. Jenny returned in moments with a blanket, followed by a cup of tea. Whilst she busied herself preparing the bath, she stole the odd glance at Miranda. The girl looked dreadful, deathly pale, with red puffy eyes, and a dirty, tear-stained face. Jenny kept her counsel and asked no questions – there would be plenty of time for that. Once the bath was run, she helped Miranda into the bathroom, gave her a towel and a robe to wear when she was bathed, and then left her alone.

When Miranda emerged some half an hour later, although still terribly pale, she looked better. Her face was clean and shiny and she had washed her hair.

'Would you like a hair dryer?' Jenny asked.

'No, I'll just sit by the fire, if that's all right,' Miranda replied, shyly.

'Yes, of course. I'm making some scrambled eggs, I'll bring them to you on a tray by the fire.'

'I couldn't eat anything,' Miranda said.

'You'll do as you're told,' Jenny replied, and disappeared into the kitchen to avoid any argument.

The scrambled eggs were demolished without protest, as were several cups of coffee. Still sitting by the fire, the food and warmth brought back some colour to Miranda's cheeks. She looked almost normal Jenny observed, with satisfaction.

'Now,' she said, briskly, 'while you were eating, I put on the electric blanket in the spare room. All you have to do now, darling, is to crawl there. We'll talk tomorrow – tonight you need to sleep.' Miranda looked up at Jenny, her eyes full of pain and bewilderment. Jenny hesitated. '. . . or would you rather talk tonight?'

'I've got to tell someone,' Miranda said, hesitantly, 'and you seem to be the right person, the only person.'

'Better out than in, certainly,' said Jenny, cheerfully. 'There, let me take your tray and I'll fetch us both a brandy to keep us awake.'

Back by the fire again, Jenny fixed her attention purposely on her brandy glass. 'Now, Miranda, tell me all about it.'

Miranda hesitated, but then began, quite fluently, to tell the story of her assignment at Joe Chang's. She managed well – even the part about going topless – but when she reached the stage in the story where Joe had come to join her on the bed, she seemed incapable of continuing.

'You let him make love to you, I take it?' Jenny said. Miranda nodded briefly. 'But it wasn't as simple as that?' Jenny suggested. Miranda shook her head but remained silent. 'Look, darling, if I'm to help, you've got to tell me everything. An old sinner like me is quite unshockable. Just imagine you're talking to yourself, but for heavens sake, you must talk about it.'

'He . . . he made me do things. I . . . I did things I've never dreamed of, I didn't know and, oh Jenny,' Miranda began to cry, great sobs shaking her body. 'I can't understand it, how I could have behaved like that and . . . and all the time we were being photographed, and Eric . . . Eric was there watching, only I didn't know that until this afternoon.'

Jenny let out a long, low whistle. 'What things did you do, Miranda?'

'I can't tell you, I can't possibly tell you.'

'You must.'

Haltingly, Miranda described everything she could remember of what had taken place. Sometimes she could not bring herself to discuss the details, but Jenny questioned her until she did. Slowly the full sordid story emerged and Jenny realised that, without doubt, Miranda had been set up in a series of poses, clearly with a hard porn magazine in mind. At last she relented. 'OK, darling, that'll do – you poor old love, what a time you've had.'

'But how could I have done those things? How could I.' Miranda, having relived the whole incident was more distraught than ever.

'You were drugged.'

'Was I? I thought I might have been – or was it just the champagne?'

Jenny shook her head vigorously. 'No, Joe Chang must have slipped something into your drink. How did you feel this morning?'

'Dreadful, but I thought that was just because of . . . well, you know.'

'Headache, sickness, double vision?' Miranda nodded. 'Look, sweetheart, what you've got to realise is that the person on the bed with Joe Chang was not you. For your future piece of mind and self respect, it's vital that you understand that.'

Miranda frowned. 'I don't think I'll ever be able to see it like that. It was my body.'

'Darling, tell me, why do you think people take drugs?'

Miranda shrugged. 'As a means of escaping, I suppose.'

'Precisely. They can't stand the people they are, or the circumstances in which they find themselves, so they take something which lifts them up and away from their normal selves. That's what happened to you. Yesterday, drugs mixed with alcohol, and used for the first time . . .' Jenny glanced up quickly at Miranda. '. . . I assume you haven't experimented with anything before?'

'No, never.'

'So, as I was saying, mixed with alcohol, the effect must have been very powerful. It was not you, Miranda, who did those things, it was the drug. You must keep that firmly in your mind, because honestly, darling, it's the truth.' To her immense satisfaction, Jenny saw the girl visibly relax. They sat quietly for a moment, both feeling the effects of having been through a considerable ordeal.

'I realised that Eric Fairfax was a toad, but not this sick,' Jenny said at last, breaking the silence.

Miranda's head jerked up, her eyes wide with fright again. 'I-I might have killed him.'

Jenny smiled, reassuringly. 'Surely not?'

'I might have done, honestly. You see, I-I went to his office this afternoon. When I told him what I thought of him and how I would never work with him again, he produced some black and white prints of . . . well, Joe and I. I sort of went berserk, Jenny, and chucked a paperweight at him. It hit him on the head.'

Much to Miranda's amazement, Jenny let out a peel of laughter. 'My darling girl, you really have had an eventful twenty-four hours, haven't you? I bet it's not this exciting on the Yorkshire moors.' Jenny was rewarded by the ghost of a smile. 'Now,' she said, 'we've talked enough. I'll check on Eric in the morning. You go to bed, have a good sleep and leave everything to me.'

'I just don't know what to do,' Miranda burst out. 'I can't go home, I just can't face my parents after what's happened, but I can't go on modelling either. Without the PIPPA contract, I'm nothing, and anyway I could never face a camera again.'

'Bed!' Jenny commanded.

By seven o'clock the following morning, Jenny was hard at work. She had the home telephone number of one of the secretaries who was responsible for hiring models at Jackson & Smythe, and, unrepentant, she used it, knowing she would be getting the girl out of bed. Barbara Young was able to confirm that, yes, there had been some sort of incident the previous day between Eric Fairfax and the PIPPA model, but Eric had not been badly hurt.

Barbara laughed. 'She chucked something at him, and good for her, I say. He's had it coming for years.'

'Are you sure he's not seriously hurt, Barbara?' Jenny asked again.

'No. He was in the office all day, moaning about a headache. Unfortunately, I don't think she did any lasting damage.'

Jenny replaced the receiver with a sigh of relief. She poured herself a black coffee, arranged her thoughts carefully and then made the telephone call that was to make, or break Miranda Hicks.

'Mr Hardcastle's residence,' a voice said, in answer to her call.

'Could I speak to him, please,' Jenny said.

'He's having breakfast at the moment.'

'It is important,' Jenny insisted.

'Who shall I say is calling?'

'Jenny Marchant.'

'Jenny, my dear.' Lawrence Hardcastle's warm, treacly voice brought an instant smile to Jenny's face.

'Hello, Lawrence. I'm awfully sorry to disturb your breakfast. I wouldn't do it for the world, only this is important – there is a damsel in distress needing your help.'

'You, in distress? That'll be the day,' said Lawrence.

'No, not me. I'm talking about your model girl, Miranda Hicks.'

There was a slight pause. 'Ah,' said Lawrence, 'our PIPPA girl.'

'That's the one,' Jenny said, with relief. With a company the size of Hardcastle & Parker, Jenny had wondered whether the managing director would have any idea who was modelling the new range in their cosmetic division. Yet she should have known better – nothing escaped Lawrence Hardcastle. He had built his empire by dedicated hard work and painstaking attention to detail.

'Lawrence, she's run into trouble, big trouble.'

'Go on,' said Lawrence.

As briefly as possible Jenny outlined Miranda's story.

'The bastard,' Lawrence burst out. 'How old is the girl?'

'Seventeen,' said Jenny, 'but it's not just her age, Lawrence, she's such an innocent. There's plenty of seventeen-year-old tough guys about, but this one has come straight from her mother's knee.' She hesitated, wondering whether this was the moment to strike, or whether to wait until she could meet Lawrence face to face. She decided to go ahead – above all, Lawrence Hardcastle was a fair man. 'The thing is, Lawrence, clearly there's no way she can continue to work with Jackson & Smythe on the PIPPA contract, but in my view, you'll go a long way before you find a better face. What I'm asking you to do, is to give her that contract. I'll be responsible for her, if we could just find a way to avoid her having to be in contact with the agency.'

'Changing agencies in the middle of a campaign is not very clever, if that's what you're suggesting,' Lawrence said, slowly. 'On the other hand, if that's how they allow their staff to treat their models . . .'

Jenny smiled, she was making more progress than she had dared hope. 'You only need to move the PIPPA contract, the rest of your business can stay with Jackson & Smythe.'

'Yes, and in any event, from what you've told me, I can't see how I can let another young girl near that agency. Look, I tell you what, bring her over here, Jenny. Can you make it by nine?'

'At your home?'

'Yes, that's right, I don't want to frighten her. We'll keep the meeting friendly and informal. Let me have a look at her and we'll see what can be done.'

All the way in the taxi, Miranda literally shook with nerves. It had been all Jenny could do to get her up and dressed, and looking sufficiently presentable for Lawrence Hardcastle. Jenny glanced at her now, with satisfaction. The white gold hair shone, her complexion was perfect. She still looked like a girl who had been through a dreadful experience, but then that was fine – Lawrence Hardcastle's sympathy was the trump card.

In St John's Wood, the taxi swung between a pair of immense stone pillars and wound its way up a drive, lined with rhododendron bushes. Jenny tried to ease the tension. 'This is Lawrence Hardcastle's little place in London. He has a country cottage near Maidenhead, too, with half a mile of river frontage.

Miranda could not manage a reply. All her carefully cultivated self-confidence seemed to have been blown away. She wanted to get out of the taxi and run, but her legs were too weak to carry her.

Miranda's terror evaporated the moment she first laid eyes on the man who was to become her guardian angel, in the years that lay ahead. He did not make a particularly impressive figure, as he strode across the hall to meet the two young women. He was a small, somewhat round figure, with thinning grey hair, and a military moustache, but it was his eyes that made him – they literally shone with kindness and humour. He took Miranda's hand in a firm handshake. 'Thank you for coming, my dear,' he said. 'It was very brave of you. I expect what you really wanted to do was find a little dark cupboard and hide in it.'

With this simple sentence he acquired Miranda's trust. He demonstrated that he both understood how she felt and could talk about what had happened with no trace of embarrassment. 'Come through and have some coffee. Knowing how you girls go on, I don't suppose either of you have had any breakfast.'

Once they were seated, in an elegant book-lined study, Lawrence gently began to question Miranda about her family, her upbringing and her life in Yorkshire. Jenny watched fascinated as, like a flower in the sunshine, Miranda blossomed in the warmth of Lawrence's easy charm. Knowing how hard he worked, Jenny imagined that there were dozens of meetings and crises awaiting his attention, but seeing him now with Miranda, one could imagine he had all the time in the world.

'Now,' said Lawrence, at last, 'I tell you what we're going to do, Miranda. I still want you for PIPPA, that at least has not changed. . . .' Miranda's look of astonishment was clear for all to see, and Lawrence smiled at her transparency. 'I appreciate though, there is no way you can work with Jackson & Smythe – even if they offered to replace Eric Fairfax, you wouldn't trust them, and there would still be unpleasant associations for you. To be honest, I'm not terribly satisfied with them anyway. Since speaking to Jenny this morning, I've done some research and I've found an agency who specialise in cosmetics.' He glanced at Jenny. 'Simpsons, you know them?' Jenny nodded. 'They would love the account, of course, it's a big break for them but I think they're ready to handle it. They're only a small outfit, Miranda, six or seven staff at the most.' Lawrence smiled reassuringly and then leaning across, took her hand. 'Now, my dear, after the experience you've had, I want you to take a week off before starting work. I'll arrange for my accounts department to send Jenny a cheque to keep you in funds until you start earning money. So there just remains one problem – where are you going to stay?'

'With me,' said Jenny, firmly, 'for the time being, at any rate. I'm not letting her out of my sight until she's a hundred per cent again.'

'Good,' said Lawrence, springing to his feet with surprising agility. He took Miranda's arm and walked her to the door. 'You've had a simply dreadful start, Miranda, but with PIPPA behind you, you've got a wonderful future. Don't let what happened poison your life. Time, as they say, will heal, but you must help the healing process by putting what happened out of your mind. If you can't do it for yourself, do it for me. I'm putting a lot of faith in you, so don't let me down. Promise?'

'I-I promise,' Miranda managed.

'Good girl.'

In the taxi, on the way home, Miranda was in tears again. 'He was so kind, but will I ever be able to live up to his expectations? Just the thought of being photographed again, Jenny it simply terrifies me.'

'We have a week to get you back into shape, darling,' said Jenny. 'Don't worry, we'll make it.'

The repercussions from Lawrence Hardcastle's decision were surprisingly far reaching. Once the two girls had left, he telephoned Pete Smythe and arranged to meet him at the office. There he told him the full story.

'You've lost the PIPPA contract anyway,' Lawrence said. 'Whether you keep the rest of the Hardcastle & Parker account is up to you. I want all copies and negatives of those photographs, plus the video and any copies of that, in my office by five o'clock sharp. At five-five, if they're not here, you lose all our business, and if you try to sue against our contract, I'll be only too pleased to tell the press exactly why I made my decision.'

A similar ultimatum was issued by Pete Smythe to Eric Fairfax. Provided Pete had the photographs by lunchtime, Eric would keep his job. By three o'clock, the photographs and video were locked in Lawrence's office safe, together with all the copies that existed.

Confident that he had extracted all the damning material which existed, that afternoon Lawrence Hardcastle wrote a formal letter to Jackson & Smythe withdrawing all Hardcastle & Parker business from the agency, at the very moment, Pete Smythe was in the process of sacking Eric Fairfax. At six-thirty the same evening, Lawrence and Jenny met at Lawrence's home, alone this time, and ceremoniously burnt all traces of photograph and film in the rather incongruous setting of a Queen Anne fireplace.

During the three years that followed, Jackson & Smythe went into liquidation, due largely, it was reported at the creditor's meeting, to the withdrawal of the massive Hardcastle &

Parker account. Pete Smythe, unable to cope with the failure of his business, drove his car into a motorway bridge at ninety miles an hour.

In 1977, Eric Fairfax was arrested by the vice squad, for involving under-age girls in pornographic films. He was sent down for seven years and died in Bradford prison of a heart attack, on his forty-ninth birthday.

And as for Miranda Hicks. . . . Miranda Hicks became, without doubt, the most celebrated fashion model of her generation.

Chapter Six

British Airways Flight BA736, from Heathrow to Iraklion, was not without incident. Although a scheduled flight, it was two hours late taking off, due to problems with a fuel tank. On arrival at Iraklion, the passengers were forced to stand around on the blistering tarmac for half an hour, unable to go into the airport building because of a suspected bomb scare. When the passengers finally made it through passport control, they had to wait a further hour while their luggage was checked for explosives. It was at this point that it was discovered the transport arranged to take the Masons party to Ayios Nikolaos had not materialised. And it was also at this point that Clive Brewer's patience finally snapped.

They were an unfortunate combination, Miranda observed, watching Clive Brewer, marketing director of Masons, raging at Peter Samuelson, from the advertising agency. Clive was small, dapper, self-opinionated and horrifically aware of his position as the client. He was given to strutting about as he issued instructions, and his sudden bursts of temper, usually unprovoked, were quite alarming in their ferocity. Peter Samuelson, by contrast, was a great teddy-bear of a man, in his mid twenties, some ten or fifteen years younger than Clive. He was easily confused, desperately upset by Clive's rude, abrasive manner, and given to blushing and stammering whenever Clive paused in his tirades long enough to demand a reply.

'The wimp and the wally,' Jake whispered to Miranda. They were sitting on Miranda's suitcase, sipping Greek brandy, seasoned travellers of a thousand modelling assignments. The delays and cock-ups were all part of the job and experience dictated that they should never be tackled sober. A delicate balance of inebriation had kept them cheerful and relaxed, throughout the trip . . . despite Clive. 'It's going to be rough going for a day or two,' Jake observed.

'It's going to be a rough assignment,' said Miranda.

'No, no, Clive will get sorted, one way or the other. The Cretans will drive him mad. After a few days apoplexy, during which he will discover that nothing happens today if it can possibly happen tomorrow, he'll either take to the *raki* in desperation, or have a complete breakdown. Either way, we'll get shot of him.'

Miranda laughed. 'How about Peter?'

'He'll just be grateful if somebody keeps telling him which day of the week it is.'

In the end, Jake took pity on Peter, waved a few drachmas around and secured two taxis, to take them to Ayios Nikolaos – one for the luggage and equipment and one for themselves. It was nearly six by the time they reached their hotel – Minos Beach, the oldest hotel on the island.

'It never occurred to me that we would be staying at the Minos Beach,' Jake said, more to himself than to Miranda. 'I didn't think there was a chance of our being booked in here, it's normally far too expensive for commercial purposes. I suppose Masons did a special deal because the season has hardly begun.'

'You've stayed here before?' Miranda asked.

'Yes,' Jake replied shortly, clearly not prepared to volunteer any more information.

At last Peter sorted out their reservations and following two porters, the party began meandering their way down paths, lined with the most exotic shrubs and flowers. Every so often, they passed a little white-washed stone villa. 'What are they?' Miranda asked Jake.

'The hotel bedrooms,' Jake replied, still oddly grim and distant.

Suddenly the path opened out and there ahead of them lay the Aegean, deep blue now, in the evening light. Just for a moment, even Clive seemed stunned by its beauty, and they stood in silent homage, gazing at the gentle movement of the water, shimmering in the last of the day's heat.

They were allocated four tiny villas, on the very edge of the sea. Tired and travel-weary, it was agreed that they would meet in the hotel bar at eight o'clock, and in the meantime, they were left to their own devices.

Jake announced that he was going to look for suitable locations, and Miranda, who had been put in charge of the garments she was to model, carefully unpacked them, and hung them up as best she could to avoid creasing. Then she wandered out onto her balcony. It was just a few steps down to the sea, and suddenly the water seemed quite irresistible. She slipped on a bikini, flashed down the steps and dived in.

It was marvellous. Initially the water felt cold to her hot skin, but as she swam she realised it was gloriously warm. It was not just the temperature that made it so good – the water had a soft, almost silky feel. Having swum a good distance from the shore, Miranda turned on her back and gasped aloud at what she saw. Behind the hotel, mountains rose steeply in shades of blue, green, apricot . . . their peaks shrouded in early evening mist. 'Crete, I love you,' Miranda whispered across the still water. Jenny had been right, she thought, this is just what I needed. Strange though it seemed, she immediately felt at home on the island, gripped by its magic, fascinated and charmed by its strange beauty.

Dinner that evening, was not a success. Jake, who on the journey had played the role of pacifier, was morose and introspective, and his lack of intervention took its toll. Clive criticised everything – the food, the wine, the service, the mosquitoes – nothing was right. Miranda tried valiantly to charm him, but without success. Peter snapped his fingers ineffectually at apparently sullen waiters, in an effort to placate his client. Jake ignored everybody and drank heavily.

The evening finally disintegrated as they were eating glorious, golden peaches, sweet as honey. 'These peaches are terrific, aren't they, Clive?' said Peter, desperately.

'Well, at least they've got something right,' Clive conceded, 'though God knows, there isn't much skill in picking a few peaches. I expect they grow by the side of the road. Now that veal we've just had was terrible. It. . . .'

'For Christ's sake, Clive, shut up,' Jake said suddenly, his voice slurred. 'OK, so you're a pig-ignorant little shit, but is it necessary to make it so bloody obvious? You're in one of the most beautiful and romantic places on earth, and all you can do is whine. I can't bear to listen to you for another moment.' With that, he stood up, swayed slightly, and stumbled from the table.

There was a stunned silence while Miranda searched desperately for something to say. 'Poor Jake,' she said, at last, 'he's been working awfully hard recently. You mustn't take any notice of him, Clive.'

With the arrogance of the truly stupid, Clive, it appeared, was not in the least offended. 'Too much wine,' he said, sagely. 'I can't abide men who are unable to hold their drink. I enjoy drinking, of course, but I have the good sense to know when to stop. I've never put myself in the position where I was out of control – it's so coarse, and embarrassing, too.' Apparently self-satisfied and at ease, Clive leant back in his chair and lit a cigarette. Clearly Jake's remarks had not even touched him.

Miranda and Peter exchanged an amazed glance. 'I'll organise some coffee and brandy,' Peter suggested hurriedly.

'Good idea, old boy,' Clive said, affably.

The rest of the evening passed without incident. In that respect, at least, it did appear that Jake's dramatic exit had affected Clive, in that he made a conscious effort to be pleasant – too pleasant in fact. Over the years, Miranda had become highly adept in the art of rebuffing clumsy and inappropriate advances, without causing offence. Clive, flushed with brandy, had to be restrained on the way back to their villas, but they all parted good enough friends.

It was only when she was alone that Miranda had time to wonder why Jake had reacted as he had done. By nature, he was not a volatile character – in fact quite the contrary. He was well known for his ability to placate difficult clients and to get the best from anxious models. He was not a man anyone seemed to know well – he appeared to be a closed book, emotionally – but Miranda had never witnessed such an outburst before, nor seen him drink so heavily.

Jake's ill-humour persisted into the following day. Peter

had worked out a schedule of shots for the ten days of photography. He went through the programme for Day 1 over breakfast and was rewarded by both Clive and Jake disagreeing with him, but for different reasons.

Jake wanted to spend the day in and around the hotel. 'We have plenty of time to do this job,' he argued, 'I want to get a feel for the light before we start careering round the countryside.'

'Shooting at the hotel is pointless – we're not looking for beaches,' Clive insisted. 'I want to get up into the villages. I'm told they are very primitive – donkeys, ragged children – that's what I'm after.'

'Well, why don't you piss off then and look for donkeys and ragged children while I get some shots done here,' Jake suggested, smiling maliciously.

'May I remind you who's paying for this trip,' Clive said, coldly.

'Well, you're not, that's for sure.' Jake's face was like thunder. 'You're just some jumped-up little guy from Masons creative department, and God knows that's no reason to get excited.'

'How dare you . . .' Clive began.

'Look,' said Jake, 'if you don't like the way I'm proposing to take these shots, take them yourself. I'm going back to my villa to load some film, while you decide how you're going to spend your day. How about writing some postcards home – that should keep you out of mischief and allow Miranda and I to get some work done.'

Once Jake had left, hurried discussions took place between Clive and Peter, while Miranda sat drinking coffee and trying to let the whole incident wash over her. If it was going to be like this for ten days, it would be sheer hell, even in this paradise, she thought miserably.

A few moments later, Clive rose from the table and left without a word. Peter moved his chair closer to Miranda's. His face was pink and sweating, a deep frown tramlined his forehead and his eyes looked frankly terrified. Poor boy, Miranda thought. 'So, you've managed to get rid of him, then?' she said, cheerfully.

'Yes,' said Peter, 'he's gone off for the day to look for locations but he says he's going to ring head office first and complain about Jake. I don't think he'll have much luck, though. The hotel porter told me last night that making calls out of the island is not easy. Apparently people can ring us, but it's very difficult the other way round.'

'Thank heavens for that,' said Miranda, standing up. 'Shall I go and fetch Jake, so that we can get started.'

'Oh, would you?' said Peter. 'I don't seem to be very good at handling these temperamental personalities.' He smiled properly for the first time. 'Do you know, I always thought it was the models who were supposed to be temperamental, especially the famous ones, like you.'

'It's all myth,' said Miranda, laughing. 'We models are the only true professionals. As for the rest . . .' She waved her hand dismissively.

'I hope you don't mind me telling you this,' Peter stammered, 'but I used to have a photograph of you on the wall of my study at school. It had pride of place.'

Miranda gave Peter a baleful look. 'Oh Peter dear, that wasn't very tactful. There's no need to remind me just how long I've been around.'

Peter blushed to the roots of his hair. 'I-I'm so sorry, Miranda, I didn't mean . . .' he rallied a little and tried again. 'You know, you're far more beautiful in real life, and much more attractive now than you were when you were younger.'

Miranda smiled at him. 'You're very sweet. Come on, let's go and find that bad-tempered old bugger, Jake.'

It was nearly one o'clock before the first shot was set up, and by then it was incredibly hot. The paving stones burnt the soles of their feet, even the sand felt too hot to walk on. Because of the heat, trying to fix her makeup to stay in place was an almost impossible job for Miranda, and there was a dry wind which kept blowing the sand up into her eyes and turning the culottes she was wearing into unacceptable shapes. 'This is awful, Jake,' she said, plaintively.

'Don't you start moaning, I'm doing my best,' he said, warningly. 'In future we should start earlier in the morning – seven at the latest, when the light's soft. This light is too hard, which is what I suspected. It bounces off the sea and it bounces off your hair. It's altogether too harsh, there are too many shadows.' He frowned. 'Still, we'll get some shots done and I'll have them developed in Ayios Nikolaos overnight. Then, at least, we'll be able to show that little tick, Clive, what I'm on about.'

They toiled on, in what for Miranda had rarely been more unpleasant circumstances – the heat and the wind were in themselves difficult to cope with, but Jake's persistent bad-temper was by far the biggest hazard. There was no charisma between them and she knew it would show in the shots. Working under difficult circumstances for a purpose was one thing, but she knew none of the shots that they were doing would be of the slightest use. It was very disheartening.

At four o'clock, Jake called it a day, by which time Miranda had a thumping headache and was feeling vaguely sick.

'What time shall we all meet for dinner?' Pete asked cheerfully.

'I won't be coming up for dinner,' Jake replied, shortly. 'I suggest we start shooting down here again tomorrow morning at, say, quarter to seven. Is that all right with you, Miranda?'

Miranda nodded. 'Yes, of course.'

'Right, I'll see you then,' Jake said, and with a wave, he started to pick his way across the rocks – camera case and tripod dangerously balanced.

'You'll be up for dinner, won't you?' said Peter, turning to Miranda.

She looked at his hopeful face and her heart sank. 'Peter, I have the most awful headache. Would you mind dreadfully if I stayed in my villa?' He could not disguise his disappointment, and she felt appallingly guilty for leaving him to cope with Clive alone. 'It's just that we have an early start tomorrow,' she pleaded, 'and if I'm to repair the ravages of what the sun and sea have done to me today, I have quite a few hours of work ahead.'

'I think you look gorgeous, just as you are,' said Peter, his eyes full of genuine admiration, 'but of course I understand. Shall I organise some supper for you in your villa?'

'That would be lovely. Thank you.'

Miranda spent a pleasant evening alone. Peter had taken great care with ordering her supper – lamb kebab and a Greek salad, fresh fruit, yoghurt and honey and a delicious ice-cold bottle of white wine – all duly arrived as the sun set. Having missed lunch she was hungry and the wine slipped down with consummate ease. It was strange, Miranda thought, how filthy Greek wine always tasted in England, whilst here it was just right. Several times, during the course of the evening, as she sat out on her balcony, she glanced across at Jake's villa. She was tempted to go and see him, to try and find out why he was behaving so strangely, but there was no sign of life and so she assumed he had gone out. Besides which, she felt very comfortable with her own company that evening.

At a quarter to seven the following morning, Miranda, dressed in Masons' sundress and sandals, stood waiting on the rocks. The beauty of the morning quite took her breath away. The sea was like glass – far out in the bay, a small fishing boat chugged out from the harbour at Ayios Nikolaos, followed by another, and yet another, silhouetted against the dramatic backdrop of the mountains.

'What are you doing, standing all alone and smiling?' Jake's voice sounded amused and Miranda turned to him with relief. He looked terrible – his face was putty-grey, his eyes red and sunken – but at least he sounded better.

'Jake, you look dreadful,' Miranda said.

'Thanks a bundle, sweetheart, and what a thing to say to a bloke who is just about to tell you how stunning *you* look.'

'What on earth did you do, to end up looking like that?' Miranda persisted.

'Oh, I went into town last night, had a few drinks and one thing lead to another. I've had a couple of hours sleep though and a pint of black coffee. I'm all right now.'

'Well, if you say so.'

They began work. Within half an hour they had the sundress shot completed to Jake's satisfaction, and Miranda, too, felt good about it. They were working well now. She went back to her villa and changed into a bikini. Their second location was a little path, high up on the rocks – the light was perfect, the mountains and sea behind a glorious background. They had almost completed the bikini shot when there was a huffing and puffing on the steps below. Clive came into sight, his face contorted with rage. 'Who authorised this?' he demanded.

Jake straightened up from the camera and stared at him. 'What the hell are you talking about?'

'This, this . . .' said Clive, stabbing at the air in Miranda's general direction.

Jake took a deep breath. 'We tried shooting during the day yesterday and it doesn't work – the light's too harsh. This light is perfect. I've had yesterday's shots developed overnight and I'll have these developed by this afternoon. We can then compare the two, and you'll see what I mean.'

'You're wasting film and time.' Clive was clearly not prepared to listen.

'Look,' said Jake, 'I'm told you want a classy job and that's what you are going to get. You've picked a classy model and a classy photographer. Now all you have to do is sit back and enjoy it, and leave the rest to us.'

'Don't you patronise me,' said Clive, 'and don't tell me what I want. I know what I want – a photographer who will follow my instructions. I told you I wanted you up in the mountains today, yet when I go to your villas this morning, there's no one about. Still, I suppose if we leave now we won't be too much behind schedule. Would you please pack up straight away and then we can get going. Peter knows which garments we'll need.'

'We're not going up into the hills today,' Jake said. 'Miranda and I have been working since seven and we're going to stop for breakfast now. We can tackle some inside shots, during the heat of the day, and then later on, I'd like to go outside again so that we can test the evening light.'

'Test, test, test. We're not here to test, we're here to get on with the job. I must insist that from now on, we do things my way, and that means going on location today. I've found just the place.'

'I'm not going,' said Jake, 'and when I am ready to go off on location, I'll decide when, and where.' His voice was steady and relaxed – there was no trace of anger. He began dismantling his camera and packing it away into his case, his general air, dismissive.

'If that's your attitude, I'm going to ring Masons straight away,' Clive said, his voice shaking with anger. 'I'll ask for a replacement photographer – they can have one here by tomorrow. So, as far as I'm concerned, you're off the job.'

'Suits me,' said Jake. He flipped shut the catches on his case and stood up. He looked at Miranda and gave her a smile. 'See you around, doll,' he said. 'I'm going up to the hotel bar, to get smashed. It certainly beats working.' He turned and started down the steps.

Clive and Miranda watched him go in silence. 'I'm sorry about all this, Miranda,' said Clive. 'If you'll excuse me, I must go and organise the new photographer.'

The day was warming up now – it was going to be a beauty, and a delicious thought crept into Miranda's mind. 'Clive, before you go . . .' she began.

'Yes, what is it?' he asked, distractedly, already on the steps.

'If you're hiring another photographer, he won't reach us before tonight will he, even if he jumps on the next flight?'

'So?'

Presumably that means there'll be no more work today. Would it be OK if I took the rest of the day off and explored. The place just fascinates me, but all I've seen of the island so far has been the hotel.'

'Yes, I suppose so,' said Clive, grudgingly. 'But don't wear yourself out – tomorrow's going to be a long day.'

A call to hotel reception resulted in a self-drive jeep. Miranda changed into shorts and a T-shirt, and armed with a map and some friendly advice from the hall porter, less than half an hour later, she was off. She had no doubts as to where she was going. Since the moment she had arrived at the Minos Beach, she had watched, fascinated, as the colours changed and the shadows shifted on the mountains across the bay from Ayios Nikolaos. Enquiries had already told her that these were the Sitia Mountains, and now she learnt that there was a good coast road that would take her to them.

She was a competent driver, and the little jeep quite adequate, but she found the constant hairpin bends alarming. The road was hacked out of the cliff and below it, there was often nothing but a sheer drop to the sea. She drove slowly, savouring the magnificent views, enjoying the scenes in the villages she passed through. The wind kept her cool, but the dry, dusty air made her thirsty. When she came to Kavousi, a small market town, she stopped in the delightful, shaded square and had a beer. Then, realising it was lunch time, she followed it up with spaghetti and salad. Much revived, she pressed on.

She was in mountain country now, peaks towered above her, and crowded in on her in a strangely menacing way. The road began travelling inland, and as the sea breezes died away, it became unbearably hot. There was very little traffic on the road, making Miranda feel isolated and very alone in these ancient mountains. She felt humbled by them and unaccountably nervous. Once she drew the car into the side of the road, stopped and listened. When the sound of the engine died away, the silence was profound. It heightened her feeling of unease.

All her life she was to wonder what made her take the turning that day. Perhaps it was the need to get away from the mountains, or perhaps it attracted her simply because it was the only turning off that particular stretch of road. She was almost past it when she saw the tiny white signpost, with the faded letters MIRTOS scratched on it. She trod on the brakes, sending up a cloud of dust, reversed sharply and headed down what was little more than a cart track. Round the first corner, the road suddenly narrowed and dipped very steeply. Too late, Miranda realised her mistake. She stopped the car, putting it into gear for safety, and studied the map. Mirtos was clearly on the coast and less than a mile off the main road. Bearing in mind how high she was now, the road to Mirtos had to be steep. Realising it was a mistake to continue, cautiously, her foot still firmly on the brake, she put the jeep into reverse. She roared the engine, the little car hiccuped but refused to go backwards – the engine was clearly not man enough to reverse up such a steep hill. There was nothing for it but to go on.

The road wound this way and that, seeming to follow a dried-up river gorge. It became increasingly dusty and bumpy and at no point was there any room for turning. At last the village came into sight. It was clearly very poor – all the houses were one storey and extremely small, and as Miranda drove down what was presumably the main street, she saw tufts of grass sprouting out of the track. Everywhere there was an air of neglect. Abruptly the road came to an end, at what was obviously the centre point of the village. There, mercifully, was room to turn the car, though whether the jeep would ever make it back up the track, Miranda doubted. She switched off the engine and again, the oppressive silence was all around her. She was surprised no one had come out of the houses to inspect her. In the other little villages she had passed through, children had run along beside the car waving; old women, in their black dresses and shawls, had stopped their sewing to watch her; the men, silent and surly, had stared at her from the shade of the village taverna. Here there was nothing, no one.

She looked about her. On close inspection, she saw some of the doors of the houses were coming away at the hinges, and everywhere the paintwork was peeling. The land, too, had an uncared-for look. There were no goats, nor dogs, or cats – never mind people. She climbed out of the jeep and started down a little track leading out of the square. It seemed to be a street of sorts – certainly houses sprang up either side of it. Dry grasses pricked her toes, her sandals clacked on the stones, as she stumbled along, looking this way and that for some sign of life. There was none. Ahead of her, suddenly, she saw a patch of blue, and yes, there was the sea. The village was higher than she had imagined, still several hundred feet above sea level. Way down in the water, she could see a tiny fishing boat. At least there is someone left alive, she thought, smiling – here it felt as though she was witnessing the end of the world.

She turned left along the cliff top, following the path. Overlooking the sea stood yet another tiny cottage, apparently empty also. On impulse, Miranda walked up to the door which was blistered and weatherbeaten. She lifted the catch – it swung open easily. 'Hello,' she called, tentatively, as she peered inside. Her eyes gradually became accustomed to the darkness, for there were no windows. The floor was made of rough stone and in one corner, a table lay toppled over on its side. Otherwise the room was completely bare, and somehow full of sorrow. Miranda hurriedly stepped back into the sunshine, and despite the heat of the day, shuddered. It was not a happy place.

She decided to have one last look at the sea and then go back to her jeep. If all else failed, she could at least walk back up to the main road and seek some help. A normally capable, practical woman, here she felt vulnerable – nature seemed so very much the master. Leaving the path, she walked between two cottages, closer to the cliff edge, shielding her eyes from the dazzling reflection of the sun. Far away in the hazy distance, she saw what she knew must be Ayios Nikolaos. In that moment, she longed for civilisation, to be back amongst people – anyone.

A sudden reflection of light made her look farther along the cliff face. About half a mile away, a little higher than the level at which she stood, she saw a magnificent white villa, clinging to the side of the mountain. It was a fairytale place. Miranda stared at it, wondering whether the heat was making her hallucinate, and so engrossed was she that it only slowly dawned on her that she was no longer alone. There were footsteps coming down the path behind her, slow, measured, heavy. Miranda turned, her nerves badly jangled, to see a tall figure come into view. She could not make out his features properly for he stood in the shadow of one of the cottages, but his stance was menacing. Her heart began to race, the apprehension which had been building was now recognisable as terror. 'Deutch?' he demanded. His voice challenging, ringing out into the silence.

What did he mean? 'I'm sorry,' she said, 'I don't understand you.'

The figure visibly relaxed and stepped forward into the sunshine. 'Good heavens, you're English,' he said, his voice, warm, cultured.

The fear drained from her, but she remained entirely speechless, for, as he moved towards her she found herself staring at quite the most magnificent man she had ever seen. He towered over her. His hair was thick and very blond, his skin a golden brown, his eyes were bright blue, his nose aqualine, his jaw strong. He had the kind of profile that looked as though it belonged on one of the coins of Ancient Greece or Rome. Appearing from nowhere, as he had done, it almost seemed to Miranda that she had somehow disturbed a Greek god. Only his faded denim shorts and T-shirt told her that this was a man of today.

'I'm sorry if I startled you,' he said. A smile lit his face, he stepped forward and held out a hand. 'How do you do. My name is Michael Richardson.'

Chapter Seven

Miranda took the hand offered. 'My name is Miranda Hicks,' she said, her voice, to herself at any rate, sounding almost strangled.

'Of course, of course you are – I should have recognised you instantly. What an extraordinary thing to meet you here, of all places. How splendid, what a treat.'

Miranda found his obvious pleasure totally disarming. She was used to being recognised wherever she went, but Michael somehow made it sound as though meeting her had been his life's ambition. She instantly relaxed, realising though that she was easy prey to his charm. 'I've made a complete nonsense of myself,' she confessed. 'I'm working on location in Ayios Nikolaos and I've been staring at these mountains for two days. When this morning, the photographer and client fell out irrevocably, I seized the opportunity to come and explore.'

Michael grinned. 'Most people stick to the main road.'

'Then most people are sensible. I'll never get the car out, will I?'

'Yes, you will,' Michael said, 'but not without my help. I have a proposal to make which is so imminently practical in the circumstances, you cannot possibly disagree with it. I suggest I drive you back to my place, where you relax with a drink, while I'll send a couple of boys to tow your car back up the road.'

Miranda tried looking a little sceptical, but she knew she was going to accept – the man was quite irresistible. 'Where is your place?' she asked.

'Over there,' said Michael.

Miranda turned to see him pointing towards the white villa she had seen moments before. She let out a soft whistle. 'My very next question was to ask who on earth lived there. It's quite amazing – I've never seen anything like it.'

'Thank you.' Michael inclined his head. 'I'll be interested in your views on closer inspection. Shall we go?'

His slightly formal, very English manners were in odd contrast to their circumstances, and having slogged back up the street, Miranda was highly amused to see a Range Rover parked beside her dusty jeep. It seemed to complete the picture she had already formed of Michael Richardson. She laughed. 'A Range Rover, how fantastic! What on earth are you doing with it here? I feel terribly underdressed – I should be wearing my green wellies.'

He did not take the joke well. 'It's a sensible vehicle to have in Crete. It will get us out of Mirtos, which your jeep could never do.'

Miranda was suitably contrite. 'I'm sorry, I didn't mean to be rude – it's just so gloriously English. All that's missing are a couple of labradors in the back.'

'They're waiting for me at home,' he said, 'it's too hot for them to be out this time of the day.'

'You're kidding!' said Miranda.

And suddenly he, too, joined in the joke, his eyes sparkling with amusement. 'Yes, but you did catch me on a raw spot – I freely admit to being terribly proud of my car.'

The Range Rover tackled the road out of Mirtos with ease and on the way to Michael's villa, Miranda told him of the ghastly two days she had just spent.

'Are all modelling assignments this bad?' Michael asked.

'No,' Miranda said, 'but they do have a tendency to breed tension.'

'It certainly sounds like it. No wonder you buried yourself down the bottom of a dusty track.'

'Which reminds me,' said Miranda, 'why is the village deserted?'

Michael took so long to reply that Miranda turned to study him as he drove. He really was incredibly attractive, but not very happy, she suspected – there was a tight look around his mouth and eyes. 'It's . . . rather a long story,' he said at last. 'I'll tell you about it, once we're home.'

The Villa Dionissos appeared even more splendid, as they bowled through great white stone gateposts, than it had looked across the sparkling sea at Mirtos. It was a villa built for sunshine. After being hurried through the front door, Miranda was confronted by a series of little, sunny courtyards, in which fountains played and vine leaves trailed over graceful arches. Michael lead her through a great, tiled hallway, at one end of which there stood a magnificent fireplace. Then, suddenly, they were on a terrace – a terrace which made Miranda catch her breath. Immediately beneath it, the earth fell away so that it gave the impression of being suspended over the sea – some four hundred feet below.

'This terrace catches the sun from dawn until dusk,' Michael said, with satisfaction. 'Do sit down and let me get you something – a glass of wine, perhaps.'

'That would be lovely,' said Miranda.

Michael rang a bell and seconds later a rather surly-looking Greek woman appeared, dressed in the traditional black. Michael spoke to her in rapid Greek. While she listened to her instructions, the woman eyed Miranda with a mixture of interest and hostility.

'That was Thea, my housekeeper,' Michael explained, after the woman had departed. 'Her sons will fetch your car, and even more important, she will fetch us wine.'

'Your Greek is obviously fluent, but then, I suppose it would be living here.'

Michael hesitated for a split second. 'I'm a mongrel,' he said, with a slightly forced smile. My father was English and my mother is Cretan.'

Miranda immediately sensed his feeling of unease, yet hopelessly fascinated by the man, she had to know more. 'Is it difficult, being half English, half Greek?' she asked.

'Cretan,' Michael replied, sharply, 'I am Cretan, not Greek.'

'I'm sorry,' said Miranda, 'I didn't realise the difference. Please forgive me – it was sheer ignorance.' Why do I keep apologising, Miranda found herself wondering – it was not something she was used to doing.

Michael's face, so forbidding in repose, suddenly broke into smiles. 'It's me who should be asking for forgiveness. We Cretans . . .' he shrugged his shoulders charmingly, 'even we half Cretans, are proud of our island and our history. We do not consider ourselves to be part of the Greek race, or any other, for that matter. The Greeks conquered us that's all, as did many other nations over the centuries.'

'So, which nationality do you favour – do you feel more Cretan or more English?' Miranda asked.

'Until I was seven, entirely Cretan. My grandparents lived in Sitia, and my mother and I with them in a house down by the harbour – in fact where my mother still lives. I played with the village children, running around barefoot, not a care in the world – I was the same as they were. Then, when I was seven, I was sent to England, to boarding school.'

Miranda was appalled. 'At seven – what alone?'

'Oh yes, quite alone. I was sent to a prep school in Oxford – the Dragon School, you may know it?'

Miranda shook her head. 'Did you speak English?' she asked.

'No,' said Michael, 'but I learnt quickly – it was a question of survival.'

'It must have been the most dreadful experience for you. Did your father make you go?'

'Not exactly,' said Michael. Once again, Miranda realised, the shutters were down – it was not a subject he wished to pursue. She tried another tack. 'After the school in Oxford, then what?'

Michael smiled. 'Fairly predictable – Eton, then back to Oxford again.'

'Heavens,' said Miranda, 'that explains the Range Rover.'

They both laughed and were still laughing when Thea reappeared, with a bottle of white wine and a dish of olives, which she slammed down on the table before them without a word.

'Sorry,' Michael whispered, as soon as Thea had disappeared, 'she doesn't really approve of me entertaining. She prefers me working to drinking and talking – I make less mess.'

'What is your work?' Miranda asked.

'I dabble at this and that,' said Michael, dismissively. He

poured the wine and handed Miranda a glass. 'I would like to drink to your beautiful hair and your kind, brown eyes. It is also true to say that the Villa Dionissos has never entertained a more spectacular guest.'

Miranda was used to compliments, but she found his words oddly moving. She smiled. 'Thank you. It's wonderful to be here, and thank you, too, for rescuing me. I'd probably still be trying to thumb a lift, but for you.'

'Well, at least you'd be safe doing that in Crete, if not in England.'

'Is that true?' Miranda asked.

'Yes. There is little or no crime here. You can leave the key in your car, the doors of your house open all day – nobody steals. In the old days there was much rough justice, particularly in the isolated villages, but now there is no rape, no murder, no violent crime at all, with the possible exception of the odd tourist or mainland Greek.'

'That sounds horrifically biased, but if what you say is true, it sounds like paradise. Who needs the real world and all its miseries?'

Michael smiled a little wistfully. 'That's an interesting comment, and truer than you know.'

They sat in companionable silence, sipping their wine for a moment or two. Miranda was aware that Michael was watching her under hooded lids and it suddenly dawned on her that she must look an absolute mess – her hair all over the place, she was hot and dusty, too. She looked up quickly, catching his gaze. 'Would it be possible to have a wash?'

He was on his feet in a moment. 'Yes, of course. How very rude of me. I'll show you to the bathroom.'

The bathroom in question was much the same size as Miranda's entire London house. Each wall was tiled in a different design, but the basic colour scheme of terracotta, apricot and brown was constant. There were plants everywhere and a domed ceiling, partly in glass, let in just the right amount of light. Michael handed her a large, fluffy cream towel, and suggested a shower, but the moment Miranda saw the huge, sunken bath, with its gold taps, she simply could not resist it.

A few moments later, lying back in fragrant foam, staring at the reflections of light in the ceiling, Miranda's thoughts refused to stray from the subject of her unexpected host. Who was he and why live in such isolated splendour? She thought his face was vaguely familiar, but the name Michael Richardson struck no chord. There was a quality about him – exotic, she decided – a strange word to use when describing a man. She supposed it was something to do with his Greek . . . no Cretan blood, yet for all the world he looked typically English – tall, blond and blue eyed . . . except for his features – those strong, lean, proud features. It was certainly an intriguing combination.

When Miranda rejoined Michael on the terrace, he let out a long, appreciative whistle. 'I'm perfectly certain my bathroom has never been used to greater effect. You look stunning.'

'I've only washed,' said Miranda. 'Actually, to be honest, I had a bath – that bath is positively irresistible, I hope you don't mind.'

'No, of course not – it is fun, isn't it? Actually that bathroom was the most expensive room in the house to build.'

'I can well believe it,' said Miranda. She hesitated for a second, suddenly very unsure of his likely reaction. 'Would it be possible to see round your home? It's an awful intrusion I know, but I'm absolutely fascinated by it.'

'I'd consider it an honour, one guided tour coming up. There are twenty-six rooms in all, if you include the bathrooms,' Michael said, 'but I have six guest suites, and those twenty-six rooms include the servants quarters as well, so the actual living area is quite small.'

'Sorry,' said Miranda, 'but there's no way you're going to convince me that this is just a modest little place really.'

They laughed and talked as Michael showed her from room to room. The style was largely the same – big, airy rooms, usually tiled with simple, sparse furniture in the Greek style. Sometimes there were rugs on the walls, sometimes paintings. A close inspection of the paintings showed them to be mainly by Minos, the celebrated Greek primitive painter. Miranda knew his paintings were worth a fortune – there must be hundreds of thousands pounds worth of paintings alone in this place, she thought. Heaven knows what the place is worth altogether. Who *is* this man?

She was shown the guest suites, the kitchens, the wine cellar, the dining room – each new area was divided from the other by a series of courtyards. The general effect was light, airy, relaxed and quite perfect for the climate. At last, Michael paused outside a door. 'This is the inner sanctum,' he said, smiling slightly. 'I don't normally show people this room.'

Miranda realised instantly that he was not joking and somewhat hesitantly, followed him into the room. When she saw it, she cried out in delight. It was a perfect English study, book-lined walls, one or two old hunting prints, a leather-topped desk, thick piled carpets and two rather battered armchairs drawn up to a pine fireplace. It was in such stark contrast to the rest of the house, that it was positively disorientating. It was almost impossible not to believe that this was England, except for the view – for one end of the room was formed into huge, bay windows. When Miranda walked to the windows, which were all thrown open, she saw that the room was built right on the edge of the cliff. As with the terrace, there was nothing below them but a sheer drop into the sea. She turned to him, her eyes alight. 'Michael, this room is gorgeous, I love it.'

'I do too,' he said. 'Sometimes, particularly in the winter, I virtually live in here.' He pointed up to a little minstrels gallery, which covered the far end of the room and could be reached, Miranda saw, by a tiny spiral staircase. 'I have a bed up there,' he said, 'it's quite cosy.' His smile was warm, but again Miranda sensed a bleakness, almost a bitterness about him. 'Why not make yourself comfortable,' Michael suggested, 'and I'll fetch the wine. We've had the best of the day now, the terrrace gets quite chilly at night because of the wind off the sea.'

While he was gone, Miranda wandered around the room. By the window, she spied a table covered in tubes of paint and a jug of brushes. So he paints, she thought. Down on the floor, leaning face to the wall there were several canvases.

Knowing she was being unforgivably inquisitive, nonetheless, she could not resist picking up one and turning it round. She recognised it instantly – it was one of the primitive paintings by Minos. It showed a man and a dog and was painted exclusively in shades of brown. If she had doubted the style, the Minos signature, in the bottom right-hand corner, was plain to see. What took her breath away, with both surprise and excitement, was that the paint was still slightly wet.

'You're Minos,' she said, accusingly, when Michael returned with the wine.

He smiled, tiredly. 'I wondered how long it would take you to work that out.'

'I'm sorry, I should have known, but the name Michael Richardson meant nothing to me. You see, I'm such an ignorant creature when it comes to the arts. My family come from Yorkshire, we're Dale farmers, and so rather off the beaten track. All Mum and Dad ever read is *The Sun*. Music to them is Victor Sylvester, and as for paintings . . . well, we do have a reproduction Peter Scott in the front room.'

Michael laughed. 'The arts are very over-rated.'

'How can you say that, particularly as an artist?' Miranda said, accepting her refilled glass. So that explained everything – this amazing man was Minos – no wonder he could afford to live in such splendour, but why alone?

Michael sat down heavily on the arm of a chair, and regarded her thoughtfully. 'In my view, only in music can man surpass nature and even then it is debatable whether Mozart or Beethoven can better the song of a nightingale.'

'But what about all the beautiful paintings and sculptures that have been created over the years? You can't just dismiss them.'

'They just represent one man's impression of a place, a person, or whatever. Take yourself – you are a beautiful girl. Look at you, standing there, now, in the window, the light is catching that amazing hair of yours. Your expression, if I dare say so, is a little bewildered because you can't make head nor tail of me – and who can blame you for that? Your skin looks almost translucent from here, and those deep pools, we call eyes . . . have a mysterious quality to them just now. I could – or at least I used to be able to faithfully reproduce you as you look now. But how would it compare with the real thing? If one had to chose between Miranda the painting, or Miranda the person, there is no contest. Give me the person. See, already you have shifted your position, the light is different, your expression is more understanding, softer. You – now, at this moment – are true art, not the capturing of a single image on a flat piece of canvas.'

His scrutiny of her, made her feel self conscious. She hurried on. 'But to see me through your eyes, surely that would be very interesting.'

'Precisely,' said Michael. 'Interesting, but nothing more.'

'Then, why are you an artist?' Miranda persisted.

'For money, nothing else – heaven knows, I haven't painted a proper picture in years.'

'What do you mean, a proper picture? What are these, then?' said Miranda, pointing to the canvases.

'Ah, the Minos paintings.' Michael gave a mirthless laugh. 'Do you know how long they take me? Half an hour at the most. I paint them in batches. I spend a day at a time and paint five, ten sometimes, and they sell these days, so I'm told, for anything between twenty and a hundred thousand pounds. Ridiculous, isn't it?'

'Do you despise the people who buy them?'

Michael considered the question. 'Despise is perhaps not the right word, but I do consider them extraordinarily foolish, although, naturally, I am truly grateful.'

'You're very cynical,' said Miranda, realising how true the words were.

'Am I? I'm sorry.'

His manner was light and jesting, but again Miranda thought she caught a glimpse of the darker side of Michael Richardson. Again, too, she seemed to have touched a raw nerve end. She groped hurriedly for a change of subject. 'You promised to tell me about Mirtos, and why it is deserted,' she said.

'So I did,' said Michael, 'but I'll need another bottle of wine to do that.' He pressed a bell by the fireplace and moments later, Thea appeared. He began talking rapidly to the housekeeper, the strange vowels tripping easily off his tongue. His manner towards the old woman was pleasant, Miranda noticed, friendly rather than authoritative. He turned suddenly to Miranda, 'You'll stay to supper?'

'Supper! I hadn't realised the time. I'd love to, but I mustn't be back late. Tomorrow promises to be a long day.' She knew she should be leaving, but she couldn't – not now – not yet.

After the housekeeper had returned with more wine and then left them alone once more, Michael filled up their glasses and they sat together either side of the fireplace. 'Thea is preparing us a seafood *hors d'œuvre* and garlic bread. She says her son is back with your car.'

'This really is most kind of you,' said Miranda.

'Kindness doesn't come into it,' Michael replied, gruffly. 'I'm far more the beneficiary than you. We haven't had anyone here in months.'

Miranda longed to ask why, but she let the remark go. 'Mirtos,' she said, firmly.

'Oh yes, Mirtos. Crete was occupied by the Germans during the war – I expect you knew that.'

'Yes,' said Miranda, 'yes, I think so, though my history, like my knowledge of the arts, is a little patchy.'

'History . . . yes, I suppose that's what it is to you. Obviously, you're younger than me and then occupation makes a difference. It's more difficult for a country to forget war when it has been invaded – there are so many scars.'

'Yes, I can imagine,' said Miranda.

'The Cretans fought like the very devil to avoid the occupation – their resistance astounded the Germans. When, at last, the island was suppressed, bands of resistance fighters escaped into the mountains – mountains like these, but most of them were based in the south-west of the island, in the White Mountains. The groups were not entirely Cretan. There were a number of New Zealand soldiers left behind after the invasion, and British too. Later on in the occupation, British soldiers were actually parachuted in to help the resistance movement.' He paused, to take a sip of wine and Miranda knew him well enough now not to interrupt him with questions. 'The resistance fighters were very effective.

They used guerrilla tactics to make raids on the German army. Knowing the country gave them a huge advantage and there were some very heavy German casualities. It was then that the Germans hit upon the idea of reprisals.' Michael spat out the word.

'Reprisals?' Miranda asked.

'A life for a life. Every time a German soldier was killed, an innocent Cretan villager would die – a woman, even a child sometimes. The Germans would enter a village, line up the villagers and simply shoot them in cold blood.'

'So, that put an end to the resistance?' Miranda suggested.

'No,' Michael scoffed. 'This is Crete – the more they are persecuted, the harder they fight.' Miranda was moved by his obvious pride. 'There was a British officer in charge of the resistance group here in the Sitia Mountains. They made a highly successful raid on the German garrison and killed many German soldiers. Word reached the resistance that some Cretan prisoners, being kept at the garrison, were to be taken back to their home village of Mirtos to be shot in the square, to teach the people in the area a lesson.'

'How awful,' said Miranda. 'What happened?'

'The resistance planned an ambush to release the prisoners on their way to Mirtos, but unknown to them, their plan was betrayed and the entire resistance band was wiped out. So elated were the German soldiers with this victory that they went on to Mirtos and shot, not only the prisoners in their care, but the entire village.'

'You've got to be joking,' said Miranda.

'Do you think it is a thing I would joke about?' A heavy silence fell between them. 'It was why I appeared somewhat unfriendly when I saw you there this afternoon. Your fair hair made me think for a moment you might be German. This island desperately needs the tourist trade for economic reasons, but I can't bear German visitors.'

'You sound very bitter, yet you can't have been alive at the time.'

'No, I was not alive, but I was conceived the day of the raid. It was the last thing my father did before he died – to give me life. You see, he was the British Officer – the one who led the raid. His name was Jonathan, I wish I'd known him.'

The silence that followed his words was not at all uncomfortable. They sat together, these two people who had met for the first time only hours before, both lost in their own thoughts of the story Michael had told. It was Miranda who finally broke the silence. 'And your mother . . . who is your mother?' she asked.

'Her name is Tassoula, she was a doctor's daughter. My father was taken to their house with wounds, after the invasion of Crete. They kept him in hiding for several months, until he was well again, and as he recovered, he and my mother fell in love.'

'It's a very romantic tale,' Miranda suggested.

'Yes, unless I suspect you were living it, when the hardship and heartbreak must have been appalling.'

The meal arrived and they sat either side of the refectory table in the bay window, the sea breezes blowing in on them while they talked and ate. As always in Crete, the darkness came quickly and as it did so, Michael lit candles round the room. The effect was extraordinarily beautiful.

'Do you always dine here, by candlelight?' Miranda asked.

'I think you're laughing at me,' said Michael. 'I may be something of a recluse these days, but I'm not entirely cracked yet. And no, I don't dine alone, in candlelit splendour, each evening.'

Miranda watched his face, as he busied himself clearing the table. The soft lighting had the effect of smoothing away the harsh lines round his mouth. He looked younger, and if anything, even more handsome. He really was the most extraordinary looking man. She felt her heart flip within her chest – a feeling she had not experienced in years. But it was not his physical beauty that caused the feeling – instinctively she knew that. It was something to do with the curious conflicts in character that went to make up the man himself – on the one hand, his strength and on the other, his vulnerability. It was that, she realised, which she found so appealing.

Thea brought Greek coffee, thick and sweet, and they returned to the armchairs round the fireplace, and talked.

Miranda told him of her Yorkshire childhood, of her family, and particularly of Paul, her brother.

'It must be nice having him living with you,' Michael suggested.

'Do you know, you're the first person to have ever said that,' said Miranda, surprised. 'Most of my friends were appalled when they heard my teenage brother was coming to live with me – thinking, I suppose, it would cramp my style. Instead, it's been the greatest fun.'

'Your friends' reaction is not surprising,' said Michael. 'You are a beautiful and desirable woman. When people look at you they cannot help but think of relationships in a sexual sense. Sometimes I think the whole world has gone sex mad. In my view, the most important relationship that can exist between two people, is friendship.' He smiled. 'Whatever happened to friendship?'

'Do you know, you're so right, in fact my agent and I were arguing about that very subject just before I came away. In her view, a woman without a man in her life is a total flop.'

'Does that mean you don't have a man in your life at present?' His voice was casual, but he was watching her intently.

Miranda smiled. 'No, I haven't and I mean to keep it that way for a while. It's so restful!'

Michael laughed. 'I know how you feel. Why do you think I'm holed up here all alone, with no one but Thea for company? The worrying thing is if I stay here long enough, I might start to find her attractive.' They laughed together. Michael hesitated. 'I seem to remember from the gossip columns that you were married. Am I right?'

Miranda nodded. 'Yes, but my husband was killed in a helicopter crash, only five months after our wedding.'

'Jesus, that must have been rotten. How long ago did that happen?'

'Oh, a long time,' said Miranda, 'I was only twenty-one, I'm twenty-eight now.'

'You poor old lady,' said Michael, 'just thank your lucky stars you're not forty-two.'

'Is that what you are?' Miranda asked.

'Come on,' said Michael, 'I've already told you when I was born, I bet you've done the sum.'

Miranda had the grace to blush, then she grinned at him. 'Still, I bet there's life in the old dog yet.'

'Only just, God knows, only just.'

Thea returned with more coffee and a bottle of Greek brandy, and they continued to talk. To Miranda, it seemed as though they were trapped in some sort of time warp – she was starting to feel that she had always known Michael Richardson, always been in this room. The concept that they had known one another for only a few hours was quite unbelievable, that life was going on outside the Villa Dionissos, quite inconceivable.

'This stuff is amazing. I seem to be able to drink it by the pint,' she said, twirling her brandy glass, perhaps it was too much drink making her feel as she did.

'It's because there are no chemicals in it, unlike most brandies. It's just fortified grape juice, which does you no harm at all.'

'All the same,' said Miranda, leaning back in the chair and stretching, 'I ought to be thinking about going back to the hotel. I wonder what time it is?'

'Ten past two,' said Michael.

Miranda sat bolt upright. 'You've got to be joking!'

Michael shook his head and grinned. 'Time travels fast when you're having fun.'

'I have had fun,' Miranda said, sincerely. 'Thank you. Today was just what I needed.'

'Me too.' Michael stood up. 'Come on then, I'll take you back to the hotel.'

'No, you certainly won't,' said Miranda. 'You said the jeep was outside, I'll drive myself.'

'My dear girl, if you think I'm going to let you career around unfamiliar lanes in the middle of the night, with a bottle of wine and goodness knows how many brandies inside you, you have to be joking. I'll drive you back tonight and get one of my boys to deliver your jeep to Ayios Nikolaos tomorrow.'

'But I haven't even paid the hire company as yet.'

'I'll pay for it,' said Michael, firmly.

'Only if you let me pay you back.'

'All right, all right,' said Michael, 'I give in – I don't know how to protect myself against independent women.'

They spoke little on the journey back to the Minos Beach, both were reliving the hours they had just spent together, trying to piece together their feelings.

'I'll walk you down to your villa,' Michael said, as he helped her from the car, outside the hotel entrance.

'No, it's all right,' said Miranda, 'honestly. The paths are well lit and I feel like a little fresh air before bedtime.'

Michael understood immediately – he too was not ready for sleep, needing time to assess and consider the jangle of emotions that this girl seemed to have produced in him. 'I'll come and collect you tomorrow evening, and take you out to dinner,' he said. It was not a question, it was a statement. It did not occur to Michael that Miranda would refuse him, nor, indeed, did it occur to Miranda to do so.

'You'd better not make it too early,' she said. 'I expect we will be working late.'

'I'll come at eight. It'll be too dark by then for photographs.' He wanted to kiss her, but neither of them were ready, yet he knew he could not leave without some form of tangible contact. Uncertainly as a boy, he stepped forward and slipped his arms round her, pulling her gently to him so that her head rested on his shoulder. They stood thus for several moments, in the circle of each others' arms. Strangely, there was no passion, no quickening of the blood, just gentle warmth and security. At last, it was Miranda who pushed them apart, and with her hands still on Michael's shoulders, reached up and kissed him gently on the cheek. Then, without speaking, she turned and ran through the hotel doorway.

Michael did not drive straight home. Instead he took the coast road to Elounda. The road climbed sharply, round a series of hairpin bends, hundreds of feet above the sea. Just before it began to descend towards the village, Michael pulled into a passing space and turned off the engine. Scrabbling around in the dashboard, he found a cigarette. He lit it and then sat back in his seat to wait for dawn to come out of the sea, feeling more relaxed and content than he had been in years, if ever.

Miranda walked slowly down the path towards her villa, and then on impulse changed direction and took the path to the beach instead. The sea was dark, and very still. She stood on the water's edge, staring ahead through the darkness, to try and distinguish the shapes of the Sitia Mountains, but there was nothing to see. Perhaps it had all been a dream, it almost seemed like it. What a strange man he was, she thought. There were so many dark shadows, so much she could not ask him. While she had been happy for him to question her about her life, her hopes and dreams, she knew, instinctively, that she could ask him nothing, that she had to wait patiently until he was ready to tell her about himself. That he was Minos, the celebrated painter was of no consequence to her. She thought of him as Michael – the first man to have moved her in a long time. For there was one thing she could not deny, one thing that was overwhelmingly certain – when he had held her in his arms, it had felt, at last, like coming home.

Chapter Eight

Miranda, too, saw the dawn that morning, but not with the same peace of mind as Michael watched it burst out of the sea. She walked along the beach to her villa and in doing so passed Jake's. At the thought of Jake, she had a momentary pang of remorse. She had not considered him once all day, yet clearly, if Clive's tale-telling had found a sympathetic ear, Jake could well be on his way back to London by now. Yet no . . . there he was, she could see his hunched outline. He was sitting on his balcony, his head in his hands, his long, straight hair flopping forward.

'Jake,' she called softly.

His head jerked up. 'What the hell do you want?'

'Jake, it's me, Miranda.'

'I sodding well know who it is. What the hell do you want, I said?' His speech was slurred with drink.

'To talk,' Miranda suggested. It was, in fact, the last thing she wanted to do. She was tired now and ready for sleep.

'Oh, you do, do you?' He gave a mirthless laugh.

It would have been easy to leave him to his drunken ill-temper, but she felt a surge of sympathy for him, coupled, as always where Jake was concerned, with guilt. Jake had been her husband's best friend. How would David have felt if he had known she had gone to bed leaving Jake like this? Wearily she climbed up the steps to his balcony. 'What's happened today?' she asked. 'Has Clive brought in another photographer?'

'I wouldn't have thought you'd have cared one way or the other, since you shoved off the moment things got difficult.' Jake straightened up and met her eye. She could swear he had been crying – his eyes were red and puffy, his naturally pale skin even paler in the moonlight.

'I'm sorry I wasn't here, Jake, but I had to get away. I'd had more than enough of all those rows – besides which, I wanted to see something of the island. It is beautiful, isn't it?'

This remark seemed to mollify Jake somewhat. He smiled, loosely. 'Yes, it is,' he agreed. 'I came here with David once, you know.'

'David! Did you? Why didn't you say so before?'

'You didn't ask me,' Jake said. 'You never ask me much about David these days. I suppose it's because you've got over him. It's not surprising really – there have always been plenty of men in your life. Have you seen my brandy?'

'I think you've had enough,' said Miranda, 'and as for getting over David, that's where you're wrong.' Instinct told her she should leave, with Jake in this mood, but she was curious. 'When did you come here with him?'

'The year before he met you. That would be 1977 – we stayed here, at the Minos Beach.'

Miranda stared at him. It seemed so strange that he had not mentioned it before, yet she supposed it explained his anger at Clive's criticism of the hotel. 'Did you have a good time?' she asked.

'Yes, yes of course. We did some good work here, too. I'll show you the photographs when we are back in London. It was why I suggested the location to Masons, but perhaps that was not such a good idea after all.'

'*You* suggested the location?' Miranda asked.

Jake nodded. 'Rick Jennings, the Managing Director of Masons is an old chum of mine.'

'Bloody hell! Does Clive know that?'

Jake looked cheerful for the first time. 'He does now, he's on a plane back to London, after the biggest bollocking of his life.'

'You mean he's been recalled . . . by Masons?'

Jake nodded. 'It appears he telephoned Rick and started moaning about my methods and Rick told him to leave me alone. They had a good old slanging match apparently – Peter was eavesdropping – and Clive was told to report back to Manchester sharpish.' Jake grinned some more. 'I hope he's put newspaper down his trousers.'

'Jake, that's wonderful. So there's just you and me and Peter?'

'That's about the size of it,' said Jake. 'So this is why I'm out here celebrating. Find my glass, there's a good girl.' Reluctantly, Miranda handed over the brandy glass, which was hovering dangerously on the edge of the table. Jake took a hearty swig. 'So, while I've been getting Clive Brooks sacked, what have you been doing with yourself?'

'I met this fascinating man,' Miranda said.

'Oh!' There was an edge to Jake's voice. 'What sort of man?'

'Well, you'll know him, know of him – his name's Michael Richardson.'

'Never heard of him,' said Jake, dismissively.

'Better known as Minos,' Miranda said.

'The painter chap?'

'The same.'

'Bloody awful paintings,' said Jake.

'That's what he thinks, but they sell. I thought they were rather good, personally.'

'Yes, but then you would, you're clearly besotted with the fellow already.'

'Jake, don't be ridiculous, I've only just met him,' said Miranda.

'Ah, that's as may be, but I can tell by the way you talk about him.' Jake searched round on the floor for the brandy bottle, and finding it, poured himself some more, spilling most of it as he did so. 'Cheers,' he said. 'David wouldn't approve, you know.'

Miranda's heart gave a lurch, as it always did at the mention of her husband's name. 'Why ever not?' she said, lightly.

'If the gossip columns are to be believed – and there's usually no smoke without fire – he's a terrible womaniser. He's had endless affairs, with Hollywood starlets and models. . . .' Jake eyed Miranda, speculatively, for a moment. 'Come to think of it, you're probably just his type.'

'That was rather unkind,' said Miranda.

'Not unkind, just factual. He was married, too. Something happened to his wife, I can't remember what now. I just don't understand you, girl. You've been married to a good man, the best. Why can't you leave it at that?'

'Jake, for heaven's sake, I'm only twenty-eight.' Miranda was starting to feel agitated. 'I was widowed at twenty-one. What do you expect me to do, spend the rest of my life in a nunnery?'

Jake ignored the question. 'At the time, I never thought you loved him, and heaven knows I've been proved right. Within months of his death you were playing around with every Tom, Dick and Harry.'

'I was not,' said Miranda, standing up. She was trembling and close to tears. 'I never looked at another man, Jake, not for at least three years after David died.'

'Three years' fidelity!' Jake gave a hollow laugh. 'Is that the only price you feel you need to pay? David paid you the supreme compliment of giving you the whole of his life – what was left of it.'

'I expected to give him mine, too,' Miranda protested.

'Yes, but you didn't have to, did you? You took his life but gave nothing in return.'

'W-what do you mean?' Miranda's voice was shrill with shock.

'You were responsible for David's death,' Jake said, bitterly. 'But for you, he would still be alive. He didn't even know the Hardcastles. It was only through you, and your wretched marriage, that he met them, that he was staying with them that weekend, that he was in the . . . helicopter.' The word seemed to stick in Jake's throat. He stood up, swaying slightly, and walked, none too steadily to the edge of the balcony. He stood with his back to Miranda, staring out to sea.

'That's not fair,' Miranda shouted at his back. 'That's not fair. If I could have died in that crash instead of David, I would have done so – willingly. But I can't control fate any more than you can, Jake.'

'You could have left him alone and not talked him into a marriage he didn't even want.'

Miranda was astounded. 'He asked me to marry him. He pestered me for months.'

'Stop it,' Jake thundered back, turning to face her, his eyes blazing with apparent hatred. 'Get the hell out of my sight, I don't want to hear any more of this – do you understand?'

'You began it – not me.'

'Then I'll finish it, too. Piss off, Miranda. Leave me alone.'

Trembling and shocked, Miranda staggered down the steps of Jake's villa, and up the steps of her own, the lovely afternoon and evening with Michael Richardson now just a dim memory. She was sticky from the heat, yet her bones felt oddly chilled and the air conditioning, which had been left on all day, seemed to have made her room icy. She turned it off and threw open the doors, letting the warm Cretan night blow through the room. In the bathroom, she turned on the taps and squeezed some baby oil into the water, watching, abstractedly, as the globules clung together on the surface. She stripped off her clothes, gingerly stepped into the water and not until the bath was full to the overflow, did she turn off the taps and lie back. She knew Jake had been terribly drunk, and that, without doubt, he had endured a harrowing day, but how could he have said those things, and were they what he truly believed? Were they purely drunken ramblings, or in Jake's mind did he really hold her responsible for David Conway's death?

In the first two years, during which Jenny Marchant acted as Miranda's agent, her career went from strength to strength. The PIPPA campaign was an enormous success. Never for a moment did Lawrence Hardcastle regret his decision – Miranda was a natural. Her face was not classically beautiful, the mouth was too large, her nose tipped up a fraction too much. Even her glorious hair could be quite a problem – those thick, white gold curls could all too easily detract from her face and therefore PIPPA PAINTS, unless it was kept well under control. Yet there was a quality about the girl which put her in a different league from every other model – a naturalness, a joy of living, and an enormous capacity for hard work. After a gruelling session in the studio,

Miranda would shower and change, and still be fresh and eager for a store promotion.

Lawrence grew very fond of her over the months. He frequently invited her down to Maidenhead for the weekend, where his wife, May, took the girl to her heart as well. After a difficult time giving birth to their son, William, May had been advised against having any further children. To the Hardcastles, Miranda very quickly became the daughter they had never had. Secretly they hoped that one day she might make a match with William. So, backed by Lawrence's avuncular guidance and Jenny's shrewd commercial instincts, Miranda's career blossomed.

Not so, her social life – the terrible experience with Joe Chang had left her irreparably damaged so far as men were concerned. Her amazing good looks, coupled with her choice of career, meant she was constantly the butt of men's admiration. Yet she trusted no man but Lawrence Hardcastle, and rebuffed, firmly, all propositions, even of the most mild nature. Jenny chided her, warned her that her reactions were understandable, but frankly becoming a fettish – she needed an affair before she ended up weird. Around the photographic studios of London, Miranda's apparent lack of interest in men was a growing legend – and therefore an irresistible challenge to every red blooded male. Yet the more she was pestered, the more inaccessible she seemed to become.

Everything changed for Miranda the day she walked into a delapidated studio, near the World's End, Chelsea. She had not been enthusiastic about the assignment. The photographer was unknown to her, which in itself produced a natural prejudice – another legacy from Joe Chang. 'Do I have to take this job?' she had asked Jenny.

'You most certainly do, darling. It's for *Vogue*, besides which I have a feeling about this boy, I think he might well be a rising star. I've never heard of *Vogue* hiring an unknown photographer before. Hitching your horse to his wagon might be no bad thing . . . in any respect,' she added darkly.

The hallway was dark and dingy, the paint peeling, but when David Conway opened the door of the studio, Miranda stepped into a world of colour – blues, reds, emerald greens shouted at her from the walls, the floor, the ceiling. For a moment she was stunned into complete silence.

'Jolly, isn't it?'

She turned on a polite smile, which became one of genuine pleasure. David Conway was about her own height. He had light brown curly hair and the cheeky cherubic face of a choirboy. His eyes were bright blue, they twinkled at her mischievously – he looked like a child pretending to be an adult. 'It's amazing,' she said.

'Oh, I don't know about amazing, but it's fun. Hey, Miranda, meet my partner, Jake Berisford. Jake this is . . . hell, I don't need to tell you who this is – the face that launched a thousand fashion designers.'

Miranda laughed. 'Hardly. Hello Jake.'

Jake smiled and took her hand, but immediately she felt slightly uncomfortable. He could not have been more of a contrast to David – he was tall and dark, but although he was clearly about their own age, his pale, tired face had the look of an old man.

'Coffee and a chat before we start work?' David suggested.

'That would be lovely.'

He lead her into a little kitchenette just off the studio, which she was not entirely surprised to find was painted in pink and orange stripes. 'Do you drink much?' she asked.

'Not a great deal, why?'

'I was just thinking of walking into this place with a hangover, it must be hell.'

David laughed. 'I'm glad you're so nice,' he said, disarmingly. 'I've been terrified about meeting you. You see, this is make or break for me.'

'What is?' Miranda asked.

'Today, these shots we're doing. If I get it right, I'm on my way, if not – curtains.'

'Surely not,' said Miranda.

'Listen, let me explain . . .' said David, his child's face wrinkled with concentration. '. . . oh, black or white, by the way?'

'White, thanks.'

He paused, coffee spoon in mid air. 'It's an incredible

opportunity, photographing for *Vogue*. I've pestered and pestered them for months, of course, and I think they've only let me have a go because they are so heartily sick of me. The thing is now I've got my chance, I mustn't blow it.'

Suddenly, Miranda felt very confident and experienced. By now she had been photographed by every major photographer. Patrick Lichfield adored working with her, Tony Snowdon had photographed her at Kensington Palace, Norman Parkinson had called her the most fascinating face of the century. This boy was just starting out, as she had once. She smiled at him warmly. 'Don't worry, David, we'll knock 'em for six.'

And they did. The feature was aimed at promoting knickerbockers as the autumn's new fashion trend. They decided on a gamine look, teaming the knickerbockers with bright sweaters and an Oliver Twist cap. Miranda cavorted round the studio, running down stairs, leaping in the air, riding a bike, rollerskating – exuberance and all the fun of being young showed in the shots. *Vogue* gave it a double-page spread and as a result, not only was David Conway on his way, but a brand new photographer/model team was established, to take up the crown from David Bailey and Jean Shrimpton, and hold it higher than it had ever been held before. Within weeks, they were getting double bookings. . . . *Paris Match*, *Women's Wear Daily* . . . they were in demand everywhere. They toured the world, and the world loved them. They were two children, taking the staid image of international fashion and turning it on its ear. And when they fell in love, the fairy tale was complete.

David was not a particularly passionate man, which was as well, for Miranda was terrified of physical contact with anyone. Alone, in impersonal hotels, in strange cities around the world, they turned to one another, for comfort and security, their intimacy and need for one another growing daily. When finally, one night, in a hotel on the banks of the Arno in Florence, David took her, he managed to banish her terror. The blood did not surge in her veins, but there was a feeling of comfort, of being wanted and needed again, and she was deeply grateful.

It seemed a natural extension to their working life that they should marry. Miranda took David home to meet her parents, but it was not a success. Coming from a comfortable, middle-class Southern home, as he did, David had little, or nothing, in common with the Higgins. Miranda, too, could not help but see her family and old home, through David's eyes. After their exotic assignments around the world, the family kitchen, which had once represented so much cosy security in her life, now seemed shabby and stark.

They married in St Mary's Church at Henley-on-Thames in a blaze of publicity. Their reception was in Phyllis Court, on the banks of the river, and after the reception, a river launch bore them away from their guests. Lottie Higgins' increasing arthritis was the excuse Miranda's parents used for not attending the ceremony, so she was given away by Lawrence Hardcastle. The Hardcastles, having recovered from their disappointment that Miranda had not married their son, quickly took David to their hearts, and whenever Miranda and David were in England, they tended to drift down to Maidenhead for the weekend. They were a golden couple, everyone adored them, but the partnership was destined to end before it had hardly begun.

Before lunch, one Sunday, in July 1979, William Hardcastle suggested to David and Miranda that they might like to take a spin in the new family helicopter. David had accepted immediately, Miranda had hesitated. She wanted to go, but she was aware of a modelling assignment the following day which required her to wear a suntop. It was the first hot day in weeks and so she decided to stay behind and improve her tan. Miranda's decision saved her life, for minutes later, the Hardcastle's only son, and Miranda's husband were burnt to death, while everyone who loved them best, watched on, helplessly.

Tears flowed down Miranda's cheeks as she lay in the cooling bath. How could Jake say she had not loved David. He had been her best friend, she would have done anything in the world for him. To say she would rather have been in the helicopter than he, was true. So, sex between them had always been a little strained but David did not seem to mind. In any event Miranda knew it was not because she did not love him that he could not arouse her. Between them, Joe Chang and Eric Fairfax had destroyed her feelings in that respect – she knew that now.

She eased her tired, aching body out of the bath and, wrapped in a towel, went in search of her watch. It was after four. Presumably Jake would want to catch the morning light, so that meant she would have to be up at half past six. She groaned, her head aching, her eyes sore from tears and tiredness – she was going to look terrible. She climbed into bed, turned out the light and lay staring into the darkness. The thought of working with Jake for the next week was repugnant, to say the least. For the first time, lying there, she faced the knowledge that since the moment she had first met him, she had neither liked, nor trusted him. David's death had irrevocably bonded them together, but not from choice. Not for the first time Miranda wondered whether Jake was jealous of the success she and David had achieved together. Individually, David and Miranda were two talented, successful people – together they were dynamite, and such was the closeness of their professional and personal relationship, that during the last year of David's life, it had excluded everyone else. Jake had been left behind, still working at World's End, photographing mail order catalogues and second-rate commercials, while they took the world by storm.

At last Miranda slipped into sleep, only to wake an hour later, screaming and crying, reliving yet again the moment when the helicopter hit the ground and extinguished her husband's life.

Chapter Nine

Jake's greeting the following morning was cool, but friendly. If it had not been for her incredible weariness and a blinding pain behind the eyes, Miranda would have begun to wonder whether she had imagined their conversation of the previous night.

Jake wanted to photograph three garments in an olive grove he had found the previous day. A taxi took them to the location, with promises to return and collect them three hours later. The 'props' were already in position, in the form of a donkey, and a cheerful, toothless old man, with a face the colour and consistency of well-seasoned leather – and who, they quickly discovered, took enormous pleasure from watching Miranda change. Standing in bra and pants, in an olive grove, at eight o'clock in the morning, being ogled by an ancient Cretan, actually produced in Miranda her first smile of the day. As so often with modelling assignments, the situation she found herself in was absurd.

The shooting went well. Miranda pretended it was David, not Jake, photographing her. She flirted with the camera, with the old man, even the donkey. Peter, now no longer restrained by the interference of his client, was the perfect helper. He pinned the garments, where needed, loaded film for Jake, held Miranda's hairbrush and powder compact at the ready, and passed round endless cups of coffee from the flask he had so thoughtfully brought with him. But as the heat of the day came up to greet them, Miranda began to feel sick and faint. The atmosphere in the olive grove was very oppressive, the air so still that it was almost difficult to breathe. The sun beat down mercilessly, and when at last an approaching cloud of dust told them that the taxi was on its way, Miranda could have wept with relief.

The journey back to the hotel revived her a little, and at Jake's suggestion, they broke for an hour's lunch. Miranda did not feel like eating, so, instead, she took a shower, and then lay on her bed. All too soon the hour was up and they were photographing again – this time on the beach. The breeze off the sea helped a little but it was an exceptionally hot day.

'Jake, how many shots are we doing this afternoon?' Miranda asked, after about half an hour.

'We'll work for as long as we have light,' Jake replied. 'We have a lot of catching up to do, bearing in mind the fiasco of the last couple of days.'

There was a mounting crowd of people watching the photography – other holidaymakers, mostly children, fascinated to see Miranda as she turned this way and that, forcing smiles of carefree joy. She changed twice more – the headache was growing worse and she was constantly harangued by waves of nausea.

'I think we ought to give Miranda a break,' she heard Peter say to Jake – his voice seemed to be coming from a long way off.

'There's no time for anyone to have a break,' Jake snapped.

A buzzing noise started in Miranda's head. At first she thought it must be a plane overhead, but it seemed too close and too noisy for that. It was all round her getting louder and louder, and her last sight was of shocked faces as she plummeted forwards into darkness.

When she came round, she was lying on the bed in her villa, with Peter leaning over her, his big, boyish face full of concern. 'Don't worry, Miranda, you'll be all right in a moment,' he said. 'I've sent for the hotel doctor.'

She tried to sit up, but the pain in her head was unbearable. 'How silly,' she said, weakly. 'What did I do – faint?'

Peter nodded. 'It was the heat. I don't mind admitting I was feeling pretty peculiar myself and I wasn't having to stand in the sun like you were.'

'I didn't get much sleep last night,' Miranda admitted. 'That probably didn't help.' Her eyes clouded, suddenly. 'Where's Jake?'

'He's gone off in rather a sulk, and I've no sympathy with him. It was a stupid thing to do, riding you so hard. It was jolly good of you to stick it out as long as you did.'

There was a soft knock on the door and the doctor came in. A quick examination revealed that, in his view, Miranda had nothing more than a touch of sunstroke. 'A day out of the sun tomorrow, plenty of sleep, and you will be very well again, madam,' he said, in stilted English.

'But I have to go out in the sun tomorrow,' Miranda said. 'I'm working here – modelling.'

The doctor shrugged his shoulders. 'It is your decision, of course, but I think you would be very foolish, and probably make yourself even more ill.'

'What did he say?' Peter asked, coming back into the room as soon as the doctor had left. Miranda told him. 'Well, that's that, then, Jake's going to have to give you a day off.'

'He won't,' said Miranda.

'He'll have to,' said Peter, surprisingly decisive for once. 'Leave him to me, I'll sort him out – there's no way I'll let you work against doctor's orders.'

Miranda fell into an exhausted sleep, waking later to find Jake standing at the end of her bed. 'I gather you've been advised to have a day off.'

'Yes,' Miranda said, drowsily. 'Apparently I have a touch of sunstroke.'

'We've already lost two days, we can't afford to lose a third.'

Miranda could barely focus – the pain behind her eyes was so severe. She tried to rally her thoughts. 'It's not my fault we lost those two days, Jake. If you had made more of an effort to get on with Clive, things would have worked out fine.'

'Fantastic,' Jake raged. 'So it's all my fault that you're lying here, when you should be working.'

'Yes, it is,' Miranda said. 'Nobody could have worked in that heat today. Heaven knows, Jake, I've always had a reputation for being conscientious – Jesus, I can work the pants off most models.'

'That's not what I've heard recently,' Jake said, nastily. 'Rumour has it that you're not the girl you were, and certainly this little escapade would tend to confirm it.'

'How dare you,' Miranda said, struggling up into a sitting position, despite the pain. 'If you're looking for a mass walk-out, Jake, you're getting painfully near to succeeding. If you're not happy with the way I work, why not ring your precious chum at Masons and tell him I'm no good either. I'm sure, for you, they would fly out another model by the morning – someone more professional, more experienced, perhaps.' Her voice was heavy with sarcasm.

The threat clearly had its effect. 'All right, all right, take your day off, if that's what you want,' Jake said, walking to the door. 'But that leaves us just six days. It means I'll need you body and soul for every hour of light we have, if we're to finish on time.' He left the room abruptly, shutting the door none too quietly behind him.

Self-pity welled up inside Miranda and she began to cry, quietly. She felt so ill, so alone, and debilitated by Jake's now obvious dislike of her. She turned her face to the pillow and began to sob, and so involved was she in her own misery that she did not hear the door open again, nor the quiet footsteps to the bedside. 'My dear girl, what on earth's wrong?'

She knew the voice. For a moment she could not place its familiarity, but the genuine concern and warmth reached her. She turned over, careless of her tear-stained face, and found herself looking into the clear blue eyes of Michael Richardson. 'W-what are you doing here?' she asked, her mind confused by the difficulties of the day.

'We were going out to dinner. Remember?'

'Oh Michael, I'm so sorry, I'm afraid I forgot.'

He sat down on the edge of the bed and took her hand. 'It's all right, don't worry about it. The hotel receptionist told me that you were not well and that a doctor had been called. Looking at you, I can see you're obviously in quite a state. What the hell's been going on?'

Without preamble or hesitation, Miranda found herself telling Michael the full story – of the scene with Jake the previous night, of her nightmare, and of the difficult day's work, on top of little or no sleep. When she had finished, it was though a great burden had been lifted from her – she felt light-headed with relief at being able to talk about it.

'That sod, Jake, I'd like to wring his neck. What a stupid thing to do – talk about mad dogs and Englishmen . . . He's lucky you're not more seriously ill – sunstroke is no joking matter.'

'Well, at least he has agreed that I don't have to work tomorrow, so let's just hope he hasn't forgotten his promise by the morning.'

'If he's hitting the bottle as hard as you say, anything's possible, and that being the case, there's only one sensible course of action.'

'What's that?' asked Miranda, wearily.

'You're coming home with me,' said Michael.

'I couldn't possibly . . .' Miranda began.

'Yes, you could, just for tonight and tomorrow night. Thea and I can wait on you hand and foot tomorrow and I'll get you back on time for the following day's shoot – however early it is.' He smiled suddenly. 'And in case you're wondering, this isn't a clumsy attempt at seduction. It's just that these little rooms are no place to be ill – they're either stiflingly hot or freezing cold. A little cossetting for twenty-four hours will do you no harm at all.'

'It's terribly tempting,' Miranda said, weakly.

'Don't think about it anymore then, just do it. I'll go and wait on the balcony while you dress. You don't need to bring anything but a toothbrush.' He stood up and walked to the door. Then he turned and grinned wickedly. 'That is, unless you're too weak and you feel you need a hand.'

'I can manage quite well, thank you,' said Miranda, smiling back.

They felt like fugitives as they crept from the hotel. Miranda wrote a note for Jake, to say she was staying with friends for twenty-four hours, but would be ready for work at seven o'clock on Thursday morning. 'He'll go mad when he reads it,' she said, as Michael helped her into the car.

'Let him.'

Forty minutes later they turned into the driveway of the Villa Dionissos, and while Thea prepared a room for Miranda, Michael took her into his study. The windows, as usual, were wide open and the room was awash with the smell of the sea – cool and fresh. 'I feel so much better, already,' said Miranda. 'In fact, I feel rather a fraud.'

'Does that mean you'd like something to eat and drink?'

She shook her head. 'No, not to eat. Perhaps a drink, something non-alcoholic, though – I'm up to my ears in aspirin.'

From a little fridge Miranda had not noticed before, Michael took out a jug of orange juice. He poured a glass for Miranda, and a whisky for himself. She sat down on a chair by the fireplace, feeling relaxed and happy, the pain now just a dull ache. 'This room is completely self-contained, isn't it?' she said. 'Mind you, I'm not surprised – it's by far the nicest room in the house.'

'I'm glad you think so,' Michael said quietly.

'What made you build the villa here?' Miranda asked. 'I mean on this spot.'

'Can you bear to stand up – if so come to the window,' said Michael.

Miranda joined him by the open window, suddenly acutely aware of his closeness, of her bare arm against his.

'It is at this precise spot,' he said, 'where we are standing now, that my father used to live.'

'Used to live – you mean there was a house here before this one?'

'No,' said Michael. 'He lived in a cave.' Michael put a hand on her shoulder and pointed a long, brown arm. 'Look, you see further along the coast, the cliffs, they are pitted with caves. His cave was just like that.'

'It must have been an extraordinarily tough life.'

Michael nodded. 'After he died, my mother kept it like a shrine for him. She left everything that was his, which heaven knows was not much, just as he had left it on the day he died. Come, I'll show you.' He took Miranda to a cupboard at the back of the room. Kneeling down on the floor, he drew out, reverently, two or three battered saucepans, a stained and delapidated goatskin rug, and an old leather-bound book. There was a hunting knife and a few items of clothing. 'When I could have been no more than two or three,' Michael continued, 'my mother brought me here and showed me these. I can remember it so well, touching the things that had been my father's. When I'd made a lot of money, I decided to return to Crete, and buy a house. As usual, whenever I came home, the first thing I did was to come up here, to say hello to my father. The Germans took his body away, you see, there was no grave, so this was the only place we could come to. I remember it so well – gazing out to sea, wondering how I could make the cave seem important to future generations – to my child, if I had one. First, it occurred to me that it would be an idea to build some sort of monument to my father, but then I realised it might upset the local people. There is already a war memorial with his name on it in Sitia, and I did not want people to think I did not consider it good enough. Then, suddenly, the idea came to me – why didn't I live here as my father had done.' Michael grinned, ruefully. 'Only I have to admit, I do enjoy my creature comforts, hence the villa. Still I feel, in a way, I have come full circle. My mother told me, after I had made my decision, that in fact I was conceived here – so it really is back to base for me.'

It was the longest speech that Michael had made about himself since Miranda had met him, and she found it very revealing. On the surface, he seemed to epitomise the stiff, formal Englishman, yet underneath, clearly, he was an unashamed romantic. She wondered for the first time how difficult he found it to deal with the two sides of his nature – which were in such obvious contrast to one another.

'I think what you have done is wonderful,' she said, simply. 'I have to admit to being something of an agnostic, but I'd like to think your father knows what's happened here and how much this place means to you.'

At that moment Thea arrived. 'Come on,' said Michael, firmly, 'I'm not going to keep you from your bed another moment, I'll show you to your room.'

At the door to her bedroom, Michael wished her goodnight – once more a remote figure. His formality disappointed Miranda, yet under the eagle eye of Thea, it was difficult to see how he could have behaved any differently. Her bedroom was magnificent. On the floor above, and a little to the right of Michael's study, it had the same wonderful view. It was an enormous room, with a bathroom leading from it and a tiny balcony accessible from French windows. Impressed though she was with her surroundings, Miranda was too exhausted to explore. After a quick wash, she slipped between the cool sheets of the huge bed, with a great sigh of relief. As she drifted off to sleep, her thoughts, for once, were not of David, nor of the problems that lay ahead with Jake – instead she thought of a doomed, young couple, making love for the last time, in a cave on the edge of the sea.

When Miranda woke the following morning, she was unsure of where she was for a moment. The sun streamed through the window, and just for a second, it reminded her of childhood. Then memory flooded back and with it came a sense of unease. What was she doing here, with this man she hardly knew? Why did she feel so comfortable with him, so sure of him – she, who had learnt to trust no man? There was another emotion, too, that worried her – a pent-up excitement, an exhilaration when she thought of him – she tried to dismiss the feelings but they persisted. She lay for a long time, mesmerised by the beams of sunlight, slipping in and out of sleep. Once or twice she wondered whether she should get up, but the effort seemed too great.

Presently, there was a knock on the door and Thea arrived, with a breakfast tray – orange juice and Greek coffee, rolls, butter and honey. Miranda thanked her profusely in English, wishing she had even a few words of Greek, but the woman seemed utterly unapproachable. With her grey hair scraped back into a bun, her black dress and severe features, she made a daunting figure. In repose, her mouth was drawn down at the corners, and Miranda wondered whether she had ever learnt to smile.

Breakfast finished, Miranda bathed and washed her hair. In the mirror she scrutinised herself professionally. Her shoulders were badly burned, but if they were kept well moisturised, they would not peel. Her nose and forehead were too red, but foundation would correct that. Yes, the image would be intact for tomorrow . . . just. She applied plenty of moisturiser to her face, towel-dried her hair and put on a favourite old baggy T-shirt she had bought some years ago in the Kings Road. Then, taking her hairbrush, she padded off in bare feet in search of Michael. She found him on the terrace, drinking coffee and reading the paper. He jumped up when he saw her, smiling delightedly. 'So, now we have it – the real Miranda Hicks. You can keep the model girl, this one's for me.'

'How do you mean?' said Miranda.

'No makeup, hair all tousled, bare feet – oh, how I would love to paint you like that.' He hesitated, and then a cloud seemed to come into his eyes. 'No. I wouldn't, I-I don't paint portraits any more.'

'Did you used to?' Miranda asked gently.

Michael nodded. 'Yes, before the demon Minos took over.'

'I'd love to see you work,' said Miranda. 'Wouldn't you just do a sketch or two? Not of me particularly, of anything.'

Michael hesitated. 'All right,' he said, 'I'll fetch my pad.'

While Miranda sat in the morning sunlight, brushing her long curls, Michael sketched her. At first, he worked leisurely, but then with a growing confidence, as he covered page after page.

Miranda laughed at him. 'You must be the champion of the paper industry.' Michael did not reply, he was lost in his work, so Miranda continued to brush her hair in silence, surreptitiously watching him, noticing little details – the strength of the brown hand that held the pencil, the almost childlike frown of concentration, the way his hair flopped over his forehead. He wore faded denim shorts and a white T-shirt, and Miranda could not help but be aware of the strong, brown legs arranged carelessly in front of her. An impulse to go to him, to put her arms round him, came to her suddenly, and it terrified her. Once before her body had betrayed her – it would never do so again. She fought off the feeling, brushing her hair ferociously, until her scalp tingled.

'There, that's enough,' said Michael suddenly.

'Can I see?'

'No, but I'll work up something for you from these – promise.' He shut the pad firmly and she knew better than to argue with him. 'Now,' he said, 'I've mapped out the day – a little reading and talking, in the shade on the terrace here this morning, an apéritif, a light lunch, a siesta, followed by – if madam feels up to it – a little boat trip once the sun has lost its heat.'

'It sounds wonderful' said Miranda, 'as long as I'm not interrupting something – don't you want to work?'

'No, I don't want to work. To be honest I never want to work, and today you have provided me with the perfect excuse for not doing so.'

They spent a quite extraordinarily relaxed morning, talking and reading. Michael had acquired the previous Sunday's British newspapers and they pored over these, exchanging pieces of news. Then Miranda announced that she had to paint her nails ready for the following day, and Michael watched, fascinated, whilst she filed and polished, and finally applied the nail varnish with consummate skill.

'What a lot of paraphernalia you women have to go through – a quick shave and that's me for the day.'

'Yes, but me more than most,' said Miranda. 'One of the lessons my agent drummed into me when I first started out in modelling was the need to look good twenty-four hours a day, seven days a week. Think beautiful, even when you're sitting on the bog, is her great motto.'

Michael laughed. 'She sounds fun.'

'She is, you'd like her, and she's right of course. In my job you can't afford to look a mess, whether you're working or not.'

'You couldn't look a mess if you tried.' He smiled thoughtfully. 'You know, beauty makes such a mockery of politics.'

Miranda frowned. 'How do you mean?'

'Well, politicians the world over are hell-bent on making us all equal – equal opportunities, equal lifestyle . . . yet when Nature is handing out a bonus, she's not nearly so even-handed. Being beautiful must make such a difference to a person's outlook on life, it must affect everything.'

'You should know,' Miranda said, before she had a chance to think. Then realising what she had said, she blushed hugely.

Michael was delighted. 'Not only have you paid me a compliment, you're actually embarrassed about it – how splendid! I must fetch us a drink to celebrate, it has to be apéritif time.' He returned with a bottle of champagne and poured them two glasses. 'To beautiful people everywhere.'

'Beauty inside and out?' Miranda queried.

'Ah, now that's another thing altogether. Beauty outside is easy to spot, inside – in my experience – it is a fairly rare commodity.'

'There you go again, Michael, you are so very cynical about people. Why?'

At her words, Michael stood up abruptly and walked over to the rail of the terrace. He seemed to be staring out to sea, his back towards her. Just when she had decided that yet again she had said something to upset him, he turned round. 'On the whole, I've come not to like the human race very much. It's why I live here, and leave the island so infrequently these days. On Crete, the people are honest and straightforward. If they like you, they'll tell you so – if they dislike you, they'll tell you so. If they're sad, they cry – if they're happy, they sing and dance. It's the deviousness of the so-called civilised world that upsets me most. I've spent a great deal of time in LA – tinsel city, tinsel people – God, how I hate it.' He paused, and then fixed Miranda with a look that started her heart racing. 'But you, Miranda, you've come from a world which should have screwed you up years ago. You don't conform to type, you're not full of empty devices to push yourself into the limelight. You're intelligent, you can still discern the difference between truth and falsehood. You don't call perfect strangers, "darling," you don't drink too much, and I'm perfectly certain you did not get where you are today by lying on your back for the right people. I think you've made it because you're good at what you do. You disturb me, Miranda Hicks, you disturb me very much.'

'You're a fine one to talk about not conforming to type,' Miranda said, trying to fend off the growing tension between them. 'I've never met anyone like you, you have to be a one-off.'

'Two oddly unique people – so where do we go from here?'

Miranda felt a tightening in her stomach, she was not sure whether it was apprehension or excitement. 'I don't know,' she said lightly. 'Do we have to go anywhere?'

'Don't be flip, Miranda.'

She raised her eyes to look into his, their deep blue

reflecting the sea and the sky around him. She could not have looked away if she had wanted to. 'I'm sorry, it's just that I'm frightened,' she whispered, putting her thoughts into words, before she could stop herself.

'It's all right,' Michael said. 'So am I.'

She wanted him then, wanted him desperately to take her in his arms, but he made no move. To her own astonishment, it was she who got up and went to him. He stood rock-still while she slipped her arms round his neck, raised herself on tiptoe and gently brushed his lips with hers. For a moment it seemed as though he was not going to respond, the next, his arms were tight about her. He bent her back, as his lips fastened on hers, kissing her hungrily, in a way which seemed to touch her very soul. She did not resist him. Indeed, she returned his kisses with an ardour that shocked her and when at last she struggled from his grasp, she was trembling – they both were.

'I'm sorry,' Michael said, 'it's too soon, I realise that.'

Miranda gave a weak smile. 'It was my fault, I'm sorry too, though goodness knows why we are apologising really.'

They stood awkwardly, inches apart, two people experienced in most of what life had to offer, yet quite unable to cope with the situation. 'How about lunch?' Michael suggested. 'It would be a diversion.'

It was a stilted, awkward meal. Neither of them ate much, conversation was a series of platitudes, and although they both drank a great deal of wine, it affected them not at all. After lunch they both departed to their separate rooms, for a siesta.

Michael could not settle at all. Once he realised that sleep was going to elude him, he left the villa and walked along the cliff top, until the sun and exertion exhausted him and he collapsed in the shadow of a rock and threw pebbles into the sea.

Miranda slept, fitfully, shadows of her past came up to haunt her – her parents, her sisters, Mark, Eric, Joe, Jake, and always David – David in the shadows, watching her every move. When she finally struggled out of bed, it was after five. She showered and changed, taking her time, not sure if she was ready to face Michael again – nor indeed, of how to face him.

He was in the hall waiting for her. 'Did you sleep well?'

'Yes,' she lied, 'and you?'

'Yes, fine, fine. I have the boat ready. Do you feel up to coming out for a spin? It is quite cool now.'

'I'd love to,' she said, thinking it might at least ease the tension between them.

He lead her down steep steps cut into the cliff face. At the base of the cliff, a small stone jetty jutted out into the sea, at the end of which was moored a red and white speed boat. Miranda refused Michael's offer of help, and climbed into the boat unaided – afraid now of even touching him.

Soon, they were zipping across the water, seeming hardly to touch the surface of the sea. The wind rushing to greet them, the spray splashing into their faces. About half a mile from the coast, they came into the lee of a small island. Michael stopped the engine. 'Do you feel like a swim?' he asked.

'I'm still very sunburnt and I mustn't be all dried up for tomorrow. You go ahead, I'll watch.'

He stripped off his T-shirt. Except for a slight golden fuzz, his chest was hairless like a boy's, but broad and very brown. Miranda turned her eyes away, trying to ignore the feelings it aroused in her. He climbed onto the runningboard, poised on the boat's prow, and executed a perfect dive into the water. When he surfaced, the hair was swept back from his face and he looked younger, less austere. 'It's gorgeous,' he shouted, 'are you sure you won't come in?'

Miranda shook her head, but even at the moment of her refusal, the deep inky-blue water seemed to be beckoning her. 'All right,' she called, 'just for a few minutes.' Hurriedly, she stripped off her shorts, and in T-shirt and pants followed Michael's dive over the side.

The water was different this deep. It was smoother in texture and there was much more movement. The sea seemed to be gently rocking her backwards and forwards, like a great cradle. When she broke the surface, she found Michael beside her. 'It's wonderful,' she cried. 'How deep is it here?'

'In miles or fathoms?' Michael asked.

'Miles – fathoms don't mean a thing to me.'

Michael considered the question, treading water. 'About half a mile, I suppose.'

'Heck,' said Miranda, 'you mean I've got all that water underneath me – it's rather daunting, isn't it?'

'Yes, and it's full of huge, slimy fish coming to get you,' said Michael, swimming to her and catching her around the waist. Miranda screamed, putting her hands on his shoulders for support. 'Stop wriggling, I've got you,' he said.

She could feel the length of his body under the water, as he held her to him. He kissed her, a gentle salty kiss, which sent a warmth coursing through her body. She drew herself away and then using his shoulders levered herself high out of the water. She transferred her hands to his head and ducked him, twisting out of his arms as she did so, so that he did not drag her down too. Laughing, she began swimming round to the other side of the boat.

'You little devil,' said Michael, coughing and spluttering. 'I'll get you for that.' He was a powerful swimmer and caught her in no time. 'Every time you duck me, you have to be kissed,' he said, holding her tight.

'You might tempt me to duck you again,' Miranda said, softly.

'That's rather what I was hoping.'

They fooled around in the water for some minutes, until Miranda was exhausted. Clutching the side of the boat, she heaved herself out, panting with exertion. 'I'm supposed to be ill,' she said, accusingly.

He pulled himself out beside her and they sat on the stern of the boat, legs trailing in the water, as they shared a towel to take the salt from their eyes.

'You look better, a lot better,' Michael said.

'I feel it.' They were sitting very close together and Miranda knew she should move. She sought diversion in words. 'It's been the most extraordinary day, in a way it seems to have gone on for ever.'

'I don't want it to end,' Michael said. 'I don't want you to go back to work tomorrow.'

'I have to.'

'I suppose so,' said Michael, glaring moodily at the water, 'but you're not to take any more stick from that bloody photographer. Look at the state he had you in yesterday – that's not going to happen again. I'll come and wrap his camera around his neck if he doesn't treat you with more consideration – a great deal more.'

His distress was so obvious that Miranda put a hand on his arm, intending to say something consoling. Instead, her touch sent a shiver through them both and in an instant she was in his arms again. The wet T-shirt clung to her, as they kissed and Michael's hands slid inside it, gliding over her breasts, down to the flat of her stomach. Then, abruptly, he drew away with a sharp intake of breath. His voice was hoarse. 'I'm taking you home now,' he said roughly.

They did not speak, as the boat sped across the water towards the cliffs. The villa looked beautiful as they approached it, the white walls now no longer white, as they picked up and reflected the pinks and oranges of the sunset. The sea had become a dark navy, the cliffs golden, but Miranda and Michael had eyes for none of it.

As the boat coasted up to the jetty, Michael leapt ashore and threw a rope round the bollard. Then he took Miranda's hand and helped her out. Still holding her hand, he hurried to the stone steps and began climbing them, two at a time.

'Michael, for heaven's sake,' Miranda said, fighting for breath.

He paused, only for an instant, to scoop her into his arms, and then continue bounding up the steps, with the same easy grace – as though her weight was of no significance. At the top of the steps he did not release her, but strode across the villa courtyard, through the side door and down the corridor to the study. He kicked open the study door and at last set her down in the middle of the room. His chest was glistening with sweat, his shoulders heaving with exertion. He closed the study door and turned the key in the lock. Then, slowly, deliberately, the expression in his eyes quite unreadable, he walked across the room towards her.

Chapter Ten

He had almost reached her, when she stepped back, seeming to shrink from him.

'No, Michael, I can't. . . .'

He seized her roughly by the shoulders. 'Look at me, Miranda, no, look at me, properly.' Slowly she raised her head to meet his gaze. 'I know it's too soon, we have so much to learn about each other yet. There has been a lot of pain, many things that have happened to us both which we find difficult to share with anyone. Yet there is this physical need in us – it's so strong – it dominates us. I know you feel it too – tell me you feel it too.'

At his words, a warmth began creeping through Miranda's body again. This feeling, over which she had no control, both frightened and thrilled her. She nodded her head, afraid to put her thoughts into words.

'There's so much I want to tell you, so much to say, yet now all I can think of is holding you, loving you . . .' He shook her slightly as if angry with the power she already exercised over him.

She was watching his mouth as he spoke. She knew she should reply – offer some words of either reproof or reassurance, yet all she could think of was his mouth . . . the full sensuous lips, not set in their usual firm line, but almost tremulous with desire. She longed to feel them on her.

'Say something, Miranda, anything, please.' His voice sounded strangled.

She forced her eyes to meet his again, and in a voice she barely recognised as her own, she said at last, 'I want you, too.'

It was the trigger, the culmination of everything they had said to one another since the moment he had taken her hand in Mirtos. His gasp at her words was audible, and gently, he drew her to him, holding her carefully, with infinite tenderness. Now that this thing was decided between them, there was no rush – the urgency remained but for the moment, at least, they were master of it.

At last he drew away, and taking her hand, he led her up the stairs to his bed. At the top of the stairs hesitantly, they turned to one another, for all their experience, unsure of how to handle the next move.

'I'm going to undress you,' Michael said. He smiled slightly. 'Or you'll catch your death of cold.' He peeled off her damp, salty T-shirt, her shorts, her pants, until she stood naked before him. Her skin was pale gold, her breasts full, the nipples already hard with desire.

As he gazed at her, his control evaporated. He let out a groan, scooped her into his arms and almost threw her onto the bed. He followed her, his mouth on hers, his hands exploring her, drowning in the scent and feel of her body. His lips travelled to her breasts – they tasted of salt and as he sucked on them, Miranda's body arched to meet his, her hands frantically working on the button of his shorts. He helped her and was soon as naked as she. Now it was Miranda's turn to look at him. They lay still and silent for a moment, while tentatively she explored his body – first with her eyes, then her fingers – touching, savouring. 'You're beautiful,' she whispered, her body beginning to move, her caresses driving him now to the edge of the precipice.

There was no time for anything but the simple act – their mutual need was too great. As he entered her, they both cried out, and began to move together as one body. Again and again he thrust into her, waiting instinctively for the moment when she was ready. When he came, with a great roar, shuddering with ecstasy, he was rewarded by the mirror image of Miranda's quivering body, climaxing in perfect unison with his own.

When they awoke, they crept like naughty children, hand in hand along the corridor to Miranda's bedroom, afraid in case they should encounter Thea. Once in the safety of her room, they had a noisy boisterous bath, which was cut short by the need to make love again. This time they did not hurry, they took their time to get to know each other's bodies, to feel the texture of each other's skin. Their anxiety to please one another was of paramount importance. It was quite unlike anything either of them had known before – giving pleasure was suddenly far more important than taking it, the whole experience so precious, so unique, it was as though they were inventing love for the first time. When at last they climaxed, weary and sated, Miranda cried openly, and Michael found, to his amazement, that the tears on his face were not hers, but his own.

Night had fallen, the day long gone, but neither of them noticed. Time was meaningless, all thoughts of past and future driven from their minds by the enormity of what had happened to them. They slept again, deeply, utterly fulfilled, at peace with the world and each other.

The soft apricot light of early morning woke Michael and for a moment he wondered where he was, the room was unfamiliar. Then he remembered and a feeling of sheer joy swept over him. Smiling, he turned and reached out a hand – the space in the bed beside him was empty. He sat up, his dream suddenly shattered. Miranda was not in the room, but a shaft of light under the bathroom door told him where she was. He relaxed a little, lay back on the pillows and waited for her. She seemed to be a long time and Michael, never a patient man, at last sprang from the bed and pounded on the bathroom door.

'Good morning, Miss Hicks. How are you this morning?' he called, cheerfully.

'I'll be out in a minute. We need to talk.' Miranda's voice sounded cold and distant, and Michael felt a sudden clutch of fear. Something was wrong, he had known it the moment he had reached out and found himself alone. Yet what could be wrong, after the night they had just spent together?

Michael used the moments while he was waiting for her to fetch a dressing gown from his bedroom. The bed was still in crumpled disarray from their love-making and it reassured him. Nothing could be wrong, it was just these new feelings making him feel unsure and vulnerable. He washed and cleaned his teeth, poured two glasses of orange juice and carried them back to Miranda's bedroom.

By the time he reached the room, she was out of the bathroom. Apprehension clutched at his stomach as he saw her. She sat on the end of the bed, fully clothed, her suitcase packed and by her feet. She looked pale and strained, in the morning light.

He bent and kissed her, trying to ignore her lack of response. 'Darling, what on earth are you doing?' he said, handing her the orange juice. 'Why are you all dressed and packed up?'

'I'm working today, remember?'

'Oh shit, I forgot.' He grinned boyishly at her, sitting beside her on the bed, but his sense of imminent loss only heightened. 'Actually, I think I can be excused for forgetting everything, after last night. What time is it now?'

'It's half past five,' Miranda said. 'I'm not due to start work until seven, but not knowing what sort of mood Jake will be in, I want to make sure I'm ready.' Her face was still set and cold. There was no sign of a loving gesture or any warmth of feeling towards him at all.

'Darling, what's wrong?' he said. 'It's not just the job, is it?' Miranda shook her head and standing up, walked away from him towards the window. Michael stood up and followed her. 'What is it then, I can't stand this-this change in you.'

'I-I don't think we should see each other again.'

It was as though someone had struck him in the stomach. 'What did you say?'

'You heard what I said,' Miranda replied. She kept her face averted and turned from him. The gesture angered him and seizing her arm, he spun her round to face him. 'What are you talking about?' he said, floundering like a fish out of water, desperately seeking to understand the appalling thing which apparently was happening to him. 'Darling, this is just the beginning for us. Last night . . . oh God, last night was so wonderful – wasn't it, wasn't it?'

'There are other things besides sex,' Miranda said quietly.

If her words were calculated to hurt, then they certainly succeeded.

'You little bitch.' Michael dropped her arm as though it burnt him and turning from her, began pacing the room. 'Last night wasn't just sex for me, I was making love to you, falling in love with you – are you trying to tell me that it meant nothing more to you than a purely physical experience – is that what you're saying – is it, is it?' His voice was anguished.

Miranda kept her back to him. Even in the semi darkness he could see her shoulders were heaving – evidently she was crying. All his instincts told him he should take her in his arms, yet his pride would not let him. She was silent for several moments, obviously struggling to regain her composure.

'It's not a question of what it meant to me, it's a question of being practical. I'm only here for another week, during which time I'm going to have to work hard, very hard, if we are to complete on schedule. Then I'll be going back to my world, while you stay here – there's no point in continuing the relationship.'

'No point, no point. What are you talking about? If we love each other, of course there's a point. People have fallen in love and found a way to be together in far more difficult circumstances than ours. We are not only relatively young and healthy, we are also very rich by most people's standards. I don't understand you, I don't know how you can talk like this.' He stopped his pacing and stared at her, his anger and frustration mounting. 'Jesus, what a bloody idiot I've been to assume you are any different from all the others.'

His words clearly got through to her. 'I-I do feel a lot for you,' she said wretchedly, 'and it's for that very reason I think it's better to end things now before they become more – more complicated.' She was crying hard now and her distress momentarily stilled Michael's anger.

'I don't think you're telling me the truth,' he said, fixing her with a shrewd look. 'There's something you're keeping from me, some reason why you're behaving like this. Is there someone back home you're committed to, is that it?'

'No, no, there's no one.'

'Then for Christ's sake, Miranda, what is it? Tell me – I demand to know.'

'Demand!' Miranda said, her anger flaring to match his. 'How dare you demand anything of me. Three days ago, we hadn't even met – what right have you to speak to me like that?'

'Last night gave me the right,' Michael said, quietly. 'You gave yourself to me, completely, unashamedly – you held nothing back, I know that. I did the same, and that binds us in a way that you simply cannot ignore.'

'Stop it, stop it.' Miranda put her hands over her ears as if to blot out the sound of his voice. 'Would you please ring for a taxi, I'm going to be late in a moment.'

'God damn and blast!' Michael shouted. 'Sod the taxi, I'll run you back to the hotel, if all you're worried about is your bloody job.'

'No, no,' said Miranda, 'I couldn't bear that. Please do as I ask, please call for a taxi.'

A coldness seemed to be seeping into Michael's very bones. He let out a great sigh of defeat. 'If that's what you wish,' he said, curtly, and left the room, heading for his study.

They waited, separately, for the taxi to arrive – Miranda in her bedroom, Michael slouched in a chair in the study. He tried to make sense of what she had said, trying to see how this morning's reaction could in any way relate to their loving of the previous night. He was very tired, and his brain seemed paralysed, unable to make any sort of assessment of the situation. He knew he should be using these precious minutes before the taxi arrived, to make some desperate effort to get through to Miranda, to understand what she was doing to them and why, but somehow he could not. He heard the sound of the diesel engine as the taxi came up the drive of the Villa Dionissos. He heard the doorbell ring and the sound of Miranda's sandals on the tiled flooring, as she hurried to answer the door. He heard her return, presumably to pick up her case. He willed her to come and see him, to at least say goodbye, so he could look on her face once more. Instead, all he heard was the sound of her receding footsteps, the slamming of doors and the roar of the engine fading into the distance.

He sat motionless for a long time, shocked and sickened.

Then he stood up, and like an old man, shuffled over to his easel by the window. The sun had come up now, throwing light across the drawing board. On it lay the pile of sketches he had drawn of Miranda the previous day, oh, so long ago now. In a fit of impotent fury, he picked them up, screwed them into a ball and hurled them into the fireplace. The action wearied him, he groped his way back to the chair and sat down. Suddenly the Englishman deserted him – he was all Cretan, and putting his head in his hands, he began to sob as though he would never stop.

By the time Miranda reached the Minos Beach, her face was wiped clean of tears and her mind of all conscious thought. Her whole concentration was focused on the coming meeting with Jake and the need to somehow struggle through the day. Emotionally she felt like an empty husk, dried up, finished, and this very lack of feeling gave her the confidence to believe she could cope. She was aware that all during the journey, the taxi driver had been watching her through the mirror, obviously wondering what had caused this tearful, early morning taxi ride. She was impervious to his curiosity, indeed she was impervious to everything. Nothing seemed to matter any more.

Although it was nearly a quarter to seven, the hotel was still deserted and Miranda walked through the quiet hall out onto the path. The cool sea breeze should have come as a relief after the hot taxi, but all it did was remind her of the Villa Dionissos and the thought brought a stab of pain. When she reached her villa, Miranda opened the door, went inside and slumped onto the bed. With her clothes and books scattered around, the room seemed oddly comforting, yet it was incredible to think of what had happened to her since she had last been there – it seemed a lifetime ago. She forced her mind away from these thoughts and concentrated on the task ahead – making herself presentable for Jake, by seven o'clock.

At seven o'clock precisely, there was a knock on her door and Jake entered. He looked much better and he was smiling. 'Welcome back, I heard you come in a little earlier. How do you feel?'

'Fine,' said Miranda, after a slight pause. 'The sunburn is under control, although I'm still a little tired.'

'How's the boyfriend?' There was a slight edge to Jake's voice, despite his smile.

'Michael's no boyfriend,' Miranda said, tersely, 'and I won't be seeing him again.'

'Lover's tiff?' Jake enquired.

'Please, Jake, I don't want to talk about it. Where are we going to start today?'

'Sorry, and incidentally, I'm sorry about my behaviour the other night. I was feeling pretty pissed off about everything and I'm afraid I took it out on you. It was unforgivable.'

Miranda looked at him in astonishment. After the embittered, caustic tongue of the last few days, she had quite forgotten that Jake was capable of saying a kind word. She made an effort to meet him half-way.

'Certainly Clive wasn't the easiest person to deal with.'

'He didn't help,' Jake said, 'but it wasn't just that. Clive only compounded the problem.'

'What else is the trouble,' Miranda asked, genuinely curious and glad of a diversion. 'I can't imagine anything being much worse than Clive.'

Jake gave her a strange look. 'I'll tell you about it sometime. Come on, let's go and get some work done. I've sent Peter off for the day, saying that you and I would work better on our own. He was very suspicious, thinking I was going to be a slave driver again but if we work really hard until, say eleven, you could be off the hook until the evening. It would give you a chance for a little more rest.'

Jake's kindness continued all during the morning session. Miranda managed to keep her mind floating in some sort of vacuum, which enabled her to smile for the camera as though she had not a care in the world. As good as his word, as soon as the sun became unpleasantly hot, Jake suggested they stopped work. Refusing lunch, Miranda went back to her villa, took a sleeping pill and was gloriously and deeply unconscious until five o'clock.

They worked for as long as they could during the evening light, and mercifully, by seven-thirty, the day's work was over.

'I'll go to bed now, if it's all right with you,' said Miranda, as they climbed the hill behind the hotel.

'No, it's not all right with me,' said Jake. 'You've eaten nothing all day and if you don't have some dinner, you'll never cope tomorrow. We're going on location and it's going to be a long hot day.'

'I'm not hungry, honestly,' said Miranda, wearily. 'I'd really rather just go to bed.

'Sorry, no can do, but I'll agree to you not eating in the restaurant. I'll order something by room service and we'll eat it together, on your balcony. That way I can make sure you get something down you.'

It seemed rude to ignore his solicitous manner, and in any event, Miranda felt too weary to argue. She bathed, washed her hair and slipped into an old towelling robe. She had just finished when Jake and two waiters arrived, complete with wine, a candle and a massive selection of food. Miranda almost managed to smile. 'Good God, Jake, there's enough food here for an army.'

'I know,' he agreed, 'I just didn't want you making the excuse that I hadn't chosen anything you liked.'

They settled down on the balcony. Jake poured the wine and began tucking into the food. 'Come on, love, try.'

Miranda picked her way through the dishes, making a great fuss about pushing her food around the plate, but eating very little. At last Jake had eaten enough himself. He poured some more wine for them both, and leaning back in his chair, began lighting a cigarette.

'Could I have one of those?' Miranda said.

Jake looked up at her sharply. 'Do you know, in all the years I've known you, I've never seen you smoke.'

'A person can change, can't they?' Miranda said, defensively.

Jake shook his head. 'No, not really. If you look at your life as a whole, you will find you make the same mistakes over and over again. We never learn.'

'I hope you're wrong,' said Miranda.

Jake lit a second cigarette and handed it to her, regarding her through a haze of smoke. 'Are you going to tell me what went wrong with your playboy?'

'No,' said Miranda decisively. 'I'd rather you told me what's been wrong with you during the last few days. I think I could do with hearing about somebody else's problems, rather than my own.'

'All right,' said Jake, after a pause. 'I told you that David and I came here for a holiday. That was true, but it was rather more than a holiday, it was . . . something of a business trip.'

Now that he had mentioned her husband's name, Miranda, who had been finding it difficult to concentrate, was suddenly alert. 'Go on,' she said.

'I don't know whether David ever mentioned it to you but whereas he trained in photography, I had begun my career in publishing, with photography very much a sideline.'

'No,' said Miranda, 'he never mentioned it.'

'Fair enough – anyway, this left me with a number of friends in publishing. I had lunch with someone one day, a guy called Don Richards, whose company specialise in travel books. Back in the late seventies, people were just starting to discover the Greek islands and he was anxious to publish a definitive guide to them – maps, local history, and, of course, plenty of colour pics. He asked me whether I would be interested.'

'It sounds wonderful,' said Miranda, 'being paid to tour the Greek islands.'

'It was. David and I came out here, took some shots, sent them back to Don and were immediately offered a contract. He reckoned it was a two-year project and that we should base ourselves in Crete.'

'So what went wrong?' Miranda asked.

'You,' Jake replied.

He really had Miranda's full attention now. 'Me! How?'

'We had to come back to London to tidy things up, dipose of the studio, complete one or two outstanding jobs. Then, unexpectedly, David was offered the chance to shoot a fashion page for *Vogue*, and his agent suggested that if he could team up with you, it might give him the break he needed . . . and the rest, as they say, is history.'

'I see . . .' said Miranda, slowly.

Jake let out a sigh. 'You met, you did the shots – bang, you were stars, and bang went our Greek project.'

'David never mentioned it,' Miranda said. 'It was naughty of him, he should never have let you down like that.'

'Of course he should,' said Jake. 'He made more money in a week playing the fashion scene with you, than he'd have made out of the whole book. I wasn't angry with him, I simply transferred my resentment to you – it was the easiest way to handle it.'

'So that accounts for the fact that I've always felt we had a rather uneasy relationship.'

Jake stood up, abruptly, and walked to the edge of the balcony. 'Yes, and of course it was greatly aggravated by David's death. It is true, of course, that if he had come to Greece with me, he would be alive today, but the things I said to you the other night were quite wrong of me and I am sorry. I was very drunk.' He turned to face Miranda. 'It's just that coming back here with you seems an awful irony. This was the place where David and I were going to spend a couple of fantastic years, working on a wonderful project – instead of which, he's dead, and I'm back here taking bloody silly fashion shots of his widow. Does that make any sense to you?'

'I think so, yes – yes, of course, it does. Certainly, besides David's death, everything seems trivial. David died so young and for no reason, while we struggle on living. It places a kind of responsibility on us – on me – at any rate to make something of my life.'

'Go on,' said Jake.

Miranda hesitated, searching for the right words. 'I feel I need to live well, not necessarily, happily, but fully, effectively, and yet I don't know how to do it. David is my yardstick – every decision I take, every person I meet, I refer back to David in my mind. Would David approve of this, would David like this person?'

'Do you?' said Jake. 'Still?' Miranda nodded. 'Can you even remember what he was really like and how he would have reacted, or have you put him onto some sort of pedestal?'

Tears pricked Miranda's eyes. 'I don't know.'

'And may I ask,' said Jake, 'how does this so called referral process affect your relationships with other men, like your playboy chum. Is that why you won't be seeing him again, because he doesn't match David's standards?'

Miranda shook her head. 'No, no, that isn't the reason – not in his case – but yes, usually.' She began to cry. 'It's just that I loved David so much, Jake, and he made me feel safe – I've never felt safe since he died.'

Jake let her cry in silence for a few moments and then stood up. 'I'm going back to my villa now and I can only apologise again for my behaviour. I'll make sure the rest of the assignment run smoothly without any more dramas. Have a good night's sleep, I'll see you at seven.'

He left the balcony without another word and Miranda watched him go, her tears temporarily halted by the surprise of his sudden departure. What had she said to upset him? He was such a strange man, she did not believe she would ever understand him. She glanced across the table to where he had been sitting. He had left so hurriedly that his cigarette was still burning in the ashtray, his lighter still lying on the table. She stood up, wearily, and stubbed out the cigarette. Then she headed for bed, where a couple of sleeping pills blotted out all conscious thought.

True to his word, Jake was kind, courteous and professional during the remainder of the assignment. By Saturday it was clear they were going to finish well on time, and as the shots came back from the developer, Miranda was surprised at how good they looked. The tight band of misery in whose grip she seemed destined to remain, did not show on her apparently carefree face. She looked like a girl on holiday, having a wonderful time. Makeup obliterated the dark circles under her eyes, and eye drops made her eyes sparkle with apparent joy. It only served to heighten her feeling of disorientation. Of Michael, she thought constantly, although she made strenuous efforts to keep him from her mind, as she stood before the camera, signed autographs in the bar, and especially when she lay alone in her villa. However, images of him persisted in crowding into her mind, bringing a pain with them which could make her gasp aloud.

Again and again she went through the reasons for her decision to leave him, justifying her motives. For the first few days, she almost hoped that he would pursue her. When he didn't, she was quite unjustifiably angry with him. As the assignment drew to a close, leaving Crete seemed like an approaching death sentence. On her last night on the island she did not go to bed at all, but sat up on her balcony, watching the moon riding high over the Sitia mountains, over the Villa Dionissos, over Michael Richardson.

On the day of their departure, Jake, Peter and Miranda had a leisurely lunch in the hotel restaurant, and then took a taxi to the airport. On the journey, Miranda sat in the front seat, drinking in the sights of Crete for the last time – the olive groves, the wrinkled brown faces, the dry, arid ground, the donkeys, the barren mountains. Why did she love this place so much, she wondered – was it the island, was it Michael, was it a combination of the two? She thought of Michael's face as the countryside flashed by, of the haunted look in his eyes, which was never far away. She longed to hold him, to banish his dark thoughts, to bring laughter to his face. The pain was now actually physical, as if she was losing a limb, or some vital organ. While she was on Crete, she could just cope with the loss. Now she was leaving the island, the break with Michael was final and absolute . . . and tearing her apart.

Iraklion airport was terrible – stifling hot and overcrowded. Their flight was called and then it was announced that it would be delayed for at least half an hour.

'Let's go and get smashed,' Jake suggested, 'we've nothing else to do.'

There was no bar but they found they could buy wine in a cafeteria-style restaurant, which had no air conditioning. The tables were filthy and crowded with discarded coffee cups. Miranda felt sick. 'I think I'll just pop to the loo,' she said, 'I'll be back in a minute.'

After a long wait, she finally gained access to the only ladies' lavatory in working order. She slammed the door behind her and began washing her hands in the wash basin. Then she caught sight of her reflection in the mirror – a frightened, distracted woman looked back, an image so very different from that of the glamorous fashion model. 'Why am I leaving?' she asked the mirror. The futility of her life seemed to rise up and greet her. What was she going back to . . . to her house that was increasingly empty since the improvement in Paul's social life, to more modelling jobs – the same smiles, the same poses. Why was she running away from Michael – because she could not cope with the feelings and emotions he invoked? Did that mean that she could never be able to handle a full emotional relationship? Was she no more, in reality, than the constant reflections she saw of herself – a smiling celluloid face, of no depth, no substance. Someone had started knocking on the door, shouting in Greek – abuse presumably. She gave one last frantic look in the mirror, as if to see whether her sudden decision had changed the way she looked. Then she wrenched open the door.

At the British Airways desk, she wrote a brief note. 'Would it be possible to page Mr Jake Berisford and give him this, please,' she said.

The girl smiled conspiratorially, almost as if she knew the significance of the message. 'OK.' Miranda watched as the paper left her fingers. The decision was made now, there was no turning back.

She ran down the stairs to the airport lobby and out into the hot afternoon sun. A row of taxis was standing in front of her, she went to the front of the queue.

'Can I help you?' the driver asked, obligingly.

'Yes, please. Could you take me to the Villa Dionissos. It's just outside Sitia, I'll show you the way.'

Chapter Eleven

No practical thoughts cluttered Miranda's mind. It did not occur to her to worry that her luggage was bound for London, that Jenny would have jobs lined up for her, that Paul was expecting her home. It certainly never even entered her head that Michael would not be there, at the Villa Dionissos. She sat tense and upright in the back of the taxi. As she watched the return of the Cretan landscape, she purposely kept her mind free of thoughts, except for clocking off the kilometres, as they grew nearer and nearer Sitia. What she was to say to Michael, how she was to explain herself and her actions, was not something she could consider, and certainly she dare not dwell on his possible reaction. Instinctively, she knew that any thoughts along such lines would have her instructing the taxi driver to take her straight back to the airport. The decision was made – now she must exist in a state of limbo until she could see whether it had been the right one.

The journey seemed interminably long. The best of the day was over, the soft evening light beautiful, but Miranda was in too much of a state of mounting agitation to appreciate the scenery properly. By the time they at last drove through the gateway of the Villa Dionissos, she felt weak with tension.

'How much do I owe you?' she asked the driver, shakily.

'Four thousand drachmas,' he said.

Miranda began scrabbling in her handbag, nerves making her spill the contents all over the floor of the vehicle. She had nothing like four thousand drachmas. 'Will you accept English money?' she asked.

The driver shook his head, his face already showing signs of concern. This was the best trip he had made all week – it was still early in the season for many tourists. If the woman could not pay, he had barely enough money for the petrol home.

'Can you take a cheque? I have a card.'

'A cheque! What's this cheque?'

She waved a cheque book at him and he saw only the name of a British bank.

'No,' he said, sharply, 'no cheque – you give cash.'

She had put herself in an impossible position. There was simply no alternative but to ask Michael for the money. 'Wait here,' she said to the taxi driver. 'I will fetch money from the house.'

He nodded, distractedly, and for the first time studied the place where he had brought his passenger. It was an immense house. Whoever owned it must be very rich – perhaps he would get his fare after all.

Leaving her handbag and its contents strewn all over the taxi, Miranda climbed out on shaky legs, went to the door and pulled the bell rope. She heard the sound of the bell clanking through the house, but her heart was hammering so loudly, she could not hear if there was any movement in response. Suddenly the door opened and Thea stood there, formidable as ever. She showed no surprise at Miranda's sudden arrival.

'Is Mr Richardson in?' Thea nodded. 'I-I have no money for the taxi and the driver is waiting. Could Mr Richardson lend me some?'

Thea eyed her with undisguised disapproval, nodded again and then disappeared in the general direction of Michael's study. Miranda stood foolishly on the doorstep. What a hopeless way to arrive. She should have cashed some money at the airport, but it had been no moment for practical considerations.

It seemed an age before she heard footsteps. She braced herself, a tight smile on her face, but it was only Thea who reappeared. In her hand she held a large wad of Greek money. 'Here is the money,' she said, contemptuously.

'Thank you,' said Miranda, trying to hide her disappointment that Michael, himself, had not brought it. She turned towards the driver and as she did so, Thea made to shut the door behind her. 'W-what are you doing?'

'You go now, yes?'

'No,' said Miranda, 'I have come to see Mr Richardson. Did you tell him that?' Thea shrugged her shoulders. Whether she understood or not, it was impossible to tell. Whether she had given Michael the right message, or even explained who needed the money, Miranda had no way of knowing. She tried again. 'Did you tell Mr Richardson it was me?'

'Yes,' said Thea.

'Did you tell him I had come to see him?'

'Yes,' said Thea. She fixed Miranda with a gimlet eye. 'He gave me the money so that you would go away.'

So he did not wish to see her. A wave of despair flooded through Miranda. What now – a humiliating journey back to the airport, back to England, her tail firmly between her legs? No, not having come this far. Michael's reaction was understandable, after the way she had walked out on him. Decisively, she turned to the driver and handed him the pile of notes. 'Here is the money, will you wait for me for a little while. I will come and tell you if I need you again.'

'OK,' said the driver, rapidly checking how much she had given him. He had been dreadfully overpaid – he would wait all night for this one, if that was what she wanted.

Miranda turned to Thea. 'Where is Mr Richardson?'

'In the study,' Thea replied.

Miranda tried to smile. 'Thank you.'

Thea's look of hostility transferred itself into action – she made no effort to move aside as Miranda squeezed past her – in fact she almost blocked the way. Without pausing for thought, Miranda ran down the passage. The study door was ajar and through it music streamed – loud, very loud – a symphony of some sort. She pushed open the door and walked in. The noise of the music was deafening. Michael was sitting in the window, by his easel, paintbrush in hand. He was staring fixedly at the canvas, but making no attempt to paint. He looked older, wearied and in that fleeting moment when she was able to watch him unobserved, it seemed to Miranda that she had caught a glimpse of the essence of the man beneath the normal defensive guard.

Perhaps feeling her eyes upon him, Michael turned

abruptly and saw her. For a moment, shock registered on his face and then the inevitable mask dropped into place – his expression as unreadable as ever. He smiled. It was not a very pleasant smile. 'Oh dear,' he said, 'was the money not enough? I'll find you some more.'

'Didn't Thea tell you I'd come to see you?' Miranda shouted above the music.

'She didn't make that clear. She simply said that you required some money for the taxi.'

'I-I came here by taxi from the airport – to see you. It was only when I arrived here, I realised I hadn't enough Greek money.'

'OK, so now you've seen me. How about getting back to the airport so that you don't miss your flight.' Michael stood up, his eyes were steely.

Miranda took a deep breath to steady her nerves. 'Michael . . .' she began, and then her patience snapped. 'Oh Michael, for Christ's sake, turn that bloody music off, I can't hear myself think.'

His expression remained inscrutable. He went to the stereo and did as she had asked. He shut the lid heavily as if to demonstrate protest. 'Well, since you're here, you'd better have a drink. What would you like?'

'Nothing, nothing, thank you,' Miranda said.

'If you won't, I will.' He walked to the drinks cabinet and poured himself a hefty Scotch.

Miranda stood watching him, not knowing how to begin and well aware now that she was going to have no help at all from Michael. 'We got to the airport,' she said, talking to his back. 'We were supposed to be leaving today, this afternoon, but the plane was delayed. The others were drinking wine in the restaurant. I went to the loo and . . . Michael, I-I realised I couldn't go without seeing you, couldn't leave Crete, I mean. So, I just ran away, jumped into a taxi and . . . and here I am.'

Michael kept his back towards her. 'Good God, they'll think you've been abducted or something.'

'No, I left Jake a message.'

Michael suddenly swung round. The full force of his glorious good looks and his piercing blue eyes terrified her. If he would just hold her – take her in his arms for a moment – it would give her the strength to go on, but she knew she was still light years away from him making such a gesture. He was as wary as a wild animal.

'So, why did you want to see me?'

It was the question she had been asking herself. 'I-I wanted to explain my behaviour of the other morning. You must have thought me dreadfully rude.'

Michael gave a short, bitter laugh. 'Rude! No, being rude didn't come into it. I'm sure you had your reasons and I have no wish to pry into what they might be. What's done is done and there's no need to feel under any obligation to explain your motives to me.'

He was not prepared to help her in the slightest. She wondered, fleetingly, whether he was enjoying it, making her squirm like a fish on the end of a hook. The thought made her angry, and with anger came sudden, hot tears. She stared into his face. She remembered his head on the pillow beside hers, the feel of his long, lean body. A feeling of longing for him swept over her. She closed her eyes against it and opened them to find him still staring at her. Her true feelings flowed from her lips before she had a chance to check or consider. 'I love you.' Her voice was almost a whisper. 'I love you so much, but that night I was . . . so frightened. Nothing has ever . . . you see, never before . . .' The words choked her, tears poured down her face, but in seconds she was in Michael's arms. The moment his arms went round her, the tension eased. It flowed from her like a river, and where before there had been only cold pain, warmth spread through her and with it came a glorious release – words tumbled out. 'You see, I had this dreadful thing happen to me, when I first came to London – it has affected everything. I see that now. . . .'

Michael guided her to one of the chairs, and sitting down drew her onto his lap, resting her head onto his shoulder, cradling her like a baby. 'What happened – tell me everything about it.'

Since the night she had thrown herself on Jenny's mercy, Miranda had spoken of Joe Chang to no one – not even

David. Now the story spilled out, like poison seeping from a wound. She felt neither embarrassed nor apprehensive in telling Michael the details of that terrible day – but the relief of speaking of it at last was immense – she felt the weight of years lift from her.

'The bastards,' Michael said, in a choked voice, when Miranda had finished. 'It must have been enough to put you off men for life.'

'I-I thought it had,' Miranda said. She sat up wanting Michael to see her face as she talked, desperate for him to understand what she herself was only just starting to recognise. 'I-I didn't have another relationship with a man until I married, and David was not a very physical person, more like a brother in a way.' She gave Michael a quick nervous smile. 'Since his death there have been one or two affairs, which have come to nothing and meant very little to me at the time. You see, until the other night I had come to believe that sex was something I could never enjoy. It didn't revolt me exactly, I just looked on it as something which seemed to give men a lot of pleasure, but . . .' she groped for words.

'But you'd never had an orgasm?' Michael said.

Miranda nodded. 'With you, the other night, I-I was out of control. Instead of lying there while some man huffed and puffed and had his fun, I was no longer in control of my own body.' She shuddered. 'It was like in the studio with Joe – a tiny piece of my consciousness knew what was going on but I couldn't do anything about it.'

'It wasn't in the least like when you were in the studio with Joe. Then you were a dumb teenager, being exploited for a porno movie and drugged out of your mind. Now you're a mature woman, who, after a somewhat colourful career, has at last stumbled across the right mate – a mate, I might add, who heartily reciprocates your feelings, and who has spent the last week going mad with misery and frustration.'

'Oh Michael, I'm sorry.'

His smile was gentle now, warmth reached his eyes. He took her hands and held them in her lap. 'And so you should be sorry – not for walking out on me the other morning – I understand that now, but for not telling me the real reason.

You must always tell me your feelings. How can we share anything unless you do.'

'Have we anything to share?' Miranda asked, wistfully – her love for him written on her face now for all to see.

'In the long term, I believe we have a lifetime that should be shared. In the short term, how about sharing my bed?'

When they woke, it was quite dark and inspection of the bedside clock told them it was after midnight. Miranda pulled Michael to her, his head resting between her breasts, their arms around each other. 'Thank God I came back,' Miranda said, dreamily. 'I could so easily have funked it.'

'Sooner or later I'd have come and found you,' Michael said. 'I couldn't have gone on without you, not for much longer. I rang your hotel yesterday to see when you were checking out. I couldn't bear the idea of your leaving Crete. While you were still here, I felt we were not really parted.'

It was the mirror image of her own feelings. Miranda let out a sigh of deep contentment. To think, if she hadn't taken the taxi. . . . 'The taxi!' she shrieked, sitting up in bed, sending Michael flying. 'My God!'

'What about the taxi?' said Michael, soothingly, pulling her down beside him again and covering her with kisses.

It was some moments before she could speak. 'I left him outside, to wait for me. I wasn't sure, you see, whether you'd even speak to me, and if not, I wanted to be able to leave quickly.'

Michael began to laugh. 'You mean you told the poor sod to wait?'

Miranda nodded, stiffling a laugh. 'How awful – I'd better go and sort him out.'

'You stay where you are, madam. I'm not having you cavorting around in your current state. Look at you, you're gorgeous – all rumpled and loved. I'm not going to let you out of this bed for days – weeks even.'

'But . . .' Miranda began.

'No buts – if you're very good and do as you're told, I'll bring you back a prize.'

He returned ten minutes later, with a bottle of champagne. 'Is that my prize?' Miranda asked.

'Well, you have a choice of prizes,' Michael replied. 'Certainly the champagne is one option, the other is this.' He placed a hand between her legs, making her gasp with pleasure.

She smiled up at him, as he lay down beside her. 'Who needs champagne,' she whispered.

And so began the pattern of their life together. Days flowed into nights, time had no real relevance. In order to give them complete solitude, Michael gave Thea a fortnight's holiday. They swam and sunbathed, went out in the boat, and made love constantly – not just in Michael's great bed but on deserted beaches, in the boat, on the verandah, sometimes on the floor of the study, if there was no time for them to reach the bed. They fortified themselves with picnics, and as the tourist season was now beginning in earnest, some evenings they visited one of the many local tavernas which had miraculously sprung into life. The Villa Dionissos was their playground, the cares and sadness of their lives to date slipped away, returning them to the carefree, spontaneous joyfulness of children. It felt as though they would always be like this, but as the days slipped by, they both knew they were living a dream. The real world could not be shut out for ever. There were decisions to be made.

The night before Thea was due back from holiday, Miranda cooked a prawn paella, Michael opened champagne and they sat together on the terrace having dinner. On the first day, Miranda had sent telegrams to Jenny and Paul explaining that she would be delayed and giving her address in case of emergency. A thick envelope from Jenny had arrived two days previously and sat unopened on Miranda's dressing table. Sometime it had to be opened. All the while they had been together Michael had placed his telephone on answerphone. While Miranda had been preparing the paella he had checked it to find that it had run out of tape. There was no escape from the demands the rest of the world imposed upon them.

They talked easily through the meal, of trivial things, like two people who had known each other a long time. Michael waited until they were drinking coffee. Then he reached across the table and took her hand. 'Miranda, there's a question you must know I'm going to ask you.' She looked up at him, trustingly, with her big brown eyes. His heart lurched. She was so beautiful, he could hardly believe it was him she wanted, when she could have anyone. 'Will you . . . marry me?' he said, surprised to hear the shake in his voice.

The brown eyes were suddenly bright with tears. 'Yes, please,' came the whispered response.

In a moment, she was in his arms, both laughing and crying. 'I love you, I love you,' they said to each other – again and again. Then he was half dragging, half carrying her to their bed, to seal the agreement in the best way they knew how.

But in the morning, it was different. Thea returned and they sat at opposite sides of the table, having a formal breakfast, and Miranda put into words the thoughts uppermost in their minds. 'Where are we going to live?' she asked.

Michael waved an expansive hand. 'Why, here, of course. I know you love the house, the climate is beautiful – it is, undoubtedly, the best place for me to work.' He saw an odd expression come in her face and quickly, he tried to make amends. 'We can go to London, of course, whenever you like – to see your friends, and your relatives. My Minos paintings take me to Europe quite often, and New York too, sometimes.'

'How often have you been away from Crete during the last year?' Miranda asked.

Michael shrugged. 'Several times, why?'

'No really, Michael, I mean it, exactly how often – when and where?'

He thought for a moment, and then looked slightly uncomfortable. 'Twice,' he said, 'for an exhibition, in Paris, and then two days in London. The BBC were doing a documentary on contemporary art and I had to say a few lines.'

'Exactly,' said Miranda. 'You see, you're quite content to be here all the year round. You have your work, and presumably, although I haven't met them yet, friends and family. This is your home, but it's not mine.'

'Are you saying you do not want to live on Crete?' There was a harsh note to Michael's voice.

'No, I'm not saying that,' said Miranda. 'I'm just asking you to consider the problem. For me, there will be things I will have to give up – if I am to live here with you.'

'Give up, give up what? I don't understand you,' Michael said, impatiently.

'My career and my whole way of life.'

Michael looked at her with genuine astonishment. 'You don't mean, you'd want to continue working once we were married?'

Miranda stood up and walked over to the edge of the terrace. 'I haven't thought it out in great detail, but instinctively I feel, yes I would. Not as much may be, but I think it would be inadvisable to give it up altogether.'

'Why?'

'Because I need my own sense of identity, independence, call it what you like. You have your work which must be very absorbing at times. What am I supposed to do while you work – sit and wait for you to finish?'

'This conversation is starting to sound frighteningly familiar.' Michael's voice was tight with tension. He swept a hand through his hair, a gesture Miranda had come to know meant he was agitated.

Suddenly, her career forgotten, a wave of love and compassion swept over her. She came to him and sat down beside him, taking his hand in hers. 'You're thinking of your first wife, aren't you?' she asked, gently. 'We've never spoken of her because with you, I always feel it is better to wait until you are ready to talk.'

'Yes, you're right I was, but it was a silly remark – I'm sorry.'

'Tell me what you meant by it, tell me about your wife?'

Michael got up abruptly, letting go of Miranda's hand. 'No, it doesn't matter,' he said. 'Let's go for a swim.'

They avoided the subject of their future for the rest of the morning, but it stood between them. After the wonderful carefree days they had spent together, this day stood out in stark contrast. They kept running out of conversation, in their anxiety to talk of anything but their plans. They suddenly found that almost no subject could be discussed without it affecting what happened to them next.

After lunch, during which neither of them spoke very much, they went, as had become their habit, to Michael's bedroom for a siesta. But today, they did not make love. Instead they lay silent and awake, several inches apart, yet terribly aware of one another. At last, Miranda rolled over and put her head on Michael's shoulder. 'Tell me about your wife. After all, I've told you all about my past – I've kept nothing from you. It hurts me that you cannot tell me everything.'

There was a pause, and when at last Michael spoke, his voice sounded dreadfully tired. 'I met her at a party in Hollywood,' he said. 'She was eighteen, I thirty-one. She was one of a batch of would-be Hollywood starlets, waiting for castings, working as a waitress at night to support herself. She was pretty, small and dark and there was an attractive vulnerability about her which I did not recognise at the time as weakness. Her name was Suzy.'

'Go on,' said Miranda.

'I suppose, at the time, although I didn't know it, I was looking for a wife. Suzy had been in Hollywood for eighteen months. All she'd had was a couple of bit parts and she was finding it a real struggle to survive. I could offer her money, security – all the things she lacked. It was what you would call a whirlwind romance. We met and married within three weeks. It was crazy.'

'Do you realise the significance of that remark?' Miranda said, gently. Michael shook his head. 'It's just about how long you and I have known each other.'

Michael's arms were round her. He raised her head to his and kissed her, and as he did so the tension and strain between them disappeared. 'No,' he said, 'it was not like us at all. I love you, I adore you, and I know you. We are old enough to be sure of what we're doing. Suzy, then, hadn't a clue. Marriage was just one of the roles she hadn't played.' He drew Miranda's head back onto his shoulder. 'The marriage worked well enough for the first few weeks.' Michael gave a hollow laugh. 'But she didn't like me working. I don't know where she thought the money came from, but she resented my work enormously. She started to get . . . well, wild, so I brought her to Crete. She hated it. She already had a drink problem, and spent most of her time in a bar in Sitia – you can imagine what the locals thought of that – especially my mother.'

'So you went to Hollywood?'

'No,' said Michael, curtly. 'She did, I stayed here.'

'So then what happened?' Miranda asked.

'She went her own sweet way. I kept on my beach house in L.A. for her, paid her bills, and now and again she visited me. Less and less though was she recognisable as the person I'd met and married.' He hesitated. 'A tremendous amount of emphasis is placed on what drugs do to destroy the body, but not so much on what they do to the mind and the personality. She was no longer somebody I could relate to, because essentially her mind had gone. I don't mean she was mad, just a sort of empty shell. Thinking about it now, living from one fix to the next must have been terrible for her but at the time I didn't realise she was on heroin.'

'So when did you find out?' Miranda asked.

'When I got a cable from her agent telling me she was dead.' The stark words hung in the air between them.

'What did you feel at the time,' Miranda said. 'Did you still love her?'

'I don't think I ever loved her.' Miranda watched his face carefully, the hooded eyes still held on to their secrets – he gave nothing away. He had appeared to be gazing into space. Now abruptly, he focused on her. 'It was all such a stupid mistake.'

'Go on,' said Miranda, 'try and tell me what you feel, I know you don't find it easy.'

Michael took her hand and pressed it to his cheek. 'I feel bitter about the experience, and humiliated, too, at having made such an idiotic choice. I minded most about the other men – she . . . she slept around all over the place – a proper little scrubber. I found that very hard to accept.'

'But didn't you feel sorry for her?' Miranda asked.

Michael shook his head. 'No, not in the least.'

'She was so young,' Miranda suggested.

'She was bad, through and through. It would have made no

difference whatever her age. I couldn't have saved her from herself, whatever I'd done.'

His heartless disregard for the loss of a young girl's life deeply shocked Miranda. This, together with her natural Northern bluntness, made her dangerously outspoken. 'But surely, Michael, you feel some sort of remorse,' she persisted. 'Don't you feel guilty in any way, or responsible for what happened – don't you ever wonder if you could have done more?'

His hand was still in hers. At her words, he tore it away and in a swift movement was out of bed. He stood naked before her as she had seen him many times. This time though there was no love in his eyes – he was angrier than she had ever seen him. 'Don't ever say a thing like that to me again,' Michael shouted at her, his face set in harsh lines. Despite the fair hair and golden skin, he suddenly looked very Greek – proud, unapproachable and beside himself with fury.

Miranda was determined not to be intimidated. 'I'm sorry to upset you, but I can't help but make comparisons,' she said, coolly.

'Comparisons – what comparisons?'

'Between my brother Paul and I. When you married, you and Suzy were almost of an age to Paul and I now, yet I look on Paul as such a baby – certainly he needs a great deal of guidance and reassurance, too.'

'It's a ridiculous comparison. Paul is a schoolboy – Suzy was born old – a slag, a piece of life's garbage, with the morals of a guttersnipe.'

Miranda sat bolt upright in bed. 'How could you speak of a dead girl like that – of anyone, let alone your wife. You could say my life has been no better than hers – I bet even she didn't get mixed up with a Joe Chang. Is this how you will talk about me one day – that I had the morals of a porno movie queen.' It was as though he had touched her nerve ends with a red hot poker. Humiliation, hurt, bitterness and anger swelled in her – who was this man, to make these sweeping, condemning judgments – playing at being a god, impervious to man's frailties?

For a moment, she thought he was going to hit her. Instead, he seized her shoulders in a grip that bruised, and threw her backwards on the bed – following her down so that his body covered hers, driving the breath from her. His lips crushed onto hers, his hands transferred to her breasts, his whole body rubbing frantically against hers in a frenzy of passion. She fought him, wanting to refuse him, to hurt him for what he had said, but he was too strong for her.

He forced her legs apart, his strong fingers feeling inside her, arousing her, in spite of her protests. He continued to kiss her, his fingers driving her mad with longing so that it was actually a relief when at last he entered her. Having won, having claimed her, he lay inside her, as they both fought for breath. He raised himself slightly to look into her face. His voice was more controlled, but his eyes still glittered dangerously. 'I don't want to ever speak of Suzy again – do you understand – nor will I tolerate you playing judge and jury with regard to my feelings. The past is no consequence now – the future is what matters – our future.'

Miranda tried to speak, but as she did so, Michael's body began to move, slowly at first, and then with increasing urgency – plunging into her, deeper and deeper, until it seemed that he was in her very womb, a part of herself. She clung to him, riding the storm with him, her hair streaked with sweat, her body bruised and battered – yet never had she felt so alive. At last he came, bursting into her, with a roar of triumph like a great bull. And as he lifted her body to his for that final thrust, the dam burst in her also, the sweet sensations permeating through her whole body – leaving her shuddering with pleasure.

Still inside her, Michael fell into an instant sleep. Miranda tried valiantly to collect her thoughts, to try to piece together their earlier conversation, but in moments, she, too slept.

She woke sometime later to a feeling of glorious sensations. Michael already awake, was moving within her again. 'Oh, darling, surely not,' she protested.

'I can't ever have enough of you. I love you so much. I'm sorry I was so angry. Do you still care for me a little, just a little?'

'Come, let me show you,' Miranda whispered. And so they continued during that long night.

Despite the ecstasy of their lovemaking, things were no better between them the following morning. Once she was calm and clear-headed again, Miranda found she still felt resentful and shocked by Michael's attitude towards Suzy. His apparent inability to have understood the girl at all worried her most, coupled with his callous disregard for her premature death. Clearly, Suzy had hated living in Crete yet he assumed that Miranda would live at the Villa Dionissos without protest. And she had so much more to give up than Suzy – her own home, her career, her friends, and the question of what to do with Paul, who still had another year at school. Yet Miranda could tell that all these considerations were of little importance to Michael. It was not that he was a romantic idealist, assuming that love would conquer all – it was simply that he did not consider her lifestyle to be of any real significance. When, tentatively, she began talking about her career, as they sat on the terrace the following morning, she was painfully aware that it was not something Michael took seriously. 'The trouble is,' Miranda began, 'modelling is not really a job one can do part-time. You are either available for work, or you're not. I can't simply pick and choose my jobs – once you start doing that, it is not long before you find yourself dropped altogether.'

'Does it matter?' said Michael.

'It matters to me,' Miranda replied.

'But why? We have plenty of money and sometime, I imagine we would like to think about having a family. You'd like that, wouldn't you?' Miranda nodded. 'Then why do you need this *career*?' He said the word mockingly.

It angered Miranda. 'Laugh if you like,' she said, 'but my career has been very successful, and although it can't go on for ever, my agent reckons I'm certainly good for another five or six years. It's different for you, Michael. I know your childhood was not easy, but the one thing you never seem to have lacked is money. Am I right?'

'Yes,' said Michael, 'yes, it's true, I inherited a considerable sum from my father but I can't see that it's relevant.'

'Let me try to explain,' Miranda said, patiently. 'When I left school I had nothing and no prospect at all of achieving anything other than a mundane job in the bank, and marriage to a local boy – a miner, a farm labourer or a textile worker was the choice on offer. We would have lived in a little two-up, two-down terraced house in a back street in some grey, Northern town, and if things had gone well – and I mean really well – my husband might actually still have a job today rather than claiming social security. When I see the girls I was at school with – which I do occasionally on my trips home – I am appalled. They are middle-aged women, tired and defeated. I didn't want that, darling, but I had to fight every inch of the way to escape. Building my career was uphill from the very start, the competition was immense, the work, contrary to most people's idea of modelling, usually gruelling hard work. But I did it, Michael, and I don't mind admitting I'm proud of it.'

'Then surely,' said Michael, irritatingly dispassionate, 'if you're prepared to admit that you have achieved what you set out to do, then what is the point in continuing with it? You've proved that you could get out from under, so now it's time to move on to something new.'

'But I've been on my own for so long. I'm used to being independent. You can't expect me to give up everything – everything that was me, to absorb myself entirely into your way of life. Surely you can see that.'

'You were married before, you must have had to make adjustments, then.'

'No, not really. We weren't together very long, David and I. In any event, we worked mostly together – my career was his also.'

'Yes, I can see that,' said Michael. 'He would have been mad not to have encouraged you, with the kind of money you must have been earning together.'

Memory of David's kindness and gentle support flashed into Miranda's mind. 'How dare you,' she said, 'how dare you speak like that. If you and I are going to have any sort of future, you must recognise that I will not accept one word of criticism so far as David is concerned. He was a good man, understanding, kind, loving. You can't judge all marriages by your own disaster.' She had stung him, she could see, but she didn't care.

Hurt, he retaliated. 'David, David, David. Do you have any idea how many times you mention that man's name in a day? David did this, David did that, David the wonder boy,' he mimicked.

'Stop it, stop it, I won't listen to this.' Miranda leapt to her feet and ran from the terrace – anything to get away from the mocking voice. She ran into their bedroom, pulled on a bikini and taking her towel, left the house and went down the steps to the sea. The water felt balmy and soothing. She swam slowly, as far out as was sensible, and lay on her back looking up at the Villa Dionissos. It was beautiful – a dream home. If someone had told sixteen-year-old Miranda Higgins she could spend the rest of her life in a house like that, with a world famous artist, who she adored and who apparently adored her, she would have been ecstatic with happiness. So, what was the trouble – simply that she was no longer sixteen-year-old Miranda Higgins, and she was not prepared to blend her life into another's. Not without give and take on both sides.

Yet when she thought of her life in London, she remembered her feeling of sterility. She remembered, too, her conversation with Jenny before leaving for Crete. What would Jenny advise her to do? She smiled. Knowing Jenny, it would be – take the man and to hell with the rest of the world. Yet Jenny herself had never married, never made the commitment and always put her career first. Somewhere there had to be an area of compromise. If only they could talk about it without hurting one another. Lying there, suddenly all Miranda could think about were the things that she had said to hurt Michael. So anxious was she to protect her wretched life-style, that she had mindlessly trampled on his feelings. Filled with remorse, she began swimming strongly back towards the shore. She ran up the steps to the house, damp and dripping, towel-drying her hair as she went. She could see no sign of Michael. He was not on the terrace, their breakfast things lay as she had left them.

Almost soundlessly, Thea appeared behind her, a tray at the ready to clear away the meal. 'Do you know where Mr Richardson is?' Miranda asked, smiling at the woman.

'Working,' Thea replied, reproachfully.

The swim had left Miranda invigorated. Love for Michael warmed her as she ran down the passage to the study. Almost ashamed of her desire, after the night they had spent together, she knew she wanted him again. They would make love and then they would talk. They would sort out their silly problems. Nothing was more important than that they should be together.

She burst into the room. Michael was sitting at his easel by the window, the room in unusual disarray, with canvases lying everywhere. 'Michael, I've had such a lovely swim . . .' she began.

He looked up, his eyes blank, unwelcoming. 'You've disturbed my work to tell me that?' His voice was heavy with sarcasm.

The happy smile died on her lips, the warmth in her heart grew cold. 'I-I'm sorry,' she said, 'it's just that I've been thinking, Michael – about us. Let's talk some more about what we're going to do, I hate us falling out.' She had been walking as she talked and now she had reached him. She slipped her arms around him from behind, pressing her lips into the base of his neck. 'Please don't let's fight,' she whispered, 'I love you so much.'

'You're wet,' Michael replied. 'Look, you're dripping all over my canvas. Can't you see I'm busy. I haven't worked for over two weeks, and I have all sorts of deadlines I'm going to miss shortly.'

It was as though he had struck her. Miranda dropped her arms and stepped back. 'How long will you be working for?' she asked, in a cold, distant voice.

'Why all these questions? I don't know, all day certainly, and perhaps this evening too. It just depends how it goes. Now, if you wouldn't mind. . . .' The slam of the door told him she had already left the room. Momentarily, he looked up and then forgot her – already totally absorbed in his work, once more.

More angry than miserable, Miranda strode back on to the terrace. So was this to be the pattern of her life in the future? Hanging around all day, waiting for Michael to stop working. He had made no attempt to introduce her to anybody – neither his friends nor his family. She knew no one on Crete but him and the morose Thea, who clearly resented her. Miranda liked people, good conversation – was her love for Michael reason enough to abandon most of life's pleasures which she held so dear? If now, while their love was fresh and new, he did not consider her happiness – what hope would there ever be of him doing so?

When Michael finally stretched his aching back and threw his paintbrushes into a pot, it was quite dark. He stood up and looked around the room, at the six canvases he had completed during the day. They did not give him the thrill of his old paintings, but there was a degree of satisfaction. They represented a job completed satisfactorily, and he could not help but be flattered by the world's apparent insatiable appetite for Minos paintings. These six canvases were a set, commissioned by an American rock star. It was heady stuff to realise that a single day's work could earn him two hundred thousand dollars. He switched on more lights around the room, walked to the drinks cabinet and poured himself a Scotch. It was only then that he remembered Miranda. His total absorption in his work was something he was used to – what he did not recognise was that he also used it as a retreat from the world, when the world became too tough. He wondered, a little uneasily, what she had done with herself all day, but it did not occur to him that his complete abandonment of her was anything other than understandable. Thea could give them dinner on the terrace, he thought with pleasure. After a successful day's work he felt fulfilled and relaxed, and confident, too, that their earlier problems could be resolved. The thought of the night ahead filled him with excitement. Taking his whisky glass, he wandered out of the room.

'Miranda, darling, where are you, Miranda?' he called.

There was no reply. She was probably on the terrace he decided. Leisurely, he sauntered down the passage and on his way, encountered Thea, her face set and grim.

'Where is Miranda?' he asked, in rapid Greek.

'Gone,' Thea replied, sternly.

'Gone! What do you mean, gone?'

In reply Thea pulled a crumpled letter from her apron. 'She left you this.'

The letter was brief and impersonal. Miranda did not see any way she could become a part of his life as things were. He seemed unprepared to compromise and if he persisted in this view, she felt it pointless to continue with their relationship, since it would only cause unnecessary suffering for them both in the long term. She was returning to London, feeling it only sensible to put some distance between them. She would not contact him again – it was up to him to decide whether there was any future for them.

Michael stood stock-still on the terrace as he read the letter. His initial reaction was one of fury, he threw the paper to the ground, followed by his whisky glass, which shattered into tiny pieces. He paced up and down, shouting at Thea to get out, in response to her concerned enquiry. When he was spent, depression and misery set in. He sat slumped into a chair and sat in the darkness, gazing out over the sea.

Why were his relationships with women always doomed? What caused it? Where had it all begun?

Chapter Twelve

It was a mercy that Michael Richardson could remember nothing of his babyhood, for his first year of life was spent in appalling squalor, despite desperate attempts by his mother, Tassoula, to counteract the hardship. The Pappadis family all lived together in two caves, linked by a passageway. In one they slept, in the other, which opened out onto the hillside, they spent their days – talking, planning, eating and drinking, when they could. The people of Sitia made sure the family never starved, but they had to be careful. There was a German garrison in the town now and it was necessary that the journeys to the doctor and his family should take place at night, and with great care. The Germans were only too aware that there were many fugitivies hiding out in the mountains, and the reputation of Georges Pappadis as doctor to the Resistance was well known.

During the summer, the family had great difficulty finding enough water, and the first winter of Michael's life was exceptionally cold. But the baby had his mother's love and his grandparents' devotion and he thrived well enough.

Michael's first memory was fishing with his grandfather, in the harbour at Sitia. It was his first all-male expedition. Up until then, his main influence had been the adoring female members of his family – his mother, his grandmother and aunts. But at three, he was considered man enough to go fishing. They had fished for octopus. All his life Michael was to remember the stench of them, the dark ink they squirted all over his bare knees, the slimy tentacles, the desperate fear that he would cry as his grandfather hauled the dreadful creatures aboard.

For the most part, though, his early childhood memories were happy ones. The sun always shone, the sea was always blue. In reality, Crete was a disturbed and turbulent place. Political unrest was rife after the Germans' withdrawal. Communist guerrillas now used the mountains as their refuge. Death, destruction and hardship persisted, but Tassoula made sure the little boy knew nothing of them. He who had been born of war, deserved a childhood free from it. His life was as carefree as any of the children of Sitia – at any rate until he was seven years old. It was then that the main influence in his life became not his mother, but his father's friend and executor, Rupert Shepherd.

The name Rupert Shepherd, always struck terror in Tassoula's heart, but to the boy, the name was the equivalent of Christmas. In the early years of Michael's life, whenever Rupert visited the family, he came bearing gifts of unimaginable splendour. Living mainly in New York, he was in the land of plenty – the toys, the food hampers, even the clothes he bought, quite literally seemed to come from another world. Tassoula always accepted the gifts, but silently, almost reproachfully. For Michael, it was wonderland.

Tassoula never forgot the first time she met Rupert. He arrived in Sitia, unannounced, and presented himself at Doctor Pappadis' house as the sun was setting. Tassoula, fresh from the exertions of putting a lively two-year-old to bed, stepped out into the street to catch a breath of sea air. It was July and very hot. Rupert, toiling up the narrow street, paused, instinctively knowing that this was the woman he had come to find, and understanding immediately why Jonathan had married her. She was small and slight, with wild, dark curly hair. She wore the traditional widow's black dress, but she wore it with a natural grace that could not conceal the full breasts, in stark contrast to her slender hips. Her lips were full, her skin pale, her eyes slightly hooded. She stood, one hand on her hip, staring out to sea, her face in sad repose. He wondered whether she was thinking of Jonathan, or of her son, or of nothing other than the beautiful Cretan sunset. He waited until he was nearer, and then softly called her name. 'Excuse me, are you Tassoula Richardson?'

She turned, startled, her heart beating wildly at the sound of a voice so reminiscent of Jonathan's – so similar, in fact, that for a moment, just for a fleeting moment, she believed it was her husband returned to her. Then the tall figure approaching her assumed its true identity. He was altogether slighter than Jonathan had been, with mousy brown hair, rather sharp features and a high domed forehead, from which the hair was already thinning. His eyes were fine, honest and intelligent. They regarded her now with a mixture of interest and contrition. 'I'm sorry, I startled you.'

'Yes, you did,' said Tassoula, speaking slowly. It seemed a long time since she had spoken English.

'My name is Rupert Shepherd. I . . . was a friend of your husband.' The man held out a long, narrow hand. Tassoula took it, her face alive with interest.

'A friend of Jonathan! Really?'

'Yes, we were at school together, and then university. I am a solicitor.' His forehead creased in concentration. 'Do you understand the term?'

Tassoula shook her head, 'No, I don't think so.'

'I look after matters of law.'

'Ah yes,' said Tassoula.

'I have come from England especially to see you,' Rupert continued, 'because I am one of Jonathan's executors.' Again he stumbled over the word. 'It is my job to deal with Jonathan's will.'

'Will?' said Tassoula, anxiously.

This was going to be harder than he had imagined, Rupert thought. Bugger Jonathan – he might have taught the girl more English. Still, his Greek had been fluent and in any event, the poor young things had spent little enough time together as it was. Remembering this, he forced himself to be patient and slowly described in simple words, his role as Jonathan's executor. 'Could we go somewhere to talk?' he suggested, when he had finally convinced himself that Tassoula understand him. 'You see, Tassoula, Jonathan had a great deal of money – much money and now I must give it to you and your son to help you both.'

'Much money?' said Tassoula, clearly amazed.

'Yes. Jonathan was very rich. If I had been able to come to you sooner, I could have helped you before, but I have still been involved in the war up until a few weeks ago.' He considered for a moment explaining to her that he had been on minesweepers, and that after everyone had gone home, he had spent a further eighteen months in the Mediterranean, clearing up the debris of war. He had lost more men and ships in that period than he had when the war had been at its fiercest. Everyone had relaxed too much, become careless. It had been a bitter period for Rupert, and the language barrier gave him an excuse not to refer to it.

Tassoula was covered in confusion. 'I don't know what to think, you had better come with me, come into my home, you must meet my father.'

The meeting with Georges Pappadis was singularly unsatisfactory in that he spoke not a word of English. Tassoula did her best to explain the position, but to Georges this stranger, this foreigner, appearing unannounced, was an intrusion and a far from welcome one at that. Although they never spoke of it, he recognised and understood his daughter's suffering at the loss of her young husband. So far as he could see, the arrival of her husband's friend would only serve to rekindle memories, best forgotten.

When Rupert began tentatively to discuss the will again – and this, in turn, was relayed to Georges – the old doctor became very angry. Money matters were not for women to discuss, he insisted. The meeting threatened to fall apart completely, until a solution was found. The only man in Sitia who spoke good English was Kostis Vosaakis, the local schoolmaster, and it was agreed that he should be summoned to act as interpreter.

Kostis was a handsome, middle-aged man, a widower – his wife having died in childbirth. Unlike most of his race, he was calm and relaxed, the result, perhaps, of controlling sixty highly strung, excitable children at his school each day. Once introductions were made, his immediate suggestion was that a bottle of *raki* would do much to ease the language barrier. When Tassoula had fetched this, the three men and the girl sat together round the table, in the beginnings of a cordial discussion.

Rupert explained the position carefully to Kostis. Jonathan Richardson's parents had died in a train crash when the boy was fifteen. As an only child, this had left him with a sizable estate, approaching quarter of a million pounds in cash and shares. He also owned three properties – a flat in London, a large estate in Derbyshire, and a cottage on the Helford River in Cornwall. It was hard to tell exactly what these properties would fetch because of their contents, but it was felt that the Derbyshire estate would be worth fifty or sixty thousand pounds, at least. The money and all the property had been left to Tassoula, in trust for any children of the marriage. It was at this point that Rupert explained that the delay in advising her of this was due to his own commitments and that he had immediate authority from the other executor, a fellow solicitor, to forward any sum of money which might be useful on an immediate basis.

Tassoula listened carefully to Kostis with a mixture of amazement and apprehension as he translated what Rupert had told him. When Jonathan had died, she had assumed that this was the end of her association with England. Yes, she had given birth to a child who was half English, and it was her intention to teach Michael the rudiments of the language and to tell him as much as she could about the country and its people, and their brave contribution to the Battle of Crete. She also intended that Michael should grow up to be proud of his father, which was not difficult, as Jonathan was considered a great hero to the people of Sitia. But to Tassoula, England was a remote place. Now, suddenly it appeared that she and her son, owned a sizable piece of it and more money than she would have believed possible.

Rupert bided his time, letting the news sink in. Now he fully understood the position, Georges' attitude had changed. The atmosphere round the little table was amazed, shocked even, but friendly. It was then that Rupert dropped his bombshell. The estate in Derbyshire had belonged to the Richardson family for nearly three hundred years. Rather than dispose of it at this stage, it seemed sensible to retain it until

Michael was old enough to decide for himself what should be done. The estate made a small profit and had been run during the war by an efficient farm manager, who was happy to stay on. The man was only in his thirties and could be trusted, Rupert felt, to look after the estate until Michael was old enough to claim his inheritance. This suggestion caused a flood of excited Greek from Georges, which Rupert was relieved to hear from Kostis was Georges' total approval of the concept of holding on to land, once one owned it. This unexpected accolade, made Rupert unexpectedly brave, and carefully avoiding Tassoula's eyes, he pressed on. If Michael was to inherit an English country estate, should he not, Rupert argued, perhaps learn to be an English country gentleman – which, of course, would mean education in England.

'You're thinking of university?' Kostis asked.

'No,' said Rupert. 'I was thinking of prep school first and then on to his father's old public school.'

'Which one?' Kostis asked.

'Eton.'

'I understand.' Kostis glanced quickly at Tassoula who was straining to follow the quick exchange. 'And this would mean the boy leaving home at what age?' he asked.

'Seven,' said Rupert quietly, 'but he will be back home for holidays, of course.'

Carefully, Kostis translated the suggestion to Tassoula and Rupert watched the pain sweep into her face, and instantly regretted his suggestion. It was something he had thought out for himself on the long journey to Crete – this idea of the boy receiving a proper education. But what could he know of these people and their feelings and, of course, of the boy himself? What right had he to come in here and disrupt what was obviously a happy family. He would not press the matter, he decided.

Tassoula spoke to Kostis in Greek, her voice very low.

'Tassoula wishes to know why you consider an English education should be necessary, but I can answer that for you. Education here on Crete is very poor. Once the children are able to read and write, our job is done. Greece is in a state of civil war, there is nothing for Michael there at present. An education in England would be the best possible start in life he could have – the best gift his father's money could buy.'

Rupert's heart sank. A schoolmaster for an interpreter – in the circumstances, the worst possible choice. Of course this man would revere learning. 'It may not be sensible for him to leave his mother so young,' Rupert suggested.

'But if he is to go to Eton and then on to university, he must. Even at seven he will be behind the other boys. He will have to work very hard.' With a sinking heart Rupert could see Kostis's growing excitement.

'Mr Shepherd,' Tassoula's voice cut into their conversation, quiet and dignified. 'Mr Shepherd, what would Jonathan have wanted for his son? What would he have considered best? We never spoke of what would happen to us after the war, or of our having children. I don't think either of us expected to see peace again.'

Rupert took a deep breath, and was about to reply that he felt sure Jonathan would want the boy with his mother when, insidiously, a memory flooded back into his consciousness. He remembered he and Jonathan as children, twelve, perhaps thirteen, on two ponies cantering over the Derbyshire hills. It was early morning in late summer. They were due back to school for the autumn term in a few days. They reached the top of the hill and Jonathan reined in his horse. He was an extraordinarily good-looking boy, even then, his face flushed with exertion. 'Look at all that, Rupe – it will be mine one day.' They stood looking down on the country that lay spread out before them. 'I often come up here,' said Jonathan, 'and I'm sure I'm not the first of my family to do so. It's good to think that my grandfather, my great grandfather, his father before that, looked out over these fields. One day, they'll belong to my son.'

'Would you think it impertinent. . . .' Rupert stopped and tried again. 'Would you think it strange of me, Tassoula, to ask to see your son?'

He regretted the words as soon as he had spoken them, yet there was an instant look of understanding in Tassoula's eyes. 'No, come with me.'

They left the room, and Tassoula lead him up two flights of

rough stone steps. At a tiny wooden door she turned and put her finger to her lips, then quietly opened the door and beckoned him in. Michael lay on his back, entirely abandoned to sleep, flushed and angelic. His hair was the colour of corn, his skin golden brown. He was the replica of his father – so much so, that the sight of the child actually shocked Rupert.

'He's in the image of Jonathan, yes?' Tassoula said.

Rupert nodded, feeling an odd constriction in his throat. It seemed so dreadful that Jonathan had never seen this child, never even known of his existence. Downstairs again, at the entrance to the room where the older men waited, Tassoula put a hand on Rupert's arm. 'Tell me what is in your heart, what you think.'

'I think, had Jonathan lived, he would have wanted his son to have an English education, and to one day take up his estate in Derbyshire. But Jonathan is dead and you are now Michael's only parent. You cannot prepare your son for school in England as Jonathan could have done. You cannot teach him what he needs to know. . . .'

'But you can,' Tassoula interrupted.

Rupert hesitated. 'Yes I could, but don't try to make any decision now, Tassoula. If you can tell me of somewhere to stay, I can remain in Sitia for a few days and we can talk some more. It is not a decision you should take in haste.'

Rupert stayed in the Pappadis household for ten days, and in those ten days, the embittered man of war began to feel whole again, relax and learn the joy of living once more. He was captivated, both by Tassoula and her son. Mother and child took him everywhere – to deserted beaches, olive groves, mountain passes. He knew Crete, of course, from the endless convoys he had escorted back and forth across the Mediterranean, but never its country, never its people.

These days were poignant for Tassoula, too. She questioned Rupert endlessly about her husband and his early life, drinking in everything he had to tell her – storing it, he knew, to pass on to the boy. Her English improved greatly. She remembered words and phrases which she thought she had forgotten, but underlying the golden days, the questionmark hung in the air – was Michael to be brought up a Cretan or an

Englishman? Watching mother and child at play, Rupert wished again and again that he could withdraw his suggestion. But the words were spoken, the opportunity was there, and exactly a week after he had first arrived in Sitia, Tassoula announced one night that her son should be educated in England.

They made plans. Michael would be put down for the Dragon School in Oxford, his father's old prep school, and then Eton. He should go to school in September 1951, four months after his seventh birthday. Rupert promised to visit the family at least twice a year, to gradually prepare Michael for school. It was agreed that Kostis should teach the boy the rudiments of English and if Rupert could obtain the necessary text books, Kostis would do his best to give Michael a grounding in English pre-prep education.

Rupert's departure left Tassoula with the realisation that she had just five years of her son's life – five years during which he would belong to her, and her world. From then on, he would be a visitor, a beloved visitor, but no longer all hers. This knowledge made her behaviour towards her son somewhat erratic – at one moment, she would be angry at his babyish ways, realising how far he was from being ready to leave her. At other times, she would smother him with love. If the boy found her behaviour confusing, he did not show it. Like everything else he accepted it placidly. He was a sunny child, joyful and outgoing.

Rupert was as good as his word. In his efforts to give Kostis as much information as possible, he regularly corresponded with him, despite a heavy work schedule. His mother's family were American. His uncle, a lawyer, too, had a large practice in New York. Rupert used this contact to build a specialist knowledge of US law, and soon found himself travelling backwards and forwards to the States. But however busy, he always had time for Michael Richardson. Twice a year, he left the civilised world behind and travelled to Sitia to stay in the doctor's house and teach the boy all he could about the future that lay ahead of him. During the last summer before Michael went to school, Rupert spent a whole month in Sitia, and it was during that time he made two momentous discoveries which were to influence the rest of his life. For it was in that month that he finally recognised, and admitted to himself, what he had always known – that he was hopelessly and irrevocably in love with Tassoula. It was also in that month that he bought Michael a paint box.

Michael's first picture was, predictably enough, of his mother. The features were crude, the colours harsh, but there was an uncanny movement and fluidity to the painting. The brush strokes had a confidence which was quite out of character in a normal small child's drawing. Years later, sorting through Rupert's papers after his death, Michael found the painting, on the back of which, inscribed in the shaky hand of old age, were the words – '*This is a portrait of Tassoula, the only woman I have ever loved. Painted by Michael Richardson, aged seven years and two months, the child that should have been mine.*'

It fell to Rupert to take Michael to school for the first time. It was Rupert who comforted Michael while he was dreadfully seasick on the boat to Athens, who held his hand tight on the plane journey that terrified him, and who finally prized himself free from the little boy's arms and kissed his tear-stained face, in the Headmaster's study. His duties at an end until half-term, Rupert immediately made the tortuous return journey to Crete to comfort Tassoula and to ask for her hand in marriage. She refused him. By the time Michael returned home at Christmas he found that his mother, extraordinarily, inexplicably, had married Kostis Vosaakis, the schoolmaster. Rupert Shepherd never touched Cretan soil again.

It was soon obvious that Michael's school days required him to be something of a schizophrenic. In Crete, not even his mother seemed to want to know about his life in England. In England, his Cretan life was something he learned quickly not to talk about for fear of being teased. So during term time, he was a model English school boy, playing rugger, cricket, rowing, reciting Caesar's Gallic Wars and doing tolerably well in all of these. In the holidays, he lived the life of a Greek peasant, and as the years went by, only Rupert seemed to understand the increasing problems this caused the boy. They had another bond, too – in art. No artist himself,

Rupert had a fine collection of paintings and was quick to recognise Michael's growing talent. He encouraged the boy, arranged extra tuition for him, and in the holidays took him, one by one, to the art capitals of the world, thus helping to bridge the gap between school and home.

Despite Rupert's efforts though, these years brought Michael an increasing identity crisis – a feeling of belonging nowhere. He visited his estate in Derbyshire, but the house was cold and damp, dust sheets covering the furniture. There was an air of decay about the place. Though he tried to like it for his father's sake, it meant little or nothing to him. In 1956, when Michael was twelve, his mother gave birth to another son, Manolis. Manolis was everything Michael was not – short, dark, very Cretan – a placid, dull baby, with whom Tassoula seemed well satisfied. This strengthened Michael's feeling of isolation. He felt like a foreigner, an interloper in his own home. It was not surprising, therefore, that by eighteen, when he won his place to Oxford, to read English at his father's old college, Lincoln, he was a thoroughly dissolute, unstable young man. That was until he met Anya Ludbeck.

He met her, of all places, at a frightful literary evening, held periodically by his tutor as a particularly gruesome form of torture for students. It was a cold, wet November afternoon as Michael strode up the Banbury Road. North Oxford looked unbearably dreary, the rain was almost sleet. It made him hanker for the sun. An evening at the pub was his idea of how to spend a Sunday and he wondered how early he could slip away without being noticed.

He met Anya in the hallway. A small grey-haired man with a goatee beard, was helping her take off a voluminous mink coat. Michael judged her to be about forty. Her figure was voluptuous, but not over-blown. Her hair was jet black, and her face quite extraordinary. She was deathly pale, her skin almost luminous – the only colour being an enormous pair of apparently coal-black eyes, and full lips, painted a deep crimson. Huge diamonds dangled from her ears, her fingers were weighed down by rings, her perfume heavy and vulgar. She was the kind of woman Michael ordinarily most despised, yet he found himself fascinated by her to the point where he simply could not look away. She saw him watching her, and smiled. It was a seductive smile. She had good teeth, he noticed and her eyes were alight with humour.

'So, young man, what are you staring at?'

Michael looked, if anything, even younger than his eighteen years. In his first term at university, as a typical English public school boy of the period, he had no more experience of women and sex than the odd experimental grope at school dances. Anya was therefore confident of his response – a blush, a stammer, a hurried departure. She could not have been more wrong.

He met her gaze without flinching, smiling too. 'You,' he said simply.

She was amazed, amused, intrigued, and the first woman to appreciate that Michael Richardson was not what he seemed – that there was another side to his nature, where his proud Cretan blood was master.

'I suspect,' she said, slowly, 'that you are the only attractive man here tonight, in which case I had better snap you up quickly. I'm worth cultivating,' she patted her handbag. 'I have a hip flask of gin in here. Added to those interminable cups of tea, it makes a gathering like this almost acceptable.'

Michael grimaced. 'Gin in tea!'

'Wonderful, darling, so good for the digestion. You'll see.' She took his arm and together they joined the rest of the party.

They behaved extremely badly throughout the afternoon. Anya was liberal with the gin and they were soon hilariously drunk, enjoying it all the more because everybody else was so depressingly sober. They laughed a great deal and ignored everyone but each other, to the point of quite intolerable rudeness. In the process, they learnt each other's life stories. Anya's was pure Hollywood, and yet, as she told it, Michael found himself believing it. Her parents, it appeared, were Armenian and had fled Russia at the time of the Revolution. In the process they had become separated from their three children, who they never saw again.

'I may have brothers and sisters in Russia still,' said Anya, rolling her eyes dramatically. 'My parents fled to Egypt, where they had friends and contacts. They tried desperately to be reunited with their children, but they were lost to them. They were in despair, old before their time. They were comfortable and safe in Egypt, but they could find no peace of mind without knowing what had become of their children.' Anya laughed, unexpectedly, her eyes bright with amusement. 'Then,' she said, 'when my mother was forty-four, an extraordinary thing happened – she found she was pregnant.'

'You?' said Michael.

'Me,' Anya agreed. 'Of course, as you can imagine, I was a dreadfully pampered child. I assuaged their guilt, you see. They lavished everything on me, every imaginable thing. We were very close to the Egyptian Royal family. My childhood was magic, full of treats and gifts, and when I was sixteen, a magnificent ball was held for me at the Palace. It was there that I discovered sex for the first time. I realised that men liked me, wanted me and that was a new kind of power, an even more exciting game. It was all very pleasing.'

Michael laughed. 'I can imagine.'

'And then the Revolution came again to destroy our family,' said Anya, her eyes growing even larger. 'You would have only been a baby at the time, but there was trouble in Egypt after the war, and the monarchy was overthrown. Again my family were forced to flee, but this time, it was my parents who were left behind.'

'Heavens, what happened?' said Michael.

'They put me in the care of an English couple, who had been on some sort of diplomatic visit to Cairo, and this couple managed to smuggled me out of Egypt. I had no money with me, but I swallowed the family diamond.'

'You did what?'

Anya shrugged her shoulders. 'It was the only way I could be sure of getting it out of the country. It was the diamond on the family tiara. My father prised it out of its setting and made me swallow it.'

'How ghastly.'

Anya smiled. 'Not at all, it was the best thing that could have happened to me. When it came out the other end, I used it well. Indeed, I have a beautiful home just a few streets from here, whose entire existence I owe to that diamond.' Michael shook his head in disbelief. 'You don't believe me,' said Anya, her eyes sparkling with anger now.

'Yes, yes . . . of course I do, it's just such an extraordinary story. What happened to your parents?'

Anya's face grew sad. 'I don't know, but I would imagine they were killed. I wrote letters, of course, when I got to England, but I never heard from them.'

'So what did you do, once you were in England?'

'My friends, the diplomats, managed to get me a British passport. My great grandmother had been British. This is the most precious thing I have in the world – my passport, at last I belong somewhere. Then I married an English professor – he is that one over there.' She pointed to the tiny little man Michael had seen earlier.

Michael was sufficiently drunk now to be blunt. 'You make rather an odd couple. He's so much older than you, and. . . .'

'Enough,' Anya snapped. 'He is kind to me, very good. We live our own lives, go our separate ways, have our own friends, but he saved me, gave me stability – you understand?'

It was Michael's turn then to tell Anya his story. She was delighted with it. 'So, we are both European mongrels,' she said, at last. 'It is why we will be such friends, and friends we will be Michael, always, I know.'

They left the gathering, flamboyantly, at seven o'clock, just when tiny glasses of sweet sherry were being passed around. Michael's tutor pretended he did not know him but Michael was past caring.

'What about your husband?' he asked, as Anya took his arm and they began weaving their way down the road.

'Oh, he is all right. He will come when he's ready. He'll be happier now I've gone, I embarrass him. You will come back to my house, darling. Yes, no?'

'Yes, I'd love to,' said Michael.

The house, externally, was typical of North Oxford. A huge Edwardian building set back from the road by a sweep of drive. Anya lead Michael, not to the front door, but up external stone steps to a little conservatory tacked on to one side of the building, in a slightly idiosyncratic manner.

She waved at the house, dismissively. 'That is my husband's. It is where he works, where he teaches his students, eats and sleeps. But this – this is mine. This is where I work – it is my studio.' She flung open the door, dramatically, and ushered Michael in.

The amazing room was in studied disarray. Rugs and huge cushions with oriental patterns, littered the floor, plants hung from the ceiling and climbed up the walls. There was the heavy scent of Anya's perfume, and this together with the subdued lighting, gave the room an exotic feel. Anya rushed across the room to a little stove, which she began riddling, vigorously. 'Michael, there's wine over there and a corkscrew. Open a bottle quickly.'

By the time he had opened the wine and poured two glasses, the stove was burning brightly. Anya threw off her coat and collapsed on a pile of cushions. 'Come and sit beside me, darling, and tell me what you want to do with the rest of your life.'

It took Anya only ten minutes to pick through his jumbled thoughts and come up with the startling conclusion – 'But darling, all you really want to be in life is a painter. So, what we have to find out now is whether you have got any talent.' She was on her feet in a second. She strode across the room to her desk, picked up a pad and a pencil and threw it at Michael. Then she turned up the lighting, drew the curtains and returned to him. 'Right,' she said, 'draw me,' and before the boy's amazed eyes, she began taking off her clothes.

As with everything she did, Anya undressed with flamboyant style. Michael sat, completely still, his heart hammering in his chest, watching her as slip followed dress, stockings followed slip and finally as she removed her bra and pants. When she was quite naked, she straightened up and stood before him. 'Do you like me, darling, will I do? Yes, no?'

The white luminous skin was not just common to her face – her body, smooth and rounded, seemed to shimmer where the light struck it. Her breasts were large, but not pendulous – the nipples rosy-tipped. He could not drag his eyes away.

'Yes, no?' she repeated, impatiently.

'Oh yes,' Michael managed. Speaking was just one of his problems – he seemed to be having difficulty even breathing.

'Good, good. I will lie like this – now draw me.' Anya threw herself on the pile of cushions opposite Michael. Supporting her head on one hand, she arranged her voluptuous body to best effect. Michael's eyes moved to the curve of her hip, to her legs slightly apart, as if in invitation.

He glanced down at the pad, his fingers trembled as he tried to grip the pencil. 'I don't think I can,' he said.

'Of course you can, try – do try, darling.'

Michael took a deep breath, and looked again at the glorious body laid out before him. He straightened himself on the cushions, terribly aware of the mounting pain in his groin. Then he began to draw. The pencil seemed to be moving with a life of its own. Before him on the page, Anya's body began to take shape, but as it did so, his excitement increased. The naked body emerging on the page – beads of perspiration broke out on his forehead. He wanted her so badly, but he did not know how to start, if she would even let him. Childish tears misted his eyes, there seemed to be a buzzing in his head. Then from a long way off, a voice said, 'Come here, *mon enfant*, come here.'

He looked, afraid the words had been spoken only in his head, but he saw her lips move, and throwing the pad aside, he flew into her arms.

She pressed his hot head to her cool white breasts. For a moment they lay still, but Michael was feverish with excitement and began clumsily to kiss her, to fondle her.

'Wait, my darling, let me undress you. Take your time, unless . . . have you never made love to a woman before?'

Michael, lying back on the cushions now, shook his head.

'Ah!' Anya smiled kindly, her black eyes fathoms deep. 'Then first, we must get rid of your virginity so that we can make love properly. Help me with your clothes.'

Within seconds, he was as naked as she. He felt shy, particularly of his enormous, throbbing penis, but he dare not move as she sat beside him, gently running her hands over him. 'You have a beautiful body, Michael. It is made for love and will make many women very happy. Come, take me.'

She lay back on the cushions, opened her legs and reaching for him, guided him to the place. The moment he entered her, he went wild, plunging into her again and again, and in seconds he uttered a wild cry as his body shuddered and spasmed.

Anya let him lie quietly for a few minutes, his head buried in her breasts. Then she turned him over so that he lay on his back – he groaned, half in sleep. 'Now, darling, we will try again.'

'Again?' His eyes snapped open – he felt sated, exhausted – what did she expect of him?

Then he felt her lips on him, taking his penis into her mouth, now no bigger than a rosebud. She sucked gently, then more firmly, her hands drifting over his stomach. Down his thighs. He groaned again but this time in the beginnings of ecstasy.

When he woke, the room was in darkness, except for the light from the stove. 'Hello,' he called out to Anya. At the far side of the room, a lamp snapped on to reveal Anya heating something in a saucepan. She turned to him and smiled. She was wearing her mink coat again, but was quite naked underneath, and the sight of her instantly aroused him again. He leapt from the cushions, no longer self-conscious of his nakedness, and went to her, slipping his arms round her, inside the coat and pulling her close.

She laughed with gusto. 'So, you liked it, you want some more? Not now, *mon cher*, you're tired, it's been a big day for you. I'm making you chocolate. You're to drink it and then go home.'

'Oh, no,' Michael groaned.

'Yes,' said Anya firmly, pushing him away, with surprising strength. 'Get dressed. If I have to look at you like that any longer, I might change my mind.'

Laughing too, he went in search of his clothes, and when he was dressed, Anya handed him a large mug of steaming chocolate. 'Drink that, like a good boy,' she commanded. He sipped it. It burnt his lips, which were still sore from lovemaking, but it tasted good. 'Now,' said Anya, suddenly very businesslike, 'I have something for you.' She went to her desk and returned with a slim book and a ten pound note. First she handed Michael the book. He looked at it. '*Erotica* by Lady Maria M,' he read. 'What's this?' he asked.

'Homework,' said Anya, with a wide smile. 'Study this and it will teach you a great deal about how to pleasure a woman.'

Michael was amused. 'Who writes this stuff?'

'Why, me, of course.'

'Truly?' He was amazed.

She waved a hand, in an expansive gesture. 'How do you think I pay for all this, for my mink, for my wine. That diamoned didn't last for ever, darling, and as for my husband's university salary . . . pah, it is nothing.'

'So you write this stuff?' Michael began to laugh, tears of mirth pouring down his cheeks.

'You can laugh, if you like,' said Anya clearly upset, 'but it brings people a lot of pleasure and me a lot of money. It takes skill, talent. I use delicacy, artistry, one must not be crude – one needs only to titillate.'

'I'm sorry, I'm sorry,' said Michael, trying to control himself. 'It's just so amazing – you're so amazing. There can't be anyone else in the whole world like you.'

'I should hope not,' said Anya, crossly, though clearly mollified by his remark. 'Now you take that home, my darling, read it carefully and come back and see me at three o'clock tomorrow afternoon, when we will try again. Yes, no?'

'Oh yes,' said Michael. 'Yes, please.'

'And this,' said Anya, handing him the ten pounds, 'is for you to go and buy yourself some paints, an easel and canvases. If we are going to spend time together, it will not be all play, there must be work too.'

'I have money,' said Michael, pride immediately to the fore.

'I'm sure you have, darling,' said Anya soothingly. 'All you young men have far too much money. But I want you to take this, because I want to be the person who bought you your first canvas – don't deny me that.'

It was almost morning when Michael slipped into his rooms. He was not ready for sleep, there was too much to think about. Instead, he lay in bed and read Anya's *Erotica* in one sitting. She was right, it excited him, and up until then, he had not known such books existed. He slept for a few hours, ate lunch in college and then walked to Broad Street, where he purchased the art materials Anya had told him to buy. At three o'clock, precisely, he knocked on her studio door.

From that moment, Michael's formal education, to all intents and purposes, came to an end. He barely ever attended lectures and certainly did no work outside them. But his education in the art of good living progressed by leaps and bounds. Anya not only taught him to make love, but also to enjoy good food and wine, the theatre, opera – all those things which because of his unique parentage and his diverse upbringing, he had never experienced. The greatest gift Anya gave Michael, though, was his art. From the first frenzied sketch he had made of her that night, Anya had spotted what Rupert had seen in the child's painting of his mother, years before. There was a fluency, a feeling for people – not just how they looked, but the atmosphere they created by their presence. Anya was convinced that Michael's future lay in portrait painting. 'But before you can paint people, first you must learn to paint flesh,' she insisted.

So Michael painted her naked in every possible position and attitude, in every nuance of light. Her luminous white skin was an artist's dream, but in the years to come, Michael was to learn it was also the most difficult to reproduce properly. He learnt his craft in a hard school. Frequently, he found it too difficult to concentrate on his work. He was obsessed by Anya and her body. In a fit of frustration and excitement, sometimes he would knock his painting from the easel and take her where she lay, despite her weak protests. Gradually though, as the weeks turned into months, the obsession shifted, as Michael became more absorbed in his work, and less in Anya. She recognised this symptom long before he did and accepted it, painfully aware of its inevitability.

So absorbed was Michael that it came to him as a complete surprise when, one day, he was summoned to the Dean's study, to be told that he was to be permanently rusticated from college, since clearly he was wasting his tutor's time. A frightful fuss ensued. Rupert, at the time in New York, was informed and reproachful letters from Tassoula arrived by every post.

'So what do I do?' Michael asked Anya.

'I think you and I had better see this Rupert,' she said.

'I daren't introduce you to him, he's dreadfully straitlaced.'

'Are you ashamed of me, then?' Anya said.

'No, no, of course not. It's just that he wouldn't understand . . . well, you and me.'

'All men understand such things. Be brave, Michael, your future lies not in this stuffy university, learning about dead writers. You are an artist, we both know that, but you are going to need my help to convince this Rupert. First, we will have lunch with him, get him a little drunk. What do you say – yes, no?'

'I suppose, yes,' said Michael, doubtfully.

'After lunch, we will bring him back here and show him your work.'

'But Anya, all my paintings are of you, and in all of them you are naked. He'll know . . . he'll know about us, as soon as he sees them.'

'Of course he will know, silly boy,' said Anya. 'But he is a man, like other men. He'll have seen plenty of naked women in his time. I don't mind, so why should you?'

'He's not quite like other men,' Michael said.

'What do you mean, *mon infant*. Is he a homosexual? If so, you should not be associating with him – it's bad for you.'

'No, no,' said Michael, laughing. 'You're always so extreme, Anya. He's never married, I don't know why – perhaps it's because he works so hard, but he is very stuffy. I know he won't approve of us and I think he'll feel I've let him down dreadfully by being rusticated.'

'But you told me he has always encouraged you to paint.'

Michael laughed. 'Yes, but I don't think he looks on it as anything other than a hobby.'

'We shall see,' said Anya.

They collected Rupert from Oxford station. It was six months since Michael had seen him and in that time he seemed to have aged a great deal. He looked careworn – there was no sparkle about him.

If Michael noticed a difference in Rupert, the feeling was more than reciprocated. The gawky schoolboy had gone, to be replaced by a sophisticated and extraordinarily handsome young man – the work, Rupert immediately assumed, of his amazing female companion.

They took Rupert to the Elizabeth Restaurant, where Anya insisted on playing hostess, plying him with drink, questions and flattery. Her manner was coquettish, but restrainedly so, Michael noticed with amusement, and Rupert clearly adored her. By the end of the meal, a hectic flush had replaced his grey pallor, his hair was a little dishevelled, his tie askew and he was having a ball.

Back at Anya's studio, she poured them all enormous brandies and then commanded Michael to present his paintings. Michael was acutely embarrassed and enormously apprehensive. He paraded the paintings one by one, feeling as though he was walking the plank.

Rupert sat on one of Anya's great cushions, with a brandy in one hand, a huge cigar in the other, and a totally unreadable expression on his face. When Michael had finished, there was a considerable silence, during which Michael and Anya looked at Rupert expectantly. He sipped his brandy, drew on his cigar and then finally spoke. 'I have to congratulate you both,' he said, in a lawyer's deliciously, measured tones. 'You, madam, on your magnificient body, and you, my boy, on your very considerable talent.'

Between them, they finished the bottle of brandy with ease, during which time Michael's future was decided upon, to everyone's mutual satisfaction.

The next few years were probably the happiest of Michael's life. He was based in Florence, on a four-year art course, which specialised in portrait painting. He loved Italy and the Italians, but his life was far from restricted to that a of a college student. Anya did not abandon him. Quite the contrary – using all the influence she had over the many people she had met in her colourful life, she obtained for Michael numerous commissions. He painted politicians, actresses, academics, musicians . . . she recommended him constantly, and with spectacular results. Michael's ability was never questioned and his growing maturity helped him produce some magnificent studies. Since his subjects were nearly always famous – Anya hand-picked each one – so his reputation grew. Rupert, now living almost exclusively in New York, provided much the same function. Michael painted senators, judges, Broadway stars and captains of industry.

With the arrogance of youth, Michael found himself at ease with everyone. His natural charm and good looks helped, but his Cretan pride was perhaps his biggest asset. He was not intimidated or over-awed by any of his subjects. He expected, and therefore received, their cooperation. His style was quite unique, his portrayals always realistic, and by twenty-three, he had a reputation which can take men a lifetime to achieve.

As for women, he bestowed his favours on several of the young students in Florence but the experiences meant little or nothing to him. Only with Anya, with her warmth and companionship, as well as her skilful loving, was he ever truly fulfilled.

Of his family, he saw very little. He returned home in response to a telegram informing him that his stepfather was dead. Inexplicably, Rupert would not go with him, so he journeyed alone to find his mother and stepbrother apparently united in their grief, requiring him not at all. He felt awkward and out of place and was glad to get back to Florence.

It was Rupert who inadvertently caused the disruption which had such a far reaching effect on Michael's life. During the summer vacation of 1968, when Michael was twenty-four, Rupert secured for him a commission to paint the main characters in an American TV soap opera. The job was due to last three months, after which Michael was to return to Europe – not to Florence, but to Paris, to continue to perfect his skills. He never made it to Paris. His portraits of the soap opera characters were ecstatically received and he, personally, was an enormous success – providing a breath of fresh air on the otherwise jaded set. A brief affair with a producer's wife obtained for him the chance to paint a portrait of each of the stable of stars signed up with Twentieth Century Fox. It was expected that the job would take eighteen months, the pay was fabulous, and the chance of living in Los Angeles, quite irresistible. Michael accepted and abandoned his studies. Rupert was not pleased, and said so. Anya accepted the decision, but knew that for her and Michael it was the end – there would be different influences, a whole new way of life. She had played her part in his development and now it was time to let him go.

Yet being Anya, their last day together before Michael left for the States, was full of love. The last time they made love was as carefree and as spontaneous as ever. Michael did return to England on Anya's behalf once more. It was to see her buried, for she died of stomach cancer two years later.

Michael did not stay in Hollywood for eighteen months, he stayed for nearly ten years. Everything about the place intrigued him. It was all so over the top, so flashy and extreme, and so much in contrast to his years in England. He loved the climate, the excitement and exhilaration, but what really bound him to Hollywood was the fact it was the birthplace of the Minos paintings.

It began completely by chance. He was at a party and it was getting to the silly stage – people were jumping into the pool, fully clothed – or being pushed – and almost without exception, everyone was very drunk. An elderly man, who Michael knew vaguely by sight, suddenly grabbed his arm. 'Say, are you the guy who painted that Redford portrait, a month or two back?'

'That's me,' said Michael.

'Your name Michael, Michael something?'

'Michael Richardson.'

'That's the guy I'm looking for. I've got a job for you. Would you be at my place around eleven tomorrow?'

'Certainly,' said Michael.

It was only when Michael looked at the business card he had been given that he saw he had been talking to Chuck James, a Hollywood legend – a director with a string of box office successes behind him. He was a big wheel by anyone's standards.

Chuck's house was in a state of total chaos. The place was littered with carpenters, electricians, plumbers and hangers-on. Chuck emerged to greet Michael from a tiny little office overlooking the pool, where he was attempting to work. 'Hell, isn't it? Thank God I chose movies rather than real estate. Do you wanna beer? No, let's have champagne, I need something to take my mind off these guys and their mess.'

They despatched a bottle of champagne in record time, followed by another. Michael had not managed any sleep until four, having become involved with a particularly energetic young stunt girl, who was anxious to prove that her stunts were not restricted to the set. There had been no time for breakfast and his share of two bottles of champagne made him feel vaguely sick and extremely muzzy in the head.

Chuck talked about everything under the sun, but why he had asked to see Michael. It was only when he proposed the third bottle that Michael decided it was time to get down to business. 'Who do you want me to paint?' he asked.

'Not who, son. It's a question of what.'

'What?'

'Yep. I'm giving this house of mine a total look. In every room I'm using the same six colours – cream, gold, a kind of orange, brown, black and grey. I'm using them in a different way in each room, of course.'

'Of course,' said Michael.

'And I guess it's going to be kind of effective.'

'Oh I'm sure,' Michael agreed.

'So, I want a painting to go in each room, using those same colours.'

'What sort of painting?'

'Jeez, I don't know, that's your job. Something kind of abstract, I guess, a touch ethnic maybe, but they must have those colours and they must all be different. You can work with my interior designer, he'll show you how the colours work in each room.'

'It's . . . very kind of you to think of me,' said Michael, 'but I honestly don't think it's my sort of work. I paint portraits.'

'Don't be crass,' said Chuck. 'I like your stuff, I've seen it around, besides which, you can't afford to refuse me.'

'Why not?' Michael asked.

'Because I've got twenty-five rooms in this house and I'm proposing to pay you ten thousand dollars a picture.' Chuck was right, that clinched the deal.

Michael rather enjoyed the work, poring over the designs he had been given, in his little beach house overlooking the ocean. It was a welcome change from portraits and far more restful. He doodled with various ideas and then, one day, he suddenly realised that the colours Chuck had chosen almost perfectly reflected the paintings of the ancient Greeks. This discovery, in turn, provided him with the theme for which he had been looking. The paintings only took four or five days each. He varied them in size and subject but all bore the unmistakable Grecian style. When they were finished, Michael propped them up all round his studio. He was pleased with the result. They were bold, rich paintings, with an undeniable stamp on them. No one could doubt but that they were painted by the same artist.

Up until that moment, Michael had left the paintings unsigned – feeling instinctively that to use the name normally associated with his portraits was quite wrong. Yet to adopt a pseudonym seemed pretentious, unless in some way it could be associated with the pictures themselves. As he stood surveying them, into his mind came the name of the ancient people of Crete, the Minoans. 'Minoan,' he said aloud, then, 'of course, of course!' Without hesitation, he dipped his pen into black ink, and scrawled across the bottom right-hand corner of the first canvas, the word *Minos* – the name that was to make his fortune.

Chapter Thirteen

Several different circumstances conspired to ensure that the Minos paintings achieved maximum publicity. With a name like Chuck James, it was hardly surprising that Michael did not realise his patron had a Greek mother. Chuck naturally assumed that Michael had done his research well and discovered his origins, and so the paintings assumed a particular significance which Michael had never intended. It also helped that Chuck christened his new home with the biggest party even Hollywood had seen in a long time, and that no guest was allowed to leave without being shown the paintings. Following the party and the resultant media coverage, commissions flowed, but still the Minos reputation might have died a death had it not been for an incident which took place just a couple of months later.

Michael had been asked to undertake six Minos paintings for the foÿer of a new hotel, being built in the heart of Los Angeles. It was a sumptuous place and Michael had no qualms about demanding sixteen thousand dollars a painting, which was accepted without query. His dealings had been exclusively with the architect responsible for the job, and when the paintings were finished, the architect asked Michael to deliver them personally, and to advise where best they should be hung, for maximum effect.

Michael and Bob Chaundy, the architect, spent a pleasant morning adjusting the lighting and arranging the correct siting of the pictures. They looked well in the lobby, with its marble floors, pillars and exotic plants. When the work was finished, Bob lifted a cool box from the back of his car and he and Michael sat amongst the workmen's rubble, drinking cans of beer. Sitting, relaxed in the hot sun, Michael squinted up at the hotel.

'Omega Hotels,' he said, reading the enormous sign fixed to the front elevation of the building. 'I've heard of them, of course, but they must be doing exceptionally well to build a place like this. It will stand out even in this crazy town.'

'Yes,' Bob agreed, 'it's certainly the biggest contract we've ever handled.'

'Who owns the hotel group?' Michael asked. 'It sounds Greek with a name like Omega.'

'The guy behind it is Greek and not very old, only in his mid-thirties. He must have made one hell of a lot of brass.'

'What is his name?' Michael asked, flicking his beer can into the pile of rubble.

'Georgios Grillos,' Bob replied.

Michael turned on him, colour draining from his face. 'What did you say?'

'Georgios Grillos. Is that some kind of big deal?' Bob looked puzzled.'

'Greek, you say, not Cretan? Are you sure he doesn't come from the island of Crete?'

'Oh yeh, I think maybe he does, but that's the same thing, isn't it? Yes, now I come to think of it, he does come from Crete. The story is he got drummed out of there during the war – some kind of hassle with the Germans.'

Michael was silent for a long moment. When he spoke, his voice was shaking. 'Shit – how the hell did he do it. The bastard, the little sodding bastard. I tell you this, Bob, he's not having my paintings in his stinking hotels.'

Before Bob's amazed eyes, Michael stood up and ran through the front doors into the hotel lobby. He went to each of his paintings, ripped them off the walls and began stamping on them, sending glass in all directions. His face was almost purple with exertion and anger.

'Hey, wait a minute, are you a loony guy or something?' Bob put a restraining hand on Michael's shoulder, but he shook him off.

'That man's not having my paintings, you'll have to get yourself another artist. Thank God I asked you. To think. . . .' He was breathing heavily, as again and again he kicked at the paintings on the floor.

'Hey, Michael, will you stop that. This glass could do someone a lot of damage,' Bob shouted.

Michael stopped, his anger suddenly spent. 'Don't worry, I'll clear it up,' he said.

'No, no, it's OK, I'll get somebody to do it. You look kind of upset, and you've smashed up one hell of a lot of work. You must have a very special reason to be mad at that guy.'

'I do,' said Michael, wearily.

'Hey, come on, let's go and have a few drinks and you can tell me about it.'

They found a bar a couple of blocks away. The day was very hot and the air conditioning was a glorious relief. They settled in a corner with a bottle of wine.

'Look, I'm sorry, Bob,' Michael said, after a while. 'You were kind enough to give me the work, you spent hours of your time getting everything just right and now you have to start all over again.'

'What's with you and this Georgios Grillos. Don't you like the guy – do you even know him?' Bob asked, clearly more interested in Michael's motives than worrying about the lost paintings.

'I've never met him,' said Michael, 'but he killed my father.'

'What!' said Bob, appalled. 'Was he locked up for it?'

'No, he was only about six or seven at the time.'

'A child, and a murderer? What the hell are you talking about, Michael?'

Michael sighed and took a sip of his wine. 'It was in Crete, during the war. The island was occupied by the Germans. Georgios' father was not a Cretan, he was a mainland Greek, and unknown to anyone, he was in the pay of the Germans. He used his son, Georgios, as a messenger to advise the Germans when to expect resistance action. On the last occasion, Georgios informed on my father. He was a British officer – one of those who headed a band of Cretan guerrilla fighters. As a result of the information they received, my father and his band, were ambushed and killed, and an entire Cretan village was wiped out.'

'Jesus,' said Bob. 'How did they find out who had done the informing?'

'Someone saw Georgios coming away from the German garrison,' Michael replied, 'and put two and two together. His father was hanged, Georgios and his mother were given forty-eight hours to get off the island, or be killed too.' Michael shook his head, in disbelief. 'Now I come to think of it, I remember hearing they had ended up in America, and that Georgios had made good, but I hadn't realised he'd made it this good.'

'I guess if he was a kid you can't blame him for what happened. He was only doing what his pop told him,' Bob suggested.

'I don't think you'd feel like that if it was your father whose death he'd caused,' Michael replied.

'I guess not,' Bob said, nodding his head sagely.

The story might still have ended there, had it not been for the fact that Bob Chaundy lived with a cub reporter who worked on the *Los Angeles Times*. The story was such a good one, he could not resist telling it to her that night. She wrote it up and the editor gave it a spot in the gossip page. Next day, the story was promoted to Page 3, and soon all Los Angeles was talking about it.

Georgios, when interviewed, denied everything, saying that his father had been wrongly accused, but Michael cut a more dashing figure, and on the whole his version was what people wanted to believe. In the city where money was king, the fact that Michael had destroyed over a hundred thousand dollars worth of his own paintings tended to lend credibility. In status terms . . . the whole incident pushed him into the Big Time. Everyone wanted a Minos painting on their wall, everyone wanted him at their party – he was a celebrity.

Michael enjoyed his fame, he enjoyed the money, too. The fact that Georgios Grillos had become so successful incensed him and, subconsciously, he wanted to match that success. So much disposable income was heady stuff, for despite his inheritance, so far, there had been little enough money to throw around. His father's money had paid for his school fees and college expenses, but Rupert had kept him on a very small allowance, with true British prudence, and although the early portrait commission had brought him useful extra cash, it had hardly generated big money when travelling and expenses had been taken into account.

Now everything was different. He bought a larger beach house, a Lambourghini and entertained lavishly – indeed, spending his money just as fast as he earned it. Worried by the press reports of his lifestyle, Rupert flew over from New York, to try and sort out his affairs, but Michael would take no advice. He was hell-bent on sampling everything Los Angeles could offer him – regardless of the cost.

Michael Richardson's reputation as a portrait painter disappeared into the mists of time. Michael had become Minos – he was even called Minos now. It was as though he had been reborn with another character. In parallel with his reputation as a hell raiser, so grew his reputation with women. His affairs were very public, volatile, numerous and brief. Past loves all said the same thing. They never felt they knew him, he used them and then abandoned them on a whim. It began to seem unlikely that he would ever find anyone to share his life, that he was doomed to move from the next party to the next woman, with a plentiful supply of Minos commissions to make sure that he could do so. And then he met Suzy Shelley.

Suzy Shelley was just another eighteen-year-old would-be starlet, struggling to make a living as a waitress while she waited for the big break. What made her different from the rest, in Michael's eyes, was her uncanny resemblance to Anya. She had the same white skin, the same dark hair. Her eyes were not as fine, nor her figure as voluptuous, nor, of course, had she Anya's wit or wisdom. But Suzy was sufficiently like how Michael imagined the young Anya must have been, for him to be drawn to her. As they made love, night after night, in his beach house, in his mind he would blot out the sound of the ocean and imagine himself back in North Oxford, loved and protected by Anya's strong, white arms.

Suzy was good for his ego, too. She was pathetically grateful for his interest in her. He insisted on her giving up her waitressing job, and when he saw the filthy little room in which she had been living, he made her give that up too and move in with him. It was then only a matter of days before he asked her to marry him.

Michael liked marriage. It provided the routine that he had been lacking in his life for years. He found it made him work better, too. He and Suzy would breakfast together – she still in bed, he at a table by the window in their bedroom. Then he would leave her and work in his studio. Sometimes, if he lacked inspiration, he would stop at lunchtime. More often though, he worked through until four or five. Then he would have a swim, change, and together they would go out on the town. He liked introducing Suzy as his wife – not because she was particularly beautiful, nor come to that, because he was particularly proud of her. It was simply that he liked the idea of her belonging to him, of his no longer being alone. It was a relief too, not to have to forage in the jungle of LA to satisfy his sexual needs. It was all there for him at home. And if he did fantasise about his wife being someone else as they made love, did it matter? She seemed well satisfied. Yes, married life suited Michael. He was a happy man.

As for Suzy, she was bored, bored out of her mind. For the first few weeks it was wonderful, lying in bed in the morning, watching TV, sunbathing, going for a swim. But at eighteen, she had no personal reserves to draw on, no way of entertaining herself and time soon began to hang heavy. Because Michael knew so many famous and influential people in Hollywood, she had assumed that he would help her with her career. Indeed her agent was convinced that marrying Michael was the best thing she could have done to improve her job prospects. But Michael refused to promote her. She kept asking him to call up people he knew, but he always laughed at her, never taking her seriously.

'Darling, you don't have to worry about working now. I earn enough money for us to do whatever we want. Relax, just enjoy life. Why spend all day in a hot, stuffy studio, when you can laze around here.' She tried telling him she was bored. 'Go shopping,' was his immediate reply, 'or how about meeting a girlfriend for lunch?'

'All my girlfriends are working,' Suzy whined.

It was then that he grew impatient. 'For Christ's sake, Suzy, you can go anywhere, do anything, buy all the clothes you like – just think how your life was before we married, and stop moaning.'

Things went from bad to worse, when Michael became less interested in going out at night, increasingly favouring a quiet evening at home. He liked to go for long walks along the beach. He liked to read, to listen to music . . . to Suzy, it was all unspeakably dull. Sometimes they would spend the evening making love, or he would draw sketches of her, but somehow even this did not satisfy her. She never felt a real person to him. When she tried talking to him, he always answered in platitudes, as though his mind was not on what she was saying. She raged at him sometimes, telling him she would get more response from a dildo, but he refused to match her anger. He just laughed at her indulgently, as one would at a small child having a tantrum.

What Suzy Shelley did not know, nor could have known, is that marriage had acted as a catalyst for Michael. The man she had met and married had been Minos, the hell raiser, the party goer. Marriage had calmed him. It was returning him to his original self – he was becoming Michael Richardson once more.

She tried provoking him by not being at home when he had finished his day's work, but it seemed to worry him not at all. She would find him lying out on the deck, in the evening sunshine, a book in his hand. He would barely glance up when she came in, ask if she'd had a good time, and then return to the book, quite unruffled. She began to drink too much. One morning, having downed the best half of a bottle of Scotch, she burst into his studio and began raging at him. He kindly, but firmly, put her outside the door and locked it. From then on, she noticed, he always locked the door of his studio when he was working.

She tranferred her drinking to bars in town. It was more friendly than being alone, and she got to talk to some nice people. One day, a guy called Tony asked her back to his place for a snort. Suzy had enjoyed cocaine in a mild way before her marriage. Tony was a handsome guy. Like everyone else in town, he was hoping to be discovered. At night, he worked as a bartender and earned good money. He had a nice little apartment Downtown. That first time, they just smoked and talked, but the following day when she went back to his apartment, they made love, smoked some more and fell asleep. It was after nine by the time she got home.

The following week, Tony suggested that another couple should join them. 'It's more fun with four, sweetheart,' he said, and after a couple of joints, she agreed with him.

The sessions became longer and hazier as they experimented with sex and drugs. For Suzy, the time in Tony's flat was the true reality. The time at home with Michael was purely a way of passing the hours until she could be back with Tony again.

It was over a month before Michael was forced to recognise that something was very wrong. Initially, Suzy's sudden acceptance of his work and their quiet lifestyle together was a relief. When she began coming home later and later, with tales of how she and her girlfriend, Babs, had been to a fashion show, or taken in a movie, he wanted to believe her because it suited him to do so. But as time passed, even he could not ignore the changes in her. It began subtly, but grew increasingly dramatic. Her behaviour became apathetic. Halfway through the evening, she would fall into a deep sleep, from which he found it difficult to wake her. In the mornings, she was edgy and bad tempered. She began to look terrible, too, taking no care with her appearance. Always pale, her skin now had a deathly pallor and there were dark circles under her eyes. Sometimes when she returned home, there was a strange smell about her. When he asked her what this was, she said it was the joss sticks in the bar she and Babs had visited.

One day, unable to ignore the situation any longer, Michael followed her into town. He saw her enter Tony's apartment and waited impatiently for half an hour. Then, with a sick feeling in the pit of his stomach, he climbed the steps and knocked on the door. Inside he could hear music and laughter, but no one answered. He knocked again, ferociously this time. There was the sounding of padding footsteps and the door was opened by a man, unshaven and dishevelled, wearing nothing but underpants. 'Yeh?' he said, his hand still on the door handle, apparently to steady himself. Michael pushed him aside and strode past him into the room.

At first, he could not see Suzy for the haze of blue smoke, which hung in the air. Then he saw her, and froze. She lay before him, stretched naked on a bed. Beside her on one side, lay another girl – older, a tired blonde with sagging breasts. She was kissing Suzy hungrily, running her hands up and down Suzy's thighs. She transferred her kisses to Suzy's breasts, her fingers now moving up inside her thighs, forcing them apart. Suzy groaned, arching her body upwards. It was then that the man, who had been sitting on the bed also, watching the two girls, made his move. He slid towards Suzy, his mouth open, his eyes glazed with lust. . . .

For a moment, Michael thought he was going to throw up. Instead, he crossed to the bed, tore the man away from his wife and seizing one of Suzy's arms in a vice-like grip, he pulled her to her feet and began dragging her across the room.

'Hey, don't do that, you're hurting her.' The man in the underpants who had opened the door stepped forward.

Michael hit him, all his anger and disgust going into the blow. As his fist caught the man's jaw, he heard it crack. As the man tumbled backwards, Michael continued on his way, dragging Suzy behind him, towards the front door.

'Michael, Michael,' Suzy screamed. 'I've got no clothes on, you can't take me outside like this.'

Michael turned on her, his eyes full of hatred. 'You're a slut, nothing but a filthy little slut. It doesn't matter who sees you naked – you'll probably get a kick out of it, anyway.'

'Stop it, stop it.' She began to scream hysterically.

Michael brought back his hand and slapped her viciously across the face again and again. Only when her screams turned to sobs did he stop. Then dragging her down the steps of the apartment building, he half threw her into his car. Passersby looked on with mild interest, but nobody attempted to intervene – this was, after all, Hollywood.

Back at the beach house, Michael ordered Suzy into the bedroom to put on some clothes, and then join him on the deck. There he force fed her with black coffee and she was too frightened of him now to argue. She sat, shivering, listening in quiet acceptance while Michael ranted and raved. 'I'm going away,' he told her at last, 'I don't know if I can bear for you to remain my wife or whether I can ever touch you again. While I'm away, I want you to stay here. I'll leave you sufficient money to live on, but I tell you this, if you ever go near that place again, I swear, by God, I'll kill you.' She didn't doubt that he meant what he said.

Michael left the following morning, before Suzy was awake. If Anya had still been alive, he would have gone to her, but there was no one else for him in England now, so instead he went home . . . to Crete.

Michael stayed in Crete for three months. He found his mother touchingly pleased to see him. His stepbrother had grown into a morose, difficult man, with a marked chip on his shoulder. Even in his current nervous state, Tassoula found her elder son light relief by comparison to Manolis. To the people of Sitia, the name of Michael Richardson had always been emotive. Now he was famous, it was even more so. He was positively revered, praised and welcomed where ever he went. It was just what his bruised ego needed, and suddenly it seemed he should be making a permanent home on Crete – he was half Cretan after all. When the idea came to him of building his home on the site of his father's old hide-out, the locals were delighted. It was the kind of sentimental gesture they adored, and the workmen employed to build the house, laboured in a quite uncharacteristic way to help him achieve his goal.

He returned to Los Angeles, to find Suzy quiet and subdued, still living in their home, apparently having obeyed his instructions to the letter. She looked better. She had acquired a light tan that suited her, and a new wardrobe of clothes. She seemed almost glad to see him, and much to his surprise, on their first night back together, he found he could make love to her, simply by pretending, as usual, that she was Anya.

During the next few weeks he made an effort to be kind to her, working for a few hours each morning, and then spending the rest of the day taking her round old haunts. When he announced one day that he had plans for them to live on Crete – at any rate for part of the year – she accepted it without argument, and apparently listened with interest to stories of his boyhood.

When they arrived on the island, the Villa Dionissos was almost finished – sufficiently so, at any rate, for them to live in it. Suzy stuck it for six weeks. One morning, Michael got up to find a note saying that she could not bear to live in such an uncivilised place any longer and that she was returning to their beach house. If he wanted a divorce, she quite understood, but she would expect to be provided with a home and a reasonable income. Eighteen months later, she was dead.

Now, once again, Michael stood alone in the Villa Dionissos, with a letter in his hand from a woman who apparently also could not bear to live with him. But this time the loss was infinitely greater. For Miranda was no Anya substitute. For the first time in his life, Michael was truly in love – and Miranda was more than a lover, she was a friend – or so he had thought. Was it ever safe to trust another human being, he wondered – especially a woman. He remembered the outrage he had felt when returning from school for his first holidays, to find his mother had re-married. He had only been away three months, but already he had been replaced.

Sitting morosely alone on the terrace, it seemed to him that even his father and Anya had betrayed him by dying when he needed them. As for women in general – to make love to them was one thing, to fall in love with them was clearly folly. Letting the note drop from his hands, he stood up and went in search of the whisky bottle.

Chapter Fourteen

It was raining hard at Heathrow and Miranda had to wait twenty minutes for a taxi. Far from worrying her, strangely enough, it was almost a relief – it gave her something on which to concentrate her misery as she stood in the long, dejected queue of people. Already she deeply regretted leaving Michael, but could see no way back to him. The essence of her argument had been right, she was sure, but her gesture in leaving him was too extreme. She loved him so much, she could not bear the idea of losing him, yet here she was, running away. She wondered at the chances of him following her, but recognised the proud streak in his nature and knew that he would not. She had made a decision that only she could reverse.

The London streets looked grey and drab through the taxi window, so different from the colour and vibrance of Crete. Even the Kings Road, when they turned into it, seemed to lack its usual panache. Yet, when the taxi drew up outside her house, Miranda's heart did quicken at the sight of home – even more so when she saw lights on which meant that Paul was back from school. She gave the driver a generous tip and he carried her bags up to the front door. A smell of cooking greeted her as she opened the door, the house was reassuringly warm and cosy. So, Paul must have learnt to cook. She felt a sudden stab of guilt for having left him for so long, to come home night after night on his own. She had not given him a thought while she had been away, so preoccupied had she been with herself and Michael.

'Paul,' she called. 'Paul, I'm back.'

He must be in the bath or engrossed with homework, she

thought. Weighed down with cases, she kicked open her bedroom door, intending to leave them there and go in search of him. The sight that confronted her, stopped her in her tracks. She stood, staring incredulously, still holding the suitcases. There was a man and a woman in her bed, the duvet covered them but there was no doubt what they were doing. The man was poised over the woman, pushing into her, her hands wildly clawing at his back, as she gave little moans of pleasure. Miranda gazed wildly around her. Was she in the right house? There were her pictures above the bed, her dressing table, then who . . .? One dark head, one fair, the fair hair almost the colour of white-gold. 'Paul?' she said, horrified.

The couple seemed to freeze in the bed and then the man rolled over onto his back. The face that stared up at hers, shocked and pale, was certainly that of Paul, yet she could not equate what clearly he had been doing with her little brother. It was as though two people were involved – the boy she was staring at now, and the man of a few seconds ago. Brother and sister simply stared at one another in silence, in their shock, more alike than ever. At last, Miranda dragged her eyes away to look at the other face. Then she gasped out loud. 'Jenny!'

'Hello, darling,' said Jenny, in her rich, treacly voice. 'Sorry you caught us in *flagrante delicto*, so to speak.'

Miranda's outrage burst out of her. 'Sorry, what do you mean, sorry? I turn my back for five minutes and you seduce my brother. Of all the men in London, why did you have to choose him? He's a child, he should be doing homework – not you, and in my bed, too.' She turned to Paul. 'Get up and get out of here. You should be ashamed of yourself, though I don't hold you responsible – you're too young to know what you're doing. Have you even been to school while I've been away?'

Paul said nothing. He grabbed a pair of jeans, he must have discarded earlier, to hide his nakedness, and as he pushed past her, he gave Miranda a look that shocked her almost more than her discovery. It seemed to be one of pure hatred. Shattered by the look, she watched, bewildered, as he walked down the passageway to his bedroom, slamming the door behind him.

Turning back into the room, she found Jenny was now sitting up in bed, lighting a cigarette. Jenny smiled at her, the same amused, slightly lopsided grin, that in any other circumstances, Miranda would have found reassuring. 'Now I suppose you're going to give me a lecture about not smoking in bed,' Jenny said.

'How could you,' Miranda spat out, 'How could you?'

'Darling girl, what are you getting in such a state about. If the boy hadn't learnt the ropes from me, he'd have learnt it from someone. At least you know where I've been.' She giggled. 'Well, up to a point. Look, darling, I'm clean and wholesome and I won't break his heart. You should be grateful to me, not angry.'

'Jenny, he's a child.'

'Sweetheart, he's sixteen years' old. He's very good-looking and, how shall we put it, physically mature.'

'Stop it,' said Miranda.

Jenny ignored her. 'And if it hadn't been me, I guarantee he'd have found somebody else in the last few weeks. Giving a good looking fella a house to himself, in the heart of London, when he's mad keen to experiment with sex – well what can you expect? You should be looking on this as an act of friendship on my part.'

'You disgust me,' said Miranda.

'Miranda, darling, I know you've always had a hang up about sex, and I suppose, given your early experiences, it's not entirely surprising. The fact is though, it's a natural, healthy way for two people, preferably of the opposite sex, to spend some time together. In the case of Paul, it's far better he learns what's what from me, rather than moping around in his room playing with himself, or catching the clap from some little scrubber.'

'I'm going downstairs to the kitchen to make coffee,' said Miranda, her voice shaking. 'When I come back upstairs, I expect to find you gone.'

'All right,' said Jenny, 'if that's the way you want it, but you're going to have to mend some bridges with Paul. Treating him like a kid in front of me just now, wasn't clever.'

'How dare you start lecturing me as to how to treat my own brother. Just get out of here.'

'As you wish.'

Trembling, Miranda went downstairs to the kitchen, and once inside, she shut the door behind her. A tray was laid out on the side – two wine glasses, two knives and forks. Following her nose, the delicious smell turned out to be casserole in the oven, along with jacket potatoes. Clearly, they had been going to have a quite a feast, and she resented it. Fleetingly, it passed through her mind that she might be jealous. These two people, whom she cared about so much, having a relationship that excluded her. Then she dismissed the thought, her real concern was obvious. Paul was sixteen years' old, Jenny well over forty. It was revolting, degrading for them both. Often in the past she had laughed at Jenny's apparently insatiable sexual appetite – now she felt her brother needed protecting from it. She wondered how long it had been going on and whether her decision to stay with Michael had been the catalyst, or whether they had leapt into bed the moment she had left for Crete. Mechanically, she switched on the electric kettle, turned off the oven and began dismantling the tray. What a homecoming. Momentarily, her thoughts flitted to the Villa Dionissos. It would be evening there now, the sun poised to sink into the sea, and Michael . . . what was Michael doing, what was he thinking? She dismissed the thought hurriedly, trying to concentrate her mind on the simple task of making a coffee. As she spooned the grounds into a mug, she saw her hand was shaking. With an impatient gesture, she threw down the spoon and reached for the whisky decanter instead. A drink would steady her nerves, it had been a long and difficult day.

The click of the front door told her Jenny had left. Clutching her whisky like a lifeline, Miranda went upstairs to her bedroom. The room was immaculate. Jenny had stripped the sheet and duvet cover from the bed and folded it neatly on the floor. The bed was now freshly made up with clean sheets, the ashtray washed. All trace of what had taken place had been removed. She certainly knows her way around my house, Miranda thought, resentfully. She scooped up the sheets and went to take them into the bathroom. The door was locked. 'Is that you in there, Paul?' she called.

'No, it's one of the forty-nine other women I've got stashed around the house.' His voice, angry, sounded very young.

She sighed. 'We'd better have a talk, hadn't we?'

'I'll be down in five minutes,' he said.

Miranda stood in the sitting room, whisky in hand, waiting for Paul and wondering what to say to him. Would he want to continue his relationship with Jenny – she could not bear the thought of it. Besides any other consideration, he simply did not have the time for a heavy emotional relationship. Paying his school fees was no small task and then there was his allowance – he owed it to her to work hard.

There was a sound by the door and she looked up to see Paul entering. Was it her imagination, or had he grown up in the few weeks she had been away? He was taller, broader, he carried himself better. There was an air of confidence about him, instead of the slightly hesitant manner she was used to.

Miranda sat down slowly in the armchair by the window. 'So,' she said, her voice flat and cold, 'when did it all begin? How long has it been going on, this – this relationship with Jenny?'

'Shit, I need a drink,' said Paul, and headed towards the drinks table, to pour himself a gin.

'Stop that,' said Miranda, 'you're far too young to be drinking gin. What the hell's been going on while I've been away?'

He ignored her, making a great play of opening the tonic bottle. When he had finished, he walked over to the cigarette box, helped himself to one, lit it expertly and then came and sat opposite her – drink in one hand, cigarette in the other, his face sullen, but triumphant. She was temporarily lost for words. 'While you've been away, sis, I've been having a bit of fun and not before time.'

'What do you mean by that?'

'You're paying for my education, that's your choice not mine, and it doesn't mean you own me. I've been living in your house these last months playing life your way, because it never occurred to you that I might want anything different. You never ask me what I want, I just have to fit in with your lifestyle, so the last few weeks I've been creating one of my own. All right?'

'No, it's not all right,' Miranda thundered back. 'Would you go on like this at home? How would you expect Mum and

Dad to react if they could see you now, knew what you'd been doing this afternoon?'

'Oh, sis, don't be so hypocritical. We're both here because we wanted to escape from home and all it stands for. OK, so you man aged it on your own, but with or without your help, I'd have done the same thing eventually. Of course Mum and Dad wouldn't understand, nor approve of what I'm doing, but shit, I bet there's a lot of things you've done they wouldn't be too pleased about either.' He had touched a nerve and seeing the expression on his sister's face, he backed off a little. 'It's none of my business what you get up to, sis, but shouldn't that equally apply to me?'

'No, it shouldn't,' said Miranda. 'While you're still at school, you're under my care. What's the point of me squandering a lot of money on your education if you're not going to take advantage of it.'

'Of course I'm taking advantage of it,' Paul said, agitated now. He stood up, his cigarette forgotten, dropping ash all over the carpet. 'I'm working damned hard and I'll get to Oxford. Bloody hell, sis, come to think of it, who are you to lecture me about how much work I do? You didn't even bother to stay on at school for A levels.'

'OK, Paul, so you're the genius of the family,' said Miranda, 'but that doesn't mean you know all the answers. If you did, you certainly wouldn't have been messing around with someone like Jenny Marchant. It's revolting, Paul, she's old enough to be your mother – heavens, practically your grandmother. She's had more men in her time than most us have had square meals and. . . .'

'Don't you say another word against her.' Paul's eyes were blazing with anger now. 'I won't have it. She's a wonderful person, and unlike you, really warm and caring.'

'What do you mean, unlike me?'

'I don't know what's wrong with you, sis – you're all cold and pent up inside. It was bad luck David dying so young, I realise that, but it's as though you died too – emotionally, anyway.'

'That's a dreadful thing to say,' Miranda said, unable to keep the hurt from her voice.

Paul came and sat down again, his anger dying in his efforts to explain his feelings. 'I'm sorry, I don't mean to be unkind but we never have any fun together, you and I. We don't sit around having a good laugh – there's no – well family feeling. This house is very beautiful but it's more of a show house than a home, and as for you, I don't know you any better than a woman I might meet at a party for a few minutes.'

'But I'm your sister!'

'So, does that make it unnecessary for us to communicate? You never tell me anything – how you feel or think. You're kind, yes, but there's no warmth, whereas Jenny is really interested in what I am doing. She even laughs at my silly jokes. She's really fun to be with.'

If he had calculated to hurt his sister, Paul could not have done a better job. Distressed more than angry, Miranda retaliated. 'Well, if that's how you feel, you'd better go and live with *her* instead.'

'Yes,' said Paul, 'I've been thinking about that.'

Miranda threw back her head and laughed. 'Don't be ridiculous. She wouldn't have you, you'd cramp her style, and she couldn't bear to have an untidy teenager cluttering up her house.'

'You lived with her for six months once, when you first came to London, she told me that. You can't have been much older than I am now.'

Miranda felt sick at his words. Had Jenny told him why she had been staying with her? She looked hard at her brother, but there was nothing mocking in his tone. Vulnerable and hurt, anger suddenly seemed her only refuge. If they wanted to live together, let them get on with it. If Paul messed up his exams that was his fault. If Jenny got fed up with him, as surely she would, it would be up to her to kick him out.

'If that's the situation, then,' she said, her voice shaking, 'you'd better get on with it.'

'I'll ring her tomorrow and see what she thinks,' Paul said, tentatively.

'No. If you're going, I'd like you to go now. You've got an hour to get out of this flat and what you haven't removed by then, I'll throw out. I'll continue to pay your school fees and your allowance, but as long as your relationship continues with Jenny, I don't want to see you again – either of you. Is that clear?'

Paul stood up, his face very white – he looked as though he was close to tears. 'If that's what you want, but you're losing a good friend in Jenny. She's really fond of you, sis, she really cares about you.'

'Well, she's got a bloody funny way of showing it,' said Miranda, standing up, too. Abruptly she turned her back on her brother and gazed out into the darkening street with unseeing eyes.

Paul stood for a moment watching his sister's back. He felt he should say something, something to soften the blow of their parting, but at sixteen he had no experience to draw on. He felt hurt and bewildered, but already his thoughts were tinged with excitement. Living with Jenny would be marvellous, like one continual party. He thought of the things she did to him, the way she made him feel, and he almost ran from the room in his haste to get to her.

Miranda sat in the armchair for most of the night, willing herself to cry. The release of tension which she knew only tears could bring was what she needed but she was too strung up to cry. It seemed that her world had fallen apart. Was it only two nights ago that Michael had proposed to her and she had accepted? Then, it had seemed that the world was a wonderful place – now it contained only dark shadows. If she had been asked that night who were the people she loved most in the world, she would have answered Michael, Jenny and Paul. Now, in just the space of a few hours, she had lost them all. Was Paul right, was she cold? As for being emotionally dead, how could she be, feeling, as she did, this degree of pain? Her mind went round and round – the things she had said, the things that had been said to her, spinning uselessly like a top – unable to make any sense of what had happened. At last, just before dawn, she fell into a fitful sleep.

When she woke, the sun was streaming through the window – it was a beautiful June morning. Her head throbbed, her eyes were gritty and every bone in her body ached. She stood up, feeling stiff and shivery, and as if drawn by a magnet, she went upstairs to Paul's room. It looked like a bomb had hit it – the drawers open, the bed unmade, magazines strewn all over the floor. Essentially, though, it was empty – Paul gone. She ran a hand through her hair in a gesture of weariness – she had not slept for two nights. She left Paul's room as it was, ran a hot bath and lay in it, letting the warmth soak into her bones. What to do now, that was the thing. She knew it was dangerous to be alone. Thoughts of Michael persisted – she missed him with a keenness that frightened her. After years of being a recluse from sensuality, he had awakened a part of her that she had not known existed. Being without him seemed to cause her actual physical pain.

In normal circumstances, of course, she would have gone to Jenny, but that was out of the question now. Wearily, she climbed out of the bath, dried herself and dressed in old jeans and a sweat shirt. The house was growing warmer by the minute, it was going to be a glorious day, the English countryside would be at its best. Suddenly a thought struck her – it was so obvious she could not imagine why she had not thought of it before. She reached for the telephone. 'May! May is that you?'

'Miranda, darling. How lovely – we haven't heard from you for weeks.'

'I–I've been away on location. How are you, and how's Lawrence?'

'We're fine, but missing you. When are you coming to see us?'

Miranda gave a small laugh. 'How about now?'

'Wonderful, darling. I'll go and make up your bed. Your room's all ready, it always is, you know that.'

'Yes, I do, bless you. I'll leave in about ten minutes, I should be with you within the hour.'

'Splendid darling. I'll shove a bottle in the fridge. I have a cooked chicken and I've just picked some strawberries – we'll have lunch in the garden.'

'You're wonderful,' said Miranda, meaning it. 'See you soon.'

'Kisses,' said May, and the phone went dead.

Since the moment William Hardcastle and David Conway had died together, on the lawn of the Hardcastle's home at Maidenhead, Lawrence, May and Miranda had been bonded together – people struggling to keep each other afloat in a world that seemed intent on drowning them. William Hardcastle had been groomed from birth to take over his father's business. Far from resenting it, that was precisely what he wanted to do. He was cheerful, kind, intelligent, good-looking, he had everything to live for, his whole life ahead of him. On his death, the Hardcastles were left with a great wealth of untapped love and support to give, and this they largely transferred to Miranda. She was not only the daughter they had never had, she was also the son they had lost. They watched her career with pride and lavished on her as much care as any child could expect from any parent. Driving down the M4, Miranda was painfully aware of how little time she had spent with them in recent months. They made no demands, never badgered her for attention but she knew they missed her sorely when she was not around.

May was in the garden when she arrived. It was a beautiful old walled garden leading out from the back of the house. She wore, as usual, a battered straw hat, and by peering underneath it, one could spy a sweet, gentle face, brown and weatherbeaten from spending so much time out of doors. She was a tiny, frail little figure, but looks were deceptive, since she was surprisingly tough, and her brown eyes twinkled with intelligence, and humour. She always reminded Miranda of a robin, but for the thatch of white curls.

At the sight of Miranda, May dropped her basket and secateurs, and flung her arms round the girl's neck, almost swinging from it due to the considerable discrepancy in their height. 'Darling, darling, how lovely. You look gorgeous, so brown. You lucky girl, where have you been? No, don't tell me, we'll discuss it over lunch. Oh blast, I've lost my gin. Can you see it anywhere?'

A drink problem was the legacy that William had left his mother. She could get through every day, provided the alcohol level was maintained at a delicate balance. Too little, and she sunk into a deep depression, too much and she became sentimental and cried a great deal. Undoubtedly, it would kill her one day, but not for a long while yet, Miranda hoped.

'There it is, May,' she said, 'by the raspberry canes.'

'So it is, how silly. Give it to me sweetheart, would you?' May took a hefty swig and then taking Miranda's arm, they began to walk back towards the house.

The next few minutes were spent busy in preparation for lunch – chicken mayonnaise had to be assembled, salad washed, strawberries culled and the wine poured. Then, without being told, Miranda carried the tray out to the terrace at the back of the house. The Hardcastles could not leave the house where their son had died, but nor could they sit at the front on the lawn or by the swimming pool. Gradually, over the years, Lawrence had gently suggested alterations which had turned the back of the house into the front. It was a subtle compromise that had worked well. While Miranda topped up the glasses, May doled out the food. They sat either side of the big refectory table which had been used for so many barbeque parties in the old days, when William was alive. Silently, they raised glasses to each other, the toast never spoken but always understood.

May regarded Miranda, shrewdly, through her bright little eyes. 'Now I come to look at it, you don't look too good, darling. Suntanned yes, but otherwise rather under the weather, I would have said.' Miranda opened her mouth to speak. 'No, don't tell me,' May said, 'let me work it out. You're miserable and you haven't had enough sleep. Am I right?'

'Spot on, as usual,' said Miranda, smiling.

'Right,' said May, 'let's start with the easy one. Why haven't you had enough sleep?'

'The night before last I was travelling back from Crete and last night I had a row with Paul. I've actually had two nights on the trot without going to bed.'

May chose to ignore the reference to Paul. 'Well, that's something we can put right. I rang Lawrence and told him you were coming, so he will be home early tonight. We'll have supper as soon as he's home, fill you full of wine and then you'll sleep like a babe – you'll see.'

'You are kind,' said Miranda.

'Kind! Rubbish. Now, the miserable bit, are you ready to talk about that yet?'

'No, not yet,' said Miranda.

'Fair enough,' said May. 'I'm dying to show you my new motorboat. Lawrence bought it for me for my birthday. He says it's unsinkable.' She let out a peel of laughter. 'We'll see if he's right after lunch, shall we?'

Miranda joined in the laughter. May's erratic behaviour in boats was a Thames legend. She was always colliding with other craft, getting stuck in locks and once even managed to go over a weir.

The afternoon slipped by in a happy mixture of sun, wine and idle chatter. When they returned from their trip on the river – unscathed, largely because Miranda had insisted on taking the tiller – they found Lawrence waiting for them.

Lawrence Hardcastle had benefited from the passage of time. He was one of those men who had been a singularly unattractive youth, but for whom a receding hairline and slight paunch actually improved his appearance. Now, he seemed to have grown into his overlarge features and looked not unlike a very distinguished Mr Pickwick. Miranda hugged him warmly. 'Missed you,' she said.

'Missed you too, sweetheart.' He held her at arm's length. 'Brown as a berry and as beautiful as ever.'

'A little world-weary though,' said May, trotting up behind them. 'She needs cosseting for a few days.'

Lawrence smiled fondly at his wife. 'And you're going to hate doing that, darling, aren't you?'

'Awful,' she said, 'but I'll bear up – somehow.'

They had cocktails on the verandah, then a delicious supper of cold cucumber soup, followed by spare ribs and salad. After dinner, Lawrence insisted on Miranda drinking a large brandy, and by nine o'clock she was more than ready for bed. She slept like a log, but when she woke in the morning, the image of Michael seemed to hang in the air, clutching at her stomach, tearing at her heart.

Miranda stayed with the Hardcastles for three days. On the second day, Jenny telephoned. Miranda was sunbathing when May came pottering out from the kitchen. 'Jenny Marchant on the phone for you.'

'Could you tell her I'm not here?'

'Certainly not,' said May, 'it would be a lie.' On some things May was completely intractable.

With a heavy heart, Miranda got up and walked into the house. 'Yes,' she said, coldly.

'It's me, darling. How are you?'

'I'm fine,' said Miranda.

'Good, good.' There was a pause.

'Is that all you rang to say?' Miranda asked.

'No, not exactly. I thought I'd just let you know that Paul was with me and that he's OK.'

'I know Paul is with you, he told me he was going,' Miranda said.

'I realise that's what he said,' Jenny's voice was a touch impatient, 'but I thought you might be worried in case I'd thrown him out. Paul said you seemed to think I wouldn't want him around.'

'And do you?'

'Yes,' said Jenny, suddenly sounding self-conscious. 'Yes, I do, Miranda. He's a nice kid, I like him very much. We have fun.'

'Well, when the novelty of having a schoolboy lover wears off, you can always send him back to me, I suppose,' Miranda said viciously. 'In the meantime, I've told him I don't want to see him, and that applies to both of you.'

'Miranda, you're being very silly, in fact very immature. It's not. . . .'

'I can take criticism from a lot of people,' Miranda interrupted, 'but not any longer from you. Frankly, the way you're going on, you're in no position to criticise anyone about anything.'

'OK, so what about your work, we're going to have to talk about that?'

'I'll find another agent,' said Miranda. 'I probably should have done it years ago.' It was an unnecessarily cruel thing to say, and the moment she said it, she regretted it. Jenny had worked tirelessly to build her career, to prop up her flagging ego and keep her sane when everything was falling apart. But the words were out, and now they could not be unsaid.

'Fair enough,' Jenny said. Her voice had a horrible hollow sound to it and suddenly, the phone went dead. Miranda let out a ragged sigh and replaced the receiver.

'I heard all that,' said May, bustling into the kitchen, 'because I was eavesdropping.'

Despite her feelings, Miranda could not help but smile. 'May, you are incorrigible.'

'Am I? Good, because if you're at least feeling well disposed towards me, perhaps it's time we had a talk about your miseries. This seems as good a moment as any. What do you say?'

'Why not?' said Miranda.

'Right,' replied May, firmly. 'I'll fetch a bottle.'

It took two bottles of wine to lubricate the whole story that began with Jake, starred Michael and finished with Jenny and Paul. May asked a number of questions, but mostly she just listened.

When at last Miranda had finished, May lay back in her chair, head cocked on one side. She took so long to say anything at all that Miranda was beginning to wonder if she had fallen asleep.

'Well, dear,' said May, at last, 'it's all very straightforward really. You're running away from this Michael character – whether for the right or wrong reasons we have yet to decide – but in any event you are very upset by it and you're taking out your feelings on poor Jenny and Paul.'

'I am not,' Miranda said. 'Heaven's above, May, you can't approve. How would you have felt if William had involved himself in an affair with a woman in her forties, when he was only sixteen?'

'I wouldn't have felt happy about it,' May admitted, 'but I'd have been a great deal less upset if I'd known the woman was Jenny. Lawrence and I have known Jenny a long time, you know Miranda – a lot longer than we've known you. She's a naughty girl but her heart is in the right place. Still, Jenny and Paul are not really the point at issue, are they? It's you and Michael. If you want my honest opinion, I think you're mad. I believe you've fallen in love for the first time in your life and it's frightening you half to death.'

'Are you saying I didn't love David? Surely you're not saying that.'

'Well, no. You loved him in a way,' May looked slightly evasive, 'but we're not talking about David now. David's dead and has been for seven years. We are talking about someone who is very much alive, and by all accounts, loves you too.'

'I never expected to hear you talk like this, May,' Miranda said.

'Well, no, perhaps not, but I'll tell you this, Miranda. If I had been younger when William was killed, I would not have hesitated to have had another child if I could. That child would not have been brought up in William's shadow, with endless references to his dead brother. For us, for Lawrence and I, it would have been a new beginning, a new life. I would have loved that child every bit as much as I loved William, and in doing so, I would not have been disloyal. In my case, a new love is not possible, in yours it is. It seems to me that you're throwing away your one chance of real happiness, but then I'm a romantic old woman.'

'But surely. . . .' Miranda began.

May held up her hand. 'No, stop, don't let's talk about it any more – it will upset us both. I have told you my views, now let's change the subject.'

Miranda was surprised. In the past, May had been endlessly willing to discuss her emotional problems. This sudden refusal to continue the conversation was out of character. She felt let down, abandoned and bewildered by May's unexpected attitude.

The next day was Saturday and the weather broke. It was wet and surprisingly chilly and it was time, Miranda decided, to go home. She dreaded returning to her house alone, but it had to be done sometime. So after lunch, she said goodbye to May and Lawrence and drove back up to Chelsea. The house depressed her, but determinedly, she set about cleaning and tidying Paul's room, turning it back into the impersonal spare room it had once been. It was after eight by the time she had finished. The rain had stopped, the evening was clear and the sky a beautiful pale blue. She felt tired but oddly purged from her work and went down to the kitchen to make herself a sandwich.

The doorbell ringing surprised her – it was an odd time of the evening to call unannounced. Then she realised it was probably Paul. In his hurry to leave, he had forgotten his beloved cassette collection. It was waiting for him in the hall for she knew he could not bear to be parted from it for long. Steeling herself, she went down the stairs. She would be dignified and cool, not let him know how he had hurt her. She opened the door with a tight little smile, and looked up into the face, not of her brother Paul . . . but of Michael Richardson.

Chapter Fifteen

No one would ever know what it cost Michael to make the trip to London to find Miranda. Loving her was not enough. He had to overcome his immense pride – as much a part of him as the air he breathed. He struggled against coming, questioned his motives a thousand times – alone at the Villa Dionissos, on the plane, even in the taxi from Heathrow. It had been Jenny Marchant who had finally proved the catalyst. A telephone call to Masons requesting Miranda's whereabouts had put him in touch with Jenny. It was ridiculous that he did not even know Miranda's address, but it had never been relevant before. Jenny had listened to his garbled explanations of how he wanted to get in touch with Miranda, and it was Jenny who had said simply, 'Yes, of course, I'll give you her address, but please, go to her quickly – she needs you.' Three words, but they were enough. . . .

Something of his struggle must have shown in his face, as he stood before Miranda. No explanations were necessary – she simply cried out his name and threw herself into his arms. He held her tight, there on the doorstep, and then gently drew her inside and closed the door on the world. They did not speak, words an unnecessary burden. As if sleepwalking, Miranda led him up the stairs to her bedroom, and there, quickly, with trembling fingers, they undressed and climbed onto the bed. As their naked bodies fused together, in unison they let out a long, deep sigh of immense relief.

They made love as never before. Their tears mingled as they clung together, their bodies no longer functioning individually but as one, as were their hearts and souls. They were desperately tender and gentle with one another, recognising each other's hurt, and awed by the knowledge that they alone were the only people on earth who could heal each other's wounds.

At some stage, they grew hungry, and Miranda went in search of food, returning with cheese and fruit and a bottle of wine. They sat in bed, having a picnic, and for the first time talked of the future. Their hours of lovemaking had affected them like a drug. They were dazed, quiescent and there was none of the usual aggression. All they wanted was to make each other happy.

'I'll open the batting,' Michael said, when he had poured the wine. 'You will agree, we can't live apart.'

'Not happily,' said Miranda.

'Not at all,' said Michael. 'So it's accepted then that we have to live together?' Miranda nodded, watching him as he talked. A wave of love for him swept over her. She abandoned her wine and leaning forward, clung to his bare chest. 'Hey,' said Michael, laughing, 'we're trying to have a conversation. This is important, this is where we fell out last time, remember.'

'We won't do that again,' said Miranda. 'I'll live wherever you want.'

'Do you mean that?'

She drew away from him. 'Yes, I do. I haven't had the chance to tell you yet, but when I arrived back in London, I found my world here had completely blown apart. This so-called splendid life of mine, which I couldn't give up, doesn't exist any more. I belong to you. If that means living in Crete, it's fine with me.'

'Oh, darling,' Michael whispered. He took her hand. 'You've just made, more or less word for word, the speech I was going to make to you. The Villa Dionissos holds no magic for me now, if you're not there. I'd rather live anywhere in the world with you, than alone in Crete.'

Miranda shook her head vehemently. 'There's no need, honestly. Let's make our permanent home in Crete – it's really what I want, too, now.'

'Promise.'

'Promise.'

As they kissed, Miranda wondered fleetingly whether her

row with Paul and Jenny had made the decision easier. Perhaps it had, but what did her motives matter, as long as they were together?

'I'm frightened to death of losing you again,' said Michael. 'I'm not letting you out of my sight until you're my wife, I'd like to make that quite clear.'

The urge to be in each other's arms again was too great. They abandoned the remnants of their meal and all further attempts at conversation, and wrapped around one another, fell into a deep, contented sleep.

Breakfast was a time for decisions. They decided that they would marry in London, immediately, as soon as they could obtain a special licence. 'We can always have a Greek wedding later, if you wish,' said Michael. 'I was brought up in the Greek Orthodox Church, but when I came to England, I sort of became C. of E. I'm a mongrel in religion, too.'

'So are most of us,' said Miranda.

After breakfast they telephoned Miranda's parents. They seemed pleased, if surprised with the news but decided they would not come down to London for the wedding – as always the farm and Lottie's arthritis provided sufficient excuse for them not to leave Yorkshire. 'Tell them we'll come up to see them,' Michael whispered.

'Are you sure?' said Miranda, putting her hand over the mouthpiece.

'Of course I'm sure. I have to check up on your origins to see what sort of creature I've married.'

They then spent a frustrating half-hour trying to get a call through to Crete. Eventually they succeeded. Michael had a long conversation with his mother. As he spoke in Greek, Miranda could understand not a word, but his tone was serious and he smiled hardly at all, while she watched him anxiously. Finally he replaced the receiver.

'I wanted to speak to her,' Miranda protested.

'I know, but she's a little upset.'

'Why – oh Michael, doesn't she approve?'

'Well, not exactly. She's worried because she hasn't met you, because we're marrying in a registry office and because . . .' he hesitated.

'Because of what?' Miranda asked.

'Because I told her you were a model. In my mother's world, a model's even worse than an actress. She sees history repeating itself. She's worried you'll be another Suzy.'

'Did you ever tell your mother how Suzy died?'

Michael shook his head. 'No, we managed to hush it up. The official verdict was heart failure, that's what everyone believed, including my mother.'

'Should we wait, go back to Crete first and talk to her?'

Michael shook his head. 'No, I can't wait, not even for my mother.'

'It seems strange,' said Miranda, a little wistfully. 'Here we are about to take this enormous step in our lives, without any of our family here to witness it.'

'Does it worry you?' said Michael.

'A little,' Miranda admitted.

'What about your sisters and brother?' Michael suggested.

'My sisters are very involved with their families. I think it would be easier to see them when we go North.'

'And Paul?' Michael persisted.

'No, I'm not asking Paul.'

'Why?' Michael demanded.

Miranda then told him the full story of Paul and Jenny and he listened in silence until she had finished. 'I do understand your feelings,' he said, 'and I think you were right to make your protest. However, things have changed rather a lot in the last twenty-four hours and I think you should ask him to come to the wedding even if you don't include Jenny.'

'He wouldn't come without Jenny,' said Miranda, with absolute certainty – recognising that Paul's stubborn loyalty was a mirror of her own.

'I'm not going to fight with you,' said Michael, 'not ever again.'

Miranda laughed. 'That, I don't believe. But seriously, forget my family for a moment. What about yours? Isn't there anyone you want to ask?'

'Only Rupert and he's in New York. There's no point in him coming over specially. Still we have to ask someone. We need witnesses, apart from anything else.'

'We'll ask the Hardcastles,' said Miranda, suddenly. 'Now they will approve, and you'll adore them.'

It took them only a week to arrange everything – the disposal of Miranda's house, her car and her furniture. All her worldly goods were either sold, shipped off to Crete or stored at the Hardcastles, but Miranda felt no regrets about the dismantling of her lifestyle. She wrote Jenny a curt note, telling her that she was getting married, going to live in Crete, and that all enquiries for work should be turned down. It was the end of a brilliant career, which had been built and nurtured for over ten years, but Miranda found no difficulty in writing the letter. She was in a daze of love, only feeling half alive, as she laboured during the day, until she could once more fall into Michael's arms.

Michael had hired a suite at the Dorchester, so that they did not have to sleep amongst the chaos of Miranda's packing. It was the lap of luxury – a huge bedroom, with a balcony overlooking Park Lane, a bathroom with a sunken bath, a pretty little sitting room. It was their whole world, the time they spent there, magical.

The wedding morning was perfect – bright sunshine and blue skies. They made an incredible-looking couple as they walked across the foyer of the Dorchester. Every head in the room turned. Miranda was dressed in an ice-blue jump suit, her hair gleaming, face alight with happiness. Michael, for once, wore a suit. It was beautifully cut, emphasising the breadth of his shoulders, and in the palest grey, it set off his deep tan. Miranda could not keep her eyes off him. A chauffeur-driven Bentley took them to Chelsea Registry Office, where May and Lawrence Hardcastle were waiting for them, together with what seemed to be the world's press.

'Oh no,' groaned Miranda, as the car drew up and a surge of photographers leapt forward. 'How on earth did they find out?'

'God knows,' said Michael, 'but if this is your last piece of publicity darling, let's go out in a blaze of glory. Smile for the nice gentlemen.'

She could have done nothing else, so happy was she . . . she seemed to be floating on air. If the photographers jostled her, she did not notice as she glided up the steps on Michael's arm. May was waiting for her, the two women kissed and May gave her a small bouquet of forget-me-nots, which perfectly matched her suit.

'How on earth did you know, May?' Miranda asked, amazed.

'I cheated dreadfully, dear. We booked into the Dorchester, too. I found out your room number and bribed the maid to tell me what colour you were wearing.' She turned her attention to Michael. 'So, this is the young man who's been causing all the trouble.' She smiled, coquettishly. 'I can certainly see why.' Everyone laughed.

'Is it permitted for the bridegroom to kiss the bride's adopted mother?' Michael asked.

'Most certainly,' said May, offering her cheek.

Afterwards Miranda could remember nothing of the service, simply the feel of Michael's hand in hers, warm and reassuring. The ring, he slipped on her finger, which they had only bought the previous day, felt heavy and strange. It was a long time since she had worn a wedding ring.

Then they were out in the sunshine again, blinking in the sudden light. The crowd had swelled, attracted by the press and a small ragged cheer went up as they appeared. Miranda posed at the top of the steps, as always the professional. She slipped an arm through Michael's and turned an adoring face to his. They kissed and the crowd went wild.

Then the questions came thick and fast. 'Will you be giving up your career, Miss Hicks? Minos, Minos, have you painted your wife yet? Where will you live? Where are you going on honeymoon? How many children do you want? What does it feels like marrying a famous model? What does it feel like marrying a famous artist?' They answered the questions patiently, in good humour – the press adored them, and they adored each other. The crowds increased, and Miranda made the charming gesture of throwing her bouquet into the midst of them. It was caught by a little girl of eight or nine. The child pushed her way through the crowd. 'I want to be a famous model like you,' she told Miranda, solemnly.

Miranda bent and kissed her. 'Work hard then and perhaps

you will be,' she whispered back. The child beamed with delight – already feeling very special.

Only when the autographs started did Michael call a halt. 'It's our wedding day,' he said, appealing to the crowd. 'No one should have to work on their wedding day.'

'Please sign this one, just for me, it's for my little boy. Just this one, Minos, I'll frame it and hang it on the wall. Miranda, Miranda, here, please sign this. . . .'

Eventually, ushering May and Lawrence into the car, they escaped.

'Phew,' said Lawrence, straightening his tie. 'This is a little more glamorous than our wedding day, isn't it, darling?'

'Where were you married?' Michael asked, as the car drew away, the crowds still waving and shouting.

'France. A little country chapel in Burgundy country, during the war. I fought with the Free French. I was in the resistance and May was a nurse, working underground. Our comrades kept a look out while the local padre married us. He did the whole job in about two minutes flat, we were all so frightened of being shot.'

'Really!' Michael was entranced. 'My father worked in the resistance in Crete.'

'Did he?'

'He was left behind after the invasion. He could have got out but he so loved Crete and its people he stayed, and then he met my mother.'

'I was dropped in after France fell,' said Lawrence. 'I'm Jewish, you see. I had a very personal axe to grind.'

'Do you know,' said Miranda, 'in all the time I've known you both, I've never heard that story. It makes me feel very humble when I think of the number of times small and unimportant things have upset me and I've moaned on to you about my troubles. And all the time you've both lived with all the danger.'

Lawrence leaned across and took May's hand. 'It's a long time ago, in another world, but I'll charge you two with this – be as happy in your marriage as May and I have been and you'll not be doing so bad.'

'We'll try,' said Michael, quietly.

The revelation as to the circumstances of the Hardcastles' wedding seemed to bond the two couples together. Michael had arranged a private room at the Dorchester, where they drank champagne and ate a sumptuous lunch – they laughed and talked together like old friends. While the men were making a great business of choosing the right cigar to accompany their port, May leaned across to Miranda. 'You've done the right thing, at last, darling – he's just the man for you. I'm so pleased – well done.'

Just for a moment, Miranda was tempted to leap to David's defence, to say that she was being given a second chance, not at last finding the right man. But it was her and Michael's day, so she let it pass.

Lunch drifted into the evening and still the champagne flowed. 'What about dinner in the Grill Room?' Lawrence suggested.

'No, darling – certainly not,' said May, sagely. She was, by now, extremely drunk and starting to become tearful. 'It's time we let these two be alone together. They've been very sweet, but they must have been dying to get rid of us for hours.' She hiccuped slightly, and wiped her moist eyes.

'But surely an early dinner. . . .' Lawrence began.

'No, my darling. Don't you remember what it was like?'

Lawrence looked at her and smiled. 'Yes, I remember what it was like. Come on then, old girl, we'll have a supper on a tray, in front of the telly – heavens above, it's all we're fit for.'

A little later, Miranda and Michael stood by their open bedroom window. It was a beautiful clear, dark night and below them, Park Lane was still busy. 'I almost wish my life could end now,' Miranda said, softly.

'Hush, my darling, don't say things like that.'

'It's just so perfect. I want to take this moment and make it last for ever. If our lives could stand still now, we would have found paradise.'

'No,' said Michael, 'that's not how you should look on things.' He cupped his hands round her face and lifted it to his. 'Our life together is just beginning. This is the watershed, it's what happens from now on that is important.'

'Kiss me,' Miranda whispered.

They stood by the window, kissing, until their mutual need dictated that they should move to the bed. They lay on their sides, facing one another, smiling into each other's eyes.

'Will it be different, do you think, now we're married?' Miranda asked, her smile seductive, her eyes bright with amusement.

'It?' said Michael, knowing perfectly well what she meant.

She felt him hard against her, and still not taking her eyes from his, she began caressing him and rubbing her breasts against his chest. 'This, I mean this,' she whispered.

Michael began to moan with pleasure, his arms tightened round her, his breathing uneven. 'I think,' he gasped, 'that is a question I should be in a position to answer in about twenty-five years' time. Ask me again at our Silver Wedding.' He kissed her and in seconds they were lost in their own fiery world.

The story of the marriage was all over the press the following morning. In the *Daily Mail* it even made the front page. By ten o'clock their room was besieged with telephone calls requesting interviews, and the hall porter confirmed that photographers were staked out all round the hotel entrance.

'If only somebody important would get assassinated, they would leave us alone,' Michael grumbled, as they sat in bed over the remains of their breakfast.

'Michael, don't – how awful.'

'Well, have you got any better ideas? Wimbledon doesn't start for another week. The lovely weather has driven all the Royals out of London, our current cricket performance is so unspeakably dreadful, it's better not to report it, and Parliament has shut shop for the Summer recess – there's nobody left to talk about but us.'

Miranda laughed. 'So what do you propose?'

'Let's go to Yorkshire.'

'Today?'

'Why not today? I'm certain the average national daily reporter believes wholeheartedly in the concept that everything stops at Watford. There's no way they will follow us to the frozen North.'

'You're right,' said Miranda. 'I'll ring Mum and Dad.'

They hired a Mercedes, and with the help of the hotel management, crept out of the back entrance. 'This is going to be wonderful for my reputation,' said Michael. 'They'll think I've kept you in the bedroom for days.'

'When we get home, I'd be very happy for you to do that.' The word home slipped easily from Miranda's lips. She meant Crete, and Michael knew it and was pleased.

They had plenty of chance to talk on the journey. 'Do you know,' said Miranda, 'we've never really discussed children in any depth.'

Michael hesitated for a moment. 'No, we haven't.'

'You would like some?'

'Yes, yes, of course.'

'You don't sound very enthusiastic.' Miranda turned and looked at him as he drove. His face had the closed look she had become used to seeing when a subject was difficult for him in any way. 'You're clamming up on me, darling. What is it about kids that upsets you?'

'Nothing.' He turned to her, took her hand and squeezed it. 'I'd love children, your children. Let's have lots, a dozen may be.'

'Come on,' said Miranda, 'two will do.'

'And the sooner the better,' said Michael. 'I don't want to be mistaken for their grandfather.'

'I hardly think that's likely,' said Miranda.

'I'm forty-one. Seriously, perhaps we should get a move on. How do you feel about that?'

'I'd love to have your baby,' Miranda said, simply, 'whenever you like.'

It was early evening by the time they reached Bradford. Miranda had booked them into the Queen's Hotel, knowing that Michael would not find it easy staying at her parents' house. She smiled to herself at the thought. His life was too pampered, he was too used to luxury. The little attic bedroom, with its bare boards, and the nearest lavatory and wash basin two floors below, was hardly Michael's style.

'I'd like to check into the hotel and change,' he said. 'I feel a bit travel-stained after the drive.'

'Oh, darling, we haven't time.'

'Surely we have,' said Michael. 'It's only six.'
'They eat early.'
'This early?'
Miranda nodded, amused. 'You're moving into a different world up here, my boy. It's tea rather than supper, and it's served sharp at half past six.'
Michael looked genuinely amazed. 'Nonetheless, I think I should change.'
'Darling, Dad will come in from the yard in a shirt and a pair of corduroy trousers, held up at the waist by baler twine. He will have washed his hands under the tap in the stable, none too thoroughly. If he remembers, he'll take off his wellingtons by the back door, and sit down at the table in his socks. Mum wouldn't dream of taking off her apron when she serves the meal. If it's a warm night, the back door will be open and the chickens will wander in and out. It's – how shall we say – fairly casual.'
'You've convinced me,' said Michael. 'Good God, I wonder what they're going to think of me?'
As it happened, Miranda was wrong about almost everything. The meal had been laid out in the front parlour, and the whole family assembled in their best finery. Lottie was wearing a new summer dress of sprigged cotton, purchased from Lewis's the day before. Jack had been forced into a jacket and tie, and looked hot and uncomfortable. Ann and Sarah were there, together with their various children and husbands, both men looking as equally constrained as Jack. Only Michael looked cool and comfortable in a T-shirt and jeans, and instantly felt shamefully under-dressed.
As was the Higgins way, the greetings and congratulations were unemotional. Everyone kissed Miranda, but seemed relieved when it was over and were similarly self-conscious about shaking Michael's hand. Sherry was passed round and everyone stood about awkwardly. Michael, in a moment of inspiration, started asking Jack about the farm and soon he had talked himself into a guided tour.
Once the men had left the room, the tension eased. 'He's a real looker, Miranda,' Ann said. 'He's like a Greek god.'
'He is half Greek,' said Miranda, laughing.
'I know, I read about it in the papers.'

'I never get used to that, you know,' said Lottie, smiling at Miranda, 'reading about you in the papers, I mean. It's as though you're two different people. I always look out for your pictures, of course. I've kept them all – all the ones I've found, but it doesn't really seem like you, somehow.'

'I know what you mean,' said Miranda. 'I feel like that too, sometimes.'

'Are you happy, girl?'

'Very.'

'Good.'

And that was the full extent of the maternal enquiries concerning the wisdom of Miranda's match.

With great forethought, Michael had brought with them half a dozen bottles of champagne. They were warm, having been in the car all day, but they did a great deal to relax the atmosphere. Supper was steak and kidney pudding, followed by apple pie. Miranda had once admitted that they were the two things she missed most in London, and since then, Lottie had faithfully cooked them for her every time she returned home.

It was while they were washing up that Lottie raised the question that Miranda had been expecting. 'What about our Paul then, is he all right in those digs you found for him?'

Miranda had to tread carefully, taking the lead from her mother. 'Oh, he sent you his new address then, did he?'

'Yes. He said that as you were getting married, he had found somewhere else to live, and that you'd introduced him to a woman who had letting rooms, and who would generally look after him and see to his needs.'

Miranda could barely suppress a smile. The little devil. 'Yes, he's all right,' she said. 'In fact, he's being very well looked after. Don't worry about him, Mum, he's growing up a lot.'

'He's going to end up just like you, never coming home,' said Lottie, wistfully.

'It's your fault,' said Miranda, slipping an arm round her mother's shoulders. 'It's all those tales you used to tell us when we were kids, about your days in the theatre – it gave us itchy feet.'

'That's what Jack says,' said Lottie. 'He says it's all my fault.'

'Mum, I'm only joking.'

'I know, love, but I don't think your dad is.'

They stayed for three days and after the initial awkwardness, it was clear that the Higgins approved of Michael. Miranda was surprised, remembering how difficult her first and only visit with David had been. Michael might have come from a totally different world to the Higgins but somehow he seemed to fit in quite naturally.

'I suppose we'll see even less of you now you're living abroad,' Jack grumbled, as they were loading the car. He said the word abroad with suspicion, as if it was alien to him, which it was – he had barely been out of Yorkshire during his lifetime, never mind out of the country.

'No,' said Michael, firmly, 'you'll see more of her, I'll make sure of that. She won't be dashing all over the world on modelling assignments any more. We'll have more time, more leisure. We'll come and see you often. Perhaps you would even come and visit us in Crete?'

'No,' said Jack, firmly, 'no, I don't think so.'

'Well, we'll see. The offer's open though, always.'

'You really are an old charmer,' Miranda said, as they drove away.

'They're nice people, I like them.'

'Yes, they are,' Miranda agreed, 'but I always feel a little awkward with them, somehow.'

'Guilt,' said Michael. 'Your father's a wonderful man, salt of the earth, but it's from your mother you get your drive and up to a point, your looks, too. She must have been a cracker when she was young. The trouble is you've done all the things she would have liked to have done, you know it and you feel guilty about it.'

'Perhaps you ought to have been a psychiatrist,' Miranda suggested, dryly.

'Cheeky. Come here and kiss me.'

'You get arrested for doing this sort of thing in public, in Yorkshire, you know,' said Miranda.

'I'll take the risk.'

Despite the fact that Michael had booked their airline tickets under false names, they were beset by photographers the moment they arrived at Heathrow, and had to be hidden away in the VIP lounge. They had to run the gauntlet of them again at Iraklion, and when they reached the Villa Dionissos, they found Thea's two sons desperately trying to ward off a full complement of *paparazzi*. Miranda was ushered quickly inside, while Michael faced the cameras and made a short appeal. They might have come home, he said, but they were still on their honeymoon and deserved a little peace and quiet.

Within a few hours of reaching the villa, all signs of the press had disappeared and with relief, they realised, they were yesterday's news.

Chapter Sixteen

It was with considerable trepidation that Miranda went with Michael to meet his mother. In her mind, she imagined Tassoula to be someone rather like Thea, and Thea had been far from friendly when Michael explained that Miranda had returned as his wife. Miranda had done her best. She had asked Michael to tell Thea that she would learn Greek so that they could talk, and that the routine running the house should remain unchanged. She even added that she was very grateful to have someone like Thea to help her. But none of these comments produced a smile or indeed, any responsive chord.

The house overlooking Sitia harbour, surprised Miranda by its size. It was fashioned from beautiful old apricot stone. There were shutters on the windows, like a French chateau and an imposing mahogany door of immense height. Michael thumped on the door and within seconds it was opened by a stooping, elderly man, his face brown and seamed, his hair white.

'Nicko!' said Michael, embracing the old man and bursting into a flood of Greek. Then he turned to Miranda. 'This is Nicko, he was my grandfather's assistant, helping out mainly in the dispensary. Now, he looks after my mother – he is a true family retainer.'

Miranda held out her hand. 'Hello, Nicko,' she said.

Nicko responded with a warm and toothless grin, as he took Miranda's hand, with a small bow. It was the first time she had felt truly welcomed in Crete.

The inside of the house was terribly dark, so dark that Miranda had to strain her eyes to see anything at all. This was partly because all light had been excluded, but also because the house was full of what appeared to be old Edwardian furniture. 'My grandfather was a great admirer of large chunks of English furniture, as you can see,' Michael said, with a grin. 'He was not concerned with their beauty, nor indeed their function, purely their size.'

Tassoula was waiting for them in a small room at the back of the house, which was lighter than the rest, since large French windows opened out onto a walled garden. She was sitting at a small table and when they entered, she rose and stepped forward to greet her son. She was quite different from how Miranda had imagined. In Crete, everyone seemed so poor, so much the peasant – but not this woman. She was quietly, but elegantly dressed, and though in her sixties, her skin was relatively unlined and her eyes bright and clear. She was tall, much taller than the average Cretan woman and wafer-thin, where normally their figures slipped – a combination of too much sugar and too many babies. In fact, she was almost exactly Miranda's height and as the two women shook hands, they were eyeball to eyeball. Her hair, swept up into a bun, was iron-grey. She had heavy eyebrows, darting up and out at an angle, and Michael's hooded eyes and strong aquiline nose. Her lips were full and generous, but deep lines were etched down her face from nose to mouth and her eyes were troubled. This is not a happy woman, Miranda thought. She smiled warmly. 'It is very good to meet you,' she said. 'Michael has told me so much about you and I have been looking forward to this day for a long time.'

Tassoula gave the ghost of a smile and an inclination of the head to show she had understood, but she said nothing. At that moment Nicko shuffled in carrying a tray. So bent and stooped with rheumatism was he that Miranda longed to take the tray from him, but was too intimidated to do so.

The three of them sat around the table while Nicko ponderously poured out glasses of *raki* and laid before them a plate of sweet, sticky honey cakes. Only when he had left did Tassoula speak for the first time. 'I hope you will both be very happy.' They raised their glasses solemnly. 'We must touch glasses,' said Tassoula, looking directly at Miranda. They chinked glasses and drank. 'Do you do that in England?' Tassoula asked.

'Yes, sometimes.'

'In Crete when we drink, we like all our senses satisfied,' said Tassoula. 'Taste is not enough. We pick up the glass, that is touch, we raise it high and study it, that is sight, we sniff it so, that is smell, then we touch glasses so there is something to hear. We always do it.'

'I like that,' said Miranda, smiling. 'Thank you for explaining.'

'Ah, you have much to learn, child, much to learn.'

'Will you help me?' Miranda asked.

Tassoula glanced at Michael. 'Perhaps.' There was an awkward pause. 'What religion are you?' Tassoula asked. 'Catholic?'

'No,' said Miranda, 'I'm not really anything – Church of England, I suppose, but I only go to church at Christmas, sometimes not even then.' This was clearly not the right thing to say.

'Why is that, don't you believe in God?'

'Mother, I've explained to you a hundred times, the church is not so important to people in England, as it is here in Crete.'

'I know, I know,' said Tassoula, looking impatiently at her son. 'I only asked. I have a right to ask, I am your mother.'

'I tell you one thing,' said Michael, 'the English priests are far better people than the Greek *pappas*.'

'Are they?' said Miranda, thinking of the austere figures dressed in black, with their long beards and distinctive hats, she had seen walking in the streets of Ayios Nikolaos.

'Yes,' said Michael, 'the *pappas* are terrible rogues. They drink, have women, play cards, smoke and swear. Despite it all, the older people revere them, but not the young. They are not impressed.'

'That is a bad thing to say, Michael,' said Tassoula. 'Very bad!'

'No, it's not, Mother, it's the truth and you know it. We are not trying to impress Miranda with our ways and our life here. She is a part of us now, she needs to understand about Crete – the good and the bad, and the Greek priests are all hypocrisy. In England, the priests care about the people. They visit the old, the sick, they lead good lives, marry, stay faithful – if not, they are thrown out of the church.' Tassoula looked mutinous but remained silent. Michael smiled encouragingly at her. 'Tell me about Manolis.' For a moment Miranda's mind reeled – who was Manolis? – then she remembered, Michael's half-brother.

At the mention of her younger son's name, Tassoula's brow knitted and her eyes clouded. 'Not good, not good. He read in the papers of your marriage, and as always he . . . he . . .' she struggled for the word.

'Resents?' suggested Michael.

'Yes, he resents you being famous.' Tassoula turned to Miranda. 'Manolis has not been happy since his father died. Kostis and he were very close.'

'How long ago was that?' Miranda asked.

'A long time ago now. Manolis was little more than a child.'

'Still, at least he had a father,' said Michael. It was an unfortunate remark. Inwardly Miranda squirmed, wishing the words could be withdrawn.

Tassoula turned sad eyes on Michael. 'I, too, would have liked it otherwise. It was not easy raising you alone, only to hand you over to the English. Some people are able to give away their children without sadness, I cannot.' Her voice was almost venomous, and Miranda sensed there was something here she did not understand.

Anxious to relieve the tension Miranda said, 'What does Manolis do? What work I mean?'

'He drives a taxi.' Tassoula raised her eyes to heaven. 'The son of a schoolmaster, the grandson of a doctor, drives a taxi! Michael would have given him all the money in the world so that he could be qualified in Athens, in London, anywhere!'

'But he would never take my money,' said Michael, 'our money,' he corrected, looking at his mother. 'My father left all his money and land to us jointly, to use as we so wished. It was as much my mother's as mine and I know my father would have liked her to use it on her other son. My mother was only twenty-two when father died, he would not have expected her to remain single, I'm sure.'

Miranda suddenly had a brainwave. 'I was widowed at twenty-one,' she said to Tassoula. 'I don't know if Michael has told you I have been married before.'

'No, he has told me nothing, except that you are a model.'

'My – my husband was killed, in a plane crash.'

Tassoula eyed her solemnly. 'Did you have children?'

'No, no children, we had only been married a few months.'

'So,' said Tassoula, briskly, standing up. 'You have known sadness, great sadness, both of you. Be sure you bring no more sadness to yourselves or any one else. I must rest now.' There were no goodbyes, no good wishes, she glided from the room leaving Miranda and Michael alone.

'She's a little intimidating, isn't she?' said Michael.

'You're not kidding. How did I do, what did she think of me?'

Michael grinned and slipped an arm round her. 'She couldn't help but think you're wonderful.'

'Smoothy!' said Miranda.

'Come on, darling, it's time I took you home, we haven't been to bed all day.'

The first days of their marriage were idyllic. Miranda had plenty to keep her occupied while Michael worked. Her furniture had arrived from England and this needed to be spread around the various rooms. Now that the Villa Dionissos was her home too, Miranda found most of the rooms rather impersonal, and she spent many happy hours shopping for fabric, cushions, and the odd piece of furniture to give the place added warmth. As Michael had his study, she decided it would be a good idea to have a room of her own, too. She had a very special affection for the spare room in which she had slept on her first night at the villa, and this she turned into a charming light, airy sitting room – very chintzy and feminine like her house in Chelsea had been. She bought a writing desk and put up many of her old pictures and ornaments. Michael loved the room.

Then there was her Greek. Determined to learn the language as quickly as possible, she employed Micos Theophillos, who came up to the villa three afternoons a week to instruct her. It was a long time since Miranda had applied herself to any form of education and she found herself to be a slow learner, but she was determined to persevere. Thea, she soon discovered, knew and understood a great deal more English than she was prepared to admit, and grudgingly helped Miranda to learn the Greek name for various fruits, vegetables and meat, so that she could do her own shopping. As far as she could tell, Thea had worked more or less, twenty-four hours a day when Michael had lived alone – and for what seemed a pittance of a wage. Miranda insisted that Thea's wages should be increased dramatically, since she was now looking after two people, and that she should stop work every day at five-thirty so that Miranda could have the kitchen to herself, to cook the evening meal – the exception being if they were entertaining.

Far from being grateful, Thea seemed to resent the change, protesting to Michael that her wages were too high and that she had nothing else to do in the evenings. Miranda was adamant, though – she and Michael did need time alone. However, she was aware that the more she ingratiated herself with Thea, the more the woman seemed to resent her.

Life was not without its problems, though. Within a week of their arrival, Miranda suggested that Michael should ask his mother, brother and sister-in-law to dinner. Tassoula accepted, but Manolis refused to come, which in itself put a dampener on the evening. Miranda spent hours preparing the meal. They began with cold soup, then roast beef and Yorkshire pudding, followed by syllabub and cheese. Tassoula appeared to enjoy the food, but conversation was stilted and difficult. No Greek was spoken, in deference to Miranda, but Michael and his mother talked of local politics for much of the time which meant nothing to Miranda. She had already noticed the Cretans' preoccupation with politics – there appeared to be nothing they liked to talk of more and she realised that at some stage she was going to have to get involved.

That evening, particularly, Miranda was very aware that the relationship between Michael and his mother was not an easy one. Michael seemed restrained, almost nervous in his mother's company, and Tassoula gave the impression of being oddly resentful of her son. Afterwards, Miranda asked Michael about it, but he was evasive. 'I suppose it's just because we have spent so many years apart – my formative years, at any rate.'

'Give me a child 'til he's seven, and I'll give you the man,' Miranda quoted.

'Maybe, but it doesn't seem to have worked with us. I think it must be the contrasts in lifestyle which have caused the problem – I mean as between Crete and England.'

'Are they so different?' Miranda asked. 'I didn't know what to expect when it came to meeting your mother. Half of me imagined that she would be living in a little one storey stone shack in the middle of an olive grove, with a goat tethered outside. OK, so she seemed very foreign to me, but her house and the way she lives is not that different from England, surely?'

'I suppose it's attitude of mind,' said Michael. 'Certainly, I found the contrasts very confusing.'

'Poor darling.' Miranda slipped her arms round his neck. 'You must have done, but not any more. So far as lifestyle is concerned, from now on we make our own – just the way we want it.'

He looked at her anxiously. 'Are you enjoying living here?'

'Yes, I am,' Miranda answered almost truthfully.

'I detected a note of reservation there. Am I right?'

'Possibly,' Miranda admitted. 'It is strange in many ways, and I suppose I'm finding it hard to adjust to the fact that I'm not very acceptable to your family.'

'Of course you're acceptable to them, darling, as you put it. They are very wary of you at the moment simply because they've never met anyone like you before – even Manolis will come round in the end – he won't be able to resist you.'

'And I suppose I've been spoilt,' Miranda said, thoughtfully. 'Certainly, in the last few years, everyone has known who I am, and I've got the VIP treatment everywhere I go. I'm shamefully used to being squired around and dreadfully pampered. Here, I'm nobody and I supposed it's inevitable that I will have to make adjustments.'

'You're a very wise lady,' Michael said, kissing her, 'but

you're wrong – you're not nobody, you're my wife.'

Miranda threw back her head and laughed. 'There we go, you see. What chance does women's lib stand on this island? How about being somebody in my own right, not just your wife?'

'Sorry,' said Michael, 'but it does stand for quite a lot on this island – the name Richardson is very much respected.'

'And I'm proud that now it's my name too,' said Miranda, gently.

The following day, Thea began adopting an unpleasant habit which, initially, Miranda thought she was imagining. Every time she addressed a remark to the old woman, Thea would turn away and appear to spit – not once, but three times. It continued for two days until Miranda could stand it no more.

'Thea, will you stop that, it's a disgusting habit,' she said. Thea put on her not-understanding face. 'I know you understand what I'm saying, I must insist that you do not spit in the house. It's revolting. What on earth is the point of us cleaning the place, if you're going to spit all over it? Please stop it.' Thea remained mute, but her eyes were rebellious. She left the room, but as Miranda peered round the door to see her go, she saw Thea spit three times as she walked down the corridor.

Over dinner that night Miranda tackled Michael about it. 'Oh dear,' he said, 'it's the Evil Eye.'

'Good grief,' said Miranda, 'what's that?'

'Just superstition, nothing to worry about.'

'What do you mean, nothing to worry about? You can't make a comment like that without explaining it.'

Michael sipped his wine, leaning back in his chair. 'The Evil Eye is rather like voodoo. It's what the Cretans visit on one another. If you have an enemy, you are supposed to think bad thoughts about him and then he will drop dead, his olive trees will die, or whatever.'

'How awful. Does it work?'

'I don't know,' said Michael. 'There are all sorts of tales, of course, to prove conclusively that it does, but I have no personal experience of it. It's why the Cretans don't ever offer much praise. I should perhaps have mentioned it to you before. For example, my mother could not have told you that you were a wonderful cook the other evening because extreme praise is thought to attract the Evil Eye.'

'And how do you keep the Evil Eye away?'

Michael smiled. 'Wear turquoise beads, keep garlic around the place . . .' he hesitated, 'or spit three times.'

'So Thea thinks the Evil Eye is being aimed at her?'

'Presumably,' said Michael. 'I'll talk to her about it tomorrow, don't worry.'

But Miranda did worry. Thea's strange behaviour seemed to crystallise the feeling of hostility that she felt surrounded her. Loving Michael, being loved by him, created a wonderful haven, but their relationship was not old enough, nor strong enough yet, to withstand too many knocks. Thea's hostility was a threat, at least it felt like it to Miranda.

The following day, Miranda had been out shopping in the morning and returned to find no lunch prepared. 'Where's Thea, where's lunch?' she asked.

'I've given her the day off and told her to go away and think things out,' said Michael. 'Come on, we'll go into Sitia.'

'Why, what happened, was it about the spitting?'

'Yes. Come on, we'll talk about it over lunch.'

They ate at the Paragadi Restaurant, right on the harbour front at Sitia. The food was surprisingly good, the view beautiful, but Miranda was in no mood to appreciate either. 'Come on,' she said, once they had ordered, 'out with it. What happened between you and Thea?'

Michael looked embarrassed. 'This is a silly situation,' he said, 'and it's all my fault. I told everyone you were a model, because it was true and because I thought that your face probably would be familiar to people, even here.' He hesitated. 'The trouble is, what I hadn't realised is that so far as the Cretans are concerned, a model is a prostitute. Thea has got it into her head that you are a bad woman, and so is protecting herself against you.'

'Oh charming,' said Miranda. 'Well, I hope you've explained that she's wrong.'

'Well, of course I have, but it's not that simple, or rather it is that simple and that's the problem. To the Cretan, a woman who parades around in front of a camera is a prostitute and that's the end of the matter.'

'Michael, that's awful, it's not fair.' Miranda bit her lip, tears coming into her eyes. She knew she was being stupid but the whole situation made her feel desperately vulnerable – the ghost of Joe Chang was forever with her, just below the surface.

Michael saw her distress but did not understand its cause. 'Hey, come on,' he said, 'it doesn't matter. Don't get upset about it. Who cares what anyone thinks.'

'I care,' said Miranda. 'It's all very well for you, you're accepted here, you're part of this island. I'm not, but if I am to spend my life here, I have to find a way of belonging. I've always been part of a community, at home in Yorkshire, of course, but also in my job – the modelling world is very small. We all know each other, the photographers, the agents, the models, even the clients. It is like a big family. I need a sense of belonging, Michael.'

'Are you saying that you and I are not enough?' His face had a dark shadowed look, but Miranda was too upset to be tactful.

'Yes, I suppose I am, put like that. Surely you don't believe that, say, two people could be washed up on a desert island and be happy alone, with each other's company, for ever?'

Michael smiled and slipping a hand under the table, ran it up the inside of Miranda's bare leg. 'I wouldn't mind being washed up on a desert island with you, my darling.'

'Michael, I'm serious.'

'And so am I. I've spent all my life searching for you, Miranda, my whole bloody life. Now I've found you, why the hell should I want to share you with anyone else? OK, so these people are going to take a little time to get used to you. Is that surprising? And why does it matter so much to you? You have me, I have you, we live in a splendid house, overlooking one of the most beautiful seas in the world. We have plenty of money, security, we have both proven to be a success in our careers. What more do you want, darling – blood?'

'You just don't understand do you?' said Miranda, angrily.

'No, I don't.' They were almost shouting and several tourists at nearby tables looked up with interest.

Miranda noticed and dropped her voice. 'Look, you've uprooted me like a plant. OK, you were careful to keep the roots intact, you even left a little soil clinging to them, in the form of my furniture and bits and pieces. But it's not enough, Michael, to now simply keep me watered. I need to be replanted.'

'Oh, don't be silly, darling, you're talking in riddles. Come on, let's get out of here, I can't bear washing our dirty linen in public like this.'

Of course, when they got back to the villa they made it up, spending the heat of the afternoon in glorious abandon on their huge double bed. But it was their first quarrel since they had been reunited and it left a scar and a slight feeling of unease between them.

The following morning, Thea served them breakfast as usual. When Miranda discussed the arrangements for lunch there was no spitting and afterwards Miranda broke the rules and interrupted Michael at his work to ask what had happened between him and Thea.

'She now understands that models are models and prostitutes are prostitutes, and that models do not attract the Evil Eye because they are good people, and therefore she is safe,' said Michael.

'But what did she actually say when you told her this?'

'Look, darling, let's drop it, this has caused enough trouble between us already. Thea now understands that you are not a bad person and that's all there is to it.'

'I'm not used to being treated like some ignorant child,' Miranda said, angrily.

'Then don't behave like one.'

The next few days passed without incident, except that Miranda had a growing feeling of unease. The heat was unbearable. How she longed for August to be over so that there was a little relief from the burning sun. Her head ached a great deal. The mosquitoes seemed to love her skin, which was now covered in unsightly bumps and lumps, and for days on end she seemed to have an upset stomach. She felt tired and listless, and suspended her Greek lessons, finding she no longer had the energy to concentrate. Now that the villa was more or less as she wanted it, there was little for her to do. Each day seemed a routine of mundane chores – the market, lunch, a siesta, preparing dinner, eating it, clearing away. . . . Michael, by contrast, seemed to be at his most creative, gloriously happy in his work, producing painting after painting. Miranda, knowing little or nothing about art, could see, nonetheless, that there was a quality about these new paintings and that, without doubt, Michael was producing some of his best work. She was proud of him, of course, but she felt excluded. In a desperate effort to keep busy, she began writing long letters home, to her parents, to the Hardcastles, even to Jake. Their replies made her homesick, their world seemed so removed from hers.

It was during the last week of August that one day Michael came home from Iraklion, having been there to buy paints. He returned mid-afternoon, having lunched in town, and instead of coming to their bedroom, where Miranda was having a siesta, he went down to the jetty and had a long swim. Miranda woke to find him towelling himself dry. 'You've been swimming?'

'What does it look like?' Michael snapped.

Miranda sat up in bed, surprised at the irritable response. She tried again. 'You should have woken me,' she said, 'I'd loved to have come with you.'

'I wanted to be alone.'

'Why, Michael? What's wrong?'

'Nothing, nothing. I'm off down to the study, I'll see you at supper.'

'No, you don't,' Miranda said, 'something is wrong. I'm not going to let you go and shut yourself away, until you tell me what it is.'

'Just leave me, could you?' Michael said. 'I'd honestly rather be alone.'

'No, I couldn't. We've agreed to share our lives, that means our troubles, too. Brooding on your own isn't going to solve anything. Come here, darling, sit down and tell me what this is all about.'

Michael sat down on the bed, slipped his arms round her and kissed her. His lips tasted of salt. Clasped close to his naked chest Miranda felt weak with love for him, but she resisted the urge to suggest they discussed the problem in bed. She disentangled herself from his arms. 'Don't sidetrack me,' she said, smiling. 'Tell me what's wrong.'

Michael let out a heavy sigh. 'Georgios Grillos is back in Crete.'

Miranda frowned, the name meant nothing to her. 'Who is he?'

'Only the boy who killed my father. He was the child sent to the German garrison to tell them of the planned ambush. It was he who betrayed my father to the Germans and killed him as surely as if he'd shot him dead himself.'

Miranda was lost for words for a moment, trying to assimilate both the tale and the passion in which it was told. 'You say back in Crete? You mean he left the island?'

'Yes, yes,' said Michael impatiently. 'His father was hanged for being a traitor and the boy, Georgios, and his mother were forced to leave the island. I knew Georgios had become a hotelier – once I nearly hung my paintings in one of his hotels, until I realised who he was. Now, he dares to come back here. With the increase in the tourist trade, it is his intention to build a big hotel outside Iraklion and another at Ayios Nikolaos.'

'It is perhaps not very tactful of him to come back to Crete,' Miranda suggested. 'There are plenty of other Greek islands he could have chosen.'

'Tactful! You speak of tact, did you not understand what I said?'

'Yes, of course I did, at least I think so. But you cannot blame a small child for what happened. Clearly, that must have been the view at the time or his father would not have been killed, and the boy set free.'

'Of course I blame him. To betray his countrymen to the Germans was unforgivable.'

'Do we know anything about the father – Georgios's father, I mean?' Miranda asked quietly.

Michael shrugged his shoulders. 'From what I have been

told, he was a brute. He was not a Cretan, he came from the mainland and married a Cretan girl. The locals never liked him, he was always drunk and abusive, but certainly he got his revenge for his unpopularity.'

'Was he the sort of man who would beat his wife and children?'

'Yes, probably.'

'Then is it small wonder that Georgios did as he was told. He was probably far more frightened of his father than of anything else on earth.'

'That's no excuse.'

'How can you say that?' said Miranda. 'You never grew up with a brutish father, beating you day and night.'

'I never grew up with a father at all, thanks to Georgios Grillos.'

'OK, OK,' said Miranda, trying to keep Michael calm. 'So you resent him coming back, I do understand that, but there's no point in getting steamed up about it.'

Michael stared at her, his eyes wild. He looked more Cretan than she had ever seen him. 'Are you mad? I'm going to stop him. There is no way that man is ever going to build a hotel on Crete – not ever.'

'But how will you stop him?'

Michael shrugged his shoulers. 'I have ways.'

'What ways?'

'Planning, I can bribe the planning people. Then the workmen, I'll make sure no one will work for him. I can stop him, I *will* stop him.'

'Michael, it all happened so long ago, over forty years. Think what these hotels would do for the island – the building of them would provide much needed labour and then once they're open, they will have to be staffed. They will attract more tourists, who in turn will patronise the local bars and tavernas.'

'And that, you think, is the most important thing. It doesn't matter that the man's a murderer, just so long as he brings plenty of money to the island. Is that what you're saying?'

'No, it's not what I'm saying. I'm saying that you can't call a terrified little boy, a murderer.'

Michael stood up, abruptly, and went to stand by the open window – apparently staring out of sea. 'Call him what you like,' he said, quietly, 'but he was responsible for my father's death, and had my father lived . . .' he hesitated, 'and had my father lived, I would have not spent so much of my life feeling so damnably alone.' The words ended in almost a whisper. The big shoulders, already hunched, began to shake and to her horror, Miranda realised that Michael, proud, defiant Michael, was crying. She jumped from the bed and ran to his side, slipping her arms round him. 'You're not alone any more, you have me.'

Michael looked down at her, making no attempt to disguise the wetness on his cheeks. His gaze searched her face hungrily. 'Have I, have I really?'

The following morning, events drove all thoughts of Georgios Grillos from Miranda's mind, for when she woke up, she was sick. The emotional upheavals of the last few months had made her periods erratic, but a quick calculation made her realise that she appeared to have missed two. Without saying a word to Michael, she went to see Hans Annis, the Dutch doctor in Sitia, to whom she had been recommended.

He examined her carefully. 'It looks to me like we have a baby coming, yes? Are you pleased, is it what you want?'

'Oh yes, it is,' said Miranda. 'How soon can you confirm it?'

'I will get the lab to test your sample this afternoon. Can I ring you later?'

'Oh, would you?'

When Michael came out, grim faced from his study that evening, he found a bottle of champagne waiting for him on the terrace, together with a plate of smoked salmon. 'Champagne, wonderful. Smoked salmon, even more wonderful, and a small miracle on Crete. Are we celebrating something?' Miranda nodded. 'What, tell me what, I can't stand the suspense.'

'Your fatherhood, my motherhood.'

For a tiny instance, a strange look flashed into Michael's eyes, then his face broke into smiles. He threw his arms round Miranda, covering her with kisses. 'I can't believe it, I can't believe it. Is it really true? Are you sure? When did you find out?'

Miranda laughed, breathless from the kisses. 'Darling, honestly, one would think you didn't know how babies were made. Considering how we go on, is it terribly surprising that I'm pregnant?'

Michael grinned, sheepishly, obviously delighted with the remark. 'No, I suppose not. When is it due?'

'The end of March, beginning of April.'

'Perfect. The best month of the year in Crete is May.'

'I-I think I'd like to go to London for the birth,' Miranda said, casually. Michael frowned. 'But don't let's talk about it now,' she added hastily. 'Tonight is for celebrating, there's plenty of time to make plans.'

Their meal was a huge success, Michael clearly beside himself with happiness. They argued amicably about names, preferences as to the sex of the baby and what it would be when it grew up. When, finally, they sank into bed and began to make love, Michael showed a new tenderness, a gentleness he had never displayed before and which Miranda found almost unbearably touching.

The next morning, while she was writing joyous letters home to her family, it suddenly occurred to her that neither of them had thought of telling Tassoula their news. She managed to contain her impatience until Michael's lunchtime break and then tackled him on the subject.

'I'll telephone her this evening,' he said.

'Why don't we both go and see her and tell her personally?'

'No, no, I'll ring her, that will do.'

'But wouldn't it be good opportunity for me to try and get to know her better. Grandmothers are always notoriously soppy about their grandchildren. Perhaps it will make her feel better disposed towards me.'

'Certainly, we'll do that some time. I'll tell her the news over the phone and then we'll go and see her at a later date.'

'But why at a later date?' Miranda persisted. 'Why not now, when we've just heard the news?'

'Miranda, let me handle my own mother my own way, please,' said Michael.

'You know, I really don't understand you sometimes,' Miranda said. 'What have you got to handle? We're simply telling her something which should be wonderful news. It's our baby, why can't we tell her together?'

'Look, I'm tired, I didn't sleep awfully well last night. Can we just drop it?' He smiled a little wanly. 'There's plenty of time for you two to get together, for baby talk.'

The thought of a cosy talk with Tassoula about babies seemed impossibly remote to Miranda, but she was wise enough not to express her views. That evening Michael confirmed that he had spoken to his mother and that she was very pleased for them both.

The days continued to hang heavy for Miranda. Michael was very preoccupied. If he was not painting, he was off on mysterious errands to Iraklion, which Miranda knew were all concerned with his vendetta against Georgios Grillos. Her morning sickness persisted, indeed it seemed to be getting worse – she suspected because of the heat. She dare not go into the sun now since it had the affect of making her eyelids swell up and her skin was altogether more sensitive to the sun than normal. She needed a woman friend desperately, someone to whom she could moan about her symptoms. Thea was quite hopeless. Having expressed surprise but no pleasure at the prospect of a baby, she now never referred to it. In desperation, Miranda plagued Michael for introductions to his friends.

'Surely,' she said, 'you can introduce me to someone who speaks a little English. What about the friends you had when you were small?'

'I no longer know the children I grew up with. I lost touch with them when I went to school in England. Since I've been back in Crete, I haven't really encouraged much social life. I had enough of parties and people in Hollywood to last me a lifetime, and my work is not the most social kind.'

'You mean you never go out to dinner with people or have friends here?'

He was defensive. 'Yes, yes, of course, occasionally.'

'Well then, introduce me to one of them, anyone.'

'So, I'm not enough for you, we're back to that again, are

we?' Once again, the need to reassure him drove the heat out of Miranda's argument. It was beginning to dawn on Miranda just how much of a recluse Michael had been before she had stumbled into his life. Whether it was, as he said, a reaction against Hollywood, or whether like her, he was an alien even in his own country, it was hard to tell. Whatever the cause, his life was an unnatural one and somehow Miranda felt she had to find a way to break out of it – for both of them.

The Georgios Grillos case was clearly building towards some sort of climax. Michael painted hardly at all during September, spending every day in meetings or furiously writing letters. When Miranda asked him what was happening, he always evaded the question. 'You don't agree with what I'm doing,' he said, 'so there's no point in my telling you about it. It will only cause arguments between us.' Once again, as with his painting, she was excluded.

Then, towards the end of September, an invitation arrived. A new exhibition of Minos paintings was to be on show in the Louvre, from the middle of October through until after Christmas. It was hoped that Michael would come and open the exhibition. Miranda was overjoyed, it was her chance to get back to the civilised world. She adored Paris, and Paris in the autumn was wonderful.

'All right,' said Michael, 'we'll do it.'

'Can we go a few days before the exhibition opens so I can buy some new clothes? Some of my current ones are rather under strain.'

'Of course, of course you can, darling. We'll spoil you dreadfully.'

'Oh Michael, I can't wait.'

All Miranda's old enthusiasm came back. They planned a two-week trip. Ten days in Paris and then a flying visit to London before coming home. 'And by the time we're back in Crete it will be really cool, and by the time the heat comes back, you'll be bouncing a baby on your knee, not having to carry it round in there.' He ran a hand gently over her belly.

The bookings were confirmed, the cases were packed. It was just two days before they were due to leave when Miranda had a show of blood. In panic, Michael summoned Dr Annis, who was quite adamant. 'If you want this baby, no trip to France. You must go to bed and not move for at least a week. Then perhaps you can have a little walk each day, but only when I've given you permission.'

'But I must go to Paris. I can't bear it, I've got no maternity clothes and I need to get away.' Miranda's voice sounded desperate, even to herself.

'OK go, but expect to lose your baby, because assuredly, you will.'

There was clearly no decision. After the doctor had gone, Miranda lay in bed and wept while Michael sat helplessly beside her. 'I'll have to go, darling. They'll have printed all the brochures by now saying I'm coming, and my agent will have arranged interviews and television appearances.'

'Oh I know, I know,' Miranda said, bitterly.

'I needn't be away for very long, nothing like as long as we were planning to be. I'll ring my agent right away and tell him what's happened. I'd like to see you back on your feet before I go, and then I'll be away for just four or five days at the most.'

While Miranda was confined to bed, Michael made an enormous fuss of her, but she felt listless and depressed. The air conditioning worked valiantly, but it could not combat the overwhelming heat which persisted this year even into October. Against doctor's orders, she took three or four showers a day, but she still seemed unable to keep cool. When Hans Annis returned to see her, the news was not encouraging – her blood pressure was far too high. 'You'll have to stay in bed, at least for another week,' Doctor Annis insisted.

'But I can't,' said Miranda, 'Michael's going to be away. Stuck here on my own in bed all day, I'll go mad.'

'I'll let you go as far as the terrace, provided once you're there, you stay put. Do we have a deal?'

'Oh yes, that would be wonderful,' said Miranda, feeling like a prisoner suddenly, unexpectedly, released. At least from the terrace she could watch the fishing boats and the ever-changing colour and texture of the sea.

On the morning of Michael's departure, she saw him off cheerfully, not wanting him to take the image with him of her miserable and depressed. After he had gone, Thea sullenly cleared away the breakfast things, answering in monosyllables Miranda's desperate attempts at conversation. After she had shuffled away to the kitchen and Miranda was left alone, she lay back on her sunbed and gazed out to sea. In the early morning mist, the opposite coast, where she knew Ayios Nikolaos lay, was completely obscured. It looked as though the sea went on for ever. The air was very still and heavy, there was no sound at all – she had never felt so alone in her whole life.

Chapter Seventeen

'Could I speak to Mrs Vosaakis, please,' Miranda said, slowly and carefully, to make sure she was understood.

'You wait,' said a voice which Miranda recognised as Nickos.

'Hello?' Tassoula's voice, even in the briefest of greetings, sounded wary.

'Hello, it's Miranda. I was ringing to see whether you would like to come and have lunch with me. Michael's away at the moment, in Paris, and I've had a bit of a scare with the baby, so I'm not allowed to go out.'

'Baby, what baby?'

Miranda could not believe her ears. 'The baby I'm expecting. Michael rang and told you about it.'

'He did not,' said Tassoula, emphatically.

'But he must have done, he said he had spoken to you and you were pleased.'

'I know of no baby.' She was quite adamant.

'But what possible reason could he have for not telling you, and for pretending to me that he had?'

'He had his reasons no doubt,' said Tassoula.

'But what could they be?'

'You'd better ask him.'

Despite Tassoula's unfriendly manner, Miranda tried to pull herself together. 'Anyway, now that you do know, would you like to come to lunch with me and celebrate?'

'No,' said Tassoula. 'Not while there is this – this misunderstanding. When Michael returns, ring me and then perhaps something can be arranged.'

All pride had left Miranda now. 'But it's while he's away

that I need some company,' she said. 'I'm awfully lonely here.'

'You should have thought of that before you came to Crete.' Tassoula's voice was hard and uncompromising. 'Crete is a quiet place, it is not London or New York. Here we still enjoy our own company.'

Even despite the rebuff, it was all Miranda could do not to beg her to come. She wanted to say, I'm frightened of losing my baby, frightened of being here without a friend, please help me. But pride, at last, took the upper hand. 'I'll ring you when Michael returns, as you suggest,' she said, coolly and replaced the receiver without saying goodbye.

Her mind was in a turmoil. Why had Michael not told his mother about the baby, and why had he lied to her and said that he had? It did not make any sense. They were legally married, in love, strong and healthy – it was the most natural thing in the world to have children. Surely any normal woman would have been pleased for them. So why the secrecy and deceit? As well as feeling confused, she felt terribly hurt. As far as she was aware, she had withheld nothing of herself from Michael, and certainly she had never lied to him. The hostility she felt generating from Michael's family, and from Thea, now seemed to have stretched its tentacles to include Michael as well – as though he too, was caught up in some kind of conspiracy. The more she thought about it, the more black her depression became. She was tempted to telephone Michael in Paris, yet it hardly seemed a subject they could discuss over the phone. Instead, she would have to wait patiently until his return.

For three days she lay alone on the terrace by day, and in bed by night. She slept badly, and when she did sleep, she was constantly beset by wild, confused dreams. She tried to make constructive plans. With Michael's blessing, she decided, she would ask her sister Ann and family over for Christmas. Recognising it was quite possible she would not be allowed to travel until after the baby was born, she would send for all the relevant mail order catalogues and then place orders for babyware and equipment which her sister could organise for her. Then, once she was a little better, she would find a local dressmaker and have some maternity dresses made. Then, there was the baby's room to be selected and decorated. There was so much to do, if she could just summon up enough energy and enthusiasm to start work. But at the back of her mind, all the time, was Michael's deception. She felt paralysed, unable to concentrate her mind on anything until she had found out why he had behaved as he had.

It was during the morning of the day before Michael's return that Thea appeared suddenly on the terrace and told her that there was a man to see her.

'What man?' Miranda asked. Thea looked blank. 'Ask him to come and see me on the terrace, and bring some wine and two glasses.' She was so desperate for company, she did not mind if it was the plumber, she was determined to delay him in talk.

The man who walked out on to the terrace was small and spare. He arrived with great speed, but despite his obvious agility, his grey receding hair suggested to Miranda that he was at least fifty. He dressed with more style and taste than anyone Miranda had so far seen on the island – in white trousers, a lightweight blazer and a crisp shirt and tie. He was clearly Greek by appearance and a successful one at that. 'Mrs Richardson? How do you do?'

'How do you do,' said Miranda, holding out her hand. 'Forgive me for not getting up but I am under doctor's orders to stay where I am for a few weeks.'

'That's all right.' His accent was American 'You stay right there – I'm sorry to intrude, only I wanted to see your husband.'

'I'm afraid he's in Paris,' said Miranda, 'but perhaps I can help.' At that moment Thea appeared with the wine, dumped it on the table and departed. 'In any event,' Miranda said, 'please have a glass of wine with me, I could do with company.'

The man met Miranda's eyes squarely. His gaze was hypnotic and she found she simply could not look away. 'I don't know how you'll feel about offering me that glass of wine when I tell you who I am.'

'Try me,' said Miranda, surprised.

'Georgios Grillos.'

There was a long silence between them, and at last it was

Miranda who spoke. 'After a shock like that, I think you'd better pour us both a glass of wine, don't you?'

Georgios grinned, a great smile that almost split his face in two. 'That's very generous of you, Mrs Richardson, I appreciate it.' He carefully poured out two glasses and handed one to her.

'Please sit down,' said Miranda. 'Presumably you wanted to talk to my husband about your hotels.'

Georgios sipped his wine. 'There'll be no hotels, Mrs Richardson, that's what I wanted to tell your husband – that he'd won. I've quit. He's stitched up Planning and I can't find a single Cretan builder who will work for me. He's done a great job, depending on whose side you're on.'

'I-I don't know what to say,' said Miranda.

'Don't say anything,' Georgios said. 'You cannot commiserate with me and be loyal to your husband. I knew I was taking a risk in trying to come back here, but it's my home, see. I may sound like an American, think like an American, do business like an American, but I sure as hell don't look like one.'

Miranda laughed. 'No, you don't.'

'I'm Cretan. I love this island and I hadn't realised how much until I came back. I thought the hotels would be a good thing for the people and would provide me with an excuse to visit now and again.'

Miranda, still hurt from Michael's deception, allowed herself a moment's disloyalty. 'Forgetting the ethics for a moment,' she said, 'I agree with you about the need for good hotels. The average Cretan is brilliant at running a little taverna, a gift shop, or a bar, but a hotel needs so much organisation. While some might say that your hotels would spoil the island, it's certainly big enough to absorb them. And then there's the work they would bring – if all the young people are to be stopped from leaving Crete in order to go in search of jobs, work needs to be provided for them. I know all about that. I come from Yorkshire, in England. There, exactly the same thing happens – the one idea the young people have when they grow up is to move away, because there is no work for them.'

'Precisely,' said Georgios. 'You are a woman after my own heart. Still, there is nothing to be done, I cannot waste any more time or money here. I'm catching a plane back to the States tonight.'

'Tell me,' said Miranda, 'I'm fascinated. How did you become so successful? You must have had a very difficult start.'

'Hard work,' said Georgios. 'My mother was never well, not after what had happened, so I learnt about hard work early. I did everything – shoeshine boy, paper round, the works. Then when I was old enough, I borrowed some money and opened a little taverna, not amongst the Greek community like everyone else was doing, but in Greenwich Village. Do you know New York?'

'Yes, I do,' said Miranda.

'Well, with all those students and artists, I guessed it was a natural place to have a Greek restaurant, where they could eat and drink themselves silly, for just a few dollars.'

'And did it work?'

'Oh, yes. Soon I had a chain of restaurants and then I sold them out to a hotel group in return for a seat on the Board and a stake in the group. From there, I learnt about being a hotelier. Once I had learnt everything I could, I resigned, sold my shares and with the capital started my own group, Omega Hotels.'

Miranda laughed. 'You make it sound easy.' She could not help but warm to the man.

'Sure as hell, it wasn't easy and I had some luck – though, boy, after the start I had, I reckon I earned that luck.'

'It's odd, but it's just occurred to me,' said Miranda, 'that the incident that drove you out of Crete deprived both you and Michael of your fathers.'

'Yeh, that's true, though I don't think your husband quite sees it that way.'

'No,' said Miranda, 'but you can hardly blame him for that.'

'No, I don't blame him for how he feels, but I think he's wrong to carry on with this bitterness in his heart. It does him no good. I'm not bitter about what he had done to me in the last few weeks. There is no point – what's done is done. He should not have let his bitterness against me fester all these years. The person who suffers most is himself. Here, let me charge your glass.'

'Thank you,' said Miranda.

They talked then, generally, of Crete and Cretan ways. Despite Georgios' long absence from the island – or perhaps because of it – he was very well informed. In fact, he was far more forthcoming than Michael ever was, on talking of customs, history, politics – anything that Miranda wanted to know. The contents of the wine bottle sunk, their conversation was informative and enjoyable . . .

So it was only a natural extension of everything they had been saying for Miranda to ask, 'Tell me, why is it that Michael's family are so against me? I suspect it's not just his family but the community as a whole. I don't think I'm being paranoid – Thea, our housekeeper, clearly loathes me and the local shopkeepers are never friendly. What can I have done to offend them? Is it just because I'm foreign?'

'No, no, it is not that,' Georgios replied, quickly. 'It is because you have rejected Michael's child.'

The words hung in the air between them. 'What did you say?' Miranda asked, faintly.

Georgios set down the glass and looked at her strangely. He said the words again, slowly. 'Because you have rejected Michael's child.'

'I don't know what you're talking about,' said Miranda.

Georgios was about to scoff, and then looking into her face again, he saw that she was in earnest. 'You mean . . . you didn't know?' Miranda shook her head, unable to speak. 'Hell, I guess it shouldn't have been me who told you,' said Georgios, but despite his words, he had a sense of elation.

'T-tell me about it,' Miranda managed, in a small voice.

'OK. You know Michael was married before, to an American, an actress, I can't remember her name.'

'Suzy Shelley,' said Miranda.

'Yeh, if you say so. From what I understand, the marriage between her and Michael was rather stormy. They had a row and he came back to Crete, and she followed him a few months later to have their baby. It was born here, at the Villa, I think.'

Miranda's eyes were round with shock. 'Then what happened?'

'The wife, she took off again, without the baby and Michael had it sent to a foster mother on the other side of the island, near Khania. Then the wife died and Michael, he stays on here alone.'

'What happened to the baby?'

'The baby is still in Khania, as far as I know. What the local people can't understand – at least this is the gossip I've heard – is why, now he's married, he hasn't brought the child here to live. They think it must be your fault – that you do not want another woman's child.'

'I can't believe this. I don't believe it.' Miranda shook her head, as if to reject his words.

'Hell, look I'm sorry, I didn't mean to upset you. I guess I thought you knew.'

'No, I didn't know,' said Miranda. 'So-so how old is the child now?'

'I don't know, five, six may be.'

'It's incredible.' Miranda put her head in her hands, pressing the tears back into her eyes, determined not to make an exhibition of herself in front of Georgios. 'Do you know whether it's a girl or a boy, or what is its name?'

'No,' said Georgios, standing up. 'I don't know any of the details.' He was impatient now to go. He did not want to stay here and witness this woman's scene. 'Look, Mrs Richardson, I'll leave you now. I'm real sorry to have upset you, but thank you for your hospitality. You'll tell your husband I'm leaving the island, will you?'

Miranda nodded. 'Can you see yourself out?' she asked.

'Yeh, of course. Don't you worry now – everything will turn out OK.'

The moment he had left the terrace, Miranda burst into tears. Another secret, this time an enormous deception. What else was there to find out, what else had Michael kept from her? She felt as though in just four days, he had become a complete stranger to her. How could he not have told her he had a child, and more important, why had he kept the truth from her?

Georgios Grillos left the Villa in high spirits. He had known Michael was away. Had he been at home, Georgios was sure he would not have been admitted. He had wanted to meet the wife, to talk to her, to see if she let slip any piece of information, any weakness which Georgios could use later against her husband. Georgios had suffered highly damaging publicity when Michael in his blind rage, had torn down his paintings from the foyer of the Omega Hotel in Los Angeles. Now he had suffered again at Michael's hands – this time far more seriously. It had been his heart's desire, to come back to Crete, but Michael Richardson had thwarted him.

Georgios had intended the meeting with Miranda to be only an information gathering exercise. Instead, it had worked out better than he could possibly have dreamed. Not only had he found the chink in Michael Richardson's armour, he had struck a fatal blow. The wife had been unhappy clearly and dissatisfied when he had arrived, or she would not have been so eager to talk to him – and now she knew about the child. Georgios did not give the marriage more than a few months.

By the time Michael was due to arrive back from Paris the following evening, Miranda had worked herself into a passion of rage. He had rung from Iraklion to say the plane had landed safely and he was on his way home. He sounded relaxed and happy, and Miranda managed to answer his questions with platitudes, without bursting into a hail of accusations. Because she still could not move around a great deal, it was agreed that Thea should cook dinner for them and then leave it for Miranda to serve. Michael arrived in a great flurry, with endless packages. He flung his arms round Miranda, kissing her with prolonged passion, seeming not to notice her lack of response, and then piled high their bed with parcels he had bought in Paris.

'Open them, please open them,' said Michael, like a child at Christmas. 'I've bought you millions of clothes. I hope you like them, I hope they fit, I'm terrified.'

'Let's look at them later,' said Miranda. 'Thea has dinner ready now.'

Michael looked crestfallen. 'Can't dinner wait?'

'No.'

'Is something wrong?'

'Yes,' said Miranda, 'but let's go to dinner, we can talk later.'

'Damn dinner. What's wrong?' Michael had her by the arm. 'What's happened? The baby, is the baby all right?'

'Oh yes, the baby's all right, but then I wouldn't expect you to be too concerned, bearing in mind what an expert you must be on the subject of babies.'

'What do you mean?' said Michael, but his expression betrayed him. He already knew what was coming.

'Why didn't you tell me you already had a child, and why is it living at the other side of the island, instead of with you? Why did you not tell your mother that I was expecting a baby? You have lied to me, over and over again – why Michael, for Christ's sake, why?'

Michael's grip on her arm tightened. 'Who told you?' he demanded.

'Does it matter who told me? What I want to know is why *you* didn't tell me. Can you imagine how much it has hurt, knowing you have kept so much from me?'

'Just calm down,' said Michael. 'Arrangements have already been made to have the child adopted. An English couple want her and once the documentation is through, she can go to them. It should only be a matter of a few weeks.'

'You're giving her away, you're giving your child away?' Miranda's surprise and horror were such that the anger drained from her.

'No, I'm not, I'm not,' said Michael. 'The child isn't mine. It's Suzy's yes, but not mine.' It was as though the words had been wrung out of him.

Miranda sat down on the bed. 'I think you'd better tell me the whole story, don't you?'

Michael, too, sat down on a chair, by the window. He hunched forward, his head averted so that Miranda could not see his face. 'I told you our marriage, Suzy's and mine, did not work out, that we were parted before she died.'

'Yes,' said Miranda.

'It – it wasn't quite as simple as that. While we were still living together in LA, I followed her one day, to a flat Downtown, and found her involved in a sort of orgy. There were several couples all fooling around with each other on the bed and they were into drugs of some sort, I don't know what. Anyway, I couldn't bear it. I left her, came to Crete, and started to build this house. When I went back to LA, she seemed to be a reformed character and we tried living together again. After a while, as I've told you, I even brought her here, but she hated it. She couldn't bear the solitude, she said.'

'It's hardly surprising,' Miranda could not contain herself – the story was starting to sound so familiar. 'How old was she at the time?'

Michael thought. 'Twenty, twenty-one perhaps.'

'This certainly isn't a suitable life for a twenty-year-old, twelve months of the year.' Miranda's voice was edged with bitterness.

'Do you want me to tell you the story or are you just simply trying to score points?'

'Go on,' said Miranda.

'Anyway, she left me and went back to LA. Frankly I assumed that would be the last I'd see of her. I let her have my beach house and gave her an allowance. Then, I wrote and suggested we divorced – there seemed little point in doing anything else.' He sat up and leaned back in his chair, the hooded eyes devoid of expression. 'Then, almost precisely nine months later, she turned up on my doorstep, heavily pregnant. She literally arrived in a taxi, complete with suitcase. I had written to her about money matters in the months we had been parted, but she had never mentioned the baby. The story, of course, was that it was mine, but the dates didn't stack up. We had not made love for several weeks before she left Crete – we were not on good terms by then. Her story was that I'd got drunk one night, and that I'd made love to her, just before she returned to the States. She also claimed that the baby was late, but I don't believe her, I think she had been expecting the father of the child, whoever he was, to stand by her. When it came to the crunch, he wouldn't and so she came back to me and tried to pin fatherhood on me.'

'Is that what you genuinely believe, or is it what you want to think?' Miranda asked.

'It's what I believe.' Michael stood up and began striding the length of the room, his face like thunder.

'So what happened then?' Miranda asked.

'Suzy made it quite clear, after the birth, that she did not want the child – a girl. I told her I didn't either because it wasn't mine. We argued a great deal. She was in hospital at Iraklion and eventually, the doctors sent me away because they said I was upsetting her and she needed her rest. Typical medical profession – they did not understand the problem.'

'Why, what happened?' Miranda asked.

'No sooner were our backs turned and she was gone. She discharged herself from hospital, went to the airport and was away.'

'Leaving the baby?'

'Leaving the baby. So, I had to do something about her. I found a woman at Khania, who was widowed, and her children all grown up. She speaks English as well as Greek, so hopefully she is teaching the child both languages.

'Don't you know?' said Miranda, appalled. 'Haven't you ever been to see her?'

'No, I've never seen her,' said Michael, defensively.

'Do you even know her name?'

'Yes, of course, I had her christened. Her name is Katarina, and I gave her her mother's maiden name, Shelley. Her name is Katarina Shelley.'

'And how old is she exactly?'

'She is five, nearly six.'

'Is she fair or dark?'

Michael stopped his pacing and looked at Miranda impatiently. 'Why?'

'I'm just asking.'

'She's fair, I believe. Her foster mother used to send me photographs until I asked her to stop.'

'Yet you told me Suzy was very dark. Does that not perhaps suggest that Katarina's father is fair?'

'I suppose so.'

'So, in that respect at least, you could be her father,' Miranda said.

'I could not. I've told you, I could not. I know just the kind of man her father is, one of those deviates, one of those depraved, drug-sodden dregs of humanity Suzy used to hang around with. I am supporting the child financially, which in the circumstances is generous. I can't be expected to do more.'

Through a jumble of confused emotions, a thought suddenly struck Miranda. 'But I was told that the reason your mother and everyone is so against me is because I've rejected your child, your child, Michael. Have you told them that Katarina is not yours?'

'I was told, I was told,' Michael mimicked. 'Who told you these things, where did you get this information? It's about time you answered some questions.'

'I'm answering no questions,' said Miranda, 'until I have the truth. You've lied to me about this all the way down the line, Michael. I need every stone unturned, every detail explained. You owe me that much.'

'All right,' said Michael. 'Yes, I did allow my family, and indeed, everyone else to assume the child was mine.'

'Why did you do that if you were so certain she was not?'

'Must you persist with these questions?'

'Yes, I must.'

'OK, have your pound of flesh, revel in my folly if that's what you wish – because I was ashamed.'

'Ashamed?' echoed Miranda.

'Yes, ashamed. In Crete being cuckolded, having one's wife make love to another man, is a terrible disgrace and a reflection on one's manhood. Not so long ago, certainly less than fifty years ago, a woman who was unfaithful to her husband would be stoned to death, or at the very least turned out of her village and her children taken away from her. Things are less barbaric these days but the attitude remains. I was ashamed to admit to my family that the child was not mine, yet nor could I bear to have her with me. My work means I need solitude, it also requires me to travel a great deal. It has been easy to explain away a foster mother.'

'But did they not think it odd that Suzy had left the baby?'

'I told them that she had gone back to America to sell the house and tidy up our affairs. Then she died, so there were no more questions.'

'But the fact that you never see the child, that she lives so far away . . . how do you justify that?'

'I've simply told the family that it was better for her to have a simple life with her foster mother, while mine was so unconventional.'

'. . . . But that one day you hoped you would settle down and then you could have the child to live with you.' Miranda finished for him. 'Is that right?'

'Something like that.'

'Which is why I've been the butt of all this anger. Good God, Michael, they must think I'm such a bitch. Yet I'd have loved any child of yours. Regardless of the circumstances, I'd have loved her like my own.'

'But she's not my child,' Michael thundered back.

'But she could be,' said Miranda, 'even you have to admit that, and even if she isn't, what right have you to condemn a little American girl to living the life of a Cretan peasant, not knowing who her mother or father are.'

'Without me, she'd have ended up an orphanage,' Michael said.

'And probably better for it. She'd have been adopted whilst still a tiny baby and would have a proper mother and father now, and a true feeling of identity, instead of this half life you've wished upon her.'

'I, too, realise it would be better for her to be adopted,' Michael said coldly. 'As soon as you and I met, as soon as I realised we had a future together, I also realised I needed to regularise the position with regard to Katarina. As I mentioned when we began this unfortunate conversation, I have found an English family who wish to adopt her. It is just a matter of paperwork.'

'You speak of her as though she's a commodity, not a living little girl with feelings. How carefully have you vetted this family?'

'They are friends of friends. They will look after her well.'

'But are they the right people? Is it sensible to uproot her at her age?'

'I had to do it at only a year older than she is now,' Michael said.

'Fine. So does that make it right? You're the first to say that it was the most traumatic experience of your life. You, of all people, should be wary of taking such a step on behalf of the child.'

'It is my decision and I have made it,' said Michael, 'and now I would like a few answers. Who told you this story?'

Miranda's greatest desire at that moment was to hurt him. Their eyes met, angry, devoid of love. 'Georgios Grillos.'

Michael visibly blanched. 'What!'

'You heard,' said Miranda.

'How did you meet him? The doctor told you not to leave here, not to go anywhere.'

'He came here to see you, to tell you that you have won and that he was leaving the island. We got talking.'

'You invited him into this house?'

'He was already in the house before I knew who he was, and I have to say, Michael, he's a pleasant, likeable man.'

'You can say that about the man who killed my father. What sort of woman are you?'

'A woman who has loved you very much and who now feels horribly betrayed,' Miranda answered.

Michael ignored her. 'So, Grillos has caused this trouble between us. Not content with what he did to my father, he now tries to meddle in my marriage.'

'It was nothing like that,' said Miranda. 'We got talking about Crete, and its people, and I asked him why I was so unpopular, and what I could do to make myself more acceptable to your family.'

'You asked such a question of that man?'

'It's a question I've asked you often enough,' Miranda bit back, 'and you would never tell me because you couldn't, because, as I now know, you knew the reason. As it turned out so did Georgios. He was not meddling, he was simply answering my questions.'

'So now, I suppose he knows that I had not told you of the child?'

'I could not disguise my shock.'

'Wonderful,' said Michael, 'so, doubtless, he will have told everyone.'

'Probably yes, and why not, since it's the truth. You're so eaten up with your own pride, your own self image Michael, it has never occurred to you to look at things from my point of view. How do you think I've felt in the last weeks and months – rejected by your family, not a friend in the world and not understanding why. I know I've lead a spoilt life, I know I'm used to being complimented and admired, but no woman could stick this. Frankly, I'm not surprised Suzy left you.'

He hit her. A vicious blow across the cheek which sent her falling backwards onto the bed. The moment he did it, he was on his knees beside her. 'Oh darling, I'm sorry, I'm so sorry. I didn't mean it, I really didn't mean to do it. Are you all right? It's just you shouldn't have said that.'

Miranda dazed, more from shock than from the blow, struggled into a sitting position. She pushed him away and stood up. 'So that, I take it, is the real Michael Richardson,' she said, her eyes blazing. 'The man who drives a young girl to drugs, the man who rejects a child who could well be his own, the man who hits his pregnant wife. . . . If that's the man I've married, I want no more of him.' She turned and ran from the room, tears streaming from her eyes. She stumbled into the passage and anxious just to get away, she ran through the garden door and started down the steps towards the beach. She was trembling with shock, weak from having been in bed for so long, and blinded by her own tears. It was small wonder, therefore, that she stumbled. As she fell, she heard a thin, high scream, which seemed to come from someone other than herself. She hit the ground with a thud which winded her, so that she had to fight for breath. As she lay in the darkness, panting, the pain began – searing pains which seemed to be ripping her belly in two. Just before she lost consciousness, she felt a warm wetness trickling between her legs.

Chapter Eighteen

The darkness parted, like a curtain, but the light that filtered through was indistinct and moving shapes swam before her eyes. Sounds reached her consciousness but she could not identify them. Suddenly, a face loomed over her, the features were blurred – she blinked, they cleared a little. 'She's coming round,' said a female voice she did not recognise. She blinked again and found herself staring into the face of Hans Annis. 'Mrs Richardson. Can you hear me?'

'Yes,' she said.

'You had a nasty fall, my dear, but you're all right, nothing broken.'

Miranda smiled weakly, more to please the doctor than anything. Clearly he was anxious that she should feel happy about things. 'Good,' she said. The effort of speaking was great. The frown of concentration cleared from her brow and she was beginning to slip into the darkness again, when a terrible thought struck her. Her eyes snapped open. 'The baby. What about the baby?'

'You lost the baby, I'm afraid, my dear.'

'I what?' She had heard the words the first time, but she needed them to be repeated.

'Don't worry, you go back to sleep now.'

'I what?' she insisted, making agitated movements with her hands. Someone caught her hands and held them tight.

'You lost the baby, but it was probably for the best. You would have had difficulty keeping this one anyway. There'll be others.'

'I don't want others, I want this one.'

'Sleep, my dear, you'll feel better if you do.'

'I want this one,' Miranda said, weakly, 'this one.' She fel a tear escape from the corner of her eye. She wanted to brush it away, but the effort of moving her arm seemed too great Exhaustion won the battle, and, mercifully, she slipped into sleep.

When she next woke, it was apparently night time. She realised she was in one of the guest rooms on the ground floor of the Villa. It must have been where they had carried her after the fall, she supposed, but she could remember nothing. There were two people in the room who gradually materialised into Michael and a nurse. The nurse washed her face and smoothed her pillows. She was Greek but she appeared to speak good English. Michael smiled at her but otherwise watched anxiously in silent attendance. Miranda knew she should feel angry with him, very angry, but she could not remember why. It stopped her smiling back, though. It was all so confusing, the easiest thing was to sleep.

The next morning, however, memory was restored to her, with horrifying clarity. While the nurse helped her into the bathroom and back again, she chatted ceaselessly, but Miranda heard nothing of what she said – she was reliving, moment by moment, the happenings of the previous evening.

'Please answer the question if you can, Mrs Richardson.' The voice broke through into her consciousness.

'I'm sorry,' she said, leaning back on the pillows. 'What did you say?'

'I'm going to fetch you a little breakfast now, what would you like?'

'Nothing.'

'You must try something. The doctor said it was very important for you to eat, you need to build up your strength. You suffered a little concussion, you know, so it will take you a while to feel better.'

'Bring me anything then, I don't mind, whatever you like.'

'And I'll fetch your husband, too.'

'No,' said Miranda vehemently, 'no, I don't want to see him. Please don't let him in here.'

'Very well, Mrs Richardson, if that's what you want,' said the nurse, her eyes reproving.

Miranda refused to see Michael for two days, while she vainly tried to sort out her feelings. The problem was she was so tired, her head ached dreadfully and nothing really seemed important any more, now that she had lost her baby. How she had wanted the baby, she realised. Hans Annis visited her twice a day and repeatedly reassured her that there was no problem, that there would be other children.

'Was it a boy or a girl?' she asked on the second day.

'It was a boy,' the doctor told her gently.

Her son, denied the chance of life. Never to laugh, to play in the sunshine, to grow to be a man. When she was not asleep, she cried most of the time, but still she flatly refused to see Michael.

On the third day, she felt stronger and with the regaining of her strength, came the realisation that she could no longer live in a state of limbo. There were decisions to be made, what decisions she did not know, but in any event, it seemed sensible to see Michael.

The nurse was ecstatic at her request, and within seconds, Michael was propelled into the room. He looked dreadful, unshaven, with dark circles under his eyes. He smelt heavily of whisky. Miranda could do nothing but speak her mind. 'You look awful,' she said.

'Sorry.' He ran a hand round his chin. 'I was going to shave this morning, only when Nurse said you would see me, I didn't want to delay an instant in case you changed your mind. How are you feeling?'

'Much as I imagine all women feel when they lose their baby. It-it was a boy.'

'I know,' said Michael. 'Hans told me. You realise what this means, don't you? It means that Georgios Grillos not only killed my father, he has also killed my son.'

Miranda let out a weary sigh. 'Don't be ridiculous, Michael, he didn't kill your son. I fell, and in any event, Dr Annis had serious doubts as to whether the baby would have gone full term.'

'That may be what he told you, but I don't believe it. Georgios Grillos killed my son – history has repeated itself, I just can't believe it.'

'Our son,' Miranda corrected. 'He was our son, remember?'

'Our son, my son, your son. What does it matter how we describe him. He's dead. If that man walked into the room now, I'd kill him, I swear it, I'd kill him. I ought to go to America and find him. If I was any sort of man, I'd do that.'

'And that would put things right, would it?' said Miranda, her voice heavy with sarcasm.

'No, it would not put things right, but it's what he deserves, and I could live with myself then.'

Miranda stared at her husband, as if seeing him for the first time. There was no warmth, no loving gestures to help her through her grief, and certainly no acknowledgement that he had been partly responsible for the miscarriage. If he had not hit her, she would not have run from the room like that. So eaten up was he with rage and revenge that he could not even see the situation as it was. If anyone was responsible for the baby's death, Miranda thought, it was Michael. It was Michael's deceipt that had caused the row, Michael hitting her that had driven her from the room. At that moment she hated him. 'That's as may be, but I do not think I can live with you at all.'

'What?'

'Do you realise that since you've come into this room, you have not even acknowledged the fact that I, too, might be upset about the baby's death, that I might be grieving quite as much as you? Just think what I've been through in the last few days – the appalling shock at finding you already had a child, then that terrible row when you hit me, then the physical trauma as well as the mental anguish of losing the baby. Yet all you can talk about is revenge. You're so cold, you seem to be able to think of no one else's feelings but your own. What has made you how you are, when you, of all men, have so much to give?'

'So, now you lecture me. Hans told me I must be gentle with you, humour you, but I don't think I can stand here while you assassinate my character and tear me limb from limb. I am what I am, I can be no different. If you don't like it then I'm sorry, very sorry, but there is nothing I can do to change.'

'Then I think you'd better leave me alone,' said Miranda,

for staying in this room, you can do me nothing but harm.'

There were no tears after he had gone. She felt clear headed and calm. She called the nurse, asked for a pot of coffee and then requested to be left alone. She sat quietly in bed, sipping her coffee and thinking of all she knew about this man who had been her husband for just a few short months. The more she went over the events, the more she thought about their life together, the more certain she became that she and Michael had no future. She did not rush over the decision, it was too important for them both. She thought about it carefully all day and during most of a long night. The following morning, despite her lack of sleep, she did not feel tired, and with the doctor's permission she got up and pottered around the house. Thea was unusually attentive, and almost vocal. Miranda wondered whether it was because she had lost the baby, or because rumours had filtered back to Thea that she had not known of Michael's other child. Either way, it was a relief to feel that the hostility had gone.

Now it was October, the weather had suddenly become cooler, indeed the evenings were quite chilly. The release from the heat gave Miranda a surprising degree of vigour. She had forgotten what an energetic person she used to be, and this fact alone tended to harden her resolve. There was no evidence of Michael and Thea confirmed that he was incarcerated in his study. She was glad, she was not ready to face him yet.

Finally, her mind was made up. It was early evening when she knocked on the door of the study and entered. Michael had lit the fire, the room exuded warmth and comfort, the flickering light from the fireplace casting shadows around the walls. For a moment, Miranda faltered. She imagined cosy evenings round the fire, during the Cretan winter that lay ahead – they had been so much in love, surely. . . . Then she looked at Michael. He was shaved and neatly dressed. Though pale, he seemed sober, the anger apparently having left him. However, when he spoke, his voice was steely. 'I suppose you've come to tell me you're leaving.'

He had thrown down the gauntlet and she could not help but pick it up.

'Yes, that's right.'

His voice, his expression, betrayed no emotion. 'I imagined that would be the case. Decide which flight you want, and I'll arrange it for you. I assume you're going to London.'

'Yes,' said Miranda, 'I thought I'd go the day after tomorrow.'

'Yes, it would be sensible to have another day's rest. Thea will help you with your packing, of course.'

'I shan't want the furniture,' Miranda heard herself say. It sounded as though they were discussing a shopping list, not the break-up of their marriage.

'As you wish. It can stay here, I'll look after it, you can always send for it if you want it. I assume you want a divorce.'

'That's up to you,' said Miranda, 'after this, I can't see myself running the risk of ever marrying again, and needless to say, I don't expect you to be responsible for me in any way. I have the money from my house – I can buy another – and, of course, the ability to earn my own living.'

'It isn't necessary to be so independent, I have no shortage of money, as you know.'

'It is necessary to be so independent – for me.'

'Well, you can always change your mind,' said Michael.

She felt that there was something else which should be said, but she could think of nothing. Part of her wanted to run from the room, to escape from him at all costs. Yet part of her wanted him to beg her to stay, to tell her he loved her, to take her in his arms again. The whole situation seemed unreal, yet they appeared to be locked into it, with no possible means of escape. They stood like strangers. There was only ten foot of floor between them but it could have been a thousand miles for all their ability to communicate. They stood tense, eyeing one another uncertainly.

'The clothes I've brought you back from Paris,' Michael said, 'please take them.'

'No,' said Miranda, 'I don't need them now I'm no longer pregnant. Perhaps you could give them to your sister-in-law.' He said nothing. 'I'd better go and get organised,' said Miranda. 'I'll see you before you go.' He turned from her, as if dismissing her from his presence. Without hesitation, she left as quietly as she had arrived, except now she was more determined, more resolved.

That night she sat down and wrote three letters, one to her mother, one to the Hardcastles, and one to Tassoula. In the letters to her mother and the Hardcastles she was very brief. She told them simply that her marriage was over, that she had lost the baby she was carrying, and that therefore she was returning home. She added that the details of the experience were painful and so on her return, she did not wish to discuss them. She would be taking up the threads of her old life and as soon as she had found a flat and could give them an address, she would do so. The letter to Tassoula took her longer. She told her that she was leaving Michael, and of her miscarriage. Bearing in mind that Michael was her son, she said nothing derogatory about him – simply that their relationship had broken down and that there was no hope of getting together again. She finished by saying – '*I loved your son very much and I'm only sorry that due to the circumstances, and the misunderstandings between us, you and I did not have a chance to get to know one another. All good wishes for the future to you both. Miranda.*'

The following day passed in a flurry of activity. Thea was a tower of strength, not letting Miranda lift a finger. Her eyes were very red and she sniffed a lot, so it appeared she was upset. Was it, Miranda wondered, because she was leaving. She doubted it, and because her relationship with the woman was so fragile, she could not find a way of asking her what was wrong.

She saw Michael briefly during the day. He came to tell her that her flight to London had been booked for midday, the following day, that a car would take her to the airport, and that he had arranged with the airport officials that she need arrive only ten minutes before take off, to avoid waiting around in view of the fact that she had been ill. It was a thoughtful gesture and Miranda appreciated it, but could find no words to say so.

On her last night in Crete, she had supper in bed, and try as she might she could not drag her thoughts away from the glorious nights that she and Michael had spent together at the

Villa Dionissos. She wondered what he was thinking, alone in his study. What was his degree of regret, or, indeed was there any? Would he simply be relieved to see her gone?

In the morning, there was no time for thought. Having had to resort to sleeping pills the night before, she slept late and was barely ready when the car arrived at ten-thirty sharp. Michael banished Thea and her sons so that Miranda did not even have time to say goodbye to them. He loaded her cases into the car himself, while she stood in the porch awkwardly, watching him. Michael, grim-faced, spoke to the driver and handed him some notes. Then he came round to the passenger side of the car. 'You have plenty of time to get there,' he said, 'and I've paid the driver.'

'Thank you,' said Miranda, coming forward. They stood together awkwardly, by the car door. 'I-I'm sorry,' she suddenly felt compelled to say, 'only . . . I don't think I could ever trust you again.'

'I understand,' said Michael. 'Goodbye. Safe journey.'

Tears leapt into Miranda's eyes as she turned away. 'Goodbye,' she said in a muffled voice, hurriedly climbing into the back of the car. She did not see them drive away from the Villa Dionissos, nor did she see Michael waving goodbye. She could see nothing for her blinding tears.

The flight to London was uneventful, but by the time Miranda arrived at Heathrow she was worn out. Her plans were uncertain other than that she had decided to stay in a hotel for a few days. Wearily, she waited for what seemed like an age, for her bags to appear. She humped them onto the trolley which hurt her still tender stomach muscles. Her head ached, the hours of air conditioning had made her feel a little faint, but resolutely, she pushed the trolley through Customs, holding on to it more for support than anything else. Then she was out into the terminal building, and through bleary eyes, started looking for signs to the taxi rank.

'Miss Hicks?' A man in a grey suit and cap stepped forward. Extraordinarily, he was holding a card with 'Miranda Hicks' printed on it.

'Yes,' said Miranda, uncertainly.

'I have a car waiting for you. Let me take your luggage for you, madam.'

'A car, waiting for me? But-but nobody knows I'm here. Whose car is it?'

'It's a hire car, madam. It was arranged by your husband, he thought you might be tired on your arrival.'

'My husband, but . . .'

'I understand he telephoned from Greece, yesterday. Would that be right, madam?'

'Yes, yes,' said Miranda, amazed.

'Just come this way, the car's outside,' the chauffeur said, soothingly.

The hire car turned out to be a magnificent bottle-green Rolls Royce. Dazed, she allowed the chauffeur to hand her into the car and stow away the luggage. Then, before driving away, he came back to the passenger door. 'Your husband felt a little champagne might revive you.' Before Miranda could speak, he leaned in, unbuttoned a table bar, removed a half bottle of champagne from a tiny fridge, popped the cork and filled a glorious crystal goblet. 'I'll leave the champagne in the bucket here, madam, to keep it chilled,' he said. Then opening another cupboard he drew out a package. 'And your husband asked us to give you this.' It was a single red rose, sheathed in polythene; the card was addressed to Miranda Hicks. Putting down her champagne, she opened the envelope. '*Good luck*,' read the message, '*and be happy. M.*' A sob escaped from Miranda's lips. The chauffeur was still standing by the door, his eyes averted. She wondered why he did not go away. 'Thank you,' she managed. 'Could you leave me alone now, please.'

'Excuse me, madam. I'm sorry but I need to know where you want to go.'

Miranda started to say The Dorchester and then she checked herself. Like the terrified sixteen-year-old girl of so many years before, there suddenly seemed only one logical place to go. Only this time she did not have to look up Jenny Marchant's address. She knew it by heart.

Chapter Nineteen

Jenny's reaction was typical. A quick survey of Miranda's tear-stained face and the chauffeur struggling up the steps behind her, with a mountain of suitcases, told the whole story. 'Do you know something, darling, age is giving you a degree of commonsense. At least this time you chose to arrive when I was at home, and at a civilised hour.' Miranda tried a smile, but burst into tears instead. Jenny flung her arms round her and guided her through the front door. 'Before you say a word, darling,' she whispered, 'where on earth did you find that gorgeous chauffeur?'

'Oh Jenny,' said Miranda, tearfully, 'you have no idea how good it is to see you.'

'Then stop making my dress all wet and tell me what to do with Jeeves out there. Do I have to pay him anything?'

'No, no, I don't think so.'

'OK, then I'll just go and thank him personally, as they say, and I'll be right back.' She returned moments later. 'He refused all my offers, damn it,' she said, smiling. 'Hey, come on – now what's it to be, coffee, brandy?'

'I've just had some champagne,' said Miranda.

'Then, darling, we'd better have some more.'

'We're not celebrating anything, in fact quite the reverse.'

'Then that's all the more reason to have champagne. Do you want a pee or something?'

'Yes please, and I'd better wash my face.'

'There's a distinct sense of *déjà vu* about all this,' said Jenny, heading for the kitchen.

When Miranda emerged from the bathroom, the champagne was poured. 'Where's Paul?' she asked. 'Is he here?'

'No, he's down the road with Maisie.'

'With Maisie?'

Jenny laughed. 'Don't panic, darling, I know she sounds like a tart but, in fact, she's the mother of my daily. Paul has a little basement flat in her house. Maisie adores him, does all his washing and cooking, in fact he's never had it so good. He only has to smile at her and she'll do anything in the world for him. That boy will go far.'

'But what happened – between you and him, I mean?' Miranda asked.

'Just what you wanted. He met a nice, wholesome sixteen-year-old, at a disco. Not only is she, shall we say, a few years younger then me, she's also a great deal prettier than I have ever been.'

Miranda frowned. 'D-do you mind? I mean . . . did he behave badly?'

'Certainly not. He behaved with all the customary charm I've come to expect from your family. Darling, I understand how you felt at the time, but there was no way I was going to have a long term affair with a schoolboy. Every young man, ideally, needs to lose his virginity to an older woman. It's done wonders for his confidence, it's cleared up his spots, and when he takes his new little girlfriend to bed, he's going to know what to do, even if she doesn't.' Jenny grinned. 'And in answer to your next question, it's not a service I provide for every schoolboy who crosses my path, but your Paul is rather special – in fact he's quite the most delicious young man I've ever met.'

'I-I'm sorry I said those things.'

'Don't be, but you must make it up with Paul. He'll be over later.'

'You still see each other then?' Miranda was amazed.

'But, of course. He pops in several times a week – for a meal or just a chat. We're rather like Darby and Joan these days.'

'He probably won't be pleased to see me.'

'Darling, looking at the state of you, a family reunion is just what you need. Now, are you going to tell me what's happened or am I going to guess?'

'M-Michael and I have split up,' Miranda said, 'and, and I've just lost a baby, a boy, a son.'

'Oh, you poor old love, how dreadful for you. Tell me, is this thing with Michael just a temporary aberration? Are you over-reacting because of losing the baby?'

'No, no it's nothing like that, it's permanent. It has been building for some time, only I hadn't realised it.' Miranda's voice shook as she spoke.

'Are you sure?'

'Quite sure.'

'Do you want to talk about it?'

'No.'

'Fair enough. So, are you saying you're back in London permanently?'

'Yes, and I'll need somewhere to live, and some work.'

'You do stretch the ingenuity of your poor old agent. I've just officially retired you.'

'Then you'll just have to resurrect me again.'

It was not going to be that easy, Jenny thought, but certainly, she was only too aware that it was not the moment to say so. 'Well, you have no problem with accommodation,' she said, brightly, 'you can stay here, for as long as you like, you know that. In fact, I can't think why I don't turn this place into a hotel – for the exclusive use of the family Higgins.'

'Oh, I'm sorry. I can easily go somewhere else, it's just that I thought I needed to talk, and now I'm here I don't want to – God, what a pain I am, Jenny.'

'Stop moaning,' said Jenny. 'Let's take your cases into the spare room and then you can have a rest and a bath, or whatever. Paul will be here about eight o'clock. He's coming for a bite of supper.'

Paul was shocked by the sight of his sister. Finding her at Jenny's at all was surprise enough but seeing her in such a state was still more alarming. All his boyhood, she had been a sort of goddess. His mother would show him pictures of her in countless glossy magazines. Sometimes between the children's television programmes she would flash on to the screen in a commercial, and walking home from school past the newsagents, he would often see her face staring back at him from the newsstands. As he and his contemporaries reached puberty, his friends suddenly became interested in his famous sister. Paul could have obtained a great deal of notoriety and popularity by giving away signed photographs and inventing stories of Miranda's amorous adventures. But it was out of the question – to him her image was untouchable. She was his sister, and yet she was not – in fact she was always far more real to him on the front cover of a magazine than she ever was on her rare trips home. When it was suggested that he should go and live with her, it was like a dream come true. Yet, as the weeks went by and he assimilated his life into hers, he found himself no nearer obtaining any real intimacy with her. She was as remote sharing her life with him, as she had been staring from the front cover of a magazine. However, seeing her now, drawn and pale, her eyes puffy from crying, her hair a mess, her clothes creased from travelling, he felt a rush of excitement – not because he wanted her to be unhappy, or to look awful, but because, suddenly, she was vulnerable and as such was, for the first time, to him, a real person.

'Hi, sis, great to see you,' he said. Jenny had already whispered to him in the hall that he was to be kind to his sister, and his few clashes with Jenny had already taught him never to argue with formidable women.

'Oh Paul, it's lovely to see you.' Miranda came forward and put her arms round him, hugging him in a way he could never remember happening before.

'It's really nice to see you, too,' he said, carefully, 'but what on earth are you doing here?'

'I've left Michael, it didn't work out.'

'I'm sorry,' said Paul, 'I really am, that must be rough.'

'And she's lost her baby, too,' Jenny chipped in.

This was yet a further revelation to Paul. Somehow he could not imagine his glamorous sister pregnant. 'A baby! Poor old sis, you've really had an awful time, haven't you?' Miranda found his genuine concern very touching.

Jenny had cooked a delicious casserole and Miranda picked her way through it as best she could. By now they were all a little drunk, and it made the atmosphere very warm and relaxed. Paul was in terrific form and he and Jenny were obviously extremely comfortable with one another.

'I'm sorry I was so awful to you two,' Miranda said.

'That's all right,' said Paul, 'but honestly, sis, Jenny is the best thing that ever happened to me.' He grinned. 'Every boy should have one.'

Jenny smiled, laughed even, but there was a slight flinching at his remark and Miranda, hypersensitive to pain, guessed that it had not perhaps been so easy to hand Paul over to his young girlfriend as Jenny had lead her to believe. She struggled desperately to say something nice, something reassuring. 'When I consider what a mess I've made of my life, I don't know how I ever had the nerve to be critical of yours,' she spoke directly to Jenny. 'You really do have the knack for successful living. In all the years I've known you, I've never seen you falling apart at the seams, yet I seem to do it with monotonous regularity.'

'It's my professional attitude to life,' said Jenny, lightly. 'Now, for heaven's sake, darling, don't start flaying yourself in public, there's no need. You're back, you're in one piece, you've had a dreadful experience, but it's behind you now. Just think positive about the future.'

The words were easily spoken but Jenny knew they would be less easy to put into practice. Firstly, the change in Miranda's appearance was significant. After the Joe Chang incident, and then later, after David's death, Miranda had the advantage of extreme youth on her side. Now she was almost thirty and the emotional and physical dramas she had experienced, seemed to have drained her. Her skin had lost its bloom, her hair its lustre. She had lost weight, so that her face was gaunt. It was no longer a question of a few days' rest to put her right. Then there was her mental attitude. During that first evening, it was evident to Jenny that Miranda had lost her sparkle. Jenny's private view was that she had left that on Crete with Michael Richardson.

Over the first few days, Jenny tried, repeatedly, to find out what exactly had happened between Miranda and Michael, but Miranda could not, or would not, talk about it. This was unusual, she normally found no problem in relating her troubles. As the days passed, Jenny, never normally given to romantic notions, came to the conclusion that Miranda would never be whole again without Michael – she seemed no longer to be an individual, but half of a whole. When she ventured to suggest such a theory, Miranda nearly walked out of the house. Indeed, that was the other problem. Miranda's normally even-tempered self, seemed to have disappeared. She was moody, irritable and reduced to tears at the slightest thing. Quite apart from the problems of trying to re-launch her career, Jenny found it far from easy just living with her. Her relationship with Miranda was like walking a tightrope – one false move and she seemed to crack up before her eyes. There was absolutely no point in approaching the advertising agencies and photographers, to say Miranda Hicks was back – not in her current state . . . so, in desperation, Jenny went to see Lawrence Hardcastle.

She arrived at his offices at midday, by appointment, and he took her straight out to lunch. He eyed her across the table. 'You look weary, you naughty girl – have you been burning the candle a little too avidly?'

'No, I wish it was that,' Jenny said, 'I've been looking after that adopted daughter of yours – that's what is wearing me out.'

'How is she?' said Lawrence. 'We knew she was back, of course, and to be honest May's a bit upset that she hasn't been in touch yet.'

'Well, you tell May from me, she's had a lucky escape. At the moment, Miranda is being absolutely impossible.'

'What can I do?' Lawrence asked, simply.

'Rather like thirteen years ago, I think you and I, Lawrence, have got to undertake a major repair job.'

Lawrence listened carefully to Jenny's description of Miranda. 'Do you think there's any point in my having a word with Michael? I got on very well with him at their wedding – he's a nice fellow.'

'If she was eighteen, yes, but she's nearly thirty, Lawrence, and Michael, I understand, is in his forties.' Lawrence nodded. 'They are two mature people – there is no way we can start meddling in their lives. I've thought about contacting him, too, but I honestly don't think anything can be gained from it. If their relationship is this volatile, perhaps it is better that they are apart. It's exhausting, even for the bystanders.'

'Then it seems to me,' said Lawrence, 'what she needs is a complete change of scene and a permanent job which can absorb her mentally as well as physically. Flitting from modelling assignment to modelling assignment, even assuming you can get her back on the circuit, is not going to absorb her. She's done it for too many years and it will give her too much time to brood.'

'What are you suggesting?' said Jenny. 'Some sort of promotion work?'

'Yes, something like that. You've got enough on your plate, playing nursemaid - leave it with me for a few days, I'll see what strings I can pull.'

Tony Harris's office was not exactly palatial bearing in mind that its occupant was sales director of a large manufacturing company. But by rag-trade standards, it was a principality in its own right. It had four walls, a door that closed - and in moments of desperation even locked. It had a threadbare carpet, several delapidated armchairs and an old cutting table, to serve as a desk. The telephone line was exclusively Tony's, and with the door shut, he could barely hear the sound of one hundred and fifty sewing machines fighting a battle for supremacy with Radio Two. Tony was working on some costings and if he could just have another ten minutes to himself, he knew the job would be done. He hated costings - he was a salesman, not a bloody accountant. His phone rang. 'Yeh,' he barked, angry at the interruption.

'Tony. How are you, Cock?'

There was a moment's pause while Tony disentangled his mind from the figures, and set about recognising the voice. 'Lawrence! Shit, times must be hard if you're bothering to ring the likes of me. You move in circles that are outside my league these days, mush.'

'Don't be daft. How's Rachael and the kids?'

'Rachael - she bullies me as ever. I'm not a free man, Lawrence, you know that. And the kids, I never see them, except at Passover, and then only if they remember. After such a good Jewish upbringing. . . .' Tony shook his head sagely. 'Still, I blame their mother, they're almost as frightened of her as I am.'

'I won't hear another word against that wonderful woman of yours,' said Lawrence. 'You must come over and have dinner with May and me sometime.'

'Is that what you rang me to say – come over and have dinner sometime? Fine, yes I will. Can I get back to my figures now?'

'No, you can't. Listen, Tony, I've heard rumours – you're opening up some shops in The States – is that correct?'

'That's right, but you're not supposed to know about it until the press launch. How did you find out?'

'I have my sources,' said Lawrence.

'Oh, you wise guys make me sick.'

'So it's true?' said Lawrence. 'Good.'

'Yeh. I'm going out myself to open them, actually. I'll be away about six months. Naturally, I'm only going because it's a chance to get away from the wife.'

'Whereabouts are you opening the shops?'

'The main branch will be in New York, then one in Houston and one in LA. We're just testing at this stage but if it works, I want one of our stores in every major city in the States.'

'That's what I like about you, Tony,' said Lawrence, 'no ambition. Listen, what are you doing about publicity?'

'How do you mean?'

'Well, presumably you want your garments modelled – in store, at the fashion shows, for the media. . . .'

'Yeh, of course. I'll get me some models when I'm over there.'

'American models, wearing British clothes – not clever,' Lawrence said.

'Models are all the same.'

'Possibly, for the catwalk, I agree with you, but for promotion you want someone intelligent, who can talk to people, who will work hard, and above all, who will project the right image – and she won't be able to do that sounding like a native New Yorker.'

'Look, Lawrence, I don't know what you're trying to tell me, but could you cut the crap and spit it out.'

'How about taking Miranda Hicks with you?'

'Jesus, you have to be joking.'

'I'm not,' said Lawrence. 'She'd give you just the right image out there – very English, very classy. Her face is well known in the States – she would lend an enormous amount of credibility to your merchandise.'

'I'm not arguing with you,' said Tony, 'but there's no way I can afford that sort of budget – she must cost a fortune.'

'The other way of looking at it is to say you can't afford not to take her,' said Lawrence. 'Let's face it, your outlay in terms of stock, premises and staff, is going to be enormous, compared with the kind of promotion budget I'm suggesting. And she'll do most of the work for you – she knows how to hassle the media, and I know what I'm talking about. She launched PIPPA for me, you know.'

'Yes, I remember, and I hear what you're saying, but what do you think she'd cost, body and soul?'

'Fifty grand a year.'

Tony let out a whistle. 'That, mush, is way out of my league.'

'You said it would be only six months, that's twenty-five grand – it's nothing.'

'I can't do it.'

There was a pause. 'OK,' said Lawrence, 'let's put it another way, what could you afford?'

'Ten grand for the six months, top wack.'

'All right,' said Lawrence, 'you pay ten, I'll pay the fifteen, only I want the fifteen to look as though it comes from you.'

There was another silence while Tony knitted his brows, anger mounting. 'I'm not going to help you cheat on May. You sort out your own smutty little games, sonny, I want none of it.'

'Tony, it's nothing like that,' said Lawrence, tiredly, 'I want to help the girl, but I'm not involved with her, never have been.'

'You want to pay fifteen grand for a girl to keep her knickers *on*?'

'Tony, she's more like a daughter.'

Tony let out a roar of laughter. 'Oh, my God, Lawrence, now I've heard it all, you might at least try to be original – what do you think, that I've got no smarts?'

'Her husband was in the helicopter with William,' Lawrence said quietly. 'He died, too. May and I have sort of adopted her since. We all helped each other through that time.'

Tony let out a sigh. 'Shit, I'm sorry, of course, I remember now. OK, I'll take her, but why come to me? Why subsidise the salary? That girl could get a job anywhere.'

'She's had a bit of a rough time, her second marriage has just broken up. Yes, of course she can go back on the modelling circuit, but I'd like to see her get right away from England – a new job, new people, a new challenge.'

'She's not going to start throwing wobblies on me, is she?' said Tony, suspiciously. 'This is a delicate operation, I can't carry passengers, and I certainly can't cope with women throwing hysterics – I have enough of that at home.'

'She won't and she's good, worth every penny, believe me,' said Lawrence, hoping to God he was right.

'OK,' said Tony, 'I'll take your word for it.'

'You don't need to see her, do you?' said Lawrence.

'No, she smiles at me every night from at least half a dozen hoardings on my way home.'

'When will you need her?'

'We fly out on the second of November. Ask her to send me her vital statistics here at the factory and we'll have some garments made up for her.'

'Thanks, Tony.' Lawrence put down the phone with mixed feelings. On the one hand, he was elated – it was just the sort of job he had in mind for Miranda. Against that, he was nervous. Last time he had been responsible for changing the course of her life, it had lead, ultimately, to her husband's death. This time, he could only hope it would bring her the lasting happiness he so wanted for her.

'New York!' Miranda said. 'For six months. No, I don't think so, no I couldn't.'

'Why?' Jenny demanded.

'I just couldn't cope at the moment. I need to be as far as possible back to base, with familiar people in familiar surroundings.'

'You know New York very well,' Jenny said. 'Heaven's above, you've worked there often enough.'

'Yes, but I've never actually lived there. As you well know, these impersonal international hotels are the same the world over, whether you are in New York, Dublin, Paris or London, it makes no difference.'

'You have friends in New York,' Jenny persisted, 'and this is no ordinary job. ENGLISH GARDEN have a big future. Lawrence knows their sales director very well, and he says they are not going to be satisfied until they have taken the States by storm. It's a unique opportunity to be in on the ground floor of something really exciting.'

'I realise that, and I am grateful to you and Lawrence for finding me this opportunity. Thanks, but no thanks. I'm sure ENGLISH GARDEN will be able to find somebody who can do the job quite as well as me.'

Jenny took a deep breath. 'Oh, there'll certainly be no problem with that.'

Miranda's head jerked up at the remark. 'There's no need to be bitchy,' she said.

'I'm not being bitchy,' said Jenny, aware of the tremendous gamble she was taking, 'just realistic. Frankly, darling, you're very lucky to have been offered that job. Finding you work is just not that easy any more.'

She really had Miranda's full attention now. 'What do you mean, you've never had any trouble in the past – we've always been able to pick and choose.'

'But things are different now.'

'How can they be?' Miranda said, incredulously. 'I've only been out of action for three months – well four, I suppose.'

'Four months is a long time in our business, and it's not as simple as that. You were at the top of your profession and you quit. It's like the Queen deciding to abdicate – how easy do you think it would be for her to change her mind and get her crown back again?'

'What exactly are you saying?' Miranda's voice was hostile.

'I'm saying that you're hanging around here, feeling sorry for yourself and expecting the star treatment, while everyone else is knocking themselves out to help you. You're behaving like a *prima donna* when you've absolutely no reason to do so any more. Only three months ago you told me you no longer wanted me to represent you because of my relationship with your brother. Then, presto, you turn up here, expect a roof over your head and my undivided attention and loyalty. As it so happens you've got them both, but the way you're going on, not for much longer. I don't know what went on between you and Michael, because you're not prepared to tell me, but whatever it was, it's had a very bad effect on you as a person. The world doesn't revolve around you Miranda, you need to recognise that. You should also perhaps consider that you don't have the exclusive rights on hurt feelings either.'

'I don't understand,' Miranda said, her anger having been replaced by distress. 'I'm not behaving any differently from how I've always behaved. Maybe I do expect a lot of people, but then I give a lot, too.'

'Do you?' Jenny said. 'I don't think I've ever really seen you give yourself.'

'That's not true,' said Miranda, really agitated now.

'Perhaps it has not always been the case,' Jenny admitted, 'but since David died, you've certainly operated only on the surface. I've always got you good jobs, you have been admired and appreciated wherever you went, but the moment the going gets even slightly tough, you run away, which is what I suspect has happened with you and Michael Richardson.'

'What happened between Michael and me is none of your bloody business,' Miranda said, viciously.

'I realise that, but you and your career are my business, and I'm telling you this, if you don't accept this job in New York, I'm not prepared to represent you any more. I have an office full of paperwork waiting for me downstairs. You think it over and let me know your decision by three o'clock this afternoon. I'm not prepared to keep ENGLISH GARDEN waiting any longer than that.'

It was a side of Jenny that Miranda had never seen directed at her before. She knew Jenny could be ruthless, but with

Miranda, she had always been soothing, encouraging, always prepared to iron out the problems. But apparently not any more. It seemed to Miranda, suddenly, as though everyone was against her. Michael with his cruelty, Jenny with her sudden change of attitude – even her mother, when she had spoken to her on the phone, had been full of criticism at her decision to leave Michael. May Hardcastle had sounded a little distant, too – when Miranda had finally telephoned her. She sat alone, in Jenny's sitting room for the rest of the morning and into the afternoon, trying to stop her thoughts straying to Michael and to concentrate on the decision that lay ahead. At three o'clock she went down to Jenny's office. 'You can ring ENGLISH GARDEN and tell them I'll do it.'

Jenny looked up from a mound of papers, her expression unreadable. 'Good girl, so that means you've got just a couple of weeks to get yourself into trim. You'll have to work hard – you look a real mess at the moment. I want the works – gymnasium every day, sunbed, hair fixed and massages. There's no need to worry about a wardrobe, ENGLISH GARDEN will provide that, but you must be in a lot better shape than you are at the moment.'

Miranda stood rooted to the spot, absolutely astounded. Jenny had never spoken to her like this before. 'Do you have any other orders,' she said, sarcastically.

Jenny looked up. 'No, not at the moment, but I must stress the need to really work on your appearance. Lawrence had quite a job ensuring that you would not be called for an audition, because if Tony Harris had seen you as you are now, believe me, you wouldn't have got the job.'

Miranda left the room, tears stinging her eyes. She felt an overwhelming sense of loneliness, and from nowhere came a sudden longing for David. If only he had lived – he had understood her, and she him – they had been a perfect partnership. That, at least, she told herself, was something she could hold onto, something that could not be destroyed. . . .

Chapter Twenty

'Miranda, there's a press launch on Thursday which I want you to attend.' One week after Miranda's acceptance of the ENGLISH GARDEN job, Jenny was still being distant and aloof.

'I can't face a press launch, not at the moment,' Miranda said.

They were having breakfast together, both buried behind their respective newspapers. Jenny lowered hers. 'It's for PIPPA PAINTS. Lawrence wants all the PIPPA girls there, to show the changing face of PIPPA over the years.'

'I can't believe he really wants somebody as old and as out of shape as me,' Miranda said, her voice heavy with sarcasm. 'You'll just have to tell him I'm too busy preparing to go to New York.'

'You owe Lawrence,' Jenny said, vehemently. She knew of Lawrence's deal to subsidise the ENGLISH GARDEN fee – indeed she had agreed to charge no commission on Lawrence's subsidy. Now she was sorely tempted to betray a confidence. Lawrence had been impossibly generous and yet Miranda was not even prepared to give him half a day of her time.

'I'm very fond of him, and he's been jolly good to me, but it works both ways,' Miranda said, somewhat complacently.

'In my view, the credit balance is well on his side,' said Jenny. 'Anyway I'm not arguing with you. I'm simply telling you it's important that you are there and that Lawrence has specifically asked me to ensure that you come.'

The room was crowded and overheated. Miranda was exhausted, her head thumping. No one had anticipated the press reaction to her sudden reappearance – no one, that is except Lawrence Hardcastle, and he was more than pleased with the way the promotion party was going. PIPPA PAINTS would be mentioned in every national the following day, running as a by-line to the story that Miranda Hicks, estranged from her husband, had returned to modelling. His reasons for insisting on her appearance were not entirely commercial. He needed to satisfy himself that she could still stand up to the press, that her experience had left her tough enough to cope. Poor girl, she must be exhausted, he thought, but it didn't show. Her eyes sparkled, her amazing hair shone and she had a smile for everyone. She was still the trouper she had always been, whatever private pain she now bore. Jenny joined Lawrence carrying two glasses of champagne. She handed one to him. 'She's done well, hasn't she? Really socked it to 'em.'

'Yes. They gave her more attention than I expected.' He grinned and nodded towards the knot of other PIPPA PAINT girls, standing desolately around, talking to a bunch of eager young advertising executives. By contrast, the other side of the room was thronged with people – photographers and the press all trying to have a few words with Miranda. 'I suppose we'd better go and save her,' Lawrence suggested.

Jenny shook her head. 'Let her save herself – that girl needs toughening up. I've realised during the last week or two, that I, you – all of us – have pandered to her far too much over the years. Losing David was a terrible tragedy and because of it, we've tended to single her out for special treatment. The result is that now, basically, she's a spoilt brat.'

'A charming, kind, caring spoilt brat,' Lawrence said, gently.

'Yes,' Jenny conceded, 'but seriously, Lawrence, we have over-protected her, as one would a child, and as a result, I can't help feeling responsible for the break-up of this marriage.'

'That's ridiculous.'

'Is it?' said Jenny. 'In the past, when the going's got tough, I've always baled her out. There was no one to bale her out in Crete. She lost her baby and probably her husband wasn't as understanding as he might have been – it happens the world over. What does Miranda do? At the first hint of trouble she comes running home to Momma,' Jenny grinned at Lawrence, 'and Daddy here.'

Lawrence sighed. 'I suppose you could be right.'

'I am right.'

The hubbub continued. Again and again Miranda avoided the direct question as to what had gone wrong with her marriage, describing it simply as a sad mistake. They probed, prodded, needled her with questions, but she knew better than to lose her temper. Since she was seventeen, it had been drummed into her that she could not afford to have the press as her enemy, but never had this golden rule been so sorely put to the test. Suddenly, she felt a hand on her elbow and turned gratefully, expecting it to be Lawrence come to save her. Instead she found herself looking into the dark, haunted eyes of Jake Berisford.

'Jake, good heavens, what a surprise.'

'Hi, Miranda, I've come to take you away from all this – you've more than given this bunch their pound of flesh. Tell them sweetly you've got to move on and I'll take you out to dinner to escape the mob.'

'You're a lifesaver,' said Miranda. 'Ladies and gentlemen,' she shouted, but it was hopeless trying to be heard above the noise.

'Silence please,' Jake boomed. Amazingly the noise died away.

'Ladies and gentlemen,' Miranda said, 'I really am awfully grateful for your interest and attention, but I think I've answered every question I can and should perhaps remind you that this a PIPPA PAINTS party. There are some gorgeous PIPPA girls over there, just waiting for you – all of whom are, I might add, a great deal younger than I am.' There was an appreciative guffaw of laughter.

'What did I tell you,' Jenny said to Lawrence, 'she can handle it on her own when she has to.'

The bistro was quiet and soothing in contrast to the PIPPA party. Miranda collapsed into a chair opposite Jake, leaning back and closing her eyes for a moment. 'Bless you, Jake, you're wonderful.'

'A drink,' said Jake, 'you need a drink.'

'Wine, and buckets of it, please,' Miranda said.

The evening began well. They discussed Jake's career which currently revolved round photographing a five-hundred page recipe book. He groaned at Miranda. 'I've lost nearly a stone in weight, I can't stand the sight of food. If ever you have a weight problem, just surround yourself with tables of food, day after day, it works a treat.'

'I'll remember that,' said Miranda, with surprising warmth. 'If Jenny is to be believed, middle-age spread is only just around the corner for me.'

They discussed Miranda's job in the States. 'It sounds ideal,' said Jake, 'fresh faces, a new start, it's just what you need.'

'I suppose it is,' said Miranda, without much enthusiasm.

It was not until they reached the coffee stage that the subject of Crete was touched on. They had both drunk a great deal of wine by this time, which in Jake's case, as Miranda well knew, always made him more aggressive.

'Of course I knew it wouldn't work,' he said, suddenly.

'What wouldn't?' Miranda asked.

'Your marriage to that Minos person.'

'Why and how could you know such a thing?' Miranda asked, immediately on the defensive.

'Well, it was obvious. The Greeks all treat their women abominably, and he, in particular, has an appalling reputation as a womaniser.'

'He wasn't unfaithful to me, if that's what you mean,' Miranda said.

'My dear girl, you can't have a clue whether he was or he wasn't.'

'I'm sure he wasn't,' Miranda protested.

'All right – but don't tell me you had the same tender loving care from him as you did from David.'

'They're entirely different sort of men,' Miranda said, surprised to find herself leaping to Michael's defence.

'Certainly that's true, but it's no good ricocheting from

relationship to relationship, expecting to find someone you can love as you loved David. I've told you that before. It's simply not going to happen. It's wrong to expect to replace him, quite wrong, quite wrong.'

'You're making it sound as though I'm being disloyal to David.'

'Well, aren't you?' said Jake. His eyes seemed slightly askew, he brushed his unruly hair away from his face with a nervous gesture.

'I don't think so.' Miranda was becoming angry. 'Think what you're condemning me to, Jake. Are you saying that my life is effectively over?'

'Mine is,' Jake mumbled. His head was now in his hands, his elbows on the table.

'What did you say?' Miranda asked, leaning closer to catch his words.

'I said, mine is.'

'I don't understand what you mean,' said Miranda. 'Are you saying that you lost someone dear to you when you were young, someone whom you've never been able to replace?'

Jake raised his head, his eyes bloodshot and puffy, and stared at Miranda. There was no anger in him, indeed his expression was kind and compassionate, and it confused Miranda still further. 'Miranda are you really so blind, or is it that you are not prepared to admit the truth?'

'Jake, I don't know what you're talking about.'

Jake ran a hand through his hair. 'Miranda, I loved David, too.'

'Well, of course you did,' Miranda said, soothingly. He was clearly drunker than she had realised.

'No, no you still haven't got it, have you? David and I – we were lovers.'

Shock galvanised her into an immediate reaction. 'Oh, don't be so ridiculous, Jake.'

'I'll try it again,' Jake said, patiently. Suddenly he did not seem at all drunk. 'David and I were lovers, we had a homosexual relationship. Now do you understand?'

Miranda's hands flew to her mouth to stifle a scream, her eyes were wide and frightened. 'I don't believe you, Jake.

You're drunk, you're making it up. Why torment me in this way – it's so cruel.'

'Whether you believe it or not, of course, is your choice. I never intended to tell you. Indeed I promised David I wouldn't and certainly I would not have broken that promise while he was alive. Although I was insanely jealous of you, I would not have done anything to ruin your marriage, I loved him too much for that.'

'Stop it, stop it,' said Miranda, 'you don't know what you're saying. David and I . . . we, well we had a normal relationship.'

'Did you, did you really?' said Jake. His eyes seemed to be burning into hers, and Miranda was the first to look away. 'Look,' said Jake, 'perhaps I'd better improve your education on the subject of gays. There are committed gays, as I am.' He smiled faintly. 'Committed fags are simply not turned on by women. That's me – never have been, never will. David, however, was bisexual – in other words, he swung both ways.'

'Don't, please,' Miranda stood up. 'I can't stay and listen to any more of this.'

'What do you think it's been like for me?' Jake said, ignoring her protests. 'David and I had a wonderful relationship until you turned up.' His words were like a drug, Miranda wanted to drag herself away but she could not do it. She sat down again. 'He was ambitious, that was the trouble, such an enthusiast, he would not be satisfied with what we had. He wanted fame and fortune, not realising that they were no substitute for happiness. The search for it killed him in the end.'

'You're trying to debase our relationship, David's and mine,' Miranda said, in a half whisper. 'You're trying to ruin my memories. Good God, Jake, David and I had little enough time as it was. Why try and destroy the one thing I do have left – sweet memories of a brief, but very happy marriage.'

'You didn't love him as I loved him, nor did he love you as much as me. He couldn't be unfaithful to me, you know. When you went off on that tour of Europe, the one where he proposed to you, he told me first what he was intending to do, and that therefore, he and I had to end our affair. I begged him for his own sake, not to try and suppress his homosexual feelings, but he said there wasn't room for us both in his life. He was too honourable, you see, he either had to belong to you or to me. He made the wrong choice, that's all.'

'I don't believe any of this,' Miranda said again. Still she could not move, it was as though she was hypnotised.

'It's – it's why I've kept in touch with you all these years,' Jake said. Now he had started to talk, he seemed quite unable to stop. 'It was not very noble, I know, but I needed reassurance that I had meant more to David than you had done. You see he is – the love of my life, there'll never be anyone else, not really. You straight people think you have problems finding a suitable mate when you have all the establishment vehicles behind you – dances, restaurants, pubs and a far larger number of people to choose from. Divorced or widowed, it's quite expected for you to be on the look-out for a partner. For us, even before AIDS, it was underground. All this talk of coming out is a farce. David was ashamed, you know, ashamed of me and of our relationship. He thought it would affect his career if people knew, and he was right, it probably would have done. I'll never find anyone else, I haven't even looked, I never will.' A tear slipped down Jake's cheek which he made no attempt to brush away. He continued to stare helplessly at Miranda and in his face she saw the most terrifying of all expressions – absolute sincerity.

She left him then, without a word. She could think of nothing but getting away, blotting out the words that had been spoken. Mechanically, she hailed a taxi and gave Jenny's address.

The lights were still on in the flat when she entered. Jenny was lounging in front of the television, a glass in hand. 'Hi, babe,' she said. 'You were wonderful tonight, absolutely brill. Would you like a drink to celebrate?'

'No thanks,' said Miranda.

Something in Miranda's voice made Jenny turn round and look at her more closely. 'Hey, what's with you, sweetheart, you look as though you've seen a ghost? Didn't you have a good time with Jake?'

'Yes, fine,' said Miranda. 'I – I think I'll just go to bed if that's all right.'

'Yes, of course. Sure you're OK?'

'Yes, I'm fine.'

She went through all the motions of preparing herself for bed, climbed between the sheets and turned out the light. Only then did she let her mind focus on what she had just been told. She wanted to recoil from the revelation, bury it as some impossible hideous game of Jake's, calculated to upset her. But she could do none of those things, because in her heart she knew it was true.

Chapter Twenty-One

She could remember the night so well – their first night, hers and David's. It was also her first night in Florence. They had arrived mid-afternoon, by train from Milan, where they had been photographing in a studio for an Italian magazine. Now the magazine wanted some outside shots, and what better backdrop than Florence.

Miranda's initial impression was of disappointment. They were booked into a hotel just downstream from the Ponte Veccio, on the edge of the Arno. 'Yuck,' she said to David when she saw the river, 'it's a revolting colour, sort of like yesterday's custard.'

He laughed. 'It's all the dead cats, sewage, rotting vegetables . . .'

'Stop, stop please,' said Miranda, 'you're spoiling all my illusions.'

'I shouldn't be,' said David, 'the whole of Europe is a sewer. The French, the Italians, the Spanish . . . just think about their idea of hygiene – well, just look at their loos,' he shuddered, and Miranda laughed.

They were standing, leaning over a parapet outside their hotel, gazing down into the river. The sky, which had been a glorious blue all day, was showing signs of the evening to come. Sounds of the city were all around them, and as she gazed this way and that, Miranda began to catch the magic that is Florence. 'What are we doing this evening?' she asked, excitedly.

'A hot bath and an early night,' David replied, teasing her.

'Don't you dare suggest such a thing – don't forget it's back to London tomorrow. This is my first and only night in

Florence, and the last night of our trip. You have to make it very special, David, you have to.'

He grinned boyishly and made a mock bow. 'Your word is my command, my lady.'

As it happened, they got very little further than the Ponte Veccio. They wandered over the bridge, stopping at all the little stalls. David bought Miranda a silver bracelet, Miranda bought David a silk handkerchief. Well pleased with their purchases, they finished their crossing of the bridge and found themselves outside, what appeared to be, the perfect restaurant – and it was. They gorged themselves on seafood, pasta and bottles of Chianti. They were in a holiday mood – just one more day's shoot, and then home for a well-earned rest. They had been on the road for five weeks.

Six months later, in the same restaurant, they would have been mobbed by autograph hunters, their faces as well-known in Italy as they already were in the UK. That night they attracted more than their share of attention, but simply because they were young and beautiful, full of fun and energy. The waiters fawned over them, the other diners smiled at them – they were quite irresistible. After dinner, a little drunk, a little tired, but very happy, they wandered back over the bridge, hand in hand, and sauntered along by the edge of the Arno. In the moonlight, the water looked beautiful and Miranda said so. David stopped, put his hands on her shoulders and turned her round so that she faced him. 'Not as beautiful as you, my love. The moon, the stars,' he grinned, 'the custard river and even Florence herself – you can keep the lot, for the sight of your shining hair, and all that gorgeous bone structure.' He ran a finger gently along her cheekbone.

'There speaks the professional photographer,' said Miranda, lightly, but her mouth was dry and she trembled slightly. David, her playmate, her working partner, had never spoken like this before.

'I love you,' he said gently, 'and I'm going to kiss you.' He did so and it felt good. His lips were not searching but warm and comforting, and the feel of his body against hers, whilst a new experience, was strangely familiar. He drew away and Miranda smiled at him. 'I love you too, David.'

The little boy cheeriness had vanished. He suddenly seemed tense and anxious. 'Let's go back to the hotel.'

'I was hoping we could walk awhile,' said Miranda.

'No, no, not now, come back with me to the hotel, come back to my room, please.' His voice was urgent.

She looked at him for a long moment, 'All right,' she said, gently, her heart hammering with sudden fear.

By the time they reached his bedroom, they were both so frightened neither of them knew what to say, or do. David turned off all the lights, except the one by the bed, then he stood awkwardly on the opposite side of the bed from Miranda. 'Shall we?' he gestured towards the bed. Miranda nodded.

Hurriedly, they both undressed, climbing awkwardly between the sheets together and immediately David doused the light so that they were in total darkness. Then they turned to one another, groping to establish contact, their bodies cold and unsure.

When he touched her, Miranda felt nothing. No man had made love to her since Joe Chang, so that terror was by far her strongest sensation as David drew her to him. But it was not simply that – he did not touch her where she wanted him to. He kissed her a great deal, while his hands cupped her buttocks, squeezing and pinching them until they hurt. The feel of his erection against her stomach, aroused her a little. She wanted him to touch her breasts, to touch her almost anywhere – anything to stop the continual kneading of her small, round bottom, now sore and bruised.

At last he took her, but she was not ready for him. Dry and tense, he hurt her as he forced his swollen penis into her and began grinding away, until in seconds, he came with a cry of triumph, while she herself felt nothing but discomfort and an odd embarrassment.

Far from being disappointed, David appeared ecstatic. He thanked her for being so wonderful, so loving, so sexy . . . it made no sense to her that he should feel this way, while she felt nothing, but far from resenting it, she felt pathetically grateful. She knew the Joe Chang affair had left her crippled, yet this man still wanted her. So it did not occur to her to say anything other than 'Yes,' when moments later, David asked her to marry him.

And that remained the pattern of their lovemaking from their first night together until David's death. However, once she was used to it, she did not mind that he could not arouse her. Making love to David was not important, sleeping with David was. Night after night, they curled up together in double beds around the world, giving each other warmth, comfort, companionship and the basic animal need of feeling another friendly body in the dark.

What did worry Miranda, however, was the infrequency of their lovemaking. Predictably, she believed herself to be the cause of David's apparent lack of interest in sex. It had to be her frigidity which turned him off, yet when, tentatively, she raised the question with him, he was desperate to assure her that this was not the case. 'Darling, we're friends first and lovers second. That has always been the way with us and it's the stuff that good marriages are built on. It will mean our relationship will stand the test of time, which is more important than anything.' She accepted his explanation because it was what she wanted to hear, but she was left with a profound sense of self doubt.

In the last weeks of their marriage, she did begin to notice a subtle change which worried her. It seemed to her that David was actively avoiding any situation which might lead to their making love. Since the act itself gave her no pleasure, in theory it should not have worried her, but again the insecurities made her blame herself for his behaviour. At night, she found he lingered in his bath until she had fallen asleep, or suddenly came up with an excuse for working late in his studio, or insisted on reading in bed until all hours. Miranda knew, instinctively that it was an excuse but could not bring herself to discuss it with him. The fact remained though, that at the time of David's death, they had not made love for well over a month.

Jake's words ricocheted through her head, as she lay in the darkened bedroom in Jenny's flat. Up to a point he had been right. Somewhere deep inside her, she had known, she had always known, yet she could never have put it into words even to herself. She had needed someone else to tell her.

The following morning, Miranda woke very late and squinting at the watch beside her bed, saw it was after ten, which meant she had missed her workout at the gym. What the hell, she thought, I'm fit enough now. Since returning from Crete she had been sleeping very badly, and in her befuddled mind, all she could think of, for a moment, was that at last she had enjoyed a good night's sleep.

Then the events of the night before came crowding back into her mind, but amazingly, there was no accompanying feeling of pain – in fact quite the reverse, she felt a sense of release, of freedom. David had not been the ideal husband, the yardstick by which she must judge all other men. Without doubt, their relationship would not have withstood the test of time, as clearly, in the long term, he would not have been able to sustain a heterosexual front. Most important of all, it was not her fault that their sex life had been so unsatisfactory. Pent-up guilt and remorse seemed to be literally falling off her – it was a wonderful feeling.

She began to wonder how many people had suspected David's problem. Jenny made no secret of the fact that she had never liked him. May had always been reticent about him being the right man. Perhaps they had recognised what she had refused to do. As at the beginning of every day, her thoughts strayed to Michael. Would the knowledge she now had of David have made any difference in her relationship with Michael she wondered? It was an unbearable thought – at that moment, she so wanted to talk to Michael, to explain about David, and why her feelings had been so screwed up. But there was no way back to Michael, she knew that now. Set free from David at last, she had to make a new life for herself – and what better place to do that than in New York?

Chapter Twenty-Two

Marty Kaufman was in a panic. It was a long time since she had needed to get herself together sufficiently to do anything other than reach for the next drink, or next cigarette. She was only thirty-two, but she looked ten years older. Yet when her banker husband, Robert, had first brought her to New York, five years before, she had been young, fresh and full of fun. Since then, she had been in a state of steady decline.

She gazed around the apartment in a state of increasing agitation – where to start? Ashtrays overflowed, dirty glasses and coffee cups lay around, the carpet had not been vacuumed in weeks. Jesus, the place was a mess, she had to do something – she could not have Miranda see it like this. She went in search of the vacuum cleaner. This took her into the kitchen, and brought her up short with an even greater sense of dismay. It was a shambles. Dirty plates, still covered with dried up food were everywhere. Someone had spilled orange juice on the floor and it was unbearably sticky underfoot, the trash can was overflowing. It was an awful mess. She was on her way to the cupboard where the vacuum cleaner was kept when the house phone rang. No, she told herself, no, not yet. She rushed back into the sitting room and slowly picked up the phone, her fingers crossed, holding her breath. 'Marty Kaufman,' she said, nervously.

'Marty, it's me, it's me,' Miranda's gloriously English voice pealed down the line.

'Oh, sugar, that's great. Where are you?'

'I'm downstairs, Dumbo.'

'Oh yeh, of course, you're on the house phone. Sorry, I was

just so pleased to hear you. Hey look, the place is in a bit of a mess.'

'Don't worry,' said Miranda, 'I just can't wait to see you. I'm on my way up, is that OK?'

'Right, fine, of course.'

To cross the hall, catch the elevator and reach the Kaufman apartment took at least three minutes, Marty knew that. She dashed into the bedroom, sat down at her dressing table mirror and began dragging a comb through her hair. She looked dreadful. Her roots needed retouching, her face was chalk-white. She dabbed on some blusher and a touch of lisptick, but she was too heavy handed and ended up looking like a clown. The buzzer sounded at the apartment door, Miranda had arrived, it was too late now.

For a split second, the two women eyed one another with dismay, but for totally opposite reasons. In Marty's eyes, Miranda looked just the same, if anything more lovely. She had an added maturity, a greater depth of expression. In Miranda's eyes, Marty looked terrible – her dyed blonde hair was like straw, she looked ill, pale, plain, over-weight – she was barely recognisable. They both recovered and fell into one another's arms.

They had known each other a long time, since Miranda had first started modelling. Jenny, anxious that the very insecure seventeen-year-old should have some moral support, had sought the help of Marty, a slightly older, experienced model, to look after Miranda, and act as a confidante. Purposely Jenny had put them up for the same jobs, and over the years Marty had proved a good friend. That was until five years ago, when she had met an American banker at a party, fallen head over heels in love with him, married him in a fortnight, abandoned her career and gone to live in New York.

It had been Jenny's idea that Miranda should contact Marty again, to see if she could give her houseroom for a few weeks, whilst she searched for a flat of her own. In theory, it had seemed a really good idea, but now, confronting one another face to face, both had their doubts.

Marty grinned nervously at Miranda. 'God it's good to see you. Hey, look I'm sorry the apartment's such a mess. I was just about to clear it up but I'll do it later. What about a drink to celebrate?'

Miranda winced. 'It's only ten o'clock in the morning, Marty. It's a bit early for me. Any chance of a coffee?'

'Sure, I'll fix a coffee, no problem.'

Miranda followed Marty into the kitchen, taking in the apartment as she went. It was beautifully furnished, the kind of place where no expense had been spared . . . yet it was a tip. She could not believe the mess – then she saw the kitchen and wondered why she had worried about the sitting room. It was surprising Marty and Robert had not died of salmonella poisoning by now.

'I have coffee somewhere,' said Marty, searching through cupboards frantically, 'but I guess we've got no milk. Do you mind it black?'

'Black will be fine,' said Miranda. 'Look, here's the coffee, it was on the table.'

'Thanks,' said Marty. 'Gosh, you must think I'm awful.'

'No, no, of course not,' Miranda lied. 'Tell me, Marty, how have things been for you? What have you been up to? I've missed you so much.'

At Miranda's words, Marty stopped and stared at her for a moment. Then slowly, her face began to crumple and she burst into tears. Miranda rushed to her side and put an arm round her shoulders. 'Hey, sweetheart, what is it?'

'C-can we go and sit down,' Marty sobbed. 'I feel sort of funny. I haven't eaten much for a day or two, I guess that's it.'

Miranda gently guided her through into the sitting room and set her down on the sofa. 'Can you find me a cigarette?' Marty said, between sobs.

Miranda looked desperately around the room. There were several discarded packets and she began examining each one. 'You never used to smoke, Marty,' she said.

'I never used to do a lot of things.' Again, she was overtaken by a spasm of sobs. Mercifully, Miranda found a cigarette and gave it to Marty, who took it with trembling fingers. 'You want to know what's wrong with me, you really do?' she asked. Miranda nodded, sitting down beside her. 'I tell you what's wrong with me. What's wrong with me is that you're the first person who's cared a damn how I am – in months, no in years.'

'But Robert, what about Robert?' said Miranda.

'Oh, Robert least of all. Robert is a banker. I think he must have been born a banker and now he lives, breathes, eats and sleeps it. You wonder why this apartment is a tip, I'll tell you why – I let it get filthier and filthier, hoping that Robert might notice it and might even bawl me out. But do you know, he doesn't even see it. It just doesn't register, and nor do I any more. He works all hours, leaves here six, six-thirty, gets home anything from midnight onwards. No, I know what you're thinking – I can see the expression on your face – he's not having an affair. Jesus, Miranda, I wish to God he was, then at least I'd know what I was up against, at least I'd be faced with something I could fight. But I can't even add up my own cheque book stubs, so how can I compete with the banking world? If ever he talks to me about his business, every third word is unintelligible.'

'Have you told him about how you feel?' Miranda asked.

'Oh, I used to, a few years back, when I could still command his attention, I used to moan like crazy. I guess that's why he doesn't come home any more. Now, I just sit around here and drink, and smoke. . . . I'm the railway platform, Robert's the express train who does not call at my particular station any more.'

'Oh Marty, I'm sorry,' said Miranda. 'You should have let me know about this before, I'd have come and seen you. Still, I expect you have plenty of friends.'

'No,' said Marty, 'I've piss-all friends. I can't stand these smart New York girls, they drive me potty. Robert used to drag me along to his boring bankers' parties, but everybody there had one foot in the grave. No, I've got no real girlfriends, that's half the trouble.'

Marty's situation struck a chord with Miranda – her long, lonely days in Crete came flooding back into her mind. Yes, she understood Marty's problems only too well, and if she had been living in Crete for five years, she would probably be in exactly the same state. 'You ought to have some kids,' said Miranda, without thinking out the remark.

'Don't you think we haven't tried,' said Marty, desperately. 'That's the other thing. I'm sterile – sterile in mind and body. What a failure.'

'Are you sure?' said Miranda. 'They can do wonderful things with fertility these days.'

'We've tried everything. Robert is that kind of guy, who won't easily take no for an answer. Hell, it's no good, Miranda, I'm going to have that drink. Are you sure you won't join me?'

'Just a small one then.'

Marty rummaged in a cupboard, found two glasses and poured hefty slugs of vodka into them. 'Do you want anything with yours?' she said.

'Have you any tonic?'

'Yeh, somewhere.'

The tonic was eventually tracked down and Miranda filled her glass to the brim, to try and counteract the enormous measure of vodka she had been given. Marty, she noticed, drank hers neat.

'Yeh,' Marty continued, 'I would have liked to have been left with a little hope – you know! Perhaps, perhaps just one day things would click and I'd get pregnant. But Robert couldn't even leave me that. By the time every quack in the country had finished mauling me about, I was left with no doubts – I'll never have a child.' The vodka seemed to have a calming affect on her, she became less agitated, sitting back on the sofa quite relaxed now and dry-eyed. 'Anyway,' she smiled, 'to hell with me and my problems, what's all this with you? You said on the telephone that you'd married and it hadn't worked out. That's tough. Is it really over, or is it a trial separation?'

'It's really over,' said Miranda, 'but don't let's talk about it Marty, let's talk about the future. I'm here for six months, and I'm determined to put the past behind me. It's really kind of you to put me up for a while, but I'll find my own place as soon as I can.' Having seen the state of the apartment, Miranda suspected she wouldn't be able to stick it for more than a few days, anyhow.

It was as though Marty read her thoughts. 'Yeh, this isn't a very attractive place to stay at the moment is it, sweetheart?'

'Why don't we clear it up?' Miranda suggested.

'Hell, no, you must be all jet-lagged and things. Don't worry, it's OK. You'll get used to it. Like another drink?'

'No,' said Miranda firmly, 'and neither would you. This place is a mess, you're a mess, and you need a bossy cow like me to tell you so. Now before Robert comes back this evening, we're going to have both you, and the apartment, looking great. Come on, there's no time to be lost.' It was not unlike the lecture that she herself had been given by Jenny, just a few weeks before, and it pleased Miranda to be on the other end of it.

They worked steadily through the rest of the morning. Marty complained all the time and reached for the vodka bottle whenever she could, but by lunchtime the apartment was more or less straightened out, the spare bed made up and Miranda unpacked.

'Now,' said Miranda, 'where's your hairdresser?'

'A block away,' said Marty, who was becoming increasingly difficult and morose, like a sulky child.

'OK, let's make you an appointment for this afternoon. Will they do you a facial as well?'

'I guess,' said Marty.

'Where's your phone book then?'

Miranda made the appointment for two-thirty and then took Marty out to lunch at a little Italian place almost next door to the apartment block. Marty drank a great deal of wine, smoked numerous cigarettes, but ate hardly anything. So erratic was her behaviour that Miranda was not sure she would even go to the hairdresser unless she delivered her personally, but having done so, she staggered back to the apartment and crawled into bed.

She woke to electric light streaming into her eyes. 'Jesus, I'm sorry, I didn't realise . . .' Robert Kaufman stood in the doorway of the bedroom. He was dressed in a dark conventional suit, and still carried his briefcase. His dark hair was flecked with grey and his rather narrow face looked strained and tired. He was the kind of man who, if he had a different lifestyle, acquired a tan and relaxed a little, would be really very good-looking. As it was, one felt exhausted, just looking at him.

'Hello, Robert,' said Miranda, rubbing her eyes, still somewhat disorientated.

'Miranda, it's great to see you. I'm so sorry for crashing in on you like this, only I came home early to make up your bed and tidy the place some. Where's Marty?'

'I sent her to the hairdressers,' said Miranda. 'What time is it?'

'Just after six.'

'She should be back any minute, then. I booked her for the full treatment so it will take a while.'

'Can I fix you a drink?' said Robert.

'That would be lovely, I'll join you in a minute.'

Although she was still drugged by sleep, Miranda slipped out of bed quickly, slung on a towelling robe, gave her hair a quick brush and went to join Robert. It was a perfect opportunity to find out what had been going on and what was really wrong with Marty.

'A dry martini?' Robert said.

'That would be lovely, thanks. Tell me, Robert, what the hell's wrong with Marty?' Miranda said, seeing no point in any preamble – Marty could walk through the door at any moment.

'Jeez, so it didn't take long for you to figure out that there was something wrong,' said Robert.

'Robert, I've spent all morning cleaning your apartment. It was like a hell-hole. Even if you haven't noticed the change in Marty, you must have noticed the conditions you've been living in.'

'It's been creeping up on me slowly, I guess,' said Robert, dismissively, 'besides which I'm not here much.'

'Exactly.'

Robert turned to Miranda and handed her a glass. 'Look, sweetheart, it's great to have you staying here, but don't start lecturing me. It's been a tough old day and I have hours of work still to do before I can hit the sack.'

'All right,' said Miranda. 'Let me just ask you this question. Do you realise that Marty is only a hair's breadth away from ending up in a sanatorium?'

'You mean because she drinks a little too much?'

'A little too much! She's drinking tumblers of neat vodka at ten o'clock in the morning.'

She had his attention now. 'Are you sure?'

'Of course I'm sure, I've watched her, and because I was here, I suspect I was seeing her on a good day.'

'She's just not happy in New York,' said Robert, heavily. 'I don't know what to do with her – we can't have kids, you know.'

'She ought to have a job. She'd probably find it difficult to break into the modelling scene, but with her background and experience there are plenty of jobs she is fit for.'

'My wife doesn't need to work, I earn plenty of money for both of us,' he said pompously.

'Robert, it's not a question of money,' Miranda said, patiently. 'Marty needs some self-respect and above all, she needs something to do. Just think about it for a moment. How would you like to be holed up in this apartment all day, with piss all to do? She can't even have the satisfaction of cooking you a meal every evening, because she never knows if you'll be home in time.'

'You're giving me hassle, I did say no hassle, Miranda.'

'OK, OK, do nothing, let your wife destroy herself, but ask yourself this. Which would be the most degrading for you – having a working wife, or one who is an alcoholic depressive, who'll probably be dead before her fortieth birthday?'

'Marty's problem is not that bad, you're exaggerating,' said Robert.

'Believe me,' said Miranda, 'she's gone down hill quite a way since the days when I knew her, but she still has a long way to go, unless somebody gives her a helping hand.'

There was the sound of a key in the door. 'Drop it, right,' said Robert.

'OK.'

Marty looked a lot better. Her hair was sleek and blonde once more and her face had been carefully made up. Her jeans and shirt were still crumpled and none too clean, but the overall effect was a vast improvement. 'Hi honey,' said Marty, tremulously.

'Hi,' said Robert, 'you look nice. Look you guys, I've got to go and work now but what shall we do about supper, send out for some?'

'Yeh,' said Marty, 'I'll fix it.'

New York was not geared to making a person feel useful, Miranda thought. Less than a quarter of an hour after making the call, a boy appeared with tinfoil dishes containing a delicious variety of Indian curries. It could have been Chinese, it could have been burgers, it could have been a gourmet dinner for two, or indeed a complete dinner party – all at the press of a button.

Marty was subdued during dinner, drinking steadily but not heavily, and immediately the meal was finished, she excused herself and went to bed.

Miranda was just clearing away, when Robert came to join her in the kitchen. 'Miranda, I'm sorry I was a little rough earlier on,' he said. 'Everything you say is right. Look, while you're with us, you couldn't try and help her a little, could you? She could really use a friend.'

The bastard, Miranda thought, delegating the job – anything to avoid him having to interrupt his precious work. 'The only person that can really help her, Robert, is you,' she said, with commendable mildness.

'I have my work,' he said, 'it's the busiest time of year, I can't just . . .'

'OK, OK,' said Miranda, wearily. 'I can do without a lecture on the pressures of the banking world. Certainly I'll do what I can to help her, but the buck stops with you. You're the guy who's responsible for her, so let's both remember that.'

Miranda went to bed, her mind full of what could best be done for Marty. A psychiatrist, fully briefed on Miranda's current state of mind, would have applauded this development in her life. Fresh from losing Michael, there could be nothing better for her than to get involved in somebody else's problems. Somebody else who was weaker than herself who highlighted, even if it was only subconsciously, that she, Miranda Hicks could cope with pressure.

*

Tony Harris and Miranda liked one another the moment they met the following morning. He looked at her appraisingly as she walked into his office. 'Shit, what a cracker, and with class, too,' he said, holding out his hand.

'Shit, a man of good taste in New York, even,' Miranda mimicked in response. They laughed together like old friends.

'Seriously though, Miranda, you look great, fresh as a daisy, not even slightly jet-lagged. You must have had a good rest yesterday.'

Miranda was tempted to tell him just what sort of a day she'd had, but decided against it. 'Yes, I'm fine,' she said, 'ready for action. What do you want me to do and when?'

'That's my girl. Lawrence said you were a worker, and that, coming from the High Priest of the art, is praise indeed.'

To reach Tony, Miranda had walked off Madison Avenue through large glass doors and had run the gauntlet of a dozen workmen, sawing and hammering. From there, it had been necessary to climb a ladder to the little boxroom above the store, which was Tony's office. 'This, I take it, is the New York store,' she said, dryly.

'Indeed it is,' said Tony, 'and we're due to have it open and running in just three weeks.'

'Good grief,' said Miranda, 'three weeks is pushing it a bit, isn't it?'

'Oh ye of little faith. It's no problem. I have to get this store finished, stocked and manned, and all you have to do is the rest.'

'Great,' said Miranda, 'define the rest.'

They spent a happy hour going through the details of the promotion plans. An advertising agency, Brewers, had been appointed to handle the account and Miranda would be working directly with them.

'We'll get the New York store up and running and give it about three months. Then, if things are going well, we'll open our second in Houston, and that will take us up to six months and the end of your contract. However, if Houston does well, then we'll be looking at LA in which case, the job goes on. We've just got to play it by ear and see what happens.'

'It's exciting,' said Miranda. 'I love the idea of a British company taking the US by storm.'

'Hopefully,' said Tony, smiling at her. This girl was great. Lawrence had been right. She not only looked marvellous, she had brains too, and that irreplaceable asset – enthusiasm. 'Right,' he said, 'we'll take a cab over to Brewers now. We have an appointment,' he consulted his watch, 'in half an hour, with Nick Brewer, who is the President. You won't be working with him on a day-to-day basis, but he wants to make the initial presentation personally – you know what these guys are like. My wife, Rachael – she'd call them arse-lickers, but I wouldn't dream of saying anything so crude, not to a lady like you.'

Nick Brewer's intercom buzzed persistently, until he pulled himself away from his office window and his gloomy thoughts, and answered it. 'Yeh?'

'Mr Harris and Miss Hicks are here to see you, from ENGLISH GARDEN.'

'OK, give me a moment.' Damn, he had forgotten about them. He had been hoping to skate out for an early lunch. He was sure that food and more particularly, a drink or two, would make him feel better. It had been a heavy night – a press party, then dinner with the client, followed by a post-mortem on the party, and finally a night with a very athletic young lady, who lived in Greenwich Village and who certainly did not think that beds were for sleeping. Nick had only been divorced for five months. I can't keep up this pace, he thought. It's time I slowed down. So I'm free – do I have to keep proving it? He tidied his desk, and then going into the adjoining bathroom, flicked some cold water onto his face. Then wearily he returned to his desk and pressed the intercom button. 'Show them in, Reenie.'

They made an incongruous couple – she was almost twice his height, he – short, fat and balding, had never been a beauty. She, with her natural elegance, magnificent figure and that incredible hair, was so good to look at, he could not tear his eyes away. He recognised her, of course, and came out from behind his desk, to greet them. 'Good to see you guys. Mr Harris, Miss Hicks, it's a real pleasure, I've been a fan of yours for years.'

'Don't let's discuss how many years, please,' said Miranda, laughing.

He was an attractive man, she decided. Classically tall, dark and handsome, but he was looking a little weary, as though he had been putting too much effort into proving his attractions. 'Come and sit down,' he said. 'I'm real excited about ENGLISH GARDENS. I guess this could be one of the biggest things that's happened to this agency if we get our marketing right. . . .'

They spent an informative morning, and Nick, who had been determined to have a quiet lunch alone, found himself inviting them to join him. Tony declined, saying he must get back to the store, but suggesting that Miranda should accept the invitation, since she would be working so closely with the agency.

Over lunch, Nick completely forgot his earlier symptoms, so captivated was he by Miranda. As a poor boy, made good, he was easily impressed by power and status, and Miranda Hicks certainly had that. When he learnt of her own humble background, and that she, too, had started from nothing, it fascinated him. They were two of a kind, he told her, firmly, and promptly asked her out to dinner – which she refused.

Nick was not used to being refused by women. Most of the girls that he was involved with these days, were models, always on the lookout for jobs. He only had to mention that he was president of an advertising agency to have them falling over him. Perversely, of course, the fact that Miranda was not a pushover, made her even more attractive to him. He was not a man to be thwarted.

The days that followed were very hectic for Miranda. She was interviewed and photographed so often that the magazines, television companies, newspapers and radio stations all blended together into a blur of fatigue. Her nights were busy, too. If she was not actively involved in keeping Marty on the straight and narrow, she was having dinner with Nick Brewer. His persistence was exhausting. More often than not, it seemed easier to accept his invitation than to refuse it. He took her to some magnificent restaurants, treated her with enormous courtesy, and always returned her to the Kaufman's apartment with nothing more than a goodnight peck on the cheek.

On their fourth meeting, however, he was openly more blatant about his feelings for her, never missing an opportunity to take her hand, or touch her arm, or knee to make a point. Miranda decided it was time to make the position clear. 'I'm married,' she said, 'I should have mentioned it to you before, Nick, but it's a painful subject.'

He was clearly very taken aback. 'When you say it is a painful subject, does that mean you are seeking a divorce?'

Miranda already knew all about Nick's divorce, in fact he had talked of it endlessly. The last thing she wanted to do was to get him back onto that subject again. 'No, just separated.'

'Well, as one who's been through it, when it does come to getting a divorce, you need look no further than ask my advice. There isn't a thing I don't know about fucking divorce.' He drank deeply of his wine.

'I don't know if I want a divorce,' said Miranda. It had been a hard day and now, full of good food and wine, she felt relaxed enough to speak her mind.

'Well, honey, the offer's open.' He eyed her speculatively for a moment. 'As a matter of interest, why don't you want a divorce?'

'I don't know,' Miranda answered truthfully, 'and I'd rather not talk about it.' Nick was left with no doubts that she meant what she said.

The combination of this unexpected social life, teamed with a hectic business life, and the continuing demands of Marty, gave Miranda very little chance to think of anything, until finally, with a sigh of relief, she collapsed into bed each night. Then her mind did wander and always her thoughts turned towards Michael. The image of his face and those hooded eyes, always hovered close by, and she wondered if the pain of being without him would ever fade. She had not told Nick the truth about her views on divorce. She could not contemplate divorcing Michael for the simple reason that she still felt a part of him. She was tempted to write to him – at least to advise him where she was, in case he needed to contact her. But she decided against it. He had Jenny's address after all and he could get in touch with her that way, if he needed to do so. Keeping him out of her thoughts had to be her main objective and writing to him was not going to help that.

She was in her second week of work at ENGLISH GARDENS when an idea came to her that was so brilliantly simple, she was furious with herself for not thinking of it before. Between interviews, she dashed back to the office and Tony. Things were definitely taking shape. The shop looked gorgeous. It was, quite literally, an English garden. There was a greenhouse, a sweep of lawn, a rockery, a water garden, a bird table and an herbaceous border. Between it all, weaved little paths to take the shopper from one range of clothes to the next. The changing rooms looked like a summer house, with a thatched roof and roses climbing round the door of each individual unit.

Miranda was knocked out and Tony joined her on hearing her squeals of delight. 'Good, isn't it?'

'Good, it's fantastic, Tony, but I hope you have green fingers – how the hell are you going to keep this lot alive?'

'A full-time gardener, day and night. He was not easy to track down in New York. Not only has he got green fingers but he's English, and his name is Fred. Beat that, if you can.'

'I can't. I'm overcome with admiration,' said Miranda, genuinely. 'Which brings me to the reason for calling in.'

'You mean you're not here because you're missing me? I must call Rachael and tell her that. She's dead jealous of you.'

'I'm not surprised,' said Miranda. 'If I was married to a macho man like you, I wouldn't let him go flying off to New York unchaperoned.' They enjoyed their gentle bantering. 'In fact, Tony dear, I'm here to solve one of your problems. I presume the sales assistants you're looking for need to be English?'

'They certainly do, but it's not that easy,' Tony said. 'The problem is, there are two kinds of English girls in New York City. They are either career mad, in high-powered jobs and would not even consider the kind of lowly position I'm offering, or else they are not career mad and in high-powered jobs, which means they are married to rich men, or they're scrubbers.'

'Isn't that something of a generalisation?' Miranda suggested.

'Yeh, perhaps, but it's also true.'

'Well, I've got someone who falls into one of your categories and who needs a job.'

'You have? Tell me more.'

'Her name is Marty Kaufman. She's thirty-five, she's an ex-model, English, married to a banker and bored as hell.'

'Accent?' Tony asked.

'She's been in New York for five years and to you and me she has an accent. To the average New Yorker, however, I would think she sounds as English as they come – especially if she concentrates.'

'OK, so this sounds great,' said Tony, 'but what's the snag?'

Miranda hesitated. It was tempting to say that there was no snag, but she was not sure how reliable Marty would prove. Tony sensed her dilemma.

'Look, sweetheart, I'm the one who pays your wages, so I'm the one to whom you owe the first loyalty.'

Miranda grinned. 'OK. She's the girl I'm staying with at the moment and she does have a few problems. Her husband's a manic worker, he's never at home and so she's taken to the bottle.'

'Oh, no,' said Tony, 'I'm not having a dypso round here – we're putting across a clean-cut wholesome image – remember.'

'Wait, wait,' said Miranda, impatiently. 'Just in the few days since I've been here, she's knocked off the juice a lot. She only drinks when she's got nothing else to do. OK, so we'd have to watch her for the first few days and if she turns up here drunk even once, then, obviously, she's out on her ear. But honestly, Tony, I think you should give her the chance.'

'If I wasn't so desperate, I'd say you were nuts,' said Tony. 'As I am, I'll say you're still nuts, but let's give it a whirl.'

Miranda threw her arms around his neck and kissed him soundly. 'Tony, you're wonderful.'

'That's what Rachael always says,' Tony said, smugly.

Marty's initial reaction was predictable. 'I can't do it,' she said. 'I simply can't. I'm not good with people any more, I get shy.'

'Only because you're not used to meeting anyone these days. Look, Marty, I've sweated blood to get this interview for you. You owe it to me to give it a try.' It was a blatant rip off of Jenny's tactics, and it worked a treat.

After an enormous amount of hassle, some new clothes, and just one vodka for Dutch courage, the following day, Miranda dragged Marty to an interview with Tony.

It went well. Tony was entranced. He and Marty had been born within half a mile of one another, they discovered, and the East End humour and comradeship instantly sparked between them. So pleased was Tony with Marty that he suggested she should begin work right away. 'There's crates of clothes to unload and price,' he said. 'Some of them will need pressing and I was going to drag some kids off the street to do it, but I'd much rather you handled it. There's a lot of valuable stuff, and the exercise will help you familiarise yourself with the merchandise.'

To celebrate the appointment, Tony, Miranda and Marty went out to lunch, and Marty, Miranda noticed, drank no more than her share of the wine bottle. Watching her friend talking animatedly to Tony, it seemed to Miranda that after months of self-doubt and introspection, at last she had done something useful – and for someone else, rather than herself. Perhaps it was a turning point, an omen for the future.

Chapter Twenty-Three

Nick Brewer was unbelievably irritated. During a tough Brooklyn childhood, he had learnt that if you wanted something badly enough, and hassled for it long enough, you always got it. But it appeared the rules did not apply to Miranda Hicks. He had spent a fortune wining and dining her, sending her flowers and little gifts of perfume, champagne – anything he felt would appeal to her. Yet he was getting nowhere. Every evening he took her out, he suggested they should return to his flat for a nightcap. Every evening she refused him. She would talk in general terms about anything under the sun, but rarely about herself. Any physical approaches he made to her were met with passive resistance – far more deadly than any kind of struggle. He wanted her, yes – for her beautiful body and because he liked the idea of screwing someone famous. Mostly, though, he wanted her because apparently she did not want him – it was a challenge, a challenge he simply had to meet.

He found it humiliating to have to resort to work as the excuse for furthering his aims, but Miranda Hicks was not some dumb kid, and her strongest motivation seemed to be her job. Certainly, trading on her professionalism seemed the most likely way to success, and the press release proved the right vehicle. He approved the draft with Tony Harris and as their meeting ended, Tony said casually, 'Oh, if you have a chance, Nick, perhaps you'd just show it to Miranda before you press any buttons. She has a natural feel for the media and since promotion is her job, I'd like her to feel she is involved in the decision process.'

'Yes, of course,' said Nick, suddenly realising that this was the opportunity for which he had been seeking. He planned his move carefully. Bob Beirdoff, who was the account executive, working closely with Miranda, was invited to an evening meeting at Nick's apartment in order to discuss the press release. So was Miranda.

She was suspicious when he called her to make the appointment. 'What's wrong with your office?' she asked.

'Bob and I both have an earlier meeting out of town. It will be a hell of a lot more convenient for us to end up at my apartment – it's nearer your place, too.' Having obtained her agreement, Nick then cancelled Bob Beirdoff.

It was a freezing night, the snow of a few days earlier had compacted into ice, the air was so cold it seemed to burn the inside of Miranda's nostrils, each time she breathed. She paid off the cab and hurried into the hallway of Nick's apartment block.

Nick's apartment was quite different from how Miranda had imagined it. The brash advertising man who admitted he had no class and came from nowhere had shown considerable taste. He favoured blues and greys – everywhere the place was restful and calm.

'It's gorgeous, Nick,' said Miranda.

'Wait until you see the Manhattan skyline – come and look.' And there New York lay before them.

'You were clever to find this place.'

'Not clever,' said Nick, 'I had to work damned hard for it. I've earned every stick of furniture, every millimetre of pile on the carpet.'

His pride was something Miranda understood, it mirrored her own feelings exactly. 'If you could have your time over again, would you do anything differently?' she asked.

'Yes, I wouldn't have got married.' There was bitterness in his voice.

'What really went wrong?' Miranda asked. 'You've never told me that.'

'I married the boss's daughter. When she found out she couldn't push me around like everyone else in her life, she started giving me a hard time. The first moment I could, I left.'

'Let me see,' said Miranda, 'when would that be, when you didn't need her any more?' Her tone was light but she sensed she was close enough to the truth to make Nick feel uncomfortable.

'I did love her,' he said defensively, 'once – incredible though it seems now.'

'Why are you so bitter?' Miranda asked.

He shrugged his shoulders. 'When I first split, the family really doled out the crap. Every business venture I entered into, they tried to block me.'

'For what?'

'Just for revenge. When they thought they'd finally broken me, they lost interest, and that's when I made my move and established Brewers. They can't touch me now.'

'What hells people do create for themselves and each other,' Miranda said, thoughtfully.

'Hey, this conversation's getting a bit heavy, let's have a drink while we wait for Bob.'

Three martinis later, when Bob had still not shown up, Miranda was becoming restive. 'Look Nick, can I just have a glance at this press release and then go. I'm sorry I can't wait for Bob but I have a lot to do.'

'Why, have you got something else on this evening?'

'No, not exactly, but I do have a heavy day tomorrow.'

'Don't tell me, you want to wash your hair.'

'More or less,' said Miranda laughing.

'I tell you what,' said Nick, 'why don't we speed things up by my cooking you a quick supper, then you needn't worry about eating when you get home.'

'No, honestly. . . .' Miranda started to protest.

'Look, I'm really not trying to delay you. I tell you what, you look at the press release and I'll go raid the freezer.'

'I didn't know you were a cook,' Miranda said.

'Who needs to be a cook these days – it's all written on the packet.'

In fact, he had already prepared mussels in a cream and white wine sauce. While Miranda read through the press release, he put the bowl of mussels in the oven, heated some French bread, and pulled the cork on a bottle of champagne.

With the minimum of fuss, he also recharged Miranda's martini glass. Ten minutes' later, he laid the meal before her.

'Mussels! How lovely,' said Miranda.

'Good, I'm glad you like them,' said Nick. 'Go on, help yourself, have plenty.'

Nick poured the champagne and they attacked their mussels with relish, dipping their bread in the delicious sauce.

'Oh, this is good,' said Miranda. 'It seems an age since I've had anything but junk food.'

'Some more?'

'But what if Bob comes?'

For a moment Nick looked startled. 'Oh, well er . . . he can make do with bread and cheese.'

Miranda set down her spoon. 'Bob isn't coming at all, is he Nick?'

'Of course he is,' he protested.

'He is not. It was just an excuse to get me to your apartment. I bet when I check with Bob tomorrow – which believe me I will, unless you tell me the truth – I'll find he wasn't due here at all tonight.'

'I guess not,' said Nick, lamely.

Miranda stood up, slamming down her napkin. 'That was a rotten, beastly trick, Nick. I'd have been pleased to come to your apartment for dinner, when I was good and ready and felt I knew you better, but this underhand stuff, using work as an excuse – it stinks.'

'Tony really did want you to see the press release.'

'So – you could have posted it to me.'

'Miranda, I really wanted to be alone with you.'

'You've been alone with me plenty of times,' Miranda said.

'No, only in a restaurant, or a cab – I meant properly alone.' Nick was standing also now. He came round the table towards her. 'You know I realise this is an awfully dumb line, but you do look even more beautiful when you're angry.'

Before she could stop him, he had slipped his arms round her, his lips swooping on to hers in a long, hard kiss. Just for a moment, a brief moment, Miranda responded. She felt so starved of physical contact since Michael had awakened her to the wondrous possibilities of the flesh. But this was not

Michael, this was a stranger, someone she barely knew and certainly did not love. She began to struggle but he was holding her fast, bending her backwards, painfully. As his lips forced hers apart, with one supreme effort, she wrenched her face from his, and in doing so he lost his balance, nearly falling. It was all she needed to fight her way out of his arms. 'Don't you ever do that again, Nick, not ever. You're a bastard, do you know that? May be your strong-arm tactics work with some women but not this one.' She was breathing heavily and painfully, her lips felt bruised and swollen, and she could feel her bottom lip was slightly cut.

Nick too, was out of breath and dishevelled. 'And why not, tell me that? We're both unattached and available. Is it so terribly wrong of me to want to make love to you?'

'Yes it is,' said Miranda.

'Why?' Nick demanded, taking another step towards her. She felt a pang of fear.

'Because . . . because I still love my husband.'

The words were as big a shock to Miranda as they were to Nick. He stopped in mid-stride. 'Say that again,' he said.

'You heard the first time.'

'Then why the fucking hell are you mucking about with me, if that's the case?'

'I'm not mucking about with you,' Miranda said. 'I've accepted a few dinner dates with you and I came here tonight, if you remember, because we were supposed to be having a meeting. Now will you fetch my coat for me, please. I'm going.' She had the upper hand now, and she knew it.

Nick's expression softened. He tried different tactics. 'Oh come on, Miranda, don't be mad at me, I'm just a red-blooded guy who fancies you like crazy.'

'A two-faced red-blooded guy who's old enough to know better. My coat, please.'

He kept up the smarmy act while he helped her on with her coat, found her gloves, rang for a cab, and saw her, not only to the lift, but rode down in it with her to the hallway. By the front door he took her arm. 'You'll have dinner with me one day next week, won't you? Just to show there's no hard feelings.'

'I certainly will not,' said Miranda. 'I only wish it were possible not to ever have to see you again – frankly I can do without creeps like you.'

The mask dropped. 'Why, you little bitch.'

'Ah, that's better,' said Miranda, 'I prefer to see you in your true colours. The smoothy hard-done-by image doesn't suit you at all. Stick to playing the bastard, Nick, it's a much easier part for you because it comes so naturally.' And before Nick had time to reply, she was through the swing doors and out into the waiting cab.

Miranda felt rather pleased with herself, riding home through the still busy New York streets. She had handled Nick well, she felt, and what a prat to have played a trick like that – it was almost as corny as running out of petrol. But as she went back over what she had said, one sentence stood out from the rest . . . 'because I still love my husband.' Sitting alone in the cab, she whispered the words again. It can't be true she told herself. Please God, don't let it be true. I must get over him, I must.

She let herself into a darkened apartment – Marty and Robert were clearly already asleep. As noiselessly as possible she started for her bedroom and then realised she was far from sleep. Instead she went into the kitchen, made herself a coffee, collapsed in front of the television and began watching a late night movie with unseeing eyes. There was a strange poignancy about her feelings for Michael, she realised. Initially, immediately after she had left Crete, her primary feelings had been anger and hurt. Now, as these more violent emotions subsided, she was left with the stark reality of how much she had loved him. The bad times were fading from her mind. All she could remember were the glorious days, the rapturous nights, the look of love in his eyes as he made love to her, and the indulgent amusement as she struggled to learn to water ski, or to get her tongue round an unpronounceable Greek word. And most bitter-sweet of all, the joy of the night she had told him she was expecting his baby. . . .

There was an unreal quality about these memories, it was like watching a film show, hardly more real than the pictures now flashing before her. And as the days went by, she realised, these images were becoming more vivid, not less. She wondered how long it would be before the burden of them became intolerable.

Tony Harris had never been more frightened in his life. They had done everything they could now. It was 8.55 and the doors of ENGLISH GARDEN, Madison Avenue, were about to open for the first time. This was make or break. Crowds would come to see the place, he was sure of that, but would they buy? Would they like the merchandise? Would they even understand it, with its classic English lines? At that moment, he wanted to run away, to bury his face in Rachael's ample bosom and not look again until six o'clock, when the store closed.

Miranda sensed his terror. While the other girls busied themselves with last minute preparations, Miranda made two mugs of coffee, slapped down one on Tony's desk, and reaching into his filing cabinet, drew out the bottle of whisky and poured a slug into the top of his coffee mug.

'That's sacrilege girl, it's one of the finest blended malts.'

'It has to be a good investment,' said Miranda, gently. 'You look as though you're about to shit a brick, and you have to be the star today.'

'You were great this morning,' said Tony. 'I'm sorry I haven't had a chance to say so before.'

Miranda had done a morning stint on breakfast television, and she had been good. She had modelled three different ENGLISH GARDEN outfits and been interviewed in each of them. The interview had gone way over time, and afterwards they had been told the switchboard had been jammed with calls from people wanting to know the address of ENGLISH GARDEN. But it still did not mean a thing, Tony knew. They might come to look, but would they put their money where their mouth was – that was all that mattered. He had admitted to no one how much his future depended on the success of this move into the States. Neither of his shareholders was in favour of the scheme, and had only gone along with it because Tony had personally guaranteed the bank loan that had financed the venture. If things went wrong, not only would it cost him his business, it would cost him his home as well. He thought of that now and felt sweat break out on his forehead.

'They jammed the switchboard with enquiries,' Miranda said, for the third time, desperate to reassure him.

'But, sugar, it doesn't mean they'll buy. How often do I have to tell you that?'

'They'll buy, they'll buy. The prices are good, the merchandise is great.'

'You think it's great because you're that sort of girl. What's some hard-bitten New Yorker going to think?'

'Terrific,' said Miranda – and she was right. . . .

Afterwards, they reckoned that three thousand people must have packed into the store during the day. Fred was not amused, his garden looked very tired, but for everyone else involved in ENGLISH GARDEN, it was nothing short of a miracle. For the punters did not just walk in and walk out, they walked in and bought, bought and bought – so much so, that by eleven o'clock, Tony had to arrange for fresh goods to be air-freighted over from London in order to be able to open the following day. It was a sell-out.

The idea had been that Miranda should spend the day in a variety of different garments, walking between the customers as they shopped, showing off the merchandise. Instead, she spent the whole day either manning the tills, packing goods, or dragging out fresh supplies from the stock room. At one point even Fred had to be taken away from his beloved plants, which he was tending surreptitiously, and pressed into service on a check-out counter. It was bedlam, it was wonderful. . . . They sweated and swore, laughed and cried, not sure whether they were living a dream or a nightmare.

Their enormous success attracted the media like flies, during the day. Television cameras whirred outside, reporters tried desperately to get a quote from someone, but everyone was too busy. At five o'clock Tony had a stroke of genius. He sent Fred out for half a dozen crates of champagne, and told the waiting press that there would be an impromptu press party, to celebrate the success, once the store was closed. Afterwards, Bob Beirdoff swore that there was not a single fashion editor in New York, who mattered, who was not there. The place was truly humming, everyone gave interviews, the champagne flowed. Tony received a telex confirmation to say that the plane load of replacement stock would be arriving at the airport at four a.m. and the press decided even to cover that.

Miranda, determined not to miss a chance of maximising the publicity, took all the sales girls into Tony's office, made them remove their crumpled clothes, and dress in a new range of ENGLISH GARDEN wear. She sent them out with fresh makeup and newly combed hair, and they created yet another rush of enthusiasm from the already over-enthusiastic photographers. When Miranda, herself, finally came down the stairs from Tony's office, it was to thunderous applause. As she descended the staircase, taking her time for the sake of the photographers, she was aware of Tony and Marty standing in the crowd, arms around each other, Tony, suddenly very Jewish, and emotional, had tears pouring down his face. Marty, too, was smiling and crying. That's what it is really all about, Miranda thought. Thank God it worked – not because of the amazing total in the tills, but the fact that there are two people whose happiness largely depended on today's success – and we made it. She joined them as soon as she reached the bottom of the stairs.

'It's no good,' said Tony, wiping his tears away, 'I'm going to have to ring Rachael. I'm going to have to call Momma and tell her it's OK. Will you excuse me? Can you hold the fort, Miranda?'

'Of course, you go ahead.'

Both women watched him as he ran up the stairs, fatigue forgotten in his effort to reach the telephone. 'That's really rather special, isn't it?' said Miranda. 'I don't know how long those two have been married, but certainly their youngest son celebrated his twenty-first the other day. Right now, a lot of men would be draping themselves around the sales girls, but not Tony. He has to call the only woman who matters, even if she is three thousand miles away.'

Marty gave her friend a shrewd look. There was wistfulness in Miranda's voice, but Marty knew better than to question her. Miranda's private life, at any rate these days, was very private indeed.

Chapter Twenty-Four

ENGLISH GARDEN's success was not a one-day wonder. The phenomenal sales continued and at the end of the first week they were all exhausted – Miranda, perhaps, more than the rest, since she had been working so hard on promotion before the store opened. It was all she could do to drag herself out of bed each morning, and everything ached from the persistent running about, humping stock, helping customers, and the massive clear-up operation each night when, finally, they saw the last customers off the premises. Fred had found it necessary to take on a full-time assistant, to cope with the flowers – everyone was stretched to the very limits.

On Saturday night, when the store had finally closed, Tony called Miranda to his office and without reference to her, poured them both a gigantic whisky.

'How are you?' Miranda asked softly. 'I don't seem to have seen you for several days, except over a sea of customers.'

'I feel great, in a battered sort of way, I just can't believe it. This is way over the top of my wildest, most optimistic pipe-dreams.'

'I'm so pleased for you,' said Miranda.

'Bless you, sweetheart, and bless you, too, for all your labours. There's not a lot of people, never mind celebrated models, who would have got stuck in, as you have, the last few days.'

'It's been a pleasure – I suppose this means we'll be going ahead with Houston?'

'I think we'd be crazy not to. Once we have got this store operating in a routine way, we could perhaps fly down together and have a look.'

'That would be great,' said Miranda.

'The other thing I wanted to say to you, poppet, is that you need to have a few days off. I'm painfully aware you haven't had a day to yourself since you arrived in New York.'

'Oh I will, in a while,' said Miranda, 'when things have quietened down a bit.'

'No, not when things have quietened down a bit – now,' said Tony. 'I've taken on a couple of extra sales girls this afternoon. It's amazing how they have popped out of the woodwork, now the store's a success. Take off tomorrow, Monday and Tuesday, sleep, lie around, go for walks. . . .'

'In this weather?' said Miranda, laughing.

'Well, you know, just hang about, relax.'

'Well, if you're sure.' The idea was bliss. 'What about Marty?'

'She says she's OK to work through another week, and I'd like someone experienced to train these new girls.' He grinned. 'I'm really pleased with Marty. You know, she was telling me last night, she reckons you've saved her life.'

'Rubbish,' said Miranda.

'No, I'm serious. It's what she thinks, anyway. From where she was when you arrived in her life, she reckoned she only had one way to go. So there you go, Miss Hicks, give your halo a good shine.'

The following morning Miranda lay in bed until after eleven, luxuriating in its warmth and comfort. Then she ran herself an enormous bath and lay in that for hours, reading the papers. Although it was Sunday, both Robert and Marty were at work and it was wonderful to have the place to herself. After her bath, she made herself some breakfast, and lounged around on the sofa enjoying the peace and tranquillity. It was time to get a place of her own, she decided. She was ready for it, strong enough to cope. Up until now she had been terrified of her own company, knowing where her thoughts would lead her. Now she actively courted solitude – Michael was always in her thoughts, but at last she could welcome him there. Thinking of him had become a necessary part of her day. On a practical level, as the store had proved to be a success, she would certainly be in New York for six months, perhaps longer, and she would use Monday and Tuesday to go hunting for an apartment.

The third address the agent sent her to was the apartment she wanted. It was in an old building on 74th Street, no more than a couple of blocks from the store. It was tiny, just one room, with a kitchenette and a bathroom. The room was well designed though, with a bed that folded up into the wall, and it was quaint, with an erratic sloping ceiling, which was reminiscent of England rather than New York. Two big picture windows looked out onto the street, below which were gaily painted window boxes. The curtains, carpets and paintwork were in good order and tastefully done in shades of apricot – it was ready to walk into. The landlady was a widow, a sweet little woman with white hair and gentle, pale blue eyes. She was everyone's idea of how a grandmother should look. Her voice was gentle too, her manner hesitant. She did not seem to belong to the harsh world of New York.

'I'd like it,' said Miranda.

'Good, I was hoping you would.' The old woman smiled disarmingly. 'When would you like to move in?'

'Would tomorrow be too soon?'

'The sooner the better, so I can start charging you rent.'

It was still early afternoon when Miranda left her new apartment in high spirits, yet it was almost dark. The sky was heavy and overcast and it looked like it was going to snow again. Everywhere there were the trappings of Christmas, now only a few weeks away – decorations, Santa Claus, fairy lights and Christmas trees. Miranda adored Christmas and she felt her spirits lift as, despite the cold, she wandered down the street, savouring her new neighbourhood. She was just about to turn into Madison Avenue, when something caught her eye. It was an art gallery across the street and in the window, surely . . . she ran across towards it, dodging the traffic, causing a stream of car horns and abuse as she went. Panting, she stopped in front of the gallery window. So, she was right. There, prominently displayed in the window, were three Minos paintings, their unmistakable style had been recognisable, even from the far side of the street. She stared, her stomach churning, her heart beating rapidly. Until that moment she had chosen to forget how much Michael could affect her, but now, staring at his paintings, never mind at the man himself, she was trembling and agitated. They were not paintings she had seen before and she wondered whether he had painted them before their marriage or subsequently. She stood for a long time, memories flooding back, oblivious of the cold or the curious glances of passersby. Suddenly, snow began to fall from the sky, as though someone had turned on a tap. Without thinking, she ran to the door of the gallery and walked in.

It was like entering another world. The shop smelt of polish, of linseed oil and . . . and yes, a bowl of winter jasmine was on a table just by the door. As the sound of the shop bell died away, a figure came towards her. He was elderly, probably around seventy, with snow-white hair and a wrinkled, benevolent face. Despite his age, he carried himself well, suggesting, perhaps, a military background.

'Good afternoon, madam. Can I help you?'

'You're English!' said Miranda, smiling broadly.

'Yes, indeed, and so are you. What a delightful happening, on an otherwise very unpleasant Monday afternoon.'

'Yes, it's snowing hard now.'

'Are you here to shelter from the snow, or can I help you in any way?' The query was spoken without rancour. Miranda felt he would have been equally happy with the answer that she was sheltering from the snow. She hesitated. 'I-I saw your Minos paintings in the window.'

The man smiled, warmly. 'Ah yes, that is a new batch which have only been on display since this morning. They've already attracted considerable interest, in fact I've sold the large one.'

'H-have you any more?' Miranda asked.

'Yes.' The man turned. 'Just through here. Would you care to look at them?'

There were three more placed on stands, in an area cordoned off from the rest of the shop, but Miranda only had eyes for one of them. It was an intricate pattern of dolphins playing, the lead dolphin being ridden by the traditional boy – his hair blowing back from his face, which was creased with laughter as the great beast beneath him ploughed through the waves. By any standards, it was a lovely painting, but for Miranda it had a special significance, for she could remember the day it had been painted. Michael had worked for only a few hours that morning and then had gone into Iraklion for a meeting. While he was away, she had wandered into his study and found the painting standing on the easel, drying. She had loved it instantly and it had seemed especially significant that he had chosen to paint a child on that day, for it had been the same evening she told him she was carrying his baby. At the sight of the painting now, on a cold December day in New York, Miranda all but broke down. She bit her lip hard, turning her head away so that the man could not see her expression. 'I'll just have a general look round, if I may,' she managed to say in a strangled voice.

'Yes, of course,' he said. Then, as if sensing her mood, he added, 'I'll leave you alone, I'll be in my office if you want me.'

Once alone, Miranda made strenuous efforts to pull herself together. She blew her nose, wiped her eyes and began walking aimlessly round the rest of the gallery. But within ten minutes, she was back to the dolphins. Well under control now, she stared at the painting for a long, long time – her head full of memories of balmy evenings, wonderful skies, the blue sea, the feel of Michael's arms around her. Rightly or wrongly, she knew she had to have the painting. She popped her head round the door of the office. 'How much is the dolphin painting?' she asked.

The man looked up sharply and smiled. 'Yes, it's one of my favourites. Let me see, it's only a small painting – thirteen thousand dollars.'

'I'll take it,' she said, decisively, not daring to think what a devastating effect it would have on her bank balance.

'Wonderful!'

They conducted their business swiftly. Miranda tried very hard not to imagine how her mother would react at the thought of spending so much money on a painting.

'It's still snowing outside,' the man said, 'it would be probably unwise to take it with you now.'

'Beside which,' said Miranda, 'you'll want to clear my cheque first.'

'Oh yes,' the man said vaguely.

Really the English were impossible – so vague about money, Miranda thought. 'Actually,' she said, 'it would be more sensible if I collected it tomorrow anyway. I've just rented myself an apartment, up the street from here, and I'm moving in tomorrow.'

'What's the address, Madam?' Miranda told him. 'Well, why don't I drop the painting round to you tomorrow evening then, when I close the shop?' He smiled, shyly. 'If that will be convenient?'

'That's awfully kind of you, if you're sure.'

'It would be a pleasure. Now, shall I ring for a cab? You can't walk home in this.'

When the cab arrived, he showed her to the door. 'I don't even know your name,' Miranda said, suddenly.

'I'm so sorry, let me fetch you a card.' He presented it to her, with a small bow. 'Rupert Shepherd,' he said, 'retired solicitor, art dealer and ageing connoisseur of life.'

She laughed. 'I'll see you tomorrow then, Mr Shepherd. Thanks very much.'

Rupert watched her as she climbed into the cab and drove off into the swirling snow. 'What an extraordinary thing!' he said aloud. He let out a sigh, shut the shop door and put up the closed sign. It was still an hour before he was due to close officially, but he wanted to think. He had recognised her immediately she had walked into the shop, of course – Miranda Hicks, the fashion model, and Michael's estranged wife. She was beautiful, much more beautiful than her photographs suggested, for there was a warmth about her. How could she and Michael have parted? She represented everything the boy most needed in his life, and she still cared for him – she must do – for there had been tears in her eyes when she had spotted the dolphin picture – and she had bought it, that had to be significant. He picked up the cheque on his desk and glanced at it, briefly, for a moment. Then, slowly, deliberately he tore it up and threw it in the bin.

'It's me, Rupert Shepherd.' His breathless voice came over the intercom.

'Oh, hello, fourth floor,' said Miranda. She pressed the entry button and then went to the elevator to meet him. He looked perished as he stepped out onto the landing. 'I feel dreadful,' said Miranda, 'I should never have allowed you to deliver the painting. It must be freezing out there and I bet you didn't take a cab.'

'Certainly not,' he said, 'and don't fuss me, my dear, you make me feel older than my years.' He smiled, mischievously.

'Well, come on in, anyway. It's very humble but I've nearly made it home.'

Although it was tiny, Rupert could see instantly why she'd taken the apartment – it was charming and cosy. 'Your dolphins are going to look well in here,' he said.

'Yes, I thought so,' said Miranda, 'I'm dying to see them. I thought I'd put them up over there.'

'Ah,' said Rupert, 'then I hope you'll let me help you.' He fumbled in the pockets of his old-fashioned greatcoat, and after a moment, triumphantly pulled out a little leather pouch. 'One tool kit,' he said, 'I was hoping you'd let me hang the picture for you.'

'Oh, you are kind,' said Miranda, 'what a lovely thought. I'm hopeless at that sort of thing. I'll accept, provided you let me take your coat and pour you a large drink.'

'Agreed on both counts. A Scotch, please.'

The picture was unwrapped with reverence and a lengthy discussion then took place as to its exact location. With great dexterity and considerable flourish, Rupert then mounted a picture hook on the wall and the dolphins were duly hung. The picture dominated the room. Wherever you stood, from whichever angle you looked, it was the main feature. Similar thoughts were in both Rupert's and Miranda's mind, as they stood gazing at it. Was it sensible to have such a dominant reminder of her estranged husband?

'It looks well,' said Rupert.

'Yes, it does. Here, let me freshen your drink.'

'Well, why not, this is excellent Scotch, such a welcome change after that dreadful bourbon.'

'My boss has a secret supply of the stuff,' Miranda confessed. 'It's something to do with a particularly close relationship with a customs man.'

'I think it would have to be,' Rupert agreed, 'knowing its likely price. Tell me, who is your boss and what do you do?'

'You mean you haven't heard of ENGLISH GARDEN?'

Having established that Rupert was probably the only resident of New York City who had not, but agreeing that women's fashion was not one of his keener interests, Miranda told him all about her job. Then she turned the tables on him. 'What took you from lawyer to art dealer?'

He had to answer the question carefully, but more or less truthfully. 'I've always been interested in art, I have quite a large personal collection. All my working life, I've been involved in a family solicitors' practice, with a branch here in New York and one in London. Increasingly – though I adore England – I found myself spending most of my time in New York. I like the American enthusiasm and, of course, the opportunities are tremendous. Six, no nearly seven years ago, associates of mine offered to buy out my business. It seemed sensible to accept their offer, it was a very generous one. At the time, though, I was not ready to retire so I decided to make my home in New York and open the gallery. I have to say, I've made a modest, but very adequate living, and I enjoy the work enormously.' What he neglected to tell Miranda was that this decision had also coincided with Michael's return to Crete and, therefore, his sudden requirement for a full time American agent.

'Do you know the artist?' Miranda asked casually, nodding towards the picture.

Rupert had been prepared for the question. 'Slightly,' he said. 'Yes, a nice chap.'

Miranda made no comment, turning the conversation instead to admitting her appalling lack of knowledge of the art world.

'Then I have a proposal to make to you,' said Rupert. 'Since you have now become a very valued customer, I wonder whether you would care to have dinner with me one evening, in my flat – I refuse to call it an apartment – it's situated over the gallery, and quite comfortable. Then, if you feel so inclined, I can lecture you on the history of art, and if not, I will endeavour to find other ways to amuse you.'

Miranda laughed. 'I'd love to. How very kind.'

'How about one day next week then?' Rupert suggested, and they settled on Wednesday.

Rupert's home delighted Miranda when, the following week, she arrived for dinner. It was a typical bachelor pad with rather heavy furniture, leather armchairs and acres of books and paintings. There was a smell about the room, too, of good tobacco and port. After drinks (don't let's call them cocktails), they went through to a tiny panelled dining room where they were served dinner by a cheerful black woman, called Bow.

'Bow has looked after me for years, she understands me. I don't think I could operate without her,' Rupert confided.

Dinner was traditional and excellent – potted shrimps, followed by roast pheasant, profiteroles and a very comprehensive cheeseboard. Rupert and Miranda frankly adored each other's company. Rupert was completely captivated by the beautiful young woman, with her ready humour and Northern good sense. And as for Miranda, it was wonderful to spend an evening in the company of an intelligent, amusing, cultured man, without any fear of unwelcome sexual advances. She said as much to him as they sat sipping port, tucking into a very excellent piece of stilton.

'If you're suggesting I'm past it, young lady,' Rupert said, with mock severity, 'I hope you will withdraw the remark forthwith. On the other hand, it would hardly be relevant to do so, since, of course, you are absolutely right.'

'I wasn't suggesting that at all,' Miranda said. 'It's just that I feel safe with you, I suppose. Male company is usually so much more enjoyable than female, if only sex didn't always get in the way.'

'I dare say you're right,' said Rupert, 'though I have very little experience of such matters. I'm a bachelor, you see, and most of my adventures have, on the whole, been rather shallow affairs. I'm perfectly normal,' he added, grinning, 'at least I've always considered myself to be, but on the whole, I do find a woman's mind far more interesting than her body.'

'How refreshing,' said Miranda. 'I've been married twice and I've never met a man before who felt like that.'

There was a pause, during which Rupert's expression suddenly clouded. He frowned and began playing nervously with the stem of his port glass. 'What is it?' said Miranda, instantly in tune with his feelings.

'Miranda, there's something I ought to have told you before, earlier in the evening, only . . .' he hesitated, 'I've kept putting it off because it's never seemed to be the right moment.'

Miranda's stomach gave an involuntary lurch. 'What is it,' she said, 'is something wrong? Have I said something to upset you?'

'No, no, it's nothing like that, it's just something I should have told you before.'

'I can't stand the suspense,' said Miranda, trying to ease the tension. 'Tell me what it is.'

He hesitated. 'I-I know who you are.' Miranda frowned. It did not seem much of a revelation, most people knew who she was. 'No,' said Rupert, 'I don't mean the Miranda Hicks part, I mean your role as Mrs Michael Richardson.' He paused for a moment, to let his words sink in. She stared back at him, surprise and shock evident on her face, and yet with it came the slow dawning of understanding.

'Who are you?' she said, quietly. 'Your name is curiously familiar to me, but I haven't been able to place it.'

'I'm Michael's guardian. Jonathan Richardson, his father, and I were at school together.'

'Of course,' said Miranda, leaning back in her chair. 'Michael spoke of you often, but he rarely mentioned your surname.' She hesitated, obviously trying to assimilate Rupert's revelation. 'Bearing in mind that you must know Michael and I are separated, you will have found it rather odd that I bought the dolphin picture.'

'No, I don't. I simply assumed you bought it because you still love him,' Rupert said, quietly.

'I don't know the answer to that,' Miranda said. 'I just know we can't live together. I-I was with him when he painted that picture, you see – in fact he painted it the day I learnt I was expecting a baby.'

'You've had a child, I didn't know that?'

Miranda shook her head. 'No, I had a miscarriage.'

'Oh, my dear, I'm so sorry, how awful for you.'

'It was.' They were both silent for a moment, lost in their own thoughts. 'Do you know about the other child?' Miranda asked, after a while.

'Katarina? Why yes, of course. I handle all the financial affairs in connection with her.'

'Katarina was one of the main reasons we split up,' Miranda said. The instinctive feeling of comfort she had felt with Rupert persisted, even though she now realised who he was – or perhaps because of it. 'Michael didn't tell me about her, you see, and I found out quite by chance. I couldn't believe he could be so cruel as to abandon her at the far end of the island. OK, so she probably isn't his child, but she could be and in any event he was married to her mother when she was born.'

'I see,' said Rupert, 'I hadn't realised that Katarina had caused the problems between you.' It was on the tip of his tongue to say more, but he was aware he had probably already said more than he should.

'It was only one of the things that went wrong,' Miranda said, hastily. 'I'm sorry, I-I didn't mean to say anything unpleasant to you about Michael. I know you must be very fond of him, you've been so good to him, so supportive over the years.'

'Not really,' said Rupert, 'and that's the trouble. He's never really had anyone permanently in the supporting role. He's never really belonged anywhere, nor had a permanent stable relationship, and sometimes I feel it's all my fault.' Rupert suddenly looked a great deal older, careworn and anxious. He refilled his port glass with a shaking hand, and passed the decanter to Miranda.

'How can it possibly be your fault?' she said.

'I interfered, I broke up an otherwise happy family unit.'

'How did you do that?'

'I introduced a red herring. I suggested that Jonathan would have liked his son to enjoy the same education as he had done, with a view to eventually taking over the family estate in Derbyshire. I'm sure I was right, it's what Jonathan would have wanted, but only if only he could have been alive to give Michael his support. Poor little boy – he was so very Greek when he arrived in England.'

'Cretan,' Miranda said, with a half-smile. 'Cretan, not Greek.'

'I'm sorry, my dear, you're quite right. He was so very

Cretan when he arrived in England, and only seven years' old, you know. It broke my heart to leave him at school, he was so bewildered. Up until then, he and his mother had enjoyed a very close relationship, but after one term at school, they lost it for ever. As for the estate in Derbyshire, Michael has never shown any real interest in it. We sold it years ago and I can't help feeling it would have been so much better for him to have been raised in Crete, surrounded by family and lifelong friends.'

'But he might never have become an artist,' Miranda said.

'Oh yes, he'd have found art, or rather art would have found him. There was no chance of him escaping his destiny in that respect. The fact is, though, that growing up in Crete, he'd probably be a far better artist than he is today. Some of his Minos paintings are excellent – like your dolphins. Others are just commercial nonsense, but they all sell the same and the trouble is, Michael knows it. He was a wonderful portrait painter, quite wonderful – he seemed to be able to read right into his subject's soul, but he says after all these years of being Minos, he has lost the gift. It's tragic.'

'He has plenty of time,' Miranda said, 'perhaps he'll come back to it.'

'Not in his current frame of mind, I doubt it very much.'

Miranda wanted to ask how he was, but it seemed like some kind of admission. Instead, she turned on Rupert. 'You sound as though you might be blaming me. I couldn't have stayed with him, Rupert, honestly.'

'Of course I'm not blaming you, my dear, but perhaps we should change the subject before we both get maudlin.'

During the days that followed, Miranda and Rupert fell into a routine of meeting up regularly, sometimes for a meal, sometimes just for a coffee or a drink. When a new batch of Minos paintings arrived, with some trepidation, Rupert asked Miranda if she would like to come and see them, and together they unpacked them. They were not particularly good ones but Rupert was confident of moving them with Christmas just around the corner.

Christmas was something of a problem to Miranda. Robert and Marty were insisting that she spent the day with them.

Now Marty was happy and fulfilled, the couple seemed much closer, and since Miranda assumed that on Christmas Day, even Robert would take the day off, she could not help feeling they would be better on their own, rather than sharing the festivities with a lone woman, playing gooseberry.

Rupert solved the problem. 'It's very presumptuous of me,' he said, one evening when they were enjoying a glass of wine at his gallery, 'but have you made any plans for Christmas Day?' Miranda explained her dilemma. 'Well, why don't we spend Christmas together,' he suggested. 'I'll arrange, or rather Bow will arrange, Christmas lunch here and then, if you like, we could invite your friends round in the evening.'

'That's a marvellous idea, Rupert, I'd love to do that, if you're sure.'

Rupert, Bow and Miranda had a wonderful, if absurdly alcoholic, Christmas lunch. Afterwards, while Bow insisted on washing up alone, Rupert tuned into the World Service and they listened to the Queen, both shedding a tear when the National Anthem was played.

About five o'clock, Marty and Robert arrived – hand in hand, Miranda noted. Ridiculous party games followed and sharp at six they started drinking again from an excellent punch bowl which Bow produced. She refused to disclose the ingredients, but the hot spicy smell was as intoxicating as the liquor itself. Soon they were singing Christmas carols, and anything else which came into their minds, accompanied by Rupert on a battered old upright piano. Robert, the only American amongst them, protested that the English were mad and that he had never spent a Christmas like it, but Miranda had never seen him more relaxed, nor more devoted to Marty.

The New Year came. It was still very cold, the weather grey and cheerless, but for Miranda, things had never been more hectic. During January, February and March, she commuted between New York and Houston, organising not only the promotion, but also helping Tony with the choice of merchandise, layout of the store and hiring of staff. Houston opened in April, with the same resounding success in New York. It seemed that ENGLISH GARDEN could do no wrong.

In May, Miranda was put in charge of both operations, while Tony went back to England, to discuss the future with his shareholders and above all, Rachael. They had been apart for seven months, except for the brief visit Tony had made home at Christmas. The future in the US looked assured, it was a question of deciding how far he took that future. He returned ten days' later, with the news that he had been given the green light by everyone. The shareholders were delighted with his success and were backing him a hundred per cent in any future expansion he wanted to make in the US. As a result, he had promoted his UK production manager to a director and, most important of all, persuaded Rachael to come and join him, at any rate, for a year or two.

'So, sweetheart,' Tony said, 'next stop LA. Are you fit?'

'Of course,' said Miranda, 'lead me to it.' Indeed, she did love the work, hard though it was, and with friends like Marty and Robert, and now, most important of all, Rupert, she never felt truly lonely. Very occasionally, she would accept a dinner invitation from one of the men she met in business, but it never went further than that. In a way she was happy – certainly far happier than she had been in London, before she had first gone to Crete. She often tried to analyse why this should be.

'I think it's because you have a proper job,' Rupert suggested. 'You're using your mind as well as your body now. Then, of course, it may be that you have such excellent friends, like me.'

And an excellent friend he was. At any time, day or night, Miranda felt free to call him or drop in for a chat. During the evening he had first disclosed who he was, he had promised to tell Michael, neither of Miranda's whereabouts, nor of her friendship with him. No meddling, he promised, solemnly. He kept to his word, though at times he was sorely tempted to break it, suspecting just how deep Miranda's feelings still were for her husband. Clearly, though, Michael had hurt the girl dreadfully, and Rupert knew better than most, that Michael's proud, stubborn, volatile nature could do a lot of damage. It was best that he kept out of it . . . but something changed his mind irrevocably, one early September morning.

Chapter Twenty-Five

Rupert Shepherd had not slept well. At seventy-four, he found he was needing increasingly less sleep – at least, less sleep in long periods. Instead, he had developed the shameful habit of cat-napping during the day, and had to be very careful that his customers did not catch him at it. That particular morning dawned after an unusually sleepless night. He had been awake for hours when the alarm sounded. Reaching out a weary hand, he turned it off and then promptly fell asleep. What seemed like hours later, he fought his way through layers of deep sleep to hear the sound of banging on the front door of the gallery. Still stupid with drowsiness, he stumbled out of bed and thrust his head out of the window.

'What the hell are you doing, waking a fellow up at this time of the morning?' he demanded.

A burly man in overalls stepped back and looked up at him. 'Listen here, fella, it's after nine. Most respectable people have been up long since.' He grinned good-naturedly at the sight of Rupert. 'At your age, you should know better.'

'Nine! Good grief, I'm sorry.'

'We've got a delivery for you here. Can you come down and let us in?'

'I'm on my way,' said Rupert.

It was a large, wooden crate, which the delivery men kindly carried down to the basement for the old man. Rupert recognised the markings – it was from Crete, from Michael. He always had a sense of excitement when it came to opening Michael's paintings. The boy was his protégé, after all, and although, privately, Rupert thought Minos's success was out of proportion to the degree of his talent, he knew that Michael had far more talent than Minos ever displayed. Having given the delivery men a generous tip, he hurried upstairs, shaved and dressed, and leaving the closed sign up on the door, he went down to the basement.

Quarter of an hour later, breathless and dishevelled, he almost ran up the basement steps, and rushed to the telephone.

'ENGLISH GARDEN. Good morning, how may I help you?' said a cultured English voice.

'Yes, yes. Could I speak to Miranda Hicks – she is with you, is she, not in Houston?'

'No, she's here.'

'Oh, thank God. Could I speak to her, it's awfully important?'

'Yes, of course, sir, if you wouldn't mind holding on one moment.'

'Hello?' Miranda's voice was cautious.

'Miranda, hello, it's me.'

'Rupert, thank goodness for that, I've just been told there was a strange man wanting me urgently. It frightened me to death.'

'Miranda, can you come over here right away?'

'Are you all right, has something happened, are you ill?' Miranda's voice was full of concern.

'No, no, nothing like that, but it is important you come over, now. I have something I must show you.'

'Couldn't it wait until this evening?'

'I don't think I can wait until then. Please, Miranda, I know you're busy but you work so hard, surely they can't mind you having an hour off. I wouldn't ask you unless it was important.'

'I'll be with you in twenty minutes,' said Miranda. 'Only for heaven's sake, calm down, it's not good for you.'

'I'll do my best,' he promised.

She made it in quarter of an hour. A mixture of curiosity and concern for Rupert's well-being sent her scurrying out of the shop and into a cab the moment he had rung off. It was almost eleven by the time she reached his shop and the closed sign was still up. He must be ill, she thought, but as she approached the door, it opened. He obviously had been watching at the window for her.

'Rupert, what in the world's going on?'

He took her arm. 'Come with me.' He led her to the back of his shop and then down the basement steps. His muddled basement store was nothing new to her. She had been there many times before to help him unpack consignments of pictures. She followed him carefully down the steps now, more concerned with watching him, in case in his agitation, he fell. When he reached the bottom of the steps he waited for her, and then taking her hand, he led her round the corner to the main area of storage.

It stood propped against a packing case, resting on its wrappings. It was a portrait. A portrait of a beautiful girl, painted with exquisite care, accuracy and skill. It was a portrait of Miranda and the artist's signature in the bottom right-hand corner was not Minos, but Michael Richardson. Shock froze Miranda to the spot. She knew all about her own good looks, she had tended them with care, over the years, for they had been her bread and butter. She had been complimented in every conceivable way, from flattery to imitation, but she had never seen herself like this before. There was warmth, humour and determination in her expression, yet how she knew that, she could not tell – something in the brush strokes suggested these things.

'W-when did it arrive?' she said at last.

'Just this morning. I suppose he painted it from memory, or has he ever painted you before?'

'He made a lot of sketches of me, he was always sketching me. They never materialised into a painting though,' Miranda said, 'not until now.'

'It's not for sale,' Rupert said. 'There was a note with it. He said, having painted it, he couldn't bear to have it in the house, and would I look after it for him.'

'Oh charming,' said Miranda, sarcastically. 'I'm sorry the sight of me causes such offence.'

Rupert let go of her hand, almost flinging it away from him, and turned on her, his eyes blazing. 'Don't you dare speak like that, you silly, silly girl. Are you blind? Look at that painting, look at it. Every brush stroke that's gone into it is a work of love. Can't you see that? This is no ordinary painting, it's as though he's made love to the canvas, it's the only way I can describe it. If you ever doubted for one moment that Michael Richardson loved you with all his heart, then the answer lies there. If you use your eyes, your mind, if you search your heart, you will never doubt his feelings for you again.'

Miranda could not believe the vehemence behind his words – mild, gentle Rupert, gallant and charming, the perfect Englishman. She looked from his angry face back to the portrait, and then, quite unexpectedly, surprising them both, she burst into tears, and turning, ran back up the basement steps.

He caught her by the front door, struggling with the lock. 'If I run up those stairs once more today,' he panted, 'I'll have a heart attack. I'm sorry, my dear, I didn't mean to upset you, but I know the agonies he must have been through to produce it. Look, come into my office, it's warm there, and we'll talk.' Tears still streaming down her face, Miranda followed Rupert into his office. He closed the door, sat her down by the electric fire, and perched on the desk close beside her. 'You see, he hasn't painted a portrait in over ten years, nearer fifteen. It must have been an agony for him, and without any shadow of doubt, I know the identity of the catalyst which has made him paint properly again. It is love for you. Lonely and lost without you, he has pieced those sketches together to produce that magnificent painting. Having painted it, the irony is that the sight of you on canvas has only heightened his loss.'

Miranda continued to sob. 'I don't believe you,' she gasped, 'if he loved me truly, he wouldn't have done the things he did, said the things he said.'

'Miranda, my dear, I know he can be terribly cruel, he's hurt me many times, his mother, too. But he's a damaged man, who can be healed, but only with consistent selfless love, which for whatever reason, you were not able, or not prepared to give him.'

'I gave him all the love I had,' Miranda said.

'But it wasn't enough, because it didn't include compassion and understanding.'

'How can you say that, how do you know?'

'Because I know how you were when I met you and I know how you are now. You've changed, Miranda. No one could spend as many years as you have, in the shallow world of modelling without it affecting you. You were obsessed with your own reflection. When you looked at other people, you saw only your reflection in their eyes, because it was what you were trained to do. But that's all changed in recent months – you've grown up, you're looking at people properly, for the first time.'

'You make me sound horrible,' Miranda said.

Silently, Rupert handed her his handkerchief. 'Not horrible, you have all the warmth and love that any man could ever want. But first, my dear, you've had to learn to love yourself, develop your own sense of identity – only then have you been able to turn your attention to anyone other than Miranda Hicks – celebrated model. The image builders have worked on you for too many years – I bet there have been times when you haven't even known who you are.'

Miranda's head snapped up at his words. She stared at him in amazement. 'You're quite right. How did you know?'

Rupert smiled. 'An old man's intuition, I suppose you could call it, but there is another factor.'

'What's that?' Miranda asked.

'I have studied you in some depth in the last months, because I do happen to be very, very fond of you.'

'Oh, Rupert,' Miranda stood up and came into his arms. She rested her damp face on his shoulder and held him tight. 'I can't think how I've ever managed without you.' The feeling was reciprocated but Rupert could not find the words to say so.

At last they drew apart. 'I must go back,' said Miranda. 'Thank you for showing me the painting.' She hesitated. 'I understand what you are saying, Rupert, but I can't go back to him, I don't know the way, and I don't think I'll ever be able to find it.'

After she had gone, Rupert did not have the heart to open

the shop. He felt exhausted, physically and emotionally, and suddenly very, very old. He made himself a cup of tea, noticing how his hand shook. He took a sip, wrinkled his nose and then chucked it down the sink. Instead, he reached for the brandy bottle, destroying, in a trice, the hard discipline of a lifetime, never to drink before noon. He drank the brandy in guilty gulps, relaxed a little and then he shuffled back to his office. He sat down at his desk, head in his hands. He stayed there a long time, lost in thought, unable to bear the concept of these two people he cared about so much, spending the rest of their lives, miserable and apart – perhaps not even realising the cause of their dissatisfaction with life.

So lost in thought was he, that the noise of a key turning in the lock at the front door did not penetrate through his consciousness. It was only when the office door opened that he raised his head, and then the figure standing before him held no sense of reality. He knew it could only be a phantom, created out of his own hopes and dreams. For there before him, like a golden Adonis, stood the formidable figure of Michael Richardson.

Chapter Twenty-Six

'Miranda, how are you feeling?'

Miranda was grateful for the call. Lying on her bed, alone in the apartment, she was falling prey to all sorts of dangerous thoughts. 'Hello, Rupert, I'm OK. How are you? Have you recovered from this morning's dramas?'

He laughed. 'Yes, more or less. Thinking about it, the whole experience was probably good for me – it stops the arteries furring up. Look, I'm sorry I was a little – how shall we say – tactless this morning.'

'It's absolutely understandable,' said Miranda. 'Michael is like a son to you, I know that. Whatever my feelings, there was no justification in being flip about the portrait.'

'No hard feelings, then?'

'Certainly not.'

'Listen, I tell you the main reason for ringing – apart from to apologise, that is. I'm having a little soirée tomorrow evening, to launch the new stock of pictures I've received. Could you come?'

'Oh Rupert, I don't think I can.'

His heart gave a lurch. 'Why not?'

'I'm going to Houston – actually only for the day. I'm catching a six o'clock flight out tomorrow morning, but by the time I get back, I'm going to be absolutely shattered.'

'Houston in a day, typical you. What are you going for?' He was playing for time, while he tried to arrange his thoughts.

'It's for a meeting on how to keep the sales momentum going, now Christmas is over.'

'What time does your flight get into New York tomorrow evening?'

'Hang on a moment,' said Miranda, 'I'll check my diary. Six-fifty,' she said, after a moment.

'That's fine, the party doesn't even start until seven-thirty. Look, my dear, I know you'll be tired but how can I possibly have a party if it doesn't include the most beautiful girl in New York?'

'Rupert, you're incorrigible, and flattery will get you everywhere.'

'That's what I was hoping. So you will come?'

'I'll try and make it. Anything could happen, of course – the flight could be delayed, the meeting could go on and I might have to stop over, but I'll ring you if I'm not coming.' She hesitated a moment. 'You won't be showing the portrait of me, will you?'

'No, my dear, of course not. I think that would be a little too emotive for us both, don't you?'

The day went badly from the beginning. The flight out of New York was delayed by nearly an hour so that Miranda arrived at her first meeting late . . . and that was only the start. Tony had appointed a young Texan girl graduate as merchandising manager for the Houston store. Miranda had not been overly enthusiastic about the appointment at the time – the girl was full of qualifications and theory, but had virtually no commercial experience, and the most vital ingredient of all – commonsense. The garments she had selected to promote over the New Year were quite wrong, so that Miranda had to reassemble the entire collection, in the teeth of violent opposition. By the time she had finished, she was bone weary and her head ached, and she realised that she had almost certainly missed her flight home. She left the store and took a cab to the airport – not with any real hope of catching the plane, but because she wanted to get away from the aggravation. It would probably be best, she decided, to stay at an airport hotel and take the first flight out in the morning. She must remember to ring Rupert, too – she was sure he would understand.

At the airport, she walked over to the American Airways desk, with a view to changing her flight, when she became aware of the tannoy pounding away in the background – all flights had been delayed by half an hour, because of a fuel spillage on the runway. She glanced at her watch, she was only twenty-five minutes behind schedule. She dashed to the check in. Yes, there was still time, they confirmed. Within five minutes she was seated in the aircraft, within ten, they were airborne, on their way back to New York.

They made up a little time on the flight, but it was still a quarter past seven by the time they landed at Kennedy. As she waited for a cab, her eyes gritty with fatigue, her briefcase weighing a tone, Miranda was tempted to go straight home and ring Rupert from there, pretending she was still in Houston. Then she thought of all his kindness to her. It seemed so churlish not to put in an appearance at least. I'll stay for half an hour, she thought – by half past eight, I could be home and in a bath.

The gallery was ablaze with lights when Miranda's cab drew up outside the door. Bow answered the door and smiled delightedly. 'Ah, Miss Miranda! Mr Shepherd, he'll be mighty glad to see you.'

The gallery was a sea of people and as Miranda looked past Bow, with tired eyes, she saw Rupert come forward to greet her.

'Miranda, bless you for coming.' He embraced her but suddenly, she was aware of a tension in the air – something was wrong. She drew away from Rupert and stared at him for a moment, seeking understanding, and as she did so, she was aware of another pair of eyes on her. She looked up.

He stood out from everyone else in the room, his tall, broad frame, his shock of fair hair, the deep tan, the strange and enigmatic features. Miranda clutched at Rupert's arm, more for support then anything else. 'Rupert,' she said, in a strangled voice, 'what the hell have you done?'

Michael moved through the crowd towards her. Miranda stood, her hand still on Rupert's arm, quite unable to move. When Michael reached her, their eyes locked and held. Then he turned on Rupert. 'Why the bloody hell didn't you tell me?'

Rupert removed Miranda's hand from his arm, and held it for a moment. 'Well, that's a fine start,' he said, smiling gently. 'You already have something in common – you're both hating me.' He looked directly at Michael. 'Take her away somewhere, Michael, anywhere away from this party. It's full of the most appalling bores, but they were the only people I could rustle up at such short notice. I had to think of some excuse to get you two together. I have to say it's all been very taxing for an old man.'

Miranda was still speechless. Although Michael stood a good two feet from her, she could feel his presence as though she was pressed to him. Her brain was numb, she was all sensation. Her skin tingled, her head felt muzzy as if she was drunk, her limbs felt heavy, her mouth dry. She wanted to cry, but even her tear-ducts seemed to have gone into a state of shock. They continued to stare at one another – Rupert now, like the rest of the room, nothing more than shadowy background.

'There's a restaurant across the street,' Michael was saying, 'Rupert uses it a lot. It's Spanish and quite quiet.'

'I know it,' Miranda managed in a cracked voice.

'Shall we go there?' She nodded. 'Let me take your case, it looks heavy.' He opened the door for her and they left the gallery. They walked across the road into the restaurant and, presumably, Michael asked for a table for two, but Miranda was aware of none of this. Her mind was reeling, trying to come to terms with what had just happened. She had to keep looking at Michael to believe he was real, and every time she met his gaze, she saw mirrored there, her own bewilderment. She was dimly aware that he ordered wine and bread. It arrived, and she watched his strong, brown, well-remembered hand pour wine into her glass. He raised his glass to her. 'I've no idea what the toast should be, I can't seem to think straight at the moment, I'm sorry, I'm behaving stupidly – should we just say good luck?'

'Good luck,' Miranda managed.

There was an awkward silence, which at last, Michael broke. 'How long have you known Rupert?'

'I met him almost as soon as I came to work in New York.'

'You realised who he was?'

'Not immediately, no.' Miranda made strenuous efforts to

pull herself together. 'I was walking past his gallery one day and noticed some of your paintings on display. It was snowing, so I went inside. Rupert apparently knew who I was straight away but he didn't tell me who he was until we'd met several times.'

'And he's become a friend?'

'A good friend,' said Miranda. 'I'm very fond of him.'

'Me too,' said Michael, 'though, what a thing to do to us – this was some stunt to pull.'

For the first time Miranda found she could smile. 'Yes, the old devil.'

'I thought you were still in London,' said Michael.

'I thought you were still in Crete.'

There was another difficult pauses. 'Did you see the portrait?' Michael asked. Miranda nodded. 'Did you like it?'

'How could I help it?' She met his eyes. 'I must have been photographed hundreds of thousands of times over the years – in the most flattering light, in the most flatting garments – but I've never seen anything remotely like that painting. I suspect you were probably too kind to me.'

'You were the key that unlocked the door, you know.'

'Of your painting?' Miranda asked.

'Señor, Señorita, you would like to order?' The waiter hovered, impatiently.

'I'm not hungry, are you?'

Miranda shook her head. 'I should be, I didn't have any lunch.'

'The chef's speciality for two, and some salad,' Michael said, 'and you'd better bring us some more wine.'

'Go on about your painting,' Miranda said, as soon as they were alone again. Michael shrugged his shoulders, 'Since I painted the portrait of you, I find I can do others. Yours took me a long time, nearly a year. These others – they're coming more easily.

'Who else have you painted?'

'Only two people,' Michael said, 'but I would rather show you the portraits than tell you about them.' The private man was very much in evidence and Miranda knew better than to question him more.

'And you – tell me about your work,' Michael said, anxious to move the spotlight from himself.

They talked of Miranda's job until the meal came. Both of them tried to eat it, but they had no appetite, and so picked, instead, at the salad. They had both changed in the year, since they had seen one another. Neither of them could have put it into words, but both of them saw in each other an inner calm that had not been there before. Michael, Miranda observed, was slimmer. Nothing could change the arrogant thrust of his jaw, those eyes which could be so intimidating, the haughty look, caused by his strong aquiline nose – but somehow he seemed softer.

Michael studied Miranda's face as she talked. She was tired, he could see that, there were blue smudges under her eyes. But the delicate skin, the wonderful colouring, the tipped-up nose, the dimple, those full, luscious lips, were all the same. He wanted to end this trivial discussion about work. He wanted her in his arms, where she belonged. He had been patient but suddenly, he could stand it no more. 'I'm sorry,' he said, 'but if I can't get you somewhere on your own, touch you, hold you, I swear I'll go mad. I won't do anything you don't want, only. . . .'

'It's all right,' said Miranda, 'my flat is just round the corner.'

The first thing Michael saw as he walked into her apartment was the dolphin picture. He stared at it in silence for a moment. 'Thank God you've got it,' he said. 'Do-do you remember that day?' Tears began streaming down his face. Miranda could see them, but she doubted whether he even knew he was crying, and she could not bear to see his pain.

'Of course I remember that day, and all the others.' She took him in her arms as one would a child and then made him lie down on the bed while she kissed away the tears as they fell.

'I love you, I love you,' he said again and again. 'I didn't know how much, I didn't realise until you had gone and then I did not know how to get you back.'

'Shush, shush,' said Miranda, 'don't talk.'

'You're right,' he whispered. He pulled her closely into his arms, her head resting on his shoulder, their bodies welded together as if one. Amazingly they slept, then woke together during the night, helped each other undress and made love, as though it was the most natural thing in the world. Their passion was profound but the mood of earlier in the evening persisted, for this lovemaking was tempered with gentleness and a desire to comfort. Then they slept again, waking as dawn shone through the windows, where no curtains had been drawn.

Suddenly they were very hungry, so Miranda made coffee and toast. They sat in bed together, as they had done so many times in the past, and to both of them, it felt as though the last year had not existed.

'There's something I have to tell you,' Michael said, his voice very serious. Terror gripped at Miranda's heart – was he in love with someone else? 'I-I have to go back to Crete today, I have a commitment there. It's very important – for nothing else would I go, after what's happened, but . . .'

'It's all right,' said Miranda, 'if it's important.'

She expected him to tell her of the reason for his sudden return, but he did not and it left her with a sense of unease. She wanted to repay him, to hurt him for hurting her. 'Perhaps it's just as well,' she said.

Michael looked at her. There was no anger in his eyes, as there was in hers. 'You don't mean that, you can't.'

She was instantly contrite. 'No, I don't mean that, but, Michael the problems haven't gone away, have they? They're still there, all the things that drove us apart before.'

'You're wrong, so wrong – they have gone, don't you see? It was all caused by my stupid deceit. Not only do I have no secrets from you now, the effect of the deceit, if you think about it, was very far reaching – the family's disapproval of you, the fact that I didn't introduce you to any of my friends. I was frightened to tell you about Katarina because I knew you would react as you did, and once I'd let things drift too far, I found myself caught up in the web of my own . . . well, lies.'

'What has happened to Katarina?' Miranda asked, abruptly.

'She's all right, she's fine. She has a new family.'

'Has she settled in?'

'Very well.'

'Are you sure, have you checked?'

Michael smiled, reassuringly. 'Yes, I promise.'

'Do you regret her going?'

'No, I've done the right thing, for her, I'm sure of it.'

Miranda sighed. 'I will never understand your reaction to that child, but then it's not right to inflict my views on you, and I do understand your feeling of betrayal and hurt. Perhaps it is better she is with people who love her, than with someone who can't help resenting what she stands for.' Michael said nothing. 'W-what do you think we should do now, I mean you and I?'

'I think we should try again, obviously. I'm different, darling, honestly I am, and I realise now it's unrealistic to expect anybody to live in Crete all the year round, particularly for you, with a career. We'll live wherever you like, whenever you like, as long as we're together.'

'I feel so shell-shocked,' said Miranda, 'I can't believe it's you sitting here, it feels so, so . . .' she hesitated, searching for the word.

'Wonderful?' Michael suggested, modestly.

'That'll do,' Miranda said, grinning.

They kissed, marvelling at the thrill it gave them, tempered with sweet familiarity.

'Look, my darling, one way and another, I've pressurised you enough,' Michael said, at last. 'I'll go back to Crete today and give you time to think about our future. Whatever you decide, I'll abide by that decision. If you really see no future for us, I won't pester you, I promise. But I do sincerely believe that we belong together. Send me a letter, a telegram, ring me, get in touch with me somehow in the next few days. Take your time, make sure your decision is right, and then let me know what you are going to do.' Miranda nodded, humbly grateful. 'But darling, I must ask you one thing.'

'Anything,' Miranda said.

'If you come back to me, it must be because you're coming back for good. You've left me three times now and I can't take it again. If we try again, we must stick with it and make it work. If we're not prepared for that, I'd far rather you didn't come back at all.'

'I understand that,' said Miranda, 'and I feel the same.'

'Then all that remains is for me to show you just how much I love you.'

He took the coffee cup from her hand and pushed her back onto the pillows.

Chapter Twenty-Seven

Miranda did not go with Michael to the airport, she could not bear to say goodbye. After he had gone, she sat alone in her flat, numb and lonely, until she remembered that it was a working day and it was already after eleven.

'Where the hell have you been?' Tony said, when she rang through. 'Your line's been busy all morning, and we have a crisis at Houston – Mary's walked out.' Miranda was not entirely surprised – Mary was the smart-arse graduate.

Miranda toyed with an excuse and then decided that this was a case where truth was infinitely preferable to any story she could invent. 'I-I met my husband, by accident, last night,' she said. 'We've been trying to sort out what to do with our marriage, and I'm afraid we took the phone off the hook.'

The needle went straight out of Tony. 'Sensible bloke, he should have ripped the bloody thing out from the wall. Is he still with you?'

'No, he had to fly back to Crete.'

'And are you following him?'

'That's what I have to decide. I said I'd send him a telegram.'

'Do you want to talk?'

It was tempting, but Miranda knew this was something she had to do alone. 'Thanks, but no,' she said.

'OK, but you'll need a couple of days off to sort yourself out, right?'

'That would be wonderful,' said Miranda, 'but what about Houston?'

'Sod Houston, this is more important. I'll handle that. Where are we now, Wednesday? Do you think you could make it back by Friday?'

'I'll be there?' said Miranda.

She mooched around the flat, walked in Central Park and window-shopped up and down Fifth Avenue. She ate and drank practically nothing – her feelings were all dominant, her body seemed to need nothing to sustain it. She found herself thinking, not so much of what she wanted from life, but what would be best for Michael and whether she could truly make him happy. And these thoughts, she realised, echoed Rupert's words of a few days before. She had changed. The decision she was trying to make was not about what she could get out of the marriage but whether she was fit for the job.

On Thursday afternoon, she found herself wandering through Central Park. The sun was warm and she sat on a bench, tired out by the revolvings of her confused mind. A woman, sauntering in the sun and pushing a baby-buggy, asked if she could join her. The woman unstrapped a toddler from the buggy and let him stumble around on the grass.

With a shock, Miranda realised that, had her son lived, he would have been almost exactly this age. That she and Michael had shared such a grief and yet could even contemplate spending the rest of their lives apart, seemed suddenly immoral, almost sick. Startling the woman beside her, she stood up briskly and strode off across the park, wanting to get away from the sight of the little boy and his pleasure in the sunshine.

Every evening found her wandering down Madison Avenue and by habit, she walked through the doors of ENGLISH GARDEN. The last customers were just leaving and she could hear Tony talking on the telephone upstairs in his office. He put the phone down as she entered. 'Just the girl I wanted to see.'

'Why? What's happened?'

'That was our agent in LA. I've managed to hurry the lease through. The store needs very little work on it and you've already done a fair amount on pre-publicity, so I guess we could have the place open in a fortnight – three weeks at the outside.'

'That's good,' said Miranda, 'but what's the sudden rush?'

'Because of your leaving us, you nut. I don't want anyone else opening that store but you. It's the biggest gamble of the three.'

'Leaving? Am I?'

'You mean you haven't yet sent that poor bastard a telegram?' Miranda shook her head, tears in her eyes. Tony rose from behind his desk and picking up the telephone he almost threw it at her. 'Then, for Christ's sake, girl, there's the bloody telephone, do something about it.'

Tears began dripping down Miranda's cheeks. 'Oh Tony, I love him so much.'

'I know you do, sweetheart, so for Christ's sake stop pissing around and put us all out of our misery.'

She looked at him for a long moment and then slowly lifted the receiver.

Chapter Twenty-Eight

'Are you sure you've got everything?' Rupert's face was creased with concern and it was the third time he had asked the question.

'Of course I have,' said Miranda patiently. 'I've only this overnight bag, and a few magazines to keep me occupied.'

'You ought to have some suntan cream. Crete at this time of year is still very hot.'

'I've packed a bikini and Michael will have the suntan cream.'

'He doesn't need it, he's very brown.'

'Oh, Rupert, stop.' Miranda slipped an arm through his as they walked towards Passport Control.

'Sorry,' he said, 'only I have to keep talking so that I can pretend I'm not going to miss you.'

'We'll come to see you, often, Rupert, and you'll come and stay with us too, won't you?'

'If I can find someone to mind the gallery, yes, of course.'

'Promise.' Miranda stopped and putting down her case, took both his hands in hers. 'I love you so much, Rupert, and without you, Michael and I would have made a total hash of our lives. I wish we all lived nearer one another.'

'I will come and see you, I promise, and I expect you here in New York at least twice a year.'

They walked on in silence, aware that the moment of parting was almost upon them. At the departure desk they stopped again. 'You'll take care of youself, won't you?' Miranda said.

Rupert smiled. 'Did I ever tell you that once I fell in love with Michael's mother?'

'No,' said Miranda, surprised. 'No, you didn't. You were in love with Tassoula – when did you know her?'

'When Michael was a little boy, I saw a great deal of them. I used to stay with them in Sitia because I wanted to get to know the boy well before he came to England.'

'Did you . . . did you do anything about it?' Miranda asked.

'I tried to, but she wouldn't have me. I understand why now. She adored Jonathan and by marrying someone of his kind, someone of a similar type, she'd have been disloyal in her own eyes. By marrying a Cretan, it was a different thing altogether. I was too young and stupid to understand that then, so I just let her break my heart. It's a shame, for if I'd persevered, we might have been neighbours now.'

'It's not too late you know, she's a widow.'

Rupert shook his head, vehemently. 'It's too late for me, for her, too, I suspect, thought it will be lovely to see her when I come and visit you.'

'Well, since you're so good at playing Cupid,' Miranda said, 'perhaps you could address the problem of your own love life for a change.'

'It's time you went, they've called your flight.'

Miranda slipped her arms round his neck and held him tight. When she drew away, she was distressed to see his eyes were dark with pain. 'Soon, Rupert.'

'Soon,' he mouthed back, and before she had picked up her case, he was gone, swallowed up in the crowd, afraid, Miranda knew, of showing his tears.

The flight was uneventful and on time, but the hours dragged by for Miranda. It was six weeks since she had seen Michael, and it could well have been six years. Since her telegram telling him that she would be coming back to him, they had spoken on the phone every day, clocking up the most amazing bills. Separated physically, their only communication was the spoken word, and in that period they got to know one another better than they had ever done in the short period of their married life together. They told each other of their hopes and dreams, their joys and sorrows – they had never been so close. They had last spoken that morning, while

Rupert was waiting impatiently below in a cab.

'There's one thing I haven't mentioned before,' Michael said, 'I have a surprise awaiting you. I just hope you'll like it.'

'Do you think I will?'

'Well I'm biased, but I think it's wonderful.'

'Give me a clue.'

'Certainly not.'

'You mean thing.'

'Abuse, before we're even reunited! If that's how you feel, are you sure you're doing the right thing, Miss Hicks, or do you think you should be staying in New York?'

'I'll be with you in about ten hours,' Miranda said, the words sounding unreal.

'I know,' said Michael, 'I'll be waiting for you.'

As the plane made a lazy circle over Crete, Miranda felt her heart leap. She had forgotten, in the confusion of their parting, how much she had come to love the island. She looked at it now as they came in to land, dry and arid from the summer's sun, and she longed to feel the heat again, smell the rosemary and thyme, hear the song of the cicaders and plunge into the blue sea. Then, as the wheels touched the tarmac, her mind was full of Michael – what to say to him, what he would say to her.

Disembarkation arrangements at Crete are notoriously haphazard. Everyone swarms off the plane and gallops across the tarmac to the airport building, hopefully avoiding other jets as they do so.

Miranda set off, ahead of the rest of the passengers, who were still grumbling at the prospect of the walk. The air was unbelievably hot although it was early evening, the sky that special blue that only belongs to Greece and her islands. She walked fast, carrying easily her small overnight bag. Ahead of her she saw two figures, walking towards her. Slowly, they materialised into an adult and a child. By the time she was sure it was Michael, hand in hand with a little fair-haired girl, she had already dropped her bags and had broken into a run. They began running, too, and so certain was she that the child was Katarina that when she reached them, she bent and scooped the child into one arm, before throwing her other arm round Michael, who enveloped them both. They all seemed to be crying and laughing. An American tourist appeared beside them, with Miranda's bags. 'I guess you dropped these in the rush.' He glanced at the man and child. 'Still, who can blame you, be happy.'

'We will,' said Miranda, 'thank you.'

She looked properly at Katarina for the first time, tucked snugly onto her hip. 'You're my surprise, I suppose,' she said. The little girl nodded gravely and rested her head shyly but confidently on Miranda's shoulder. Miranda looked up into Michael's face. 'Thank you,' she said, 'no one could have a better present in the world. I take it, we're Katarina's new family.'

Michael smiled. 'Katarina and I have been living together for a year now, and she was the reason I had to get back to Crete. At first her foster mother lived with us, but she went home a few months ago. The three of us – Katarina, Thea and I – have managed well enough, but we do need a Mummy, don't we, darling?'

The little girl looked up, shyly. 'Yes, Daddy,' she said, grinning. 'Especially you, you need a Mummy to keep you in order.' She looked at Miranda, with the time-honoured expression that women keep exclusively for other women, when they're talking about the vagaries of men. 'He's hopeless,' she said, wearily, 'he's so untidy, he can never find anything.'

Miranda gave a mock sigh. 'You and I are going to have to sort him out then, aren't we?'

'I could do with some help,' Katarina confided.

In the early hours of the following morning, Michael and Miranda lay in bed talking. 'Are you sure you feel all right about Katarina,' Michael said. 'I suddenly felt terrible on the way to the airport, yesterday. There was I inflicting a ready-made family on you, without even asking.'

'I think she's gorgeous, I love her already,' said Miranda. 'Do you think she likes me?'

'Oh come on,' said Michael, 'you two were inseparable last night. I was quite jealous.'

'I hope you didn't think I neglected you, only I didn't want us to be too wrapped up in each other, so that she felt I was some kind of threat. You two have obviously grown very close.'

'Yes, we have, and I have you to thank for that – you made me realise how wrong I was being,' Michael admitted. 'I feel so terrible for having cut her out of my life up until now. Sometimes when I look at her, I swear I can see a likeness to me, other times not. In the early days, it mattered, but now it doesn't matter at all. She's just Katarina, and I love her.'

'Do you know, that's the nicest thing I've ever heard you say.'

'Nicer than the things I said last night?' He rolled over, lazily, onto one elbow and kissed her.

'No, not nicer than that. Oh, I do love you, Michael.' They lay clasped in each others arms for a long while. 'When I first saw the portrait you'd painted of me,' Miranda said, after a while, 'Rupert tried to explain something to me. I didn't understand it at the time, but now I do.'

'Go on,' said Michael.

'When we first came together we were too selfish to make our marriage work. We were both trying to grab things from one another. We were so wrapped up in ourselves, so insecure, that we couldn't give unselfishly, nor recognise each other's weaknesses without dramatising them into huge faults. We grabbed at each other, without any plans, without any thought for the future, and without any consideration for each other's frailties.'

'I suppose that's true,' said Michael, 'not pleasant to hear but probably true.'

'I'm not trying to be complacent,' said Miranda, 'but I do think, painful though it's been, that the last year has been a good thing – for you and Katarina mainly, of course, but also for your work. I have changed too – doing a different sort of job, learning to live in a new city . . . when I look back on some of the scenes I caused, I feel so ashamed.'

'Not as ashamed as I feel,' said Michael. 'When you lost our baby, I didn't show an ounce of understanding.'

'Stop, stop, don't let's go on about the past, let's look to the future. What can I do now to make sure I'm accepted in the eyes of your family and friends?'

'Is that a serious question?' Michael asked.

'Of course it's a serious question.'

'Then how would the idea of a Greek wedding appeal to you?'

Miranda smiled. 'Is that a serious question?' Michael nodded. 'Then I'd love it, if it's what you want, and your family too.'

Hurried preparations were made for the wedding – Tassoula being of the view that it would be better if they were not known to be living together until the wedding had taken place, not withstanding the fact that they had already been married in Britain.

'What about your family?' said Michael. 'Would you like them to come over?'

Miranda shrugged her shoulders. 'Yes, in a way, but they haven't come to my other two weddings so there's no point in asking them now. This is for your family, Michael.'

Katarina was in a state of constant excitement. She was to be the bridesmaid, of course, and a special dress was prepared for her, using yards of lace. With her long, blonde hair and big blue eyes, she looked adorable. Miranda's dress too, had to be traditional, a combination of lace and tulle.

The wedding was set for four days after Miranda's arrival in Crete, and on the morning of the wedding, she drove, with Michael, in his car, into Sitia, with Katarina and Thea in the back, feeling nervous and self-conscious. The lace headdress and long, swirling dress suited her beautifully. Tassoula had helped her dress that morning and she knew everything was as it should be, yet she felt more nervous than she could ever remember. As they entered Sitia, the town was thronging with people.

'Why is it so busy?' said Miranda. 'It's only eleven o'clock.'

Michael looked at her and smiled. 'They've come for our wedding.'

'You're joking.'

'No, I'm not. They'll have come from miles around. You see, it will be a day of feasting. As I explained to you, traditionally there should be much feasting before the wedding, but I thought you would be too tired for that, not to mention jet-lagged. So, we're going straight into the church and we'll have the party afterwards.'

'I'm frightened,' Miranda whispered.

'Think of it as just another modelling assignment.'

'I can't.'

Katarina, hearing her words, leaned forward in the car and slipped an arm round Miranda's shoulders. 'Don't be frightened, Mummy – Daddy and I are with you.'

Miranda stared at the little girl in amazement. 'You called me "Mummy".'

'I know, I meant to. Can I call you Mummy? You are going to be my Mummy aren't you, once you and Daddy are married.'

'Yes, my darling, of course I'm going to be your Mummy. I'm your Mummy now.'

'That's all right then,' said Katarina with satisfaction.

'And what's more,' said Miranda, raising her chin defiantly, 'if I'm your Mummy, I've no cause to be frightened of anything, have I?'

'That's right,' said Michael, squeezing her hand. 'That's right, my love.'

The square outside the church was thronging with people. A carpet ran from the door of the church down into the square, at the top of which stood a ruddy-faced, white-bearded old priest, his hands clasped over his flowing robes. Michael helped Miranda out of the car and Katarina, full of importance, arranged the bride's dress, and her own. Then the three of them began a slow walk up the steps of the church. The sun shone, people called and clapped, talking excitedly, pointing and nudging one another. Just for a moment, Miranda felt a stab of regret, wishing her family could have been there, but no, she thought, this is for Michael. They reached the top of the steps, the priest stepped forward and blessed them, and then with great ceremony, turned and started to lead them into the church.

After the bright sunlight, the church seemed very dark. It was full of people, chattering Cretans, packed into every available seat – indeed whole families seemed to be camped there. Gradually, as they walked slowly up the aisle, Miranda's eyes became accustomed to the light and, suddenly, she began to see familiar faces. There, in the right-hand pew were May and Lawrence Hardcastle . . . or was she dreaming? No, she couldn't be because there was her sister, Ann, and husband and children, and Sarah, too. Then, surely not, but yes, her mother and father, and Paul – and beside him the unmistakable figure of Jenny, smiling at her wickedly.

Miranda stopped and turned to Michael. 'I don't believe this, darling – what have you done?'

'Keep walking, darling, or the locals will think you're a reluctant bride.'

'But how did you do it?' She began walking forward again. Another face was smiling at her and she realised, to her amazement it was Marty, with Robert beside her – Robert, not working! And there was Tony, on whose arm hung a small, plump, dark-haired woman, who could only be Rachael. Suddenly they were at the altar and there was the dearest sight of all – Rupert standing straight and proud beside her.

Michael bent down and whispered in Miranda's ear. 'I asked Rupert to be the *kaumbaros*.'

'The what?' Miranda asked, also in a whisper.

'The best man. It also means he has to be godfather to our first child. I hope that's all right.'

Miranda smiled, tears in her eyes. 'What do you think?' she said.

The ceremony was beautiful, although Miranda understood not a word of it. The climax was when the little white crowns, linked with ribbon, were placed on Miranda and Michael's head and then exchanged three times by the *kaumbaros*. Rupert conducted his role with enormous efficiency, as though it was something he had been doing all his life. There was no music but as a background to the service, there was laughter and small talk from the crowd at the back of the church, with occasional cries of, 'Bravo, bravo.' It was not at all solemn, just warm and full of gaiety.

Suddenly the service was over. They were propelled down the aisle and out into the sunshine again, where they were borne on a crowd of people across the square to the taverna. Great goblets of wine were thrust into their hands. Michael and Miranda linked arms and drank. 'Bravo, bravo,' everyone cried again.

From somewhere in the crowd there was the sound of a bouzouki. 'We must dance now,' said Michael.

'Help! Can I, in this dress?'

'Of course you can, my darling.'

They danced round and round the square to more cries and cheers. Then, from out of the crowd came a man Miranda had never seen before, who took Michael's place, then another, then another. Then Rupert rescued her, then Tony, then Robert – unusually flushed in the heat.

'How long have I got to keep this up?' Miranda gasped.

'It's a tradition, apparently,' said Robert. 'I'll get Michael to rescue you in a moment, shall I?'

She danced and danced and then suddenly familiar arms pushed aside her partner and she was back with Michael again. The square exploded into cheers to see the bride and bridegroom together once more.

'You're wonderful,' Michael said, as he whirled her round, 'ravishing, magnificent and you should be dead on your feet.'

'I am, at least I was, until now, until you rescued me. Now I feel I could go on for ever.'

'You can,' said Michael, 'we can, together.'

'I love you,' Miranda said, almost shouting the words in her exhilaration and joy.

They had reached the taverna and as they flashed past the glass doors, Miranda caught sight of her reflection. Tendrils of hair had escaped from her mantilla, her dress was askew, her feet dusty from dancing. The carefully groomed model had gone – perhaps for ever. She had never looked more happy in her life.

Epilogue: CRETE, June 1987

Two naked bodies lay stretched on the great bed. The sun, already high in the sky, shone rays through the open window above them. It warmed them, and kept them locked in sleep. Then, from somewhere deep in the heart of the house, the telephone began to ring. Michael heard it first, stretching, then burying his head under the pillow, to shut out the sound. His movements work Miranda. 'Michael, is that the telephone?'

'No,' he answered firmly.

'It is. Honestly, you are a lazy old sod.' She clambered out of bed, throwing on one of his shirts which lay discarded on the floor. 'I'd better go and get it,' she said. 'It's Thea's day off.' Michael grunted in response.

But once she had left the room, his eyes snapped open and he sat up. It was a beautiful morning. He loved this time of year in Crete – so fresh and bright, before the merciless sun dried everything to a crisp. He got up, and naked wandered through the house, tiptoeing past Katarina's room. The three of them had been out to a friend's party the night before and had come home far too late for an eight year old – still it was almost the school holidays. The sun had not yet reached the terrace and the stone was cold under his bare feet. He walked to the railings and gazed out across the sea, taking deep breaths and revelling in the smell of the salty air. Suddenly, his attention was caught by a sparkle in the water immediately below him. Grasping the rail, he leaned out for a better view.

'Michael, Michael, darling where are you?' Miranda's voice echoed through the house.

He turned. 'I'm here, darling, come and look, quickly.'

Miranda burst onto the terrace. 'Wait, I'll look in a minute, I have something to tell you.' Her face was deadly serious and just for a moment Michael had a feeling of disquiet. 'What is it?' he said.

'That was Hans on the telephone. He rang early because he knew we'd want to know right away.'

'Know what?'

'The tests from the lab. Oh darling, they were positive. We're going to have a baby.'

Michael let out a whoop of delight and threw his arms round Miranda, hugging her, kissing her, his tears of joy mingling with hers.

It was some time before he remembered what he had seen. When he did, he drew Miranda to the very edge of the terrace, his arm firmly round her. Together they peered over the railings.

Far below them, the dolphins were playing. . . .